The Original Inspector George Gently Collection

Alan Hunter

Constable & Robinson Ltd
55–56 Russell Square
London WC1B 4HP
www.constablerobinson.com

This paperback edition published by C&R Crime,
an imprint of Constable & Robinson Ltd., 2013

A copy of the British Library Cataloguing in Publication
Data is available from the British Library

ISBN 978-1-47210-836-4 (paperback)

Typeset by TW Typesetting, Plymouth, Devon

Printed and bound in the UK

1 3 5 7 9 10 8 6 4 2

Alan Hunter ~~was~~ ~~born~~ ~~in~~ ~~Hoveton,~~ ~~Norfolk~~ ~~in~~ 1922. He left school at the ~~age~~ ~~of~~ ~~fourteen~~ ~~to~~ ~~work~~ ~~on~~ his father's farm, ~~spending~~ ~~his~~ ~~spare~~ ~~time~~ ~~sailing~~ ~~on~~ ~~the~~ Norfolk Broads and writing nature notes for the *Eastern Evening News*. He also wrote poetry, some of which was published while he was in the RAF during the Second World War. By 1950, he was running his own bookshop in Norwich. In 1955, the first of what would become a series of forty-six George Gently novels was published. He died in 2005, aged eighty-two.

The *Inspector George Gently* series

For

ADELAIDE

A GENTLE REMINDER TO THE READER

This is a detective story, but NOT a 'whodunit'. Its aim is to give a picture of a police investigator slowly building up his knowledge of a crime to a point, not where he knows who did it – both you and me know that at a fairly early stage – but to a point where he can bring a charge which will convince the jury.

I thought it worthwhile mentioning this. I hate being criticized for not doing what I had no intention of doing.

Sincerely yours,

ALAN HUNTER

Gently Does It

CHAPTER ONE

C HIEF INSPECTOR GENTLY, Central Office, CID, reached automatically into his pocket for another peppermint cream and fed it unconsciously into his mouth. Then he folded his large hands one over the other on the guard rail and peered into the inferno below him with a pleased expression, rather like a middle-aged god inspecting a new annex for the damned.

It was something new in Walls of Death. It was wider, and faster. The young man in red leather overalls was not finding it at all easy to make the grade. He was still tearing madly round the cambered bottom of his cage, like a noisy and demented squirrel, trying to squeeze yet more speed out of his vermilion machine. Chief Inspector Gently watched him approvingly. He had always been a Wall of Death fan. He breathed the uprising exhaust fumes with the contented nostrils of a connoisseur, and felt in his pocket for yet one more peppermint cream.

Suddenly the gyrating unit of man and machine

began to slide upwards towards him: a smooth, expert movement, betraying a brain which could judge to a hair. The ear-splitting thunder of a powerful engine in a confined space rose to a crescendo. The solid wooden wall vibrated and swayed threateningly. Higher it crept, and higher, and then, in one supreme gesture, deliberately rehearsed and breathtakingly executed, shot up to the very lip of the guard rail with a roar of irresistible menace and fell away in drunken, flattening spirals.

Chief Inspector Gently smiled benignly at the ducked heads around the guard rail. His jaw continued its momentarily interrupted champing movement. The steadying quality of peppermint creams on the nerves was, he thought, something that deserved to be better known.

Outside the Wall of Death the Easter Fair was in full swing, a gaudy, lusty battleground of noise and music. There were at least five contenders in the musical field, ranging from the monstrous roundabouts that guarded the approach from Castle Paddock to the ancient cake-walk spouting from the cattle-pens, wheezy but indomitable. All of them played different tunes, all of them played without a break. Nobody knew what they were playing, but that was not the point . . .

Chief Inspector Gently shouldered his way tolerantly through the crowd. He didn't like crowds, by and large, but since he was on holiday he felt he could afford to be generous. He stopped at a rock-stall and inspected its brilliant array of starches. 'Have you got any peppermint creams?' he enquired, not very hopefully. They hadn't, so he bought some poisonous-looking bull's-eyes with orange and purple stripes to take back for the landlady's little boy.

4

A newsboy came thrusting through the crowd, challenging the uproar with leathern lungs. '*Lay-test – lay-test!* Read abaht the . . .' Gently turned, in the act of putting the bull's-eyes into his pocket. The newsboy was serving a tow-haired young man, a young man still wearing a pair of scarlet leather breeches. Gently surveyed him mildly, noticing the Grecian nose, the blue eyes, the long line of the cheek and the small, neat ears. There was a note of determination about him, he thought. The peculiar quality which Conrad called somewhere 'ability in the abstract'. He would get on, that lad, provided he survived his Wall of Death interlude . . .

And then Gently noticed the long cheek pale beneath its coat of dust and smears of oil. The blue eyes opened wide and the hand that held the paper trembled. The next moment the young man had gone, darted off through the crowd and vanished like a spectre at cock-crow.

Gently frowned and applied to his bag for a peppermint cream. The newsboy came thrusting by with his stentorian wail. 'Gimme one,' said Gently. He glanced over the dry headlines of international conferences and the picture of the film-starlet at Whipsnade: tilted the paper sideways for the stop-press. 'Timber Merchant Found Dead,' he read. 'The body of Nicholas Huysmann, 77, timber merchant, was discovered this afternoon in his house in Queen Street, Norchester. The police are investigating.' And below it: 'Huysmann Death: police suspect foul play.'

For the second time that afternoon the jaw of Chief Inspector Gently momentarily ceased to champ.

Superintendent Walker of the Norchester City Police
looked up from a report sheet as Chief Inspector Gently
tapped and entered the office. 'Good Lord!' he
exclaimed. 'I was just wondering whether we should
get on to you. What in the world are you doing down
here?'

Gently chose the broader of two chairs and sat down.
'I'm on holiday,' he said laconically.

'On holiday? I didn't think you fellows at the Central
Office ever had a holiday.'

Gently smiled quietly. 'I like to fish,' he said. 'I like
to sit and watch a float and smoke. I like to have a pint
in the local and tell them about the one that got away.
They don't let me do it very often, but I'm trying to do
it right now.'

'Then you're not interested in a little job we've got
down here?'

Gently brought out the battered bag which had
contained his peppermint creams and looked into it
sadly. 'They'll send you Carruthers if you ask them,' he
said.

'But I don't want Carruthers. I want you.'

'Carruthers is a good man.'

Superintendent Walker beat the top of his desk with
an ink-stained finger. 'I don't like Carruthers – I don't
get on with him. We had a difference of opinion over
that Hickman business.'

'He was right, wasn't he?'

'Of course he was right! I've never been able to get
on with him since. But look here, Gently, this case
looks like being complicated. I've got implicit faith in

my own boys, but they don't claim to be homicide experts. And you are. So what about it?'

Gently took out the last of his peppermint creams, screwed up the bag and laid it carefully on the superintendent's desk. The superintendent whisked it impatiently into his waste-paper basket. 'It's this Huysmann affair, is it?' Gently asked.

'Yes. You've seen the papers?'

'Only the stop-press.'

'I've just got a report in from Hansom. He's down there now with the medico and the photographer. Huysmann was stabbed in the back in front of his safe and according to the yard manager there's about forty thousand pounds missing.'

Gently pursed his lips in a soundless whistle. 'That's a lot of money to keep in a safe.'

'But from what we know of Huysmann, it's probably true. He was a naturalized Dutchman who settled down here a good fifty years ago. He's been a big noise in the local timber industry for longer than I can remember and he had an odd sort of reputation. Nothing wrong, you know, just a bit eccentric. He lived a secluded life in a big old house down by the river, near his timber yard, and never mixed with anybody except some of the Dutch skippers who came up with his wood. He married a daughter belonging to one of them, a nice girl called Zetta, but she died in childbirth a few years afterwards. He's got two children, a daughter who lives in the house and is very rarely seen out of it, and a son called Peter, from whom he was estranged. Peter's known to us, by the by — he was the mate of a lorry-driver who got pulled for losing a load of cigarettes. He gave up lorry-driving after that and got a job with a travelling show.'

'He's a Wall of Death rider,' said Gently, almost to himself.

Superintendent Walker's eyebrows rose a few pegs. 'How do you know that?' he enquired.

'Things just sort of pop up on me,' said Gently. 'That's why they stuck me in the Central Office. But don't let it worry you. Keep on with the story.'

The superintendent eyed him suspiciously for a moment, then he leant forward and continued. 'Between you and me, I think Peter is the man we're after. He's here in town with the fair on the cattle market and according to the maid he was at his father's house this afternoon and there was a quarrel. That was just before 4 p.m. and the body was found by the housekeeper at 5 p.m. At least, he was the last person to see Huysmann alive.'

'As far as you know,' added Gently mildly.

'As far as we know,' the superintendent corrected himself. 'The weapon used was one of a pair of Indian throwing knives which hung on the wall. He was stabbed under the left shoulder-blade, the knife penetrating well into the heart. Hansom thinks he was kneeling at the safe at the time and the murderer had to push the body aside to get the money. The money was principally in five-pound and smaller notes.'

'Are any of the numbers known?' enquired Gently.

'We've got a list of numbers from the bank for one hundred of the five-pound notes, but that's all.'

'Who was in the house at the time of the murder?'

'Only the maid, as far as we can make out. The

8

housekeeper had the day off till tea-time: she was out from 11 a.m. till just before five. Gretchen, the daughter, went to the pictures at half-past two and didn't get back till well after five. There's a chauffeur, but he went off duty at midday. The only other person with normal access to the house was the yard manager, who was watching the football match at Railway Road.'

Gently pondered a moment. 'I like alibis,' he said, 'they're such fun, especially when you can't disprove them. But this maid, how was it she didn't hear Huysmann being killed? People who're being knifed don't usually keep quiet about it.'

The superintendent twisted his report over and frowned. 'Hansom hasn't said anything about that. He got this report off in a hurry. But I dare say he'll have something to say about it when he's through questioning. The main thing is, are you going to help us out?'

Gently placed four thick fingers and two thick thumbs together and appeared to admire the three-dimensional effect he achieved. 'Did you say the house was by the river?' he enquired absently.

'I did. But what the hell's that got to do with it?'

Gently smiled, slowly, sadly. 'I shall be able to look at it, even if I can't fish in it,' he said.

Queen Street, in which stood the house of Nicholas Huysmann, was probably the oldest street in the city. Incredibly long and gangling, it stretched from the foot of the cattle market hill right out into the residential suburbs, taking in its course breweries, coal-yards, timber-yards, machine-shops and innumerable ancient, rubbishy houses. South of it the land rose steeply to Burgh Street, reached by a network of alleys, an ugly cliff-land of mean rows and wretched yards; northwards lay the river, giving the street a maritime air, making its mark in such nomenclatures as 'Mariner's Lane' and 'Steam Packet Yard'.

The Huysmann house was the solitary residence with any pretension in Queen Street. Amongst the riff-raff of ancient wretchedness and modern rawness it raised its distinguished front with the detached air of an impoverished aristocrat in an alien and repugnant world. At the front it had two gable-ends, a greater and a lesser, connected by a short run of steep roof, beneath which ran a magnificent range of mullioned windows, projecting over the street below. Directly under these, steps rose to the main entrance, a heavily studded black door recessed behind an ogee arch.

Gently paused on the pavement opposite to take it in. A uniformed man stood squarely in the doorway and two of the three cars pulled up there were police cars. The third was a sports car of an expensive make. Gently crossed over and made to climb the steps, but his way was blocked by the policeman.

'No entrance here, sir,' he said.

Gently surveyed him mildly. 'You're new,' he said, 'but you look intelligent. Whose car is ZYX 169?'

The policeman stared at him, baffled. On the one hand Gently looked like an easy-going commercial traveller, on the other there was just enough assurance in his tone to make itself felt. 'I'm afraid I can't answer questions,' he compromised warily.

Gently brought out a virgin, freshly purchased packet

of peppermint creams. 'Here,' he said, 'have one of these. They're non-alcoholic. You can eat them on duty. They're very good for sore feet.' And placing a peppermint cream firmly in the constable's hand, he slid neatly past him and through the door.

He found himself in a wide hall with panelled walls and a polished floor. Opposite the door was a finely carved central stairway mounting to a landing, where a narrow window provided the hall with its scanty lighting. There were doors in the far wall on each side of the stairway, two more to the left and one to the right. At the end where he entered stood a hall table and stand, and to the right of the stairway a massive antique chest. There was no other furniture.

As he stood noting his surroundings the door on his right opened and a second constable emerged, followed by a thin, scrawny individual carrying a camera and a folded tripod.

'Hullo, Mayhew,' said Gently to the latter, 'how are crimes with you?'

The scrawny individual pulled up so sharply that the tripod nearly went on without him. 'Inspector Gently!' he exclaimed, 'but you can't have got here already! Why, he isn't properly cold!'

Gently favoured him with a slow smile. 'It's part of a speed-up programme,' he said. 'They're cutting down the time spent on homicide by thirty per cent. Where's Hansom?'

'He – he's in the study, sir – through this door and to the left.'

'Have they moved the body?'

'No, sir. But they're expecting an ambulance.'

11

Gently brooded a moment. 'Whose is that red sports car parked outside?' he asked.

'It belongs to Mr Leaming, sir,' answered the second constable.

'Who is Mr Leaming?'

'He's Mr Huysmann's manager, sir.'

'Well, find him up and tell him I want to see him, will you? I'll be in the study with Hansom.'

The constable saluted smartly and Gently pressed on through the door on the right. It led into a long, dimly lit passage ending in a cul-de-sac, with opposite doors about halfway down. Two transom lights above the doors were all that saved the passage from complete darkness. A heavy, carved chest-of-drawers stood towards the end, on the right. Gently came to a standstill between the two doors and ate a peppermint cream thoughtfully. Then he pulled out a handkerchief and turned the handle of the right-hand door.

The room was a large, well-furnished lounge or sitting-room, with a handsome open fireplace furnished with an iron fire-basket. A tiny window pierced in the outer wall looked out on the street. There was a vase of tulips standing in it. At the end of the room was a very large window with an arched top, but this was glazed with frosted glass. Gently looked down at the well-brushed carpet which covered almost the entire floor, then stooped for a closer inspection. There were two small square marks near the outer edge of the carpet, just by the door, very clearly defined and about thirteen inches apart. He glanced absently round at the furniture, shrugged and closed the door carefully again.

There were five men in the study, plus a sheeted

figure that a few hours previously had also been a man. Three of them looked round as Gently entered. The eyes of Inspector Hansom opened wide. He said: 'Heavens – they've got the Yard in already! When the hell are we going to get some homicide on our own?'

Gently shook his head reprovingly. 'I'm only here to gain experience,' he said. 'The super heard I was in town, and he thought it would help me to study your method.'

Hansom made a face. 'Just wait till I'm super,' he said disgustedly, 'you'll be able to cross Norchester right off your operations map.'

Gently smiled and helped himself from a packet of cigarettes that lay at the Inspector's elbow. 'Who did it?' he enquired naïvely.

Hansom grunted. 'I thought you were here to tell me that.'

'Oh, I like to take local advice. It's one of our first principles. What's your impression of the case?'

Hansom seized his cigarettes bitterly, extracted one and returned the packet ostentatiously to his pocket. He lit up and blew a cloud of smoke into the already saturated atmosphere. 'It's too simple,' he said, 'you wouldn't appreciate it. We yokels can only see a thing that sticks out a mile. We aren't as subtle as you blokes in the Central Office.'

'I suppose he was murdered?' enquired Gently with child-like innocence.

For a moment Hansom's eyes blazed at him, then he jerked his thumb at the sheeted figure. 'If you can tell me how an old geezer like that can stab himself where I can't even scratch fleas, I'll give up trying to be a detective and sell spinach for a living.'

13

Gently moved over to the oak settle on which the figure lay and turned back the sheet. Huysmann's body lay on its back, stripped, looking tiny and inhuman. The jaw was dropped and the pointed face with its wisp of silver beard seemed to be snarling in unutterable rage. Impassively he turned it over. At the spot described so picturesquely by Hansom was a neat, small wound, with a vertical bruise extending about an inch in either direction. Gently covered up the body again.

'Where's the weapon?' he asked.

'We haven't found it yet.'

Gently quizzed him in mild surprise. 'You described it in your report,' he said.

Hansom threw out his hands. 'I thought we'd got it when I made the report, but apparently we hadn't. I didn't know there was a pair. The daughter told me that afterwards.'

'Where's the one you have got?'

Hansom made a sign to the uniformed man standing by. He delved into an attaché case and brought out an object wrapped in cotton cloth. Gently unwrapped it. It was a beautifully ornamented throwing knife with a damascened blade and a serpent carved round the handle. It had a guard of a size and shape to have caused the bruise on Huysmann's back.

'Does it match the wound?' Gently asked.

'Ask the doc,' returned Hansom.

The heavily jowled man who sat scribbling at a table turned his head. 'I've only probed the wound so far,' he said, 'but as far as I can see it's commensurate with having been caused by this or an identical weapon buried to the full extent of the blade.'

'What do you make the time of death?'

The heavily jowled man bit his knuckle. 'Not much later than four o'clock, I'd say.'

'And that's just after your Peter Huysmann was heard quarrelling with his papa,' put in Hansom, with a note of triumph in his voice.

Gently shrugged and walked over to the wall. The room was of the same size as the sitting-room opposite, but differed in having a small outer door at the far side. Gently opened it and looked out. It gave access to a little walled garden with a tiny summer-house. There was another door in the garden wall.

'That goes to the timber-yard next door,' said Hansom, who had come over beside him. 'We've been over the garden and the summer-house with a fine-tooth comb and it isn't there. I'll have some men in the timber-yard tomorrow.'

'Is there a lock to that door in the wall?'

'Nope.'

'How about this door?'

'Locked up at night.'

Gently came back in and looked along the wall. There was an ornamental bracket at a height of six feet. 'Is that where you found the knife?' he enquired, and on receiving an affirmative, reached up and slid the knife into the bracket. Then he stood there, his hand on the hilt, his eyes wandering dreamily over the room and furnishings. Near at hand, on his right, stood the open safe, a chalked outline slightly towards him representing the position of the body as found. Across the room was the inner door with its transom light. A pierced trefoil window on his left showed part of the summer-house.

He withdrew the knife and handed it back to the constable.

'What has the mastermind deduced?' asked Hansom, with a slight sneer.

Gently fumbled for a peppermint cream. 'Which way did Peter Huysmann leave the house?' he counter-ed mildly.

'Through the garden and the timber-yard.'

'What makes you think that?'

'If he'd gone out through the front door the maid would have known – the old man had a warning bell fitted to it. It sounds in here and in the kitchen.'

'An unusual step,' mused Gently. He turned to the constable. 'I want you to go to the kitchen,' he said. 'I want you to ask the maid if she heard any unusual noise whatever after the quarrel between Peter and his father this afternoon. And please shut all the doors after you. Oh, and Constable – there's an old chest standing by the stairs in the hall. On your way back you might lift the lid and see what they keep in it.'

The constable saluted and went off on his errand.

'We're doing the regular questioning tomorrow,' said Hansom tartly. Gently didn't seem to notice. He stood quite still, with a far-away expression in his eyes, his lips moving in a noiseless chant. Then suddenly his mouth opened wide and the silence was split by such a spine-tingling scream that Hansom jumped nearly a foot and the police doctor jerked his notebook on to the floor.

'What the devil do you think you're doing!' exclaimed Hansom wrathfully.

Gently smiled at him complacently. 'I was being killed,' he said.

'Killed!'

'Stabbed in the back. I think that's how I'd scream, if I were being stabbed in the back . . .'

Hansom glared at him. 'You might warn us when you're going to do that sort of thing!' he snapped.

'Forgive me,' said Gently apologetically.

'Perhaps you break out that way at the Yard, but in the provinces we're not used to it.'

Gently shrugged and moved over to watch the two finger-print men at work on the safe. Just then the constable burst in.

'Ah!' said Gently. 'Did the maid hear anything?'

The constable shook his head.

'How about you – did you hear anything just now?'

'No sir, but—!'

'Good. And did you remember to look in the old chest by the stairs?'

The impatient constable lifted to the common gaze something he held shrouded holily in a handkerchief. 'That's it, sir!' he exploded. 'It was there – right there in the chest!'

And he revealed the bloodied twin of the knife which had hung on the wall.

'My God!' exclaimed Hansom.

Gently raised his shoulders modestly. 'I'm just lucky,' he murmured, 'things happen to me. That's why they put me in the Central Office, to keep me out of mischief . . .'

CHAPTER TWO

T HE TABLEAU IN the study – constable and knife rampant, inspector passive, corpse couchant – was interrupted by the ringing of a concealed bell, followed by the entry of Superintendent Walker. 'We've lost young Huysmann,' he said. 'I'm afraid he's made a break. I should have had him pulled in for questioning right away.'

Hansom gave the cry of a police inspector who sees his prey reft from him. 'He can't be far – he's probably still in the city.'

'He went back to the fair after he'd been here,' continued the superintendent. 'He had tea with his wife in his caravan and did his stunt at 6.15. He was due to do it again at 6.45. I had men there at 6.35, but he'd disappeared. The last person to see him was the mechanic who looks after the machines.'

'He was going to face it out,' struck in Hansom.

'It looks rather like it, but either his nerve went just then or it went when he saw my men. In either case we've lost him for the moment.'

'His nerve went when he saw the paper,' said Gently through a peppermint cream.

18

The superintendent glanced at him sharply. 'How do you know that?' he asked.

Gently swallowed and licked his lips. 'I saw it. I saw him do his stunt. His nerve was certainly intact when he did that.'

'Then for heaven's sake why didn't you grab him?' snapped Hansom.

Gently smiled at him distantly. 'If I'd known you wanted him I might have done, though once he got going he was moving faster than I shall ever move again.'

Hansom snarled disgustedly. The superintendent brooded for a moment. 'I don't think there's much doubt left that he's our man,' he said. 'It looks as though we shan't be needing you after all, Gently. I think we shall be able to pin something on young Huysmann and make it stick.'

'Gently doesn't think so,' broke in Hansom.

'You've come to a different conclusion?' asked the superintendent.

Gently shrugged and shook his head woodenly from side to side. 'I don't know anything yet. I haven't had time.'

'He found the knife for us, sir,' put in the constable defiantly, thrusting it under Walker's nose. The superintendent took it from him and weighed it in his hand. 'Obviously a throwing knife,' he said. 'We've just found out that young Huysmann used to be in a knife-throwing act before he went into the Wall of Death.'

'That's one for the book!' exclaimed Hansom delightedly.

'All in all, I think we've got the makings of a pretty

sound case. I'm much obliged to you, Gently, for consenting to help out, but the case has resolved itself pretty simply. I don't suppose you'll be sorry to get back to your fishing.'

Gently poised a peppermint cream on the end of his thumb and inspected it sadly. 'Who was watching Huysmann from the room across the passage this afternoon?' he enquired, revolving his thumb through a half-circle.

The superintendent stared.

'You might print the door handle and the back of the chair that stands just inside,' continued Gently, 'and photograph the marks left on the carpet. Then again,' he turned his thumb back with slow care, 'you might wonder to yourself how the knife came to be in the chest in the hall. I can't help you in the slightest. I'm still wondering myself . . .'

'Well, I'm not!' barked Hansom. 'It's where young Huysmann hid it.'

'Why?' murmured Gently, 'why did he remove the knife at all? Why should he bother when the knife couldn't be traced to him in any way? And if he did, why did he take it into the hall to hide it? Why didn't he take it away with him?'

Hansom gaped at him with his mouth open. The superintendent chipped in: 'Those are interesting points, Gently, and since you've made them we shall certainly follow them up. But I don't think they affect the main issue very materially. We need not complicate a matter when a simple answer is to hand. As it rests, there is no suspicion except in one direction and the suspicion there is very strong. It is our duty to show

how strong and to produce young Huysmann to answer it. I do not think it is our duty, or yours, to hunt out side issues that may weaken or confuse our case.'

Gently made the suspicion of a bow and flipped the peppermint cream from his thumb to his mouth. Hansom sneered. The superintendent turned to the constable. 'Fetch the men in with the stretcher,' he said, and when the constable had departed, 'Trencham is going to meet me at the fairground with a search warrant. You'd better come along, Hansom. I'm going to search young Huysmann's caravan.'

Gently said: 'I'm still interested in this case.'

The superintendent paused. He was not too sure of his position. While the matter was doubtful, the sudden appearance of Gently on the scene had seemed providential and he had gratefully enlisted the Chief Inspector's aid, but now that things were straightening out he began to regret it. There seemed to be nothing here that his own men couldn't handle. It was only a matter of time before young Huysmann was picked up: the superintendent was positive in his own mind that he was the man. And the honour and glory of securing a murder conviction was not to be lightly tossed away.

At the same time, he *had* brought Gently into it, and though the official channels had not been used, he was not sure if he had the power to dismiss him out of hand. Neither was he sure if it was policy.

'Stop in if you like,' he said, 'it's up to you.'

Gently nodded. 'It's unofficial. I won't claim pay for it.'

'Will you come along with us to the fairground?'

Gently pursed his lips. 'No,' he said, 'it's Saturday night. I feel tired. I may even go to the pictures . . .'

The constable left in charge was the constable who had found the knife. Gently, who had lingered to see his finger-printing done, called him aside. 'You were present at the preliminary questioning?' he asked.

'Yes, sir. I came down with Inspector Hansom, sir.'

'Which cinema did Miss Huysmann go to?'

'To the Carlton, sir.'

'Ah,' said Gently.

The constable regarded him with shining eyes. 'You'll excuse me, sir, but I would like to know how you knew where the knife was,' he said.

Gently smiled at him comfortably. 'I just guessed, that's all.'

'But you guessed right, sir, first go.'

'That was just my luck. We have to be lucky, to be detectives.'

'Then it wasn't done by – deduction, sir?'

Gently's smile broadened and he felt for his bag of peppermint creams. 'Have one,' he said. 'What's your name?'

'Thank you, sir. It's Letts.'

'Well, Letts, my first guess was that there'd been some post-mortem monkeying because the knife was missing and there was no reason why it should have been. My second guess was that the party who was watching from the other room this afternoon was the party concerned.'

'How did you know the party was watching this afternoon, sir?'

'Because the room was cleaned up before lunch and it was cleaned up today before lunch – witness the tulips with dew on them and the absence of dust. Hence the marks on the carpet were made after lunch. My third guess was that the party concerned was an inside party and not an outside party, and that the odds were in favour of them hiding the knife in the house. Now a person with a bloody knife to hide doesn't waste time being subtle. It could have been in the chest-of-drawers at the end of the passage, but the polished floor in that direction has an unmarked film of dust. The only other easy hiding-place was the chest in the hall. So I guessed that.'

The constable shifted his helmet a fraction and rubbed his head. 'Then it was all guessing after all, sir?' he said slowly.

'All guessing,' Gently reiterated.

'And yet you were right, sir.'

'Which,' said Gently, 'goes to show how much luck you need to be a detective, Letts . . . don't forget that when you apply for a transfer.'

'But you've given the case a different look, sir. It could be that somebody else was in this job as well as young Huysmann.'

'Could be,' agreed Gently, 'or it may just mean that somebody's got some pretty virile explaining to do. Remember what the super said, Letts. He was quite right. It's our job to make a case, not to break it. Justice belongs to the court. It's nothing to do with the police.'

The hall, which was gloomy enough by evening light, seemed even gloomier when lit by the low-power chandelier which depended from its high ceiling. As Gently passed through it on his way out a tall figure stepped towards him. Gently paused enquiringly.

'Chief Inspector Gently?'

'That's me.'

'I'm Rod Leaming, Mr Huysmann's manager. They told me you wanted to see me.'

He was a man of about forty, big, dark-haired, dark-eyed, with small well-set ears and features that were boldly handsome. His voice was rounded and pleasant. Gently said: 'Ah yes. You were at the football match. How did the City get on?'

There was a moment's silence, then Leaming said: 'They won, three-one.'

'It was a good match, they tell me.'

Leaming gave a little shrug. 'There were a lot of missed chances. They might have won six-one without being flattered, though of course Cummings was a passenger most of the match. Are you interested in football?'

Gently smiled a far-away smile. 'I watch the Pensioners when I get the chance. Is your car ZYX 169?'

'Yes.'

'It's got mud all over the rear number plate. I thought I'd mention it to you before you were stopped. It's fresh mud.'

'Thanks for the tip. I must have picked it up on the car park this afternoon.'

'It's a clay mud,' mused Gently, 'comes from a river bank, perhaps.'

'The car park at Railway Road lies between the river and the ground.'

'Ah,' said Gently.

Leaming relaxed a little. He pulled out a gold

cigarette case and offered it to Gently. Gently took a cigarette. They were hand-made and expensive. Leaming gave him a light and lighted one himself. 'Look,' he said, forcing smoke through his nostrils, 'this is a bad business, Inspector, and it looks pretty black for young Huysmann. But if an outside opinion is any help, I'm one who doesn't think he's the man. I've seen a good deal of Peter at one time or another and he's not the type to do a thing like this.'

Gently blew a neat little smoke-ring.

Leaming continued: 'Of course, I realize there's everything against him. He's been in trouble before and the reason he was estranged from his father is well known.'

'Not to me,' said Gently.

'You haven't heard? But it's bound to come out in the questioning and it's not so very serious. You've got to remember that he was the only son; he was brought up to regard himself as the automatic heir to the business. Well, there's no doubt that Mr Huysmann was a little hard on Peter when it came to pocket money and one day Peter decamped with a hundred pounds or more.'

Gently exhaled a stream of smoke towards the distant chandelier.

'But that was merely youthful high spirits, Inspector. If Peter had had a proper allowance, it would never have happened. It wouldn't have happened then if Peter hadn't fallen in love with an office girl – she's his wife now – and if Mr Huysmann had treated the affair with . . . well, a little more feeling. But there it was, he wouldn't hear of the idea of Peter getting married and though he might have forgiven the embezzlement, he treated the marriage as though it were a personal affront. Poor Peter had a rough time of it after he left home. He wrote to Mr Huysmann on several occasions asking for small sums, but he never received a penny. I'm afraid their relations were very embittered towards the end.'

Leaming paused for comment, but Gently contented himself with another smoke-ring.

'It got so far that Mr Huysmann threatened to cut Peter out of his will and I believe he meant to do it, if he'd had time, though between you and me it would have been a gross injustice. Apart from his temper – and he inherited that from his father – there was nothing vicious in Peter at all. He's a very likeable lad, with a lot of initiative and any amount of guts. He'd have made a very worthy successor in the firm.'

'And you don't think he did it?' queried Gently dreamily.

'I'm positive he didn't! I've known him for ten years and intimately for eight – saw him every day, had him up to spend the evening, often. I'll tell you something more. If you get this lad and try to pin the murder on him, I'll brief the best counsel in England for his defence, cost what it may.'

'It will cost several thousand,' said Gently, helpfully.

Leaming ignored the remark. He breathed smoke through his nose under high pressure. 'I take it that Peter is your guess as well as theirs?' he demanded.

'My guessing is still in the elementary stage.'

'Well, I could see clearly enough what Inspector Hansom thought about it.'

'Inspector Hansom is a simple soul.'

Leaming's powerful brown eyes sought out Gently's absent green ones. 'Then you don't think he did it – you're on my side in this?'

Gently's smile was as distant as the pyramids. 'I'm not on anybody's side,' he said, 'I'm just here on holiday.'

'But you're assisting on the case? Look here, Inspector, I've been thinking this thing over. There's one thing that's going to tell a lot in Peter's favour. It's the money.'

Gently nodded one of his slow mandarin nods.

'There was forty-two thousand pounds in that safe, more or less, and they won't find it with Peter.'

'Why?' asked Gently brightly.

'Why? Because he didn't do the murder, that's why. And as soon as some of those notes that are listed start turning up, it'll be proof positive that the real murderer is still at large.'

Gently surveyed the burnt-down stub of his cigarette thoughtfully, moved over to the chest and stubbed it against the massive iron clasp. Then he raised the lid and dropped the end inside. 'It might work out if the murderer started on the right side of the forty-two thousand,' he said, 'but then again, he might start in the middle . . .' And he let the lid fall back with a bang.

Leaming stood, feet apart, watching him closely. 'At least it's a good lead,' he said.

Gently sighed. 'Police work is full of leads. It's the tragedy of routine . . . and ninety-nine per cent of them lead nowhere.' He came back from the chest. 'If you're going back to the city I could use a lift,' he said.

★　★　★

27

Leaming dropped him off at Castle Paddock. Gently shambled away, head bent, following the crescent wall at the foot of the Castle Hill, the patriarchal features of the Norman keep silent and peaceful in the dark sky above. From the other side of the Hill rose the glow and the feverish cacophony of the fair. Clark, the owner of the Wall of Death, had tempted back one of his ex-riders. The Greatest Show on Earth continued to do business . . .

In a quieter corner of the fairground Peter Huysmann's young wife stood near the door of her tiny cosmos, biting her lips to keep back tears of humiliation and helplessness. Inside were the policemen. With religious thoroughness they were dismembering and examining her private, familiar things. 'Look,' said a constable, holding up a cheap little necklet that Peter had bought her on her twenty-first birthday, 'wasn't there something like this on the list of stolen properties today?'

Gently came to Orton Place, where a great sunken gap, used as a car park, still offered mute witness of the Baedeker Raids of ten years back. On two sides of the gap blazed the windows of large stores, risen phoenix-wise. But the gap remained a gap. The streets about it were thronged with Saturday-night crowds, gay, noisy, unconscious that somewhere amongst them was a man for whom they were terrible, who feared their slightest glance, who had the mortal horror on him of being seized and dragged to their machine of death. And amongst them too went the hunters, the takers, the accusers, those to whom the killing of Peter Huysmann meant preferment. But they were unconscious of this as of the gap. Habit had staled them both. And after all, *someone* had done for old Huysmann . . . hadn't they?

'Pink!' cried an old man, as Gently drew near him, 'don't forget your pink!' Gently fumbled in his pocket for coppers. 'They did well today,' said the old man. 'Did you see the match, sir?' 'No,' said Gently. He took the paper. 'Isn't there a home match next week too?' he enquired. 'We've got the Cobblers coming, sir – it'll be a good match.' Gently nodded vaguely. 'I may see it,' he said. As he walked on he unfolded the paper and glanced over the headlines. They ran:

MISSED CHANCES AT RAILWAY ROAD
City not flattered by margin
First-half injury to Cummings

Gently pursed his lips, folded the paper and put it carefully away in his pocket.

29

CHAPTER THREE

IT WAS RAINING.
A generous stream of water escaped from a blocked gutter two stories higher and battered insistently on the zinc-shod window-sill of Gently's window. He raised his head, frowning. Waking up to rain filled him with a sort of hopelessness, a feeling that here was a day to be got over and dismissed as quickly as possible, a day when all normal business ought to be postponed. He blinked and reached out for the cup of tea that should have been there.

Down below in the little dining-room Gently was the only guest at breakfast. It was Sunday, of course . . . for the rest of the world. But there was a fire and a sheaf of Sunday papers, and the breakfast was a fairly lavish plate of bacon, egg, tomatoes and fried bread. Gently turned over a paper as he ate. The Huysmann business hadn't built up yet, there was only a short paragraph headed: TIMBER MERCHANT STABBED TO DEATH. He sifted it with a practised eye to see if his name was mentioned. It wasn't.

Feeling fuller and better, Gently donned his raincoat

and sallied forth. The rain was pelting down out of a low, monotonous sky and the streets were practically empty. In front of the pathetically gay awnings of the provision market a gang of men were shovelling bruised and rotten fruit into a lorry. Behind them rose the pale pastelled mass of the City Hall with its dim portico and slender naked tower. Gently plodded on through the city centre to the castle and the cattle market.

There was something ominous about the deserted fairground. The booths which had yesterday been wells of colour and bright lights were now blinded with screens of old canvas, taut with the rain and flapping dismally. The avenues of alleys between them had ceased to be channels of raucous delight, showed the black, cross-grooved tiles of the cattle market, threatening the ephemerality of usurping pleasure. Gently made his way to the Wall of Death. At the back was a lean-to with one side canvas. He pushed up the flap and went in.

Inside was a bench on which stood one of the red-painted motorcyles, its engine in the process of being stripped down, while another machine leaned against the end of the lean-to. Across from the flap was the entrance to the well, with the ramp up which the riders went. From this came tinkering sounds. Gently went through. Between the cambered bottom and the outer wall a man was crouched, tightening down the bolt which secured a strengthening strut. He looked at Gently suspiciously. Gently shrugged, leaned against the wall, took out his pipe and began to fill it.

Having locked the bolt with wire the man came out. He was short and stuggy, and his brown, porous face

31

looked as though it had been squeezed up in a pair of nutcrackers. He rolled a cigarette, peering at Gently sharply as he licked it.

'Police?' he asked.

Gently transferred the flame of his lighter from his pipe to the stuggy man's cigarette. 'CID,' he said casually. The stuggy man's hand trembled and he drew at the cigarette powerfully.

'Your outfit?' enquired Gently.

'You know it is.'

'You must be Mr Clark.'

'Who'd you think I was – Nye Bevan?'

Gently shook his head seriously. 'Why did Peter go to see his father yesterday afternoon?' he asked, then leaned back against the wall again to give the stuggy man time to think it over.

There was a pause of quite some moments. The stuggy man puffed at his cigarette with industrious energy, flicking it nervously at the end of each puff. Gently drew in smoke with slow deliberateness. There was a ratio of about three to one. At last the stuggy man said: 'S'pose he just went to say "hullo" to his old man.'

Gently removed his pipe. 'No,' he said, and put his pipe back.

The stuggy man's cigarette nearly burst into flames. He said: 'I don't have to tell you anything!'

Gently nodded indefinitely.

'You can't do nofink to me if I keep my trap shut. Why can't you leave us alone? I told them all they wanted to know last night!'

'You didn't tell them what I want to know.'

'Well, haven't you got enough against him, without looking for any more?'

Gently turned over his pipe and let the top ash fall into a little pool of water gathering on the floor. He surveyed the stuggy man with distant green eyes. 'There's a very good case to be made against Peter Huysmann,' he said. 'If he's guilty, the less that's found out the better. But if he's innocent, then everybody concerned had best tell what they know. But perhaps you think he's guilty?'

'Naow!' The stuggy man flipped ash in a wide arc. 'Pete never did a thing like that. You don't know Pete.' He faced Gently fiercely.

'Then the best way you can help him is to answer my question.'

The stuggy man threw down his cigarette-end and ground it to pulp beneath his foot. 'I know you!' he burst out, 'I know you and your questions! It's all very well now, but when it gets to court it will all be twisted against him. I seen it happen before. I seen the way they went to work to hang old George Cooper. All very nice they were, as nice as pie – they only wanted to help him! But what happened when they gits him in court? Every mortal thing what people had told them was used against him – every mortal thing.'

He broke off, breathing heavily through his flattened nose. 'So don't come telling me how I can help him, mister,' he concluded. 'I wasn't born yesterday, d'ye see?'

The growing pool of water on the floor made a sudden dart forward at a sunken tile. Gently moved his foot to higher ground. 'Let's put it another way,' he said smoothly. 'There's a sufficiently sound case against

Peter Huysmann to put him in dock and probably hang him. Any further evidence will simply reinforce the case. So it might be good policy to please the police rather than tease them . . . isn't that sense?'

The stuggy man's eyes blazed. 'You haven't got nofink against me, mister!' he exclaimed.

'I'm not suggesting we have. Though we might have, some day . . . it's worth remembering.'

'They was at me last night that way – says they might find the Wall was dangerous. But I know where I stand. It isn't no more dangerous here than it was at Lincoln or Newark, nor anywheres else. And I told them so.' He spat into the pool of water.

Gently sighed, and mentally cursed the large feet of Inspector Hansom, whose prints were so painfully visible. The stuggy man produced his tin of tobacco again and began the nervous concoction of a fresh cigarette. Gently lit it for him absently. The rain continued to fall.

'I saw him ride yesterday,' said Gently, apropos of nothing. 'He's a good rider.'

'He's the best man on the Wall in England,' jerked the stuggy man.

'You wouldn't want to lose him.'

'I shan't, if I can help it.'

'If he gets off he'll inherit his father's business.'

The stuggy man shot him a guarded glance, but said nothing.

'Unless he's been cut off, of course,' added Gently. 'I'm told his father intended to make a fresh will.'

The stuggy man drew in an enormous lungful of smoke and jetted it out towards the canvas flap.

'It could be he went to see him about that,' continued Gently, 'and then, in the course of the quarrel that followed—'

'Naow!' broke in the stuggy man.

'Why not?' queried Gently. 'It's the line that logically suggests itself . . .'

'He didn't go about no will!'

'You'll have a hard time convincing the City Police that he didn't. It's the obvious reason, and the obvious reason, right or wrong, is peculiarly acceptable to juries.'

'But I tell you he never, mister – he knew all along that the old man was going to cut him out!'

'Then,' said Gently, sighting his pipe at the stuggy man's heart, 'why did he go?'

The stuggy man gulped. 'I offered him halves in the Wall,' he said. 'He reckoned the old man would put up five hundred to be rid of him.'

'Ah,' said Gently dreamily, 'how you make us work for it – how you do!'

He knocked out his pipe and moved over to the canvas flap. The world outside had an arrested, gone-away look, dull and washed out, a wet Sunday. Instinctively, you would be indoors, preferably with a fire. Gently hovered at the flap a moment. He turned back to the stuggy man.

'Where's Peter Huysmann now?' he asked.

'Where you won't bloody well find him!'

Gently shrugged reprovingly. 'I was only asking a civil question,' he said.

Huysmann's caravan was small and cheap, but it had been recently re-painted in a dashing orange and blue:

neatly too. Some time and pains had been lavished on it. It stood somewhat apart from its neighbours, beside a plane tree. One entered by steps and a door at the side. Gently knocked.

'Who is it?' called a voice, subdued, coming with an effort.

'A friend,' replied Gently cheerfully.

There was movement inside the van. The door was pulled inwards. A young woman of twenty-three or -four stood framed in the tiny passageway. She was brown-haired with blue-grey eyes and round, attractive features. She had a firm, natural figure. She wore an overall. There was a frightened look in her eyes and her mouth was held small and tight. She said: 'Oh – what is it you want?'

Gently smiled reassuringly. 'I've come to be a nuisance,' he said. 'May I come in?'

She stepped back with a sort of hopeless submission, indicating a door to the left of the passage. Gently inserted his bulky figure with care, pausing to wipe his feet on the small rectangle of coconut-matting. It was a minute sitting-room which at night became a bedroom and at mealtimes was a dining-room. In the centre was a boat-type mahogany table, narrow, with wide, folded-down leaves, on which was a bowl of daffodils. There were three windows with flowered print cur-tains. A settee built along the wall on the right unfolded into a double bed and opposite it, on the other wall, was a cupboard with drawers, on which stood a row of Penguins and cheap editions of novels. Facing the door hung a framed photograph of Peter in an open-necked shirt.

Gently chose a small wooden chair and sat down. 'I'm Chief Inspector Gently of the Central Office, CID,' he said, 'but don't take too much notice of it. I don't cut much ice in these parts.' He looked around him approvingly. 'I've often thought of buying a caravan like this when I retire,' he added.

Mrs Huysmann moved across behind the table and sat down on the settee. She held herself very stiffly and upright. Her eyes never wandered from Gently's face. She said nothing.

Gently glanced at the photograph of Peter. 'How old is your husband?' he enquired.

'Twenty-nine, in August.' She had a soft, low voice, but it was taut and toneless.

'I've only met him once – if you can call seeing him ride meeting him. I liked his riding. It takes real guts and judgment to do that little trick of his.'

'You've seen him ride?' For a moment she was surprised.

'I was here yesterday. I'm on holiday, you know, but they roped me in on this business. I believe they're sorry they did now. I'm so hard to convince. But there you are . . .' He raised his shoulders deprecatingly.

She said: 'You want to ask me something.' It was between a question and a bare statement of fact, colourless, something to be said.

'Yes,' Gently said, 'but don't rush it. I know how painful it is.'

She looked down, away from him. 'They took my statement last night,' she said.

There was a moment during which the rain beat remotely on the felted roof, an ominous moment, razor-sharp: and then tears began to trickle down the tight, mask-like face. Gently looked away. She was not sobbing. The tears came from deeper, from the very depths of humiliation and fear and helplessness. She said: 'I can't tell you anything – I don't know anything . . . they took it all down last night.'

Gently said: 'They had to do it, you know. I've got to do it, too. Otherwise there may be an injustice.'

'He didn't do it – not Peter – not Peter!' she said, and sank forward with a great sigh, as though to say that had drained away the stiffness in her body. She was sobbing now, blindly, a foolish little lace handkerchief crumpled up in a ball between her hands, the shock and the pent-up horror of the night finding outlet at last. Gently moved across and patted her shoulder paternally. He said: 'Cry away now, like a good girl, and when you've finished I'm going to tell you a secret.'

She looked up at him wonderingly, eyes glazed with tears. He went on: 'I oughtn't to tell you this – I oughtn't even to tell myself. But I'm a very bad detective, and I'm always doing what they tell you not to in police college.'

He moved away to the other side of the caravan and began looking at the books. She followed him with her eyes. There was something in his manner that struck through the bitter confusion possessing her, something that gave her pause. She choked into the handkerchief. 'I'm – I'm sorry!' she faltered.

Gently took down a book. 'You've got *Mornings in Mexico*,' he said absently. 'I read an extract from it somewhere. Can I borrow it?'

'It's – Peter's.'

'Oh, I'll let you have it back. There's nothing at my rooms except a telephone directory, and I've read that.'

He came back and sat down beside her. She sniffed and tried to smile. 'I didn't mean to cry,' she said. 'I'm terribly sorry.' Gently produced his bag of peppermint creams and proffered them to her. 'You'll like these – I've been eating them off and on for twenty years. You try one.' He took one himself, and laid the bag open on the end of the table.

'Now,' he said, 'my secret. But first, you can keep a secret, can't you?'

She nodded, chewing her peppermint cream.

'It's this. I, Chief Inspector Gently, Central Office, CID, am morally certain that Peter didn't murder his father. What do you think of that?'

Her eyes widened. 'But––!' she exclaimed.

Gently held up his hand. 'Oh, I know, and you mustn't tell anybody at all. It's a terrible thing for a Chief Inspector to prejudice himself in the early stages of an investigation. I've had to tick people off about it myself. And to tell it to somebody concerned in the case is flat misdemeanour.' Gently paused to fortify himself with another peppermint cream. 'I've been a policeman too long,' he concluded, 'it's high time they retired me. Some day, I might do something quite unforgivable.'

Mrs Huysmann was still staring at him disbelievingly. 'You – you *know* he didn't do it!' she cried.

'No,' said Gently, 'I don't know it. Not yet.'

'But you said––!'

'I said I was morally certain, my dear, which isn't quite the same thing.'

She relapsed slowly into her former forlorn posture. 'Then they'll still charge him with it,' she said.

Gently nodded. 'My moral certainties won't prevent that. Peter's still in grave danger and unless I can produce some hard, irreducible facts pointing in another direction, he may find his innocence very difficult to establish. Which is why I'm here this morning.'

'But I don't know anything – I can't help you at all!'

Gently smiled at a point beyond the blue horizon. 'That is something, my dear, which we will now attempt to discover,' he said.

The rain had washed out any lurking quaintness there might have been in Queen Street. The raw brick tower of the new brewery seemed rawer, the stale flint-and-brick tower of the old breweries staler, the mouldering plaster-and-lath miserable to disintegration. Gently splashed through puddles formed in hollows of the pavement. He stopped to look at a horse-meat shop. Painted a virulent red, it had crudely drawn upon it the faces of a cat and a dog, with the legend: 'Buy our dinners here'. Up the middle of Queen Street rode a lonely sodden figure, a bundle of papers covered by a sack in the carrier of his bicycle. Behind him limped a dog, head down, tail down. At the horse-meat shop the dog raised its head and gave a low whine. But it continued to limp after its master.

Today there were only two cars outside the Huysmann house, a police car and Leaming's red Pashley. The constable on the door saluted smartly. 'Inspector Hansom is in the sitting-room, sir,' he said. Gently disrobed himself of his raincoat and left it hung dripping on the hall-stand. A second constable opened the sitting-room door for him. Inside sat Inspector Hansom at a table, smoking a cigar. Beside him sat a uniformed man with a shorthand notebook.

'Ah!' cried Hansom, 'the Yard itself! We'll have to forget about the third degree after all, Jackson.'

Gently smiled moistly, took out his pipe and began to fill it. 'Forgive me for being late,' he said.

Hansom spewed forth cigar-smoke. 'Don't mention it,' he said, 'we can accommodate ourselves to Metropolitan hours. Just sit down and make yourself at home. There'll be tea and biscuits in half an hour.'

Gently lit his pipe and sat down.

'I suppose you didn't look in at the office this morning,' continued Hansom, a glint in his eye.

'No. Should I have done?'

'It might be an idea, if you want to keep abreast of this case.'

Gently patted the ash down in his pipe with an experienced finger. 'You mean the five-pound note you found in a drawer in Peter Huysmann's caravan, don't you?' he enquired thoughtfully.

'You were at the office then?' demanded Hansom, a little clashed.

'No. But I was at the caravan this morning.'

'Then perhaps you don't know that it was one of the notes taken from Huysmann's safe?'

Gently shrugged. 'Why else would you have taken it away?'

Hansom's eyes gleamed triumphantly. 'And how do you propose to explain that one, Chief Inspector Gently?' he demanded.

Gently patted away at his pipe till the ash was perfectly level, then dusted off his finger on his trousers. 'I don't explain anything,' he said. 'I'm a policeman. I ask questions.'

'It'll take a lot of questions to make this look silly.'

'I should ask myself,' proceeded Gently, 'why Peter left a note there at all, just one. And I should ask myself whether it was likely to be one of those on your list – he had so many others.' He paused.

'And is that all you'd ask?' enquired Hansom with a sneer.

'And I think,' added Gently, 'I'd ask Mrs Huysmann if she knew how it came to be there.'

Hansom sat up straight, his cigar lifting. 'So you would, would you?' he said.

'I think I would. Very nicely, of course, so I didn't make her feel she was being kicked in the teeth by a size fifteen boot.'

'Har, har,' said Hansom, 'give me time to laugh.'

'And I should find out that Peter never had but that one note and brought it back with him yesterday in a seething temper and put it in the drawer with express instructions that it wasn't to be touched. Of course, it's technically possible that he had his pocket picked of the balance . . . perhaps that's why he was so angry.'

Hansom snarled: 'And you believe that bosh?'

'I don't believe anything,' said Gently mildly. 'I just ask questions . . .'

The ash dropped off Hansom's cigar and fell neatly on to the blotter in front of him. He grabbed it away savagely. 'See here,' he snapped, 'I know you're dead against us. I know you'd go to any lengths to get young

Huysmann off, even though you're as sure as we are that he did it. Because why? Because you're the Yard and you think you've got to show us we're a lot of flat-footed yokels. That's why! That's why you're going to upset this case – if you can. But you can't, Chief Inspector Gently, it's getting much too one-sided, even for you. By the time we've lined this case up there won't be a jury in the country who'll give it more than ten minutes – if they give it that!'

Gently leaned back in his chair and blew the smallest and roundest of smoke-rings at the distant ceiling. 'Inspector Hansom,' he said, 'I'd like to make a point.'

'What's that?' snarled Hansom.

'There is between us, Inspector Hansom, a slight but operative difference in rank. And now, if you will start sending these people in, we'll try to question them as though we were part of one of the acknowledged civilizations.'

CHAPTER FOUR

MRS TURNER, THE housekeeper, was a clean, neat, bustling person of fifty-five, dressed for the day in a black tailored suit smelling of stale lavender. She had a large bland face with small mean eyes, and her nose was the merest shade red.

She said: 'I'm sure there's nothing more I can tell you what I didn't say yesterday,' and sat down with an air of disapproval and injury.

Hansom said: 'You are Mrs Charles Turner, widow, housekeeper to the deceased. You had the day off yesterday till 5 p.m . . . where did you spend the day?'

'I told you all that yesterday.'

'Please be good enough to answer the question. Where did you spend the day?'

'I went to see me sister at Earlton . . .'

'You were at your sister's the whole of that time?' Gently said.

The housekeeper shot him a mean look. 'Well, most of it, like . . .'

'You mean that part of the time you were somewhere else.'

44

She pursed her lips and jiffled a little. 'I spent the day with me sister,' she repeated defensively, adding, 'you can ask her, if you don't believe me.'

'Right. We'll check on that,' said Hansom. 'What time did you arrive back here?'

'I got in about five to five.'

'What did you do then?'

'I went into the kitchen to see if the maid had got things ready for tea.'

'You found the maid in the kitchen?'

'She was sitting down reading one of them fourpenny novels.'

'Did she mention anything unusual that had occurred during the afternoon?'

'She said as how Mr Peter had called and seen his father, and they'd had a dust-up over something, but it didn't last long.'

Gently said: 'She could not have heard them quarrelling from the kitchen. Did she say where she was at the time?'

The housekeeper frowned. She didn't like Gently's questions. He seemed determined to complicate the most clear-cut issues. 'I didn't ask her,' she replied tartly.

Hansom continued: 'When did you go to the study?'

'I went there straight away, to ask Mr Huysmann what time he wanted tea.'

'Was that usual?' chipped in Gently.

'Yes, it was usual! He didn't have no set times for his meals. You had to go and ask him.'

'That would be a few minutes after 5 p.m.?' proceeded Hansom.

'About five-past, I should think.'

'And you knocked on the door and entered?'

'That was how he told us to go in.'

'Tell us what you saw when you entered.'

'Well, I just see Mr Huysmann lying there sort of twisted like, as though he might have had a fit.'

'Was he lying in the same position as he was when the police arrived?'

'I might have moved him a little bit, but not much. I thought as how he was took ill. I tried to get him up, but when I saw all the blood under him I knew that something horrible had happened, so I put him back again.'

'And then?'

'Then I went for Susan and told her to get the police.'

'Did Susan go into the study?'

'No, I told her not to. That was bad enough for me, who've seen dead people. I nearly went out when I got back to the kitchen.'

'A telephone message was received at headquarters at 5.17 p.m. That was ten minutes after you would have returned to the kitchen.'

'Well, there I was in a bad way, I had Susan fetch me some brandy. And then Miss Gretchen, she came back and had to be told.'

'What time did Miss Huysmann return?'

'About a quarter past five, I suppose it was.'

'At which door did she enter?'

'She came in the front, of course. Susan was just going through to phone and she see Miss Gretchen in the hall and tell her.'

'How did Miss Huysmann take the news?'

'Well, she's always a very quiet sort of girl, but she was mortal pale when she came into the kitchen. I gave her a sip of brandy to pull her together.'

'Was Susan at all surprised when Miss Huysmann came in?'

'She said: "Oh – I thought you was still in your room, miss."'

Hansom paused, leaned back in his chair and appeared to be studying the rash his cigar-ash had made on his blotter. The constable beside him scribbled industriously. Outside the rain made a soft quiet noise, like the sound of time itself. The housekeeper sat upright and rocked very gently backwards and forwards.

Hansom said: 'You have been a long time in this family, Mrs Turner. Certain private matters concerning it must have come to your notice. Can you think of anything which may have a bearing on the present tragedy?'

The housekeeper's face changed to defensive righteousness. 'There's Mr Peter,' she said, '*he's* no secret.'

'Is there anybody else connected with Mr Huysmann who, to your knowledge, may have had a grudge against him?'

'I daresay there's several people as weren't over-fond of him. He was a long way from being open-handed. But I can't think of anybody who'd want to do a thing like this.'

'Did you know that Mr Huysmann proposed to make a fresh will disinheriting his son?'

'Oh yes. He'd been talking about that ever since Mr Peter got married.'

Gently said: 'How long ago was that?'

The housekeeper thought for a moment. 'It'll be just on two years,' she replied.

'Did Peter know about it two years ago?'

'Mr Huysmann told him before he got married.'

Gently nodded his slow, complacent nod. Hansom glared across at him. 'Is there anything else you'd like to ask before we let Mrs Turner go?' he asked bitingly.

Gently placed his fingers neatly together. 'Was the safe door open or closed when you discovered the body?' he said.

'It was open.'

'And how about the outer door?'

'I think it was closed.'

'Ah,' said Gently. He leaned forward in his chair. 'At the time the murder was discovered, are you positive that Susan and yourself were the only persons in the house?' he asked.

The housekeeper's face registered surprise followed by indignation. 'If there had been anyone else I should have said so,' she retorted magnificently.

'Is there anybody not so far mentioned whom you would not have been surprised to find in the house at that time in the afternoon?'

She paused. 'Well, there's the chauffeur, but he was off duty. And there might have been someone from the yard about business.'

Gently nodded again and rested his chin on his thumbs. 'This room we're in,' he said, 'was it last cleaned before lunch yesterday?'

'You'd best ask Susan about that. It should have been done.'

'To your knowledge, did anybody enter it after the discovery of the murder?'

'There was nothing to come in here about.'

Gently leant far back into his chair, elevated his paired fingers and looked through them at the ceiling. 'During the time when you were not at your sister's yesterday,' he said, 'would you have been . . . somewhere else . . . for the purpose of taking alcoholic refreshment?'

The housekeeper's face turned scarlet. She jumped to her feet, her eyes flashing, and seemed on the point of a scathing denial. Then, with an effort, she checked herself and flung out of the room like an outraged duchess.

Gently smiled through the cage of his fingers. 'Pass me,' he said dreamily, 'there's one alibi less on my list.'

Gently was eating a peppermint cream when Susan came in. He had offered one to Hansom as a sort of olive branch, but Hansom had refused it, and after counting those that remained in the bag Gently was not sorry. He had a feeling that Norchester would not be very productive of peppermint creams on a Sunday, especially a wet Sunday, and the prospect of running short was a bleak one. Life was hard enough without a shortage of peppermint creams.

Susan was a pretty, pert blonde girl with a tilted bra and an accentuated behind. She wore a smile as a natural part of her equipment. She had a snub nose and dimples and a pleased expression, and had a general supercharged look, as though she was liable to burst out of her black dress and stockings into a fierce nudity.

The constable with the shorthand notebook sighed as she took her seat. He was a young man. Hansom ran through the preliminaries of identification and association.

'What time did the family finish lunch, Miss Stibbons?' he asked.

Susan leant her bewitching head on one side. 'It would be about two o'clock, Inspector. It was quarter past when I went to clear away.'

'Did Mr Huysmann go to his study directly after lunch?'

'I wouldn't know, Inspector. But he was there when I took him his coffee.'

'When was that?'

'It would be about half-past two, I should think.'

'What was he doing then?'

'He was standing by the window, looking at the garden.'

'Did he make any remark out of the ordinary?'

The bewitching head dipped over an errant blush. 'We-ell, Inspector . . .'

'Did he lead you to suppose he was expecting a visitor?'

'No . . . he didn't give me that impression.'

Hansom looked her over thoughtfully. He was only forty himself. 'What did Miss Huysmann do after lunch?' he asked.

'She took her coffee up to her room.'

'She apparently left the house shortly afterwards to go to the pictures. She says she left at half-past two. You didn't see her go?'

'No, Inspector.'

'Did she take her coffee to her room before you took Mr Huysmann's to him?'

'Oh yes, she came and got it from the kitchen.'

'You didn't hear the front-door bell between the time she took her coffee and the time you went to the study with Mr Huysmann's?'

'No, Inspector.'

'Nor while you were in the study?'

'No, I didn't hear it at all till Mr Peter came.'

'Because of that you were surprised to find that she had, in fact, gone out?'

'It surprised me at the time, Inspector, but after I'd thought about it I realized she must have gone out through the kitchen.'

'Why should she have done that?'

'We-ell, I don't think she would want her father to know she had gone to the pictures.'

Gently broke in: 'Was it unusual for Miss Huysmann to go to the pictures?'

Susan embraced him in a smile of melting intensity. 'Mr Huysmann didn't think it proper for girls to go to them. But she went when Mr Huysmann was away on business and sometimes she pretended to go to bed early and I would let her out by the kitchen.'

'Wasn't it unusual for her to slip out in the afternoon, when her father might enquire after her?'

'Ye-es . . . she'd never done that before.'

'You have no doubt that she did go out?'

'Oh no! I saw her come in with her hat and coat on.'

'You heard nothing during the afternoon to suggest that she might still be in the house?'

'Nothing at all.'

'Miss Huysmann deceived her father over the matter of the pictures. Do you know of any other way she may have deceived him?'

Susan placed a smooth, conical finger on her dimpled chin and appeared to consider deeply. 'He was very strict,' she said at last.

'You haven't answered the question, Miss Stibbons.'

Susan came back with her take-me smile. 'We-ell, she used to read love-stories and other books that Mr Huysmann didn't know about . . .'

Gently shrugged and extended an open palm towards Hansom. In his mind's eye the figure of the deceased timber-merchant began to take form and substance. He saw the foxy, snarling little face, the sharp, suspicious eyes, the spare figure, the raging, implacable temper of a small man with power . . . the man whose son had kicked free at any price, whose daughter was in league with the maid to deceive him: who declared the cinema improper while he ruffled Susan in his study . . . An alien little man, who had spent most of his life in a new country without making friends, shrewd, sudden, tyrannical and hypocritical . . .

Hansom continued with the questioning. 'What did you do after you had taken Mr Huysmann his coffee?'

'I cleared away the lunch things and washed up, Inspector.'

'What time would that be?'

'I couldn't say, exactly. I finished washing up about quarter past three, because there was a change of programme on the wireless just then.'

'What programme was that?'

'It was a football match.'

'At what time did it finish?'

'It was just before four, I think.'

'Who won?' put in Gently curiously. Susan flashed him another smile. 'The Rovers beat the Albion two-nought,' she said. Hansom snorted.

'Did you hear the whole programme?' he proceeded.

'We-ell, I had to go and let Mr Peter in.'

'What time was that?'

'It was just as the Rovers scored their first goal.'

Hansom drew his fingers wearily across his face. 'And what time would that be, if it isn't too much to ask?'

The constable with the notebook cleared his throat. 'Beg pardon, sir, but the Rovers scored their first goal in the twenty-ninth minute.'

Hansom stared at him.

'If the kick-off was at three, sir, it would make the time exactly 3.29 p.m.'

'Ah,' said Hansom heavily, 'so it would, would it? Thank you very much. Make a note of it. You're a credit to the force, Parsons.'

'I'm a student of soccer, sir,' said Parsons modestly.

'So am I,' said Gently.

Hansom drew a deep breath and looked from one to the other. 'Why don't you get your pools out?' he yapped. 'Who am I to butt in with my homicide? Send out for the papers and let's get down to a session!'

Parsons retired to his notebook, crushed, and Gently took out his peppermint creams.

'Now!' said Hansom, 'you appear to have let in Peter Huysmann at 3.29 p.m. Greenwich. Who did he ask to see?'

'He said he'd come to see his father, Inspector, and asked if he was in.'

'Was there anything unusual in his aspect?'

'He did seem a little off-hand, but Mr Peter is like that sometimes.'

'Did you show him into the study?'

'I told him his father was there, and then I went back to the kitchen.'

'It must have been an exciting match,' said Hansom bitterly. 'What happened then?'

'I got on with washing the salad for tea.'

'How did it come about that you heard Mr Huysmann and his son quarrelling?'

'Well, there wasn't a salad bowl in the kitchen, so I had to fetch one from the dining-room. I heard them at it as I was passing through the hall.'

'Time?'

'I don't really know, Inspector.'

'Nobody scoring any goals?'

'Not just then.'

Hansom rolled his eyes. 'I wonder if I could pin anything on those boys for withholding assistance from the police ... Was it much before the end of the programme?'

'Oh yes ... quite a long time before.'

'Did you go down the passage to listen?'

Susan gave him a well-taken look of sad reproof. 'No, Inspector.'

'Why not? It should have been worth listening to.'

'But there'd been so many of them before.'

'And then, of course, the Albion might have equalized. Did you hear anything at all of what was said?'

'We-ell, I heard Mr Peter say his father hadn't got any human feelings left.'

'And what did Mr Huysmann say?'

'He said something that sounded nasty, but he had a funny way of speaking. You couldn't always understand him.'

'And that was positively all you heard of a quarrel following which Mr Huysmann was stabbed to death?'

Susan frowned prettily and applied her finger to the dimple in her chin again. 'We-ell, when I was coming back from the dining-room I heard Mr Peter say something about he'd take it, but there'd be a time when he'd give it back.'

'Have you any idea to what he was referring?'

'Oh no, Inspector.'

'You didn't,' mused Gently, 'you didn't hear anything to suggest that the object referred to . . . *wasn't* . . . a five-pound note?'

Susan looked puzzled. 'I don't think so,' she said.

Hansom breathed heavily. 'So you went back to the kitchen,' he said. 'Well – what did you do then?'

'I finished the salad and cut some bread and butter.'

'Did you hear nothing unusual while you were doing that?'

'No, Inspector.'

'Nothing resembling cries or a struggle?'

'You can't hear anything from that side of the house in the kitchen.'

'How about the warning bell on the front door?'

'I didn't hear it ring.'

'After the sports interlude – did you turn the wireless off?'

55

'Oh no, it was dance music after that. I had it on all the while. It was Mrs Turner who switched it off when she came in.'

'How long did it take you to finish preparing the tea?'

'I'd done by ten past four. After that I made a cup of tea and some toast, and sat down for a bit till Mrs Turner got back at five. It should have been my evening off,' she added glumly.

'What happened when Mrs Turner got back?'

'Well, she took her things off and looked to see if I'd done the tea properly, then she went to ask Mr Huysmann when he'd be wanting it.'

'And then?'

'She came back a minute or two later looking as white as a sheet. "Oh God!" she said, "there's something terrible happened to the master. Don't go near the study," she said. It was awful, Inspector!'

'Mrs Turner sent you for some brandy. Where was it kept?'

'I got the decanter from the dining-room.'

Gently leant forward. 'When you passed through the hall to the dining-room, did you see anybody?' he enquired.

'No, nobody.'

'Did you hear or see anything unusual?'

'I can't remember anything.'

Gently brooded a moment. 'Mrs Turner then sent you to telephone the police. Which telephone did you use?'

'I used the one in the little place under the stairs.'

'As you entered the hall you met Miss Gretchen. Where did you first see her?'

'She was just come in. She was taking her hat off.'

'Was the door open or closed?'

'It was closed.'

'Did you hear the warning bell just before or as you were leaving the kitchen?'

'We-ell . . . I might have done.'

'Can you say for certain that you did?'

Susan bathed him in her dissolving smile. 'Yes,' she said, 'I think I can.'

Gently eased back in his chair and studied illimitable realms of space. 'Do you not think it strange,' he said, 'that Miss Gretchen should re-enter the house by the front door with its warning bell, which she was at such pains to avoid when she went out?'

For a brief second the blue eyes stared at him in complete blankness. Then they swam to life again. 'She'd got an evening paper,' said Susan, 'I dare say she'd have said she went out to buy one.'

'Ah!' breathed Gently, 'an evening paper. That's the second one that's cropped up in this case.' He waved her back to Hansom.

'The Chief Inspector has forgotten to ask you his most telling question,' said Hansom acidly.

Gently inclined his head.

'He wants you to tell him if you entered this room any time after lunch yesterday.'

Susan glanced at Gently in puzzlement.

'Well, go on,' said Hansom, 'tell him.'

Gently said: 'Not after lunch but after you cleaned the room out.'

Susan wrinkled her snow-white brow. 'I put the flowers in the window. I didn't go in after that. I don't think anybody did.'

'You've made him happy,' said Hansom, 'you'll never know how happy you've made the Chief Inspector.' And he laughed in his semi-handsome way.

CHAPTER FIVE

HANSOM WAS SMOKING again: the air was thickening with the fulsome smell of his Corona. Gently, too, was adding smoke-rings to the upper atmosphere. The constable sniffed in a peaked sort of way. 'Go on,' said Hansom, 'be a devil. Have a spit and a draw.' The constable said, 'Thank you, sir,' and fished out a somewhat tatty cigarette. Hansom gave him a light. He said: 'The super doesn't smoke, and he's the one person around here who can afford to.' Gently said: 'You'll have to transfer to the MP and get the London scale.' Hansom grunted.

They could hear the rain still, outside. There was a drain by the pavement just outside the big window which made little, ecstatic noises. To hear that made the room seem chill. 'There's the chauffeur and the manager and Miss Gretchen,' said Hansom. 'Who'd you like to have in next?'

Gently said: 'Was there anyone in the yard yesterday?'

'Nope,' Hansom said. 'Saturday.'

Gently blew a few rings. 'Let's have the chauffeur,'

he said. 'He's probably sweating on his pint before lunch. After him I'd like to see Miss Gretchen. We'll keep Leaming for dessert.'

Hansom called in the constable from outside.

The chauffeur's name was Fisher. He was a tall, broad-shouldered, athletic-looking man of thirty, dark-haired, dark-eyed, with a strong but rather brutal face and lop-ears. He had a small moustache, carefully trimmed. He wore a beach-girl tie and a cheap American-style jacket in two patterns.

Hansom said: 'What time did you go off duty yesterday?'

'About twelve or just after,' Fisher replied slowly. 'I'd just cleaned the car down.' He had a hard but slovenly voice.

'What did you do when you went off duty?'

'I had a beer in the "Lighterman".'

'And after that?'

'Had something to eat in the snack-bar – Charlie's, they call it.'

'What time did you leave the snack-bar?'

'I dunno. Might've been half-past one.'

'Where did you go then?'

'I went back to my place and had a lie-down.'

'Where's your place?'

'5A Paragon Alley. It's up the hill towards Burgh Street. It's a flat.'

'Do you live alone?'

'There's a woman comes in of a morning.'

'Did anybody see you there?'

'I dunno. There may've been someone about, but it's quiet up the Alley.'

'How long were you lying down?'

'Hour, maybe.'

'What did you do then?'

'I got on with my model.'

'What's that?'

Fisher moved his long, sprawling legs. 'I make scale model planes – it's a hobby. I'm making an S.E. 5.'

'How long were you doing that?'

'Till four o'clock.'

Gently said: 'You remember that time very precisely. I wonder why?'

Fisher stirred again, uneasily. 'I just thought I'd work on it till four, that's all. There wasn't any reason. I just thought I'd work on it till four.'

Hansom continued: 'What did you do after four?'

'I went up to the fair.'

'Did you meet anyone you recognized?'

'I saw Mr Peter go across to the Wall from his caravan.'

'Time!' snapped Gently, beating Hansom to it by a fair margin.

Fisher jumped at the suddenness of the question. 'It was twenty-five past four.'

'How do you know?'

'I just looked at my watch.'

'Why?'

'I dunno – I just looked at my watch!'

'Do you often just look at your watch, or is it only when you know you may have to account for your movements?'

'I didn't know anything – I just looked at it!'

Gently paused like a stalking jaguar. Fisher's brow

was tight and moistening with perspiration. 'What was he wearing?' purred Gently.

'He was going to the Wall – he'd got his overalls on.'

'You mean the red leather ones he rides in?'

'That's right.'

'And he was going to the Wall?'

'I said he was!'

'Then how do you account for the fact that the overalls are kept at the Wall and not at the caravan?'

'I dunno – perhaps he wasn't coming from the caravan—'

'But you said he was.'

'I thought he was – he was coming from that way—'

'How many things have you thought up to tell us?'

'I haven't thought anything – it's the truth!'

'When did you hear about the murder?'

'They told me when I came in this morning.'

'Who's "they"?'

'Mrs Turner.'

'When did it take place?'

'About four.'

'How do you know?'

'She told me!'

'But Mrs Turner didn't find the body till five. How did she know that the murder took place at four?'

'I dunno – she just told me!'

'And you just happened to be looking at the time and deciding to go out at four?'

'Yes, I did!'

'Would you describe that as being coincidental in any way?'

'I dunno, but it's true!'

Gently swam forward in his chair. 'It's true that you can give no verifiable account of your movements between 1.30 and 4.25 p.m. yesterday. It's true that you know the approximate time at which the murder took place and that Mrs Turner could not have done. And it's true that you've taken care to give your movements precise times at and immediately after the murder took place. All these things,' he added thoughtfully, 'would be equally true of the murderer himself.'

Fisher jumped to his feet. 'But I didn't do it!' he cried, 'I didn't − and you can't say I did! You're asking me all these things and twisting them round to make it seem like I did it, but I didn't, and you can't prove that I did!'

'I haven't suggested that you did,' said Gently smoothly. 'I'm merely establishing that you could, perhaps, be more helpful to this enquiry than in fact you are.'

Fisher stood breathing quickly and staring at him. 'I don't know anything,' he said, a note of sullenness in his voice. 'I've told you what I know, and you can't prove anything else.'

Gently looked from Fisher to the chair on which he had been sitting. 'Your chair,' he said, 'we had it finger-printed last night.'

The chauffeur moved away from it involuntarily.

'Do you think it possible that we shall find your prints on it?'

'You'd find them there now, wouldn't you?'

'But would they have been there last night?'

'They might be there any time. I'm about the house. I move the furniture for them sometimes.'

Gently sighed and extended his palm towards Hansom, who had been following the proceedings very attentively.

Hansom said: 'Were you or were you not in this house at the time of the murder?'

'I told you I wasn't.'

'Did you witness the murder by standing on that chair and watching through the transom lights?'

'No! I was nowhere near the place.'

'The answers you have given to Chief Inspector Gently suggest to me very strongly that you had knowledge of the crime prior to this morning. Think carefully, now. Are you sure you've nothing to add to what you've already told us?'

'No, I haven't.'

'You've told us the whole truth?'

'Yes!'

'You wouldn't like to reconsider any part of it?'

'It's the truth, I tell you!'

'And it had bloody well better be, for your sake!' bawled Hansom, suddenly dropping his official mask in exasperation. 'Now get out of here and hold yourself ready for further questioning.'

Fisher flushed angrily and turned towards the door.

'Just a minute,' said Gently. Fisher paused. 'Why did you put it in the chest?' enquired Gently confidentially.

The chauffeur stared at him with complete lack of understanding. 'Put *what* in the chest?' he asked.

Gently swam back into the depths of his chair. 'Never mind,' he said, 'run along. Do what the Inspector tells you . . .'

Hansom blasted the butt of his cigar in the ashtray and took one of his very deepest breaths. He said: 'I've got to hand it to you. I never thought there was much in that hoo-ha about the chair, but I'm beginning to have my doubts.'

'It's just guess-work,' replied Gently deprecatingly. 'The maid might have missed those marks when she brushed the carpet.'

'I'm willing to swear that fellow was in here like you said.'

'There's nothing to prove it, yet. Fisher's got an alibi that'll take a lot of breaking and you've seen what luck I've had trying to establish that there was someone else in the house.'

'He was lying. He was lying himself black in the face. I'll have him down at headquarters and see what I can get out of him there.'

Gently nodded a pensive nod.

'Not that I can see how it'll help young Huysmann,' added Hansom suspiciously. 'If Fisher is shielding him and we make him talk, that'll put the kybosh on you, good and proper.'

Gently smiled agreeably. 'Always supposing that Peter is your man.'

'You know he's our man!' snorted Hansom. 'Good grief, why not admit it? Apart from anything else, who else would want to rub the old man out?'

'Well, there was forty thousand pounds lying about.'

'That's all my eye! That could have been sprung without deliberately knocking him off first. They'd only to wait till he wasn't there. And whoever did it didn't come armed – they did it on impulse, after they got there, after they'd chewed the rag with the old man – which means it was somebody he knew. I tell you, the jury'll be solid.'

Gently's smile grew further and further away. 'There's one thing that puzzles me about our friend Fisher,' he mused.

'And what's that?'

'He didn't seem to me the type who would shield anybody . . . especially with his own neck sticking out as far as it does.'

There was something virginal and nun-like about Gretchen Huysmann, not altogether accounted for by the large silver cross that depended on her bosom. She was not a pretty woman. Her face was pale and a little long, and she wore her straight black hair divided in the middle and caught up in a flat bun. She had small, close-set ears and dark, but not black eyes, now a little reddened and fearful. There was a waxenness about her complexion. She was above medium height. Her figure, which should have been good, was neglected and bundled anyhow into a long, full dress of dark blue. She wore coarse stockings and flat-heeled shoes. She was twenty-seven.

Hansom said: 'Sit down, Miss Huysmann, and make yourself comfortable.' Gretchen sat down, but she did not make herself comfortable. She sat forward on the edge of the chair, her knees together and her feet apart. Her pale face turned from one to another of them quick, frightened glances; her small mouth grew smaller still. She reminded Gently of a plant that had grown in the dark, at once protected and neglected. In this room of three serious men with its alien smell of tobacco smoke she seemed shrunk right back into herself.

Gently motioned to the constable. 'It's getting thick in here. Open that top window.' The constable manipulated the cords that let fall a pane high up in the big window, letting in a nearer sound of rain with a welcome current of new-washed air. Gently beamed encouragingly at Miss Huysmann.

Hansom cleared his throat and said: 'I'd like you to understand, Miss Huysmann, that we fully appreciate the tragic circumstances in which you find yourself. We shall keep you here the shortest possible time and ask you only those questions which it is absolutely necessary for us to have answered.'

Miss Huysmann said: 'I'll . . . tell you all I can to help.' She spoke in a low tone with a slight accent.

Hansom continued: 'Can you remember if your father was expecting any visitors yesterday?'

'I do not know, he would not tell me that.'

'Was it usual for him to receive visitors on a Saturday afternoon?'

'Oh no, practically never. The yard is closed, everyone has gone home.'

'Did you notice anything unusual in his manner at lunch yesterday?'

'I do not think so. He did not speak to me very much at meal-times. Yesterday he said, "Your brother is in town. Take care I do not hear you have been seeing him," but that was all.'

'Were you in the habit of seeing your brother when he was in Norchester?'

'Oh yes, I see him sometimes. But my father, he did not like that.'

'Did you see your brother on this occasion?'

'I see him on the Friday, when I go out to pay some bills.'

'Did he speak of calling on your father?'

'He said he must see him before he leave Norchester.'

'What reason did he give for that?'

'He said that the man for whom he worked had offered him to be partners, but he must have five hundred pounds. So he will ask my father to lend it to him.'

'Did he say lend it?'

'Oh yes, he know my father will not give it to him.'

Hansom toyed with the little pearl–handled penknife that lay on his blotter and glanced towards his cigar case, but Gently clicked disapprovingly. Hansom proceeded:

'What time did lunch finish yesterday?'

'It was about two o'clock.'

'And what did you do after lunch?'

'First, I have a wash. Then I go and fetch my coffee from the kitchen, which I take up to my room. As I am drinking it, I get ready to go out to the pictures.'

Gently said: 'Your visits to the pictures were clandestine, I understand.'

'Pardon?'

'You were obliged to go secretly – your father did not approve.'

Gretchen looked down at the two pale, plump hands twisted together in her lap. 'It is true, I go without his permission. He think the pictures are . . . all bad. And so, I must not go.'

'Did you feel that your father was being severe in forbidding you to go to the pictures?'

'I think, perhaps . . . he did not know how they were. It was safer that I should not go.'

'You thought, at least, that he was being unreasonable.'

'I cannot say. No doubt it was very wrong of me. It may be that this is a judgment, because I do wrong.'

'Did your father ever find out that you had been to the pictures?'

'Once, he caught me.'

'What steps did he take?'

'I was not to leave my room for two days and must not go out of the house for a month.'

'And after that, I take it, you were more cautious?'

The pale hands knotted and pulled apart, but came together again immediately. 'At first, I went only when he was away on business. Then, Susan helped me. I used to pretend I had a headache and go to bed, but I creep downstairs again and out through the kitchen. It was very wrong of me to do this.'

'Miss Huysmann, when you planned to go to the pictures in the afternoon yesterday, you were surely taking an unusual risk?'

'I do not know – my father is usually in the study all the afternoon.'

'But he might easily have asked for you.'

'Oh yes, it could be so. But if Susan came to my room and find me not there, she tell him I am not feeling well, I am lying down and asleep.'

'Following the occasion on which you were caught, had you ever ventured out previously on a Saturday afternoon?'

Her small mouth sealed close. She shook her head forlornly.

'And yet yesterday you did so, without even taking the precaution of first warning Susan. Why was that?'

'I do not know. There is a film I very much want to see . . . all at once, I think I will go.'

'When did you decide that?'

'Oh . . . during lunch.'

'But after lunch you went to the kitchen to fetch your coffee. Why didn't you tell Susan then?'

She shook her head again. 'Perhaps I do not really decide till later, till I take my coffee back to my room.'

'At what time did you leave the house?'

'I think it is twenty-five past two.'

'And you left through the kitchen?'

'It was the only way, if my father is not to know.'

'Why didn't you tell Susan when you passed through on your way out?'

'I do not know . . . perhaps I did tell her.'

'Miss Huysmann, Susan was in the kitchen till half-past two, but she did not see you go out. She was surprised to find that you were out. Yet you claim to have left the house at twenty-five past two.'

Gretchen's dark swollen eyes fixed upon him, pleading and fearful. 'Perhaps it was later when I left . . . perhaps it was after half-past two.'

'How much later?'

'One minute . . . two minutes . . .'

'It was not as late, say, as four-fifteen?'

'Oh no! I was not here, no, no!'

'You were not in the house at all between, say, 2.35 and 5.10?'

'During all that time I was at the pictures.'

'Ah.' Gently sighed, and directed her back to Hansom with an inclination of his head. Hansom picked up the questioning neatly where it had been taken away from him.

'You dressed to go out while you were drinking your coffee. You left the house by the kitchen at a few minutes after 2.30. What did you do then?'

'I went straight to the Carlton cinema.'

'What were they showing there?'

'The big film is called *Scarlet Witness*.'

'Is that what was showing when you entered the cinema?'

'Oh yes, but I came in at the end, I saw only the last twenty minutes. Then there was the interval and the news, and then the other film.'

'What was that called?'

'It was *Meet Me in Rio*, with Joan Seymour and Broderick Davis.'

'When did that finish?'

'At five o'clock. I wanted to stay and to see the big film through, but it was already late, I was afraid that my father had already begun tea. So I bought an evening paper in order to pretend I had been out for one and went in through the front door.'

'This film, *Scarlet Witness*,' murmured Gently, 'is it the same one as I saw in London a fortnight ago? How does it end?'

Gretchen turned towards him, her hands snatching at each other. 'I did not see much of it . . . I do not remember. It was not very good.'

'But you saw the end of it?'

'It was . . . complicated.'

'Was it the one where they get taken off the island in a helicopter just as the volcano erupts?'

The two hands gripped till the knuckles whitened. 'No! It wasn't that one . . . I was worried about whether my father would find out, I did not see it properly.'

'They made an appeal after the one I saw – some fund for the maintenance of an aerial rescue force. Did they make an appeal here?'

'Yes – yes! There was an appeal for something. A man spoke from the stage and they sent round boxes. I put something in.'

She bent her head away from him as though his eyes reacted upon her physically. Gently shrugged and felt in his pocket for a peppermint cream. She continued, without looking at him: 'The big film came on at a quarter to two and finished at a quarter past three. The other film started at half-past three and finished at five.'

Gently said: 'Thank you, Miss Huysmann, for such precise information.'

Hansom said: 'When you re-entered the house, whom did you see?'

'It was Susan. She was coming out of the passage from the kitchen.'

'What did she say to you?'

'She said, "Oh, I did not know that you had gone out," and then she told me that something was wrong with my father.'

'Did you go into the study?'

'No, after I was told I did not feel that I could. I sat down in the kitchen and Mrs Turner gave me some brandy to drink.'

72

'Then it wasn't you who hid the knife in the trunk?' demanded Gently suddenly. Gretchen writhed in her chair. 'I know nothing, nothing about that!' she exclaimed.

'And you wouldn't know if Fisher the chauffeur was in the house during the afternoon?'

A shiver ran through her dark-clad form, her eyes widened and her mouth opened. For a moment she stared at Gently horror-struck. And then it was over, as quickly as it had begun: the eyes narrowed, the mouth closed, the lips were forced deliberately into a tight line. 'I do not know, I was not here,' she said.

Gently sagged a little in his chair. He looked tired. 'How long has Fisher been chauffeur here?' he asked.

'Oh . . . three or four years.'

'Would you describe him as being honest and trustworthy?'

'Otherwise, my father would have got rid of him.'

'I am asking for your personal impression.'

'He is honest . . . I think.'

'What are your personal relations with Fisher, Miss Huysmann?'

'I do not see him, very much. Sometimes he is in the house to move things about. One day, he drove me to service at the cathedral, because I has a poisoned foot and could not walk there.'

'He is respectful and obedient?'

'Oh, yes.'

'Was he on good terms with your father?'

'I do not know – my father was not . . . a condescending man.'

'He had no reason to harbour a grudge against your father?'

'Oh, no.'

'The maid, Susan, is an attractive girl. Is there anything between her and Fisher?'

'. . . No! Nothing whatever!'

Gently's eyebrow rose the merest trifle and he transferred his gaze to the top of the far window. 'Would it be correct to say that you were in considerable fear of your father?'

'I do not know . . . fear.'

'You had observed how Peter was treated, how he was driven out and completely disowned. Did it not suggest to you that a similar fate might be yours on some other occasion?'

'Peter took money . . . he got married.'

'But you also disobeyed your father in the matter of going to the pictures.'

'That was very wrong of me, very wrong.'

'Miss Huysmann, were you deceiving your father in any other matters, perhaps more important ones?'

'I do not know how you mean!'

'You were very isolated here. You went out very rarely. You were denied all the usual facilities for meeting people and making friends. And you are twenty-seven. Did you propose to continue in this way of life indefinitely, or had you resolved to, shall we say . . . assert your rights, in some manner?'

'I cannot understand!'

'Your visits to the pictures, for instance, were they always made alone? Was it always to the pictures that you went?'

'Always – to the pictures! – always!'

'And always alone?'

'Every time I was by myself!'

'You were never accompanied by . . . Fisher, for example?'

A hot blush sprang into the pale cheeks. 'No! Never! Never!'

'Your association with him has always been that of mistress and servant?'

'How can you ask such things! How can you ask them!' Tears welled up in the dark eyes and she covered her face with her hands.

Gently said: 'I don't like asking these things, Miss Huysmann, any more than you like being asked them. But if justice is to be done, we must have a clear picture of all the events surrounding this crime. You may think that these questions are unnecessary, you may be tempted to answer them untruthfully; but remember that they are the steps by which a man may be brought to the gallows and that no personal feelings should be allowed to dictate what you will answer.'

She cried: 'It isn't true . . . I cannot help him!'

'You wish to answer that your association with Fisher is completely impersonal?'

She raised her face from her hands, agonized and tear-wet. 'Yes, that is my answer . . . O God! Please, let me go now, please!'

Hansom said: 'That stuff about the pictures – did it add up?'

Gently leant a freshly filled pipe to his lighter. 'No,' he said, 'it didn't. She didn't go to the pictures.' He gave a few puffs and adjusted matters with his thumb.

'Then you're reckoning that she was in the house during the afternoon?'

'It could be that.'

'And Fisher was there with her and she set him on to get rid of the old man and they swiped the money just for a blind. It's not a bad line at that!' exclaimed Hansom admiringly.

Gently smiled at the far-flung Pylades. 'You've got a lurid imagination,' he said.

'And young Peter comes in and nearly messes things up. They watch him quarrelling through the transom lights, and see the old man give him a note which might be traced and realize it's a pip. Fisher goes in and does the job, and then they slide out and collect alibis. Why, it's a natural!'

'And how about the knife in the trunk?'

'Oh blast, you can surely think of something to cover that!'

Gently's smile widened to include the still-vexed Bermoothes. 'It's an interesting conjecture. There's only one element lacking.'

'And what would that be?'

'Proof,' said Gently simply, 'there isn't a grain of it.' And he blew a playful little smoke-ring over his colleague's close-cropped head.

CHAPTER SIX

LEAMING BY DAYLIGHT was as handsome as ever. When he came in he immediately produced his gold cigarette case and offered everybody one of his hand-made cigarettes. Hansom and the constable accepted. Gently had only just puffed his pipe into flavoursome maturity. Leaming took a cigarette himself, tapped it on the case, twisted it between his lips and lit it with a slim, gold-plated lighter. Then he sat down, and with a jet of smoke from each nostril indicated that he was alert and attentive.

Gently said: 'You'll be able to tell me – who got the City's first goal yesterday? Was it Robson?'

Leaming glanced at him in surprise. 'It was Smethick, actually,' he said. 'He scored from a free kick after a foul on Jones S.'

Gently murmured: 'Ah yes, in the twenty-second minute.'

A correction seemed to hover on Leaming's lips, but eventually he said nothing.

'I don't suppose we shall need to keep you very long, Mr Leaming,' Hansom said. 'We'd just like to know a few routine details.'

'Glad to help you in any way.'

'What time did you leave the yard yesterday?'

Leaming thought and answered carefully: 'At twenty past one.'

'Were you the last person to leave?'

'Yes. I usually lock up personally.'

'Is the entire yard locked up, or only the office and buildings?'

'The office and buildings. But there is a boom across the entrance to prevent unauthorized vehicles entering and parking.'

'But that would not prevent persons from entering or leaving the yard?'

'It would not – there is an unlocked side-gate in any case.'

Gently asked: 'Isn't it tempting providence to allow free access to the yard in that manner?'

Leaming shrugged and breathed smoke. 'There's nothing to steal but timber. Nobody would manhandle a load of that right across the yard to the gate – especially under the eye of Mr Huysmann. His bedroom windows look down on the yard.'

Hansom continued: 'When did you last see Mr Huysmann?'

'He left the office at about ten past one. He looked into my office to say that he was going to London on Monday.'

'Did he say what for?'

'To pay Olsens' for the last quarter's shipments. Olsens' are our agents at Wapping.'

'Was it usual for Mr Huysmann to make payment in person?'

'Oh yes, invariably. And always by cash – it was one of his eccentricities.'

'About how much would the quarterly payment amount to?'

Leaming thought unhurriedly. 'This quarter's was eleven thousand three hundred and twenty-seven pounds plus some odd shillings, less three per cent for cash.'

'Did you notice anything unusual about Mr Huysmann yesterday morning?'

'Nothing in particular. He was a little – ah – agitated because his son was in town. I believe he thought that Peter only came to Norchester to annoy him, but that's by the way. He mentioned the will again and said that after Easter he proposed to call on his solicitors.'

'Did he lead you to suppose that he expected a visit from his son?'

'As a matter of fact, he did say something of the sort, or at least something which might be construed that way. He said (he had a peculiar way of speaking): "He'll find me ready for him, Leaming, *ja, ja*, he'll find me ready."'

'And you think it might have referred to an expected visit?'

'It might have referred to his intention to change his will, of course, but since then I've wondered.'

'Would you say that he stood in any fear of his son?'

'Oh, I don't know about that. He had acted, I think, a little unwisely towards Peter, and Peter had a temper, but to say he "stood in fear" is laying it on a bit.'

'But you would say that he was apprehensive?'

'He was always nervous when Peter was in Norchester.'

'To your knowledge, had Peter ever visited him before since he left home?'

'Not to my knowledge.'

'They had never met since Peter absconded with the money?'

'Never.'

Hansom stubbed the end of the hand-made cigarette into his ashtray and reached for his cigar case by way of afters. Leaming sat watching, handsome and unabashed, while the Inspector carved the tip off a Corona and lit it carefully all round. 'Hah!' said Hansom. Leaming smiled politely.

'Where did you go after you'd locked up?' continued Hansom.

'I went home for lunch.'

'Where's that?'

'I live at Monk's Thatch, at Haswick.'

'Do you live alone?'

'I have a housekeeper, a Mrs Lambert, and a gardener who comes in daily.'

'Were they there when you went home for lunch?'

'The housekeeper was, of course, but the gardener had knocked off. He came back later and I gave him a lift to Railway Road.'

'What time did you arrive home?'

'About a quarter to two.'

'What time did you leave again?'

'It was just on twenty to three – I was rather late. It isn't easy to get to the car park through the crowds.'

'And what time did you get to Railway Road?'

'It was just turned three. I dropped Rogers (that's my gardener) off at the station end and went on to park my car. By the time I'd done that it was quarter past and I missed the kick-off.'

Gently said: 'Are you a keen City supporter, Mr Leaming?'

Leaming gave a slight shrug. 'I suppose I am, really. I never miss a home match if I can help it and I sometimes manage the near away fixtures.'

'Then you will have a season ticket, of course?'

Leaming hung on a moment. 'Actually, no,' he replied. 'For me, half the excitement goes out of a match when I watch it from a seat in the stands. I love the hurly-burly and noise of the terraces. It sets the atmosphere of anticipation. To sit on a hard seat with my knees in someone's back and someone's knees in mine, to be detached from the drama taking place by a stooping roof of girders and galvanized sheet – no, I must have my terraces, or the game isn't worth the candle.'

'I like the terraces myself,' said Gently dryly. 'I wish I was as tall as you.'

Leaming laughed, pleased, and Hansom proceeded: 'At what time did the match finish?'

'At five to five. I got away at about a quarter past and went home to tea. Shortly after six you people rang me up and asked me to put in an appearance, which I did, straight away.'

Hansom said: 'I understand, Mr Leaming, that you feel strongly convinced of Peter Huysmann's innocence. Could you tell me what reasons you have for this?'

A tiny frown appeared on Leaming's handsome brow. 'Well, I suppose I haven't got what you'd call reasons. Not things like clues and evidence and that sort of thing. It's mostly a matter of personal feeling – I just know Peter so well that to ask me to believe he's done this seems ludicrous. I wish he were here now. I wish we could talk it over quietly with him. You'd soon see what I mean.'

'Have you any reason, then, for supposing that some other person was responsible?'

Leaming spread his hands, palms downwards, and placed them on his knees. 'It could have been almost anybody, really,' he said.

'How about Fisher – does he suggest himself as a suspect?'

'He would know that there was money in the safe.'

'How would he know that?'

'There's not much that servants don't know. He wouldn't know the amount was so large, of course. That was due to payments from the City Treasury on timber contracts to their housing estates. But he could easily have discovered that payment was made on the first of this month.'

'You do not think that Peter Huysmann belongs to the killer type. What would be your estimate of Fisher?'

'I don't know Fisher as well as I know Peter,' replied Leaming cautiously. 'It isn't fair to ask my opinion.'

'We should like to have it, all the same.'

'Well, there's a streak of brutality in the man. I wouldn't put it past him.'

'Can you tell us anything of his relations with the rest of the household?'

'I don't know that I can. He was an efficient chauffeur, knew his job, didn't get drunk, was always punctual. May have chased the women a bit – but there you are.'

'The maid Susan – did he chase her?'

'He may have done, though I doubt whether he had any success. Susan is well aware of her market value.'

'It is unlikely that Miss Huysmann had anything to do with him?'

Leaming laughed. 'You couldn't know how Miss Huysmann has been brought up. She reads nothing but her Bible. She wouldn't know what to do with a man if she had one.'

Gently said: 'How long have you been with the firm, Mr Leaming?'

'It will be ten years in the autumn.'

'Did you find Mr Huysmann a difficult man to work for?'

Leaming shrugged. 'You've probably been able to form an opinion of what he was like. When I first came, I thought I wouldn't last a month, but the salary made me stick it out.'

'It was a good salary?'

'Oh yes. One must give the old man his due. He's always paid the best wages in the trade – had to, I suppose, to get anybody to work for him. But that's not quite fair, though. He had really first-class business principles. He wanted a lot for his money, but he always paid generously for it, and right on the nail. Whatever he was like at home, you could trust him in business to the last farthing. That's how he built up a firm like this. Nobody was very fond of the man, but they all liked his way of doing business.'

'And would that sum up your attitude towards him?'

'I think it would.'

'You bore him no grudge for his treatment of you?'

'Good heavens, no! It was rather an honour to be manager of Huysmann's.'

Gently laid down his pipe and fumbled around for a peppermint cream. 'I believe you are a bachelor,' he said.

Leaming nodded.

'Would that be anything to do with Mr Huysmann?'

'Well, yes, I suppose it would. He preferred his staff to be unmarried.'

'Did that mean you would have lost your job if you had married?'

'Oh, I don't know about that, though he was quite capable of going to such lengths. But I never ran the risk.'

'It could be a very irksome situation, however.'

Leaming smiled complacently. 'There are ways of alleviating it.'

Gently bit a peppermint cream in halves. 'Such ways as Susan?' he enquired.

'One could go further and fare worse.'

'Which makes you positive that Fisher was having nothing to do with her?'

Leaming's smile broadened. 'I think you can discount Fisher in that respect,' he said. 'As I said before, Susan is well aware of her market value.'

'Ah,' said Gently, and ate the other half of the peppermint cream.

Hansom took a deep breath. 'Well,' he said, 'I don't think we shall require you any more for the present, Mr Leaming. Thank you for being so co-operative. We'll let you get away to lunch.'

Leaming rose to his feet. 'I'm only too glad to have been of any assistance. No doubt the Chief Inspector has told you that if you put Peter in the dock I shall be your number one adversary – but till then, call on me for any help I can give.' He smiled at both of them in turn and moved towards the door.

'Mr Leaming,' murmured Gently.

Leaming paused obediently.

'I should like to look over the firm's books.'

Leaming's brown eyes flickered, perhaps in surprise. 'I'll bring them over for you,' he said.

'This afternoon,' pursued Gently. 'I'll come back after lunch.'

'This afternoon,' repeated Leaming evenly. 'I'll have them here waiting for you.' He turned towards the door again.

'And Mr Leaming,' added Gently.

Leaming stiffened.

'I suppose you wouldn't know where one can buy peppermint creams in Norchester on a Sunday?'

Hansom pushed his chair back from the table and stretched his long, beefy legs. The constable shut his notebook and found another stringy cigarette. Gently got up and wandered towards the little pierced window.

Hansom said: 'Well, what do you know now?'

Gently shook his head slowly, still looking through the window.

'I guess this Leaming's the only lad with a pedigree alibi,' Hansom mused. 'Hit it where you like, it gives a musical note. What was that stuff about the books?'

'It's a wet day, I thought they'd be fun.'

'You didn't scare Leaming with it. I'll bet they check to five per cent of a farthing.' He dipped the long ash of his cigar into the ashtray. 'I haven't heard anything yet to make me think that young Huysmann isn't our man,' he said. 'You've started something with Fisher and the girl, but I don't think it's going to hold up the case. Mind you, I'll crack into Fisher. I'd like to know the ins and outs of that business myself. But I don't think it'll help you. I don't think he did it myself and I don't think you stand a dog's chance of proving it.'

Gently smiled into the window. 'There's so much we don't know,' he said, 'it's like a picture out of focus.'

'It focuses sharp enough for me and the super.'

'It's taking shape a little bit, but it's full of blind spots and blurred outlines.'

Hansom said challengingly: 'You're pinning your faith on Fisher, aren't you?'

Gently shrugged. 'I'm not pinning it on anybody. I'm trying to find out things. I'm trying to find out what happened here yesterday and what led up to it, and how these people fit into it, and why they answered what they did answer this morning.'

Hansom said: 'We're not so ambitious. We're just knocking up a case of murder so it keeps the daylight out.'

'So am I . . .' Gently said, 'only I like walls round mine as well as a roof.'

Still it rained. A black twig sticking out of the grille over the drain by the Huysmann house cut a rainbow wedge from the descending torrent. Gently stood a moment looking at it as he came out. Hansom had departed in the police car, carrying with him the constable and his notebook. He had offered Gently a lift and lunch at the headquarters canteen, but Gently preferred to remain in Queen Street.

'Looks like it's set in for the day, sir,' said the constable on the door. Gently nodded to him absently. He was looking now along the street towards Railway Bridge, sodden and empty, its higgledy-piggledy buildings rain-dark and forbidding. 'Where's Charlie's?' he asked.

'What's Charlie's, sir?'

'It's a snack-bar.'

'You mean that place down the road, sir?'

'Could be.'

'It's that cream-painted building about a hundred yards down on the other side.'

'Thanks.'

He plodded off towards Railway Bridge, his shoes paddling in the wet. They were good shoes, but he could feel a chill dampness slowly spreading underfoot. He shivered intuitively. The cream-painted building was a rather pleasant three-storey house of late Regency vintage. It had wide eaves and a wrought-iron veranda on the first floor, and had been redecorated probably as late as last autumn. It was only at ground level that the effect was spoiled. The sash windows had been replaced with plate glass and the door was a mixture of glass and chromium-plate. A sign over the windows said: CHAR-LIE'S SNAX. Another sign, a smaller one, advertised meals upstairs. Gently pressed in hopefully.

Inside was a snack-bar and several lino-topped tables,

at which sat a sprinkling of customers. Gently approached the man behind the bar. He said: 'Are you serving lunch today?'

The man looked him over doubtfully. 'Might do you something hot, though we don't do meals on a Sunday as a rule.'

'Where do I go — upstairs?'

'Nope — that's closed.'

Gently took a seat at a vacant table by the door and the man behind the bar dived through a curtain behind him. It was not an impressive interior. The walls were painted half-cream and half-green, with a black line at high water mark. The floor was bare, swept, but not scrubbed. An odour of tired cooking-fat lingered in the atmosphere. The clientèle, at the moment, consisted of two transport drivers, a soldier, a bus-conductor and an old man reading a newspaper. The bar-tender came back.

He said: 'There's sausage and chips and beans and fried egg.'

Gently sniffed. 'I was hoping for roast pork and new potatoes, but never mind. Bring me what you've got.'

The bar-tender dived through the curtain again. Presently he came back with cutlery and a plate on which lay three scantly smeared triangles of thin bread, each slightly concave. 'Will you have a cup of tea to go on with?' he asked.

'Yes. No sugar.'

The tea arrived in a thick, clumsy cup. But it was fresh tea. Gently sipped it reflectively, letting his eye wander over the snack-bar and its inmates. This was where Fisher went for lunch. Fortified by a pint of beer, the chauffeur had come in to face his plate of sausage, chips, beans and fried eggs. What had he done while he waited? Read a newspaper? Talked? There was talk now between the two transport drivers.

'I got a late paper off the station . . . there's a bit in the stop-press about Scotland Yard being called in.'

'That's because the son hopped it, you mark my words.'

'D'you reckon he did it?'

'Well, you see what it said . . .'

'What did it say?'

'It said the police thought he could assist them in their investigation. That's what they always say before they charge them with it.'

'They're a rum lot, them Huysmanns . . . you don't know where you are with foreigners.'

The bar-tender sallied out with Gently's plate. Gently motioned to him to take the chair opposite. He hesitated suspiciously. 'You knew this young Huysmann?' enquired Gently blandly. The bar-tender sat down.

'Yep, I used to know him,' he said.

'What sort of bloke was he?'

'Oh, nothing out of the ordinary. You'd think he was English if you didn't know.'

'Used he to come in here?'

'He did before he went away, but he's been gone some time now. He had a quarrel with his old man before this lot happened.'

'Do you think he did it?'

'Well, I dunno. Might've done. He didn't look the sort, but you can never tell with these foreigners.'

Gently essayed a piece of sausage and chip. 'You know the chauffeur up there?' he asked through a mouthful.

'Who – Fisher?'

'That's his name, I believe.'

'Oh, he's often in here for something to eat. You know him?'

'I've run across him somewhere.'

'He's another rum card, if you ask me. He lives for women, that bloke. Thinks he's the gnat's hind-leg.'

'I heard he fancied the Huysmann girl.'

'He fancies every bloody girl. He was after our Elsie here till I choked him off.'

'Do you think there's anything in it?'

'I dunno. That girl Susan who works up there dropped something about it one night, but I don't pay any attention.'

Gently sliced an egg. 'Is she the blonde piece?'

'Ah, that's the one. She's a fancy bit of homework, I can tell you. But Fisher never got a look in there.'

'How was that?'

The bar-tender grinned knowingly. 'She's got a boyfriend out of his class. She runs around with Huysmann's manager, Leaming, his name is, a real smart feller. Fisher don't cut much ice while he's around.'

Gently doubled up a triangle of bread and butter and took a bite out of it. 'That get Fisher in the raw?' he mumbled.

'You bet it does – he'd give his arm to tumble her!'

'Mmn,' said Gently, masticating.

'I wouldn't mind a slice myself, if it comes to that.'

'Fisher been around lately?'

'He came in when he knocked off yesterday and had a meal.'

''Bout two, was that?'

'Nearer one, I should think. He hadn't got much to say for himself.'

The bar-tender was called back to serve a customer. Gently plodded onwards through the sausage. As he ate he fitted into place in his picture each new fact and dash of colour. Fisher, jealous of Leaming. Fisher, wanting to be Susan's lover. Susan, hinting at something between Fisher and Gretchen. 'He lives for women, that bloke . . . after our Elsie till I choked him off . . . Fisher never got a look in there . . . don't cut much ice while Leaming's around . . .' And Leaming had said, 'There's a streak of brutality in the man . . .'

The doorbell tinkled, and Gently looked up from his plate. It was Fisher himself who entered. Not noticing Gently, he swaggered over to the counter and ordered a cup of tea and some rolls, then stood there waiting while they were got for him. The bar-tender glanced at Gently, who winked back broadly.

Turning, Fisher saw Gently. He stopped stock-still. Gently nodded to him affably. 'Come and sit down,' he said, indicating the chair vacated by the bar-tender. 'I've thought up one or two more things I should like to ask you.'

CHAPTER SEVEN

A WHITE, EXPANSIVE April sun, low-tilted in its morning skies, looked down upon the rain-washed streets. In Chapel Field and the Castle Gardens birds were singing, thrushes, chaffinches, blackbirds, and on the steep southern and westerly slopes of the Castle Hill the daffodils looked down, proudly, consciously, like women dressed to go out.

Early traffic swirled up Princes Street and round Castle Paddock; the fast London train rumbled over the river bridge at Truss Hythe, swept out into the lush water-meadows of the Yar; passing over, as it did so, a stubborn little up-stream-making tug with a tow of five steel barges, on each of which was painted the name: Huysmann.

Onward puffed the little tug, bold as a fox-terrier, full of aggression and self-assurance, and onward crept the barges, phlegmatic, slow, till the cavalcade was in hailing distance of Railway Bridge. Then the little tug slowed down, trod water as it were, allowing the foremost barges to catch up with it. A man jumped out of the tug. He ran down the barges, jumping from one to another, till finally, coming to the last one, he loosed the sagging cable and cast her free. A shout ahead set the little tug puffing off on her interrupted journey, while the slipped barge, with the way left on her, was steered to a dilapidated-looking quay on the south bank.

Altogether, it was a smart and well-executed manoeuvre, thought Gently, watching it as he leaned over Railway Bridge. It was worth getting up early just to see it.

He crossed the bridge to watch the tug and its barges pass through the other side. A door in the rear of the tug's wheelhouse was open. Through it Gently observed a lanky figure wearing a peaked seaman's hat, a leather jacket and blue serge trousers tucked into Wellington boots. As he watched, the lanky man spun his wheel to the right. There was a tramp steamer on its way down.

Gently anticipated the warning hooter and got off the bridge. He stood by the railings to see the bridge rise, rolling ponderously, and moved further over to get a good view of the vessel as it surged by below. It was a bluff-bowed, clumsy, box-built ship, with a lofty fo'c'sle descending suddenly to deck level. The bridge and cabins aft were neat and newly painted, and the washing that hung on a line suggested that the captain had his family on board. The engines pounded submergedly as the steel cosmos slid through. There followed the bubbling and frothing under her stern. She was the *Zjytze* of Amsterdam.

Grumblingly the bridge rolled back into place and Gently, after a moment's pause, strolled over to the little glass box where the bridge-keeper sat. 'When did she come up?' he asked.

The bridge-keeper peered at him. 'Friday morning,' he said.

'What was she carrying?'

'Timber.'

'Where did she lie?'

The bridge-keeper nodded upstream to where the tug with its train of barges was edging in towards the quays. 'Up there at Huysmann's.'

'Is she a regular?'

'Off and on. She's been coming here since the war, and before that there used to be another one, but they say she was sunk in a raid. It's the same skipper, though.'

'Do you know his name?'

'It's a queer sort of name, something like Hooksy.'

'Thanks.'

Gently gave the departing vessel a last look and hurried away down Queen Street. A police car was outside the Huysmann house and Gently noticed, in a side-glance, that Leaming's car was parked inside the timber-yard. Constable Letts was on the door. 'Hansom inside?' asked Gently. 'Yes, sir. Been here for some time, sir.' Gently pushed in.

Hansom was in the hall, talking to a sergeant.

He said: 'Why, here he is, all bright and early.'

Gently said: 'There's a ship just left Huysmann's quays, the *Zjytze* of Amsterdam. Did you know about it?'

Hansom extended his large hands. 'A little bird told me about it last night.'

'And you've checked her?'

'That's sort of my job around here.'

'Well?'

Hansom took a medium-sized breath. 'They're football fans,' he said, 'like everyone else round here, only more so.'

'How do you mean?'

'They went to London to see the Gunners.'

'All of them?'

'Yeah – one big happy family. The Skipper and Ma Hoochzjy, the son who's mate, the son who isn't mate, the son who's cook, three able-bodied cousins and a grandson who's cabin boy. They lit out for town at ten o'clock on Saturday, and got back on the 11.53 last night. They spent the night at the Sunningdale Hotel in Tavistock Place – I checked it – and went to Kew yesterday to give the tulips a once-over. They think our English tulips are *vonndervul*.'

'Did you check the vessel?'

Hansom gave a snort. 'Why do you think they've got customs at Starmouth?'

Gently shook his head in slow, mandarin nods. 'I don't *want* to have Peter Huysmann arrested, but as one policeman to another . . .'

'Good Lord!' gaped Hansom.

'. . . I think you'd better have the *Zjytze* checked before she clears Starmouth.'

Hansom was already doubling to the phone. 'I'll send some men out to Rusham!' he exclaimed. 'They'll have to wait there for the swing-bridge.' And he dialled viciously.

'Of course, he may be somewhere else entirely,' added Gently, 'he may even have grown a beard . . .'

They were sawing oak in the timber-yard. The smell of it, sweet with a sharpness and heaviness, carried into the street and even into the house, while the high-pitched whine of the saws, labouring at the hard, close grain, might be heard during intervals in the traffic as far as Railway Bridge. At the quays they were already busy with the barges. Two rattling derricks hoisted out bundles of rough-sawn planks and swung them to growing piles outside the machine sheds, where shouting men were stacking them. Close by an overhead conveyor trundled sawn-out stuff to a lorry. Pandemonium reigned in the great machine sheds. There were ranked the circular saws, buzzing at rest, shrieking with rage as they met the timber, whining viciously as they settled down to tear through it; the fiendish, screaming band-saws, temperamental and deadly; the soft, shuddering planers, cruel with suppressed power; and over all the sweet wholesome smell of sawn oak, of oak sawdust, of oak stacked in neat, separated piles.

Gently wended his way cautiously through this alien world. There was something shocking and amoral about so much terrible power, all naked; it touched unsuspected chords of destruction and self-destruction. He glanced curiously at the men who fed the lusting blades. They could not but be changed, he thought, they must partake of that feeling to some extent: become potential destroyers, or self-destroyers. He wished vaguely that such things were not, that timber could be produced by means other than these. But he could think of no other way, off-hand.

He came upon Leaming checking off a consignment of finished wood. Leaming grinned at him, a band-saw close by making oral communication impossible. Gently waited until he had finished checking, by which time also the band-saw had done ripping out scantlings.

'It's like this all day!' bawled Leaming.

'Doesn't it drive anybody mad?'

'They're mad when they come here – or else they wouldn't come!'

They walked on towards the comparative quiet of the planers, stopped to see the rough-sawn planks being driven over the steel bench with its wicked concealed knives. 'Tell me,' said Gently, 'do you get many suicides in here?'

Leaming threw back his head in laughter. 'No – they don't commit suicide here. They go away somewhere quieter for that.'

'Do you get accidents?'

'Not so many as you might think.'

Gently winced as a flying chip went past his face. He was aware of Leaming quizzing him, a little contemptuous. 'You soon learn to be careful when you're working a buzz-saw – mighty careful indeed. Most accidents happen when they're sawing up a tree with a bit of metal in it – an old spike that's grown into it or something. Sometimes the saw goes through it, but sometimes it doesn't.'

'What happens then?'

'The saw goes to pieces – and the pieces go a long way.'

Gently shuddered in spite of himself. Leaming laughed sardonically. 'Anything can happen here, any time. The miracle is that nothing much does happen . . .'

They walked out of the inferno and into the yard.

Gently said: 'I suppose the old man Huysmann was rather like a buzz-saw in some ways.'

Leaming shot him a side-glance and then grinned. 'I suppose he was, though I never thought of him like that.'

'He buzzed and shrieked away happily enough until somebody put a spike in his log . . . and now nobody quite knows where the pieces will finish up.'

Leaming said: 'But there's one man with his neck right out to stop a lump.' His grin faded. 'I'd better get back to the office,' he said, and turned away abruptly. Gently stared after him, surprised at his sudden change of mood. Then he noticed somebody standing at the entrance to the office, a tall but rather furtive figure: someone who slipped inside as he realized that Gently's eye was on him. It was Fisher.

Two loaded transport trucks stood outside Charlie's, both from Leicester. Inside there was an air of briskness which had been lacking the day before. Most of the tables were occupied and in addition there was a group who stood around the fireplace (in which there was no fire) arguing. Their subject was the murder, which by now was getting front-page billing in all the popular dailies. One of the standing group held a paper in his hand. 'SLAIN MERCHANT – YARD CALLED IN', ran the headline. 'Son Still Missing . . .'

'You can say what you like,' said a transport driver, 'when they talk like that about someone, he's the one they want. They never do say anyone's the murderer till they've got their hands on him, but you can tell, all the same.'

'It don't mean that necessarily,' said a little stout man. 'I remember somebody who was wanted like that, but he got off all the same.'

'Well, this one won't get off . . . you listen to me. I'll have ten bob on it he hangs, once they get hold of him. You just read it again and see what they've got against him . . .'

There was a hush when Gently entered. Damnation, he thought, I must be growing more like a policeman every day. He ordered a cup of tea without sugar and added to it a cheese roll. The bar-tender's place had been taken by a girl in a flowered overall. She banged his tea down aggressively and retired to the far corner of the bar. Gently sipped tea and reflected on the hard lot of policemen.

Halfway through the tea the bar-tender put in an appearance. He nodded to Gently, and a moment later leant over the counter. 'Come upstairs, sir,' he said, 'there's something I think you'd like to hear about.'

Gently finished his tea and roll and went up the stairs. The bar-tender was waiting for him on the landing.

'Excuse me, sir, but you are Chief Inspector Gently of Scotland Yard, aren't you?' he asked.

Gently nodded, and sorted out a peppermint cream for digestive purposes.

'I thought you was him, when I remembered the way our friend Fisher acted when you spoke to him yesterday afternoon.'

'He was in his rights to tell me to go to hell,' said Gently tolerantly.

'Well yes, sir, I dare say . . .'

'What's your name?' asked Gently.

'I'm Alf Wheeler, sir.'

'Charlie to your pals?'

'Well, I do run this place, though there isn't no Charlie really – that's just what it's called. And I hope you don't think I was anyway disrespectful yesterday, sir, it's just I didn't know you were . . .'

'A policeman?'

'That's right, sir . . . though I ought to have guessed from the way you was leading me on.'

'Well, well!' said Gently, pleased, 'you're not going to hold it against me?'

'No, sir – not me.'

Gently sighed. 'It makes a change . . . what was it you wanted to tell me?'

The bar-tender became confidential. 'He was in here last night, sir.'

'Who?'

'Fisher, sir. He was a bit – you know – a bit juiced, and the girl Elsie and one or two of them was kidding him along, pretending they was scared of him – asking who he was going to do in next and that sort of thing. Quite harmless it was, sir – nothing intended at all.'

'Go on,' said Gently.

'Fisher, he begin to get all of a spuffle. "I could tell you a thing or two you don't know," he says, "and I could tell that b— Chief Inspector Gently something, for all his cleverness."

'"Why don't you tell us, then?" says the girl Elsie.

'"Never you mind," he says, "but you're going to see some changes round here shortly, you mark my words."

'"What sort of changes?" they say, but Fisher begin

to think he's said enough. "You'll see," he says, "you'll see, and maybe it won't be so long either."

'"Hugh!" says the girl Elsie. "I 'spect he thinks he'll be manager at Huysmann's now."

'"Manager," he says, "I wouldn't be manager there for something. And another thing," he says, "there's people cutting a dash today who may not be cutting one tomorrow," and after that he shut up and they couldn't get anything else out of him.'

Gently ate another peppermint cream thoughtfully. 'Would you say that the last remark referred to the manager?' he enquired.

'I thought it did, sir, and so did the others.'

'Have you any idea what he might have meant by "changes"?'

'Well, you know what we was saying about there being something between him and Miss Huysmann? If that's the case, sir, then he's probably thinking, now that the old man is dead, that she'll take him on and make a man of him. I can't think what else he may have had in mind.'

'And then he would be in a position to deal summarily with Mr Leaming?'

'You bet he'll put a spoke in *his* wheel when he gets the chance.'

Gently shrugged. 'It depends a lot on Miss Huysmann's attitude,' he said. 'I wonder if, perhaps, he could be referring to something else . . .?'

He went down the stairs, followed by the bar-tender. A heated discussion amongst the group round the fireplace broke off as the door opened. Gently bowed to them gravely. 'Carry on, my friends . . . don't let us interrupt you,' he said. Twenty pairs of eyes from all parts of the snack-bar turned on him in silence. He shook his head sadly and went out.

The bright sun of the street struck in his eyes, making him blink. A steady stream of traffic was making in both directions, slowing at that point to get round the two parked trucks. A few yards further back Mariner's Lane disgorged a small, hooting van. Gently read the street sign with puckered eyes; at the same time he observed a figure standing in the gateway of the timber-yard. He turned directly and began walking casually towards the lane.

Mariner's Lane threaded the jungle between Queen Street at the bottom of the cliff and Burgh Street at the top. It was narrow and steep and angular. It began at the bottom by a derelict churchyard, carved its way past walls and slum property, with occasional vistas of desolate yards and areas, and threw itself at last breathlessly into the wide upper street, a bombed-site on one hand and a salvage yard on the other. It was a mean, seamy thoroughfare, part slum and part derelict: its only saving grace was the view it commanded – over the roofs of Queen Street, over the river, over the railway yards, as far as the bosky suburbs rising out of the easting Yar valley.

Gently plodded upwards with tantalizing slowness, pausing now and then to study his surroundings. He did not look back – at least, he did not appear to look back; but he looked long and hard at each miserable series of yards, and sometimes peered curiously at sparsely furnished windows. One of the many angular turnings brought him to Paragon Alley. It was a neglected little cul-de-sac about fifty yards long, with grass and ragwort growing out between the made-up surface and the pavement. One side was derelict, the other comprised of high walls and forgotten warehouses. Gently turned into it.

For a moment he did not see how anybody could live in Paragon Alley. It seemed too completely forgotten and neglected. And then he noticed, well down on the right-hand side, a warehouse over which were two curtained windows. It had access by a paintless side-door and two worn steps, and the number was chalked on the door: 5A.

Gently brooded before this footprint in the desert sands. 'It's quiet up the alley,' was what Fisher had said, 'there might have been someone about . . .' He turned to take in the blank face of the wall that closed the alley and the sightless windows that stared across the way. From the corner of his eye he saw the figure that slid out of sight at the entry . . .

There was a face at one of the windows, a dirty little urchin's face. It stared at Gently with mock ferocity.

'Hullo,' said Gently.

'Zzzzzzzz!' said the face, 'I'm Superman. I'm going to carry you away to the Radio Mountain.'

'Well, you'll have to come out here to do that,' said Gently.

'No, I won't – I'll get you with my magnetic ray!' A piece of stick came over the window-sill and levelled itself at Gently. 'Zzzzzzzzing!' said the face, 'zing! zing! Now I've got you!'

Gently smiled affably. 'What's your name?' he asked.

'I'm Jeff, the Son of Superman.'

103

'Do you often play in these old houses?'

'Mister, this is my headquarters. This is where I bring all my prisoners, after I've paralysed them with my magnetic ray.'

'Were you here on Saturday? Saturday afternoon?'

'Course I was. That was the day I caught Professor X and his Uranium Gang.'

Gently moved over, closer to the window. 'Do you know who lives across there – over the warehouse?' he asked.

The little brow wrinkled itself ferociously. 'Course I know. He's my arch enemy. That's the hide-out of the Red Hawk, the biggest plane bandit in all England. That's where he builds his planes, mister, real ones, and then he goes out and shoots down other planes with gold in them. Oh, I've been watching him for a long time. One day I'm going to get him real good, and all the stolen gold he's got.'

'What was the Red Hawk doing on Saturday afternoon?'

'Saturday afternoon? That was when he shot down the mail-plane carrying all the gold. I tried to stop him, mister, I was firing the magnetic ray at him all the way down the alley. But do you know what I think?'

'What do you think?'

'I think he's got wise to the magnetic ray. I think he's got an atomic plate on him that stops it.'

Gently fumbled for his peppermint creams. 'Here,' he said, 'these are G-men hot-shots. They've got radio-active starch in them – they'll put sixty miles an hour on you.'

Superman took two and tried out one for effect. 'Gee

104

– thanks, mister!' he exclaimed. 'I'll get that Red Hawk now, just you see.'

Gently said: 'Now this is important, Superman. What time did Red Hawk light out to rob the mail-plane on Saturday?'

Superman injected the second hot-shot. 'He went right away, mister, as soon as he'd come back for his Z-gun.'

'When was right away?'

'Right away after dinner.'

'And what time do you have dinner?'

'Oh, when my father gets back from the factory.'

'And after dinner you came right along here to headquarters?'

'You bet, mister. I'd got a special code message from Mars that Professor X was going to attack right after dinner. I wasn't going to miss him – he's been preying on s'ciety too long.'

'Did you see the Red Hawk come back again with the gold?'

Superman corrugated his brow. 'He's mighty cunning, is Red Hawk. He brought it in the back way – through all these old houses. But I saw him, mister. I saw him come in from my look-out post.'

'What time would that be?'

'Oh . . . I don't know. He'd been gone a good while, but it wasn't tea-time. I caught Professor X before tea-time.'

Gently pondered a moment. 'You can hear them at the football up here, I should think.'

'I'll say you can, Mister! You don't ever need ask how they're getting on, not up here.'

'They scored three times on Saturday. You hear them?'

'Course I did!'

'How many had they scored before the Red Hawk came back with the gold?'

'They'd just scored the second one as he was coming back.'

'You're sure of that, Superman?'

'Course I'm sure! I went up to my look-out post to see if I could see it – you can see one of the goals, mister. And then I saw the Red Hawk creeping back through the houses.'

'What did he do?'

'Oh, he slipped into his lair with the gold and hid it with the rest, I 'spect. Then he went out again, down into the Lane, and asked somebody about the football.'

'And after that?'

'He just went off up the Lane.'

Gently administered another hot-shot. 'You're a good boy, Superman,' he said, 'you've got your head screwed on tight. What are you going to be when you grow up – a policeman?'

Superman's face wrinkled with disgust. 'Not me, mister. I'm really clever. I'm going to be the one who catches them when the police have given up . . . What's your name, mister?'

'Me?' Gently grinned. 'I'm Dick Barton Senior,' he said.

The Red Hawk stood at the entry to the alley, hands in pockets, scowling, disdaining any further concealment. The two-day growth of beard that darkened his face gave it a slightly sinister look. He still wore the beach-girl tie and American-style jacket, but had changed his slacks, which were formerly inconspicuous, for a pair of Cambridge-blue ones. He stood, as though barring Gently's egress. His eyes were aggressive and slightly mocking.

'You been asking questions about me?' he demanded.

Gently stopped, stared at him stolidly.

'Was that kid telling you a pack of lies?'

Gently remained silent.

'They aren't going to believe a kid. Nobody'll believe a kid – not that kid, anyhow. They had him in the home once. He's cracked.'

Gently said: 'Are you just going back to your flat?'

Fisher eyed him nastily. 'Suppose I am. There's nothing wrong with that, is there?'

Gently said: 'I'd like to come in and look it over.'

'Oh, would you? And s'pose I don't like policemen coming into my flat – what are you going to say to that?'

Gently shrugged. 'It's up to you,' he said. 'I could phone down for a search-warrant, if I thought it was worth it.'

Fisher swayed a little, his scowl deepening. 'All right,' he said, 'all right. You come in, Mr Chief Inspector Gently – you come in, and see where you get then.'

He led the way down the alley, Gently following a few paces in the rear. As they drew opposite the flat there was a warning cry from Superman. 'Watch out, mister! I've got the ray on him, but he's a desperate character!' Fisher made a threatening movement and Superman's face and ray-gun disappeared with great promptness. Fisher unlocked the door. There was a short section of dingy passage leading to a steep flight of steps. At the top of these was a dark landing from which opened three doors. Fisher threw them wide. 'There, Mr Chief Inspector Gently,' he said, 'go in and find some clues.'

Gently glanced around him impassively. The first room was a kitchen, combining, apparently, the duties of wash-room. The second was the bedroom, narrow, unornamented, its furniture an iron bedstead, a chair and a varnished chest-of-drawers. The third room was the living-room. It contained three chairs, a couch, a cupboard, a table and a stool. Its walls, from damp patches in which pieces of plaster had fallen, were decorated with coloured drawings of tight-skinned nudes taken from American magazines. Several nude photographs adorned the mantelpiece. The table stood under the window. On it stood several built-up scale models of aircraft, together with an untidy assemblage of balsa wood, tubes of cement, coloured tissue, piano wire and odd-shaped parts, amongst which lay a blunt-nosed skeleton fuselage. A printed sheet of balsa, partly cut out, was at the front of the table. Beside it lay an open cut-throat razor.

'Go on,' jeered Fisher, 'go right in and pull things about – I don't mind!'

Gently went in and slowly circumnavigated the room, touching nothing. Fisher watched him scowlingly from the doorway. 'You don't know anything,' he said, 'think you're so clever, coming from Scotland Yard, but you don't know a thing.'

Gently paused before the razor.

'That's it – have a good look at it! I go out cutting little girls' throats with that.'

Gently picked it up, tried the blade on his thumb and laid it down again. He turned and regarded Fisher distantly. 'What don't I know?' he asked.

'You don't know anything – that's what you don't know. You just think you do!'

'And what do I think I know?'

'You think you know I wasn't here when I said I was here, for a start.'

Gently said nothing.

'You think maybe I was at the house when it was done, don't you?'

Gently raised his eyebrows slightly.

'You think I heard them quarrelling and nipped into the other room and got a chair and watched it done – you think I could tell you how he got the knife off the wall and stabbed the old man as he was at the safe. That's what you think you know, Mr Chief Inspector Gently – that's what it is. But you don't know nothing really, nothing at all! And you're never going to know nothing, for all your cleverness.'

Gently took out a peppermint cream without moving his gaze from Fisher.

'You think you can find out things that Inspector Hansom can't find out. You've been bloody clever, haven't you? But there's as clever people about as you, don't you forget it. They know how much you can prove and how much you can't, and that's not a damn sight and never will be.'

Gently said: 'I might be able to prove that you're the father of Gretchen Huysmann's child.'

Fisher's mouth hung open. 'You'll *what*?' he gabbled.

Gently chewed his peppermint cream.

Fisher came closer. He thrust his face close to Gently's. There was anger and fear in his eyes. 'You're lying!' he spluttered, 'she isn't going to have a child!'

Gently chewed on.

'If she told you that, it's a lie – it's nothing to do with me!'

Gently swallowed.

'Anyhow, they can't prove things like that, not really. You're trying to trap me, that's what it is. You can't prove anything, so you're trying to make me say something by lying.'

Gently smiled at him seraphically.

Fisher breathed hard. 'You don't know anything!' he repeated fiercely, 'you only think you know!'

Gently placed a hand firmly on Fisher's chest and pushed him to one side. 'Think about it,' he said, 'take an hour off and think about it.'

He went down the stairs. From the top Fisher shouted after him: 'You can think what you like . . . you can't prove it!'

Gently completed his climb to Burgh Street and stood for some minutes by the bombed-site, partly to see the view and partly to get his breath back. A steep climb like that came as a warning that retirement was not so very far ahead. And then, he thought, I'll buy a cottage somewhere, quite away from all superintendents with bad cases of murder, and fish . . . Having got his breath, he set off down the hill again. Near the bottom, as he was passing the ruined shell of an old factory-building, he heard a slight movement high above his head. He jumped without stopping to look. At the same moment a fragment of masonry about the size of a football crashed on to the pavement where he had been walking, bounced once and trundled away down the steep slope.

Gently stood motionless, pressed against the wall. There was a sudden clambering and rush of footsteps on the other side. Up the hill, down the hill the wall stretched blindly, completely without access. The footsteps died away in the distance.

Gently picked up the fragment of masonry and placed it carefully at the side of the pavement. It weighed nearly half a hundred-weight. 'You can think what you like,' he quoted to himself, 'but you don't know nothing ... and you can't prove it.' He fed himself a peppermint cream and walked on down the Lane.

CHAPTER EIGHT

THE LATER LUNCH-TIME fly-sheets carried the news: PETER HUYSMANN CAUGHT. It was scanned by typists in snack-bars and discussed by housewives over their lunch-time coffee. The heavy, red-faced man who sold papers outside the bank shouted: 'Huysmann Taken Off Ship – Latest!' – and sold the thick sheaf under his arm as quickly as he could take the money. Two painters on a cradle high above the Walk heard his cry. 'Ted, get you down after a paper,' said the elder one, 'I used to know young Huysmann when he was knee-high to a tin of paint.' Ted went down the scaffolding like a monkey, but by the time he got to the pavement the papers were all sold. So he had to go round to the door of the printing shop and wait while the grumbling machines flapped out a fresh, warm-smelling edition.

'CAUGHT WHILE FLEEING COUNTRY' ran the revised headline, 'PETER HUYSMANN ON DUTCH SHIP BOUND FOR AMSTERDAM: Intercepted by Police at Haswick.' It continued: 'Peter Johann Huysmann, 28, son of the murdered Norchester timber-merchant, was discovered this morning hiding in the Dutch motor-vessel *Zjγtze*, which was returning to its home port of Amsterdam after discharging a cargo of timber at Norchester. Wanted by the police for questioning in connection with the death of his father, Huysmann was discovered concealed in a hold when the vessel was intercepted and searched by the Yar River Police patrol boat at Haswick. Captain Hoochzjy, master of the *Zjγtze*, in a statement to the Norchester City Police, denied all knowledge of the presence of Huysmann on board his vessel. Huysmann was taken to Norchester City Police Station. He was given a meal of bacon and fried sausages in the Police canteen . . .' And there was a photograph of Peter in his riding helmet, a bad one, deliberately chosen for its villainousness.

The elder painter scrutinized the photograph broodingly. He removed the tab-end of a Woodbine. 'Always something queer about that fellow,' he said, 'never quite like you and me, he was . . .'

Gently found Hansom closeted with the super in the latter's neat, bare office. 'He's got that look about him,' Hansom was saying, 'you know, it gets to be an instinct.'

The super rose as Gently came in. 'I'm glad you're here,' he said. 'Judging from the reports I've had in, you've put a finger on some complications which will need a thorough going over. At first – and I don't mind admitting it – I thought you were just being awkward. But I see now there are points here that would be a gift to the defence unless we get them straightened out first. Also, I think they will help us. If we can get the chauffeur to talk, our case is fool-proof.'

Hansom leered at Gently, but said nothing.

Gently said: 'You won't have charged him yet?'

'I'm going to charge him now, when we have him in.'

Gently said: 'May I offer some advice?'

The super glanced at him sharply, frowning. 'I'm always willing to take advice – sound advice.'

Gently's face was completely expressionless. 'My advice is not to charge him with murder,' he said.

Hansom let out a bellow. The super exclaimed: 'But good lord, Gently, it's impossible – completely impossible!'

Gently proceeded smoothly: 'I know it's a great deal to ask, and I wouldn't suggest it except for the best possible professional reasons. But, for your own sake, I advise you not to charge him.'

'I'm sorry, Gently, but it's completely out of the question.'

'You mean we should just question him and let him go?' yapped Hansom, 'just like that – with a conviction staring him in the face?'

Gently pursed his lips. 'I was not suggesting that,' he said.

'Then what are you suggesting?' snapped the super. 'To let him go now is as much as my post is worth and if I don't charge him, I can't hold him. What possible alternative have I?'

'You can hold him on a charge of unlawful possession.'

'Unlawful possession?'

'You found a bank-note in his caravan which was one of those stolen from the safe. I don't think you'll get a conviction, but it's enough to hold him on. And, it's one thing to fall down on a case of unlawful possession, quite another to fall down on a case of murder.'

'You know something that's not in these reports?' demanded the super, like the crack of a whip.

Gently sighed. 'I do,' he said.

'And what is that?'

'It's a lot of little things that I couldn't prove to your satisfaction, but they keep adding together in a way that doesn't point towards Peter Huysmann.'

'Then where do they point?'

'I don't want to be positive about that, yet.'

'You don't know?'

Gently shrugged his shoulders. 'I think it's safest to say that.'

'But, good heavens, Gently, what am I to think? You realize that there's people above me who want to know chapter and verse the reasons for my decisions? What am I going to tell them?'

'You could tell them you wanted a little more time.'

'But these reports speak for themselves.'

Gently felt around in his pocket hopefully and produced a part-worn peppermint cream. 'It's a very good case against Huysmann,' he said; 'if you could put him in dock tomorrow, you would get a conviction. Unfortunately you can't do that, and by the time you can, to the best of my judgment, there won't even be a case of unlawful possession against him. That's why I'm offering this advice, which you needn't accept.'

The super stabbed a glance at Hansom and exploded: 'Blast you, Gently! Can't you understand my position? My men have done a good job and they look to me to back them.'

Gently continued: 'If you do accept my advice it may be a help in clearing this matter up.'

'It is cleared up!' snarled Hansom.

'It will suggest to the culprit that we aren't satisfied. We may get a lead out of it.'

The super turned his back on them and fumed at the closed window. 'I wish to God I'd been a whelk-seller! I wish to God I'd stopped in the bloody Army! Would anybody in his right mind be a police superintendent?' He swung round on Gently. 'Let's get this straight – you want me to stand up my men and fob off the powers that be because you've got some blasted intuition – that's it, isn't it?'

'Not intuition,' murmured Gently, 'just judgment based on experience.'

'Intuition!' barked the super. 'Listen, Gently. Can you give me one good solid reason why Huysmann is not the murderer?'

'I think so, if you really want one.'

'*Want* one! Who am I supposed to be – the charwoman?'

Gently rubbed his chin with a stubby finger. 'An hour or two ago some interested person tried to drop some masonry on my head,' he said reluctantly. 'It was a large lump, and it wouldn't have bounced. Now why should anybody want to do that to a policeman?'

'I could tell you!' Hansom yipped.

'You mean they tried to kill you?' demanded the super.

'I'm afraid they did. Which seems to indicate that somebody has grown dissatisfied with the course of my investigations – that somebody is deeply interested in having Peter Huysmann convicted. There can't,' added Gently, 'be more than one reason for that . . . can there?'

Peter Huysmann had been fed and washed, but there had been no time to shave him. A mist of blond beard surrounded his rather long, drawn face and a darkness and sunkenness of the eyes betrayed the fact that he had slept very little in the past forty-eight hours. He was still wearing his overalls, now soiled and stained with oil: their being open at the neck gave him an unexpectedly boyish appearance. He was brought in by two constables. Parsons, the shorthand constable, had already taken his place.

'Sit down, Huysmann,' said the super, not unkindly, indicating a chair placed in front of his desk. Peter sat down with some awkwardness, placing his hands on his knees. He shot defensive glances at Hansom and Gently, who flanked the super right and left. His mouth was set in a drooped, quivering line.

The super cleared his throat. 'First of all, I am charging you, Peter Huysmann, with being in unlawful possession of property, namely a bank-note, removed from a safe, the property of your father, the late Nicholas Huysmann.'

Peter stared at him in momentary surprise, but probably supposing this to be some sort of prelude to a graver charge, said nothing. The super continued: 'Do you wish to say anything in answer to this charge? You are not obliged to say anything, but whatever you say will be taken down in writing and may be used in evidence.'

'Though not necessarily against you,' added Gently, in the pause that followed.

Peter looked from one to the other of them, still not quite able to follow the turn things were taking.

'Do you wish to say anything?' repeated the super.

Peter licked his lips. 'Yes,' he said, 'I – I'd like to tell you everything – all I can tell you.'

His voice was slightly harsh, but contained almost no accent. 'You'd like to make a statement?' asked the super.

'Yes, I'll make a statement. But I didn't take the bank-note – it was given to me.'

'You plead not guilty to the charge?'

'My father gave it to me just before I left.'

The super picked up a pencil and began doodling on a pad in front of him. 'Before you make your statement I would like to caution you once more. You are quite within your rights to say nothing and we have no power to demand that you shall. You do so at your own risk. I'm not saying this to stop you making a statement, but simply to warn you that you needn't if you feel it may incriminate you in a possibly graver charge. I can't put it plainer than that. It's up to you.'

Peter said: 'Thank you . . . but I want to tell you everything that happened.'

He licked his lips again and looked across at the constable with the notebook. Gently wondered: did they tell his wife or did she see it first in the lunch-time papers?

'You've found out how I left home,' said Peter, 'you know that my father and I weren't on good terms. It was my marriage he couldn't forgive – I was to have married the daughter of a merchant in Rotterdam, somebody rich. They'd worked it all out when I was in the cradle. When I married Cathy I just about ceased to be a son of his.

'It was pretty hard for me, never having had to get my living before. I knew how to drive a truck, so I got a job with a small transport firm at King's Lynn, and that went on for about three months. But the driver I was with got mixed up in a robbery – I lost my job and nearly went to prison as an accessory. After that I got in with the fair people and learned to do an act. It didn't pay very well, so I persuaded Clark – he's my boss – to let me practise the Wall, and I got so good at it that he took me on as his number one rider.'

Hansom said: 'What was the act you learned that didn't pay very well?'

Peter hesitated. 'It was just one of the little side-show acts.'

'Anything like knife-throwing?'

'It *was* . . . knife-throwing.'

'Ah,' said Hansom, 'little details like that help to fill in the picture, you know. Don't leave them out.'

Peter flushed, his lip quivering. He went on, a little sullenly: 'I'd written to my father once or twice since I went away, but he never answered. My only contact was with Gretchen, whom I saw sometimes when I was in Norchester with the fair. And I used to write to her, addressing the letters to the maid Susan. Then two weeks ago, when the fair was at Lincoln, Clark offered me a partnership in the Wall if I could find up five hundred pounds. It was a very liberal offer . . . the Wall would clear a hundred pounds in a good week. I told him I would see my father when we got to Norchester.'

The super said: 'What made you think your father would let you have the money?'

Peter shrugged. 'I don't know. We were just coming to Norchester again, so I thought I would give it a try. Five hundred pounds was not much to my father . . . I thought he would lend it to me. First I sent a note to my sister, arranging to see her as soon as we got into town. She wasn't very hopeful. My father was still talking of changing his will and he had been in an irritable mood of late – perhaps because he knew I was coming to town.'

Gently said: 'Could there have been any other reason why he was irritable?'

'There was business, of course . . .'

'Do you know of any particular business reason which might have caused it?'

'He used to imagine there was a leakage somewhere. But that had been going on for years . . . I think it was a delusion. My father was a very suspicious man.'

'Did he suspect anyone in particular?'

'I don't think so.'

'Do you know how the wages he paid compared with those paid by the trade in general?'

'I couldn't say exactly, but he was not the sort of man to pay more than the minimum rate.'

'Would he have paid more than that, say, to his manager?'

'No, he couldn't have done: I can remember Mr Leaming complaining that he was getting only two-thirds of what some managers were paid.'

'You are positive of that?'

'Quite positive.'

'Did it never seem strange to you that Mr Leaming should not transfer to a firm where he would be better paid?'

'He had a reason for that. Before he came to us he was with a firm called Scotchers' which went bankrupt. There was no blame attached to Mr Leaming, but he found it difficult to get a position afterwards . . . he was the first manager to last with us for more than twelve months.'

Gently nodded his mandarin nod to signify that he had done. Peter licked his lips again and continued.

'After I'd spoken with Gretchen I thought I'd try to raise the money somewhere else. There was a firm called Trustus advertising in the local paper, so I went to them and told them the position. At first I thought I was going to get it. When they understood that I was the son of Nicholas Huysmann they were very favourable. But once they realized that I was on my own and without a fixed address it was different . . . even though I brought the last balance sheet to show them. I went to another firm after that, Goldstein in Sheep Lane, but it was the same there. So I decided to go through with my original plan.

'My father was usually busy in the yard on Saturday mornings, so I waited till the afternoon, which he was in the habit of spending in the study going over his books and the like. Clark scrubbed one of the performances at the Wall so that I could have an hour off. I didn't tell Cathy where I was going because I knew she would be upset . . . it would be time enough to tell her if I got the money. I left the fairground at about quarter past three.'

'What makes you sure of the time?' interrupted the super.

'There was a performance at three – they last about ten minutes. By the time I'd got out of my overalls and straightened up it would be about quarter past. I went straight down Queen Street and knocked on my father's door.'

Gently said: 'Did you notice if there were any vehicles parked in the vicinity?'

'I can't remember any. There was still quite a bit of traffic going down to the football match.'

'Did you see anybody you recognized, or any vehicles you recognized?'

'I wasn't thinking much about other people . . . Susan answered the door, and I told her why I had come. I also asked her where Gretchen was. She told me that my father was in the study and that Gretchen was upstairs in her room. I went along to the study, knocked and entered.

'My father was sitting at the table facing the door. He rose as I entered.'

'What did he say?' demanded Hansom.

'He said something like: "You! I was expecting you to turn up one of these fine days!" I replied that I had not come to annoy him but about a business matter.'

'What did he say to that?'

'He said that I hadn't any business to come about and that I could take myself off again. I did my best to smooth him down so that he would listen to me. I admitted that I had been very much in the wrong, and that I did not expect his forgiveness, and let him give me a thorough dressing-down without saying a word.

After he had cooled off a little bit I mentioned that I was in the way of setting up in business on my own.'

'How did he take that?'

'He took it a good deal better than I expected. I went into details about the partnership, showed him the balance sheet and eventually touched on the five hundred pounds. He said, "Yes, I could see that coming," and got out the safe key. I could hardly believe in my good luck. He went over and opened the safe and took out a packet of five-pound notes. Then he came back and put them on the table between us. "There," he said, "there's five hundred pounds, my little man. Let us say that is what you were worth to me two years ago. But you've depreciated," he said, "you've gone down in the market, my son. Today, you are worth only one per cent of your value two years ago. You have taken money, ha, ha! You have run away, ha, ha! And . . . you have married!" Upon which he stripped off the top note and thrust it into my hand. "That is your value to me, my son," he said, "you have it now, and that is all you will ever have."

'For a moment I just stared at him, unable to credit it. The next, all my self-control had gone. Everything that had been stored up for two years came out in a rush . . . everything. I told him just what I thought of him. I couldn't help it. I have a very bad temper . . . we both had . . .'

'Can you remember anything of what you said?' asked Gently.

'I said that he was unnatural – that he had sold his soul – that he had no more human feelings left: and I called him names . . . hypocrite . . . miser . . . satyr . . .'

123

'Did you refer to the bank-note?'

'Yes. I told him there'd be a time when that note came back to roost . . . with interest.'

'What did you mean by that?'

'I'm not quite sure. I had some idea of returning it in such a way that he would regret it . . . I don't know how.'

The super said: 'Think carefully, now. Was there any violence on either side during this quarrel?'

'No, none.'

'Was any offered?'

'No . . . my father raised his hand once, but that was all.'

'Very well. Go on with your statement.'

'In the end I flung out of the side door and left him to it. The last thing he said was that if I ever showed my face there again he'd have me put in charge.'

'Why did you leave by the side door?' asked Hansom.

'It happened to be open, and I wanted to get out quickly. I went back to the fairground in a flaming temper. I told Cathy what had happened, which upset her, I'm afraid: it wasn't fair, but I had to let off steam somehow. Anyway, I cooled down a bit and had a cup of tea, and then went over to the Wall for my next ride.'

'What time was that?' Gently enquired.

'It was timed for four-thirty.'

'Where did you put on your overalls – at the Wall?'

'No . . . I put on this spare pair. I had them at the caravan. I tore the seam of the other pair when I took them off.'

124

'Did you see anybody you knew as you crossed the fairground?'

'I shouldn't have noticed them if I did. I saw Clark, who told me not to take it to heart too much – he said he'd got a pal in London who might put up the money for me. And then I got on with my rides. I rode at four-thirty, five, five-thirty and six. After the show at five I went back to the caravan and had something to eat . . . also, I tried to cheer Cathy up. By the six ride I'd pretty well got over it. And then I went out and bought a paper . . .

'I saw it directly because I looked at the stop-press for the football results. It struck me absolutely numb, like a blow on the head . . . it almost seemed that I must have done it myself. I felt as though I were . . . doomed.'

'Did it not occur to you that the best thing to do would be to come straight to the police?' asked the super sternly.

'But what would they think? What could they think? Everything was so much against me that I could hardly believe myself . . . The quarrel, that must have been heard by everyone in the house – perhaps other people; my relations with my father – my need of money – his intention of changing his will – it was all well known. And then, for it to have happened directly after the quarrel . . . it seemed that I was caught up in some terrible mechanism. There was only one thing left to do, and I did it.

'That evening I hid amongst some derelict buildings near Burgh Street. As soon as it was dark I made my way out of town towards Starmouth. I didn't know quite what I should do, but I felt I should be safer out in the country. I spent the night in a cart-shed somewhere and tried to think things over and make a plan. There was just a chance that the police would find the murderer quite quickly, that I might not have been suspected at all. In that case I intended to give myself up. But if they did not, then it was as good as committing suicide and I resolved that somehow I must get out of the country. At first I thought I would go on to Starmouth, but it was a long way. Then I thought of the timber-boats that came up to Norchester. Some of them were Dutch, and as you know, I am Dutch by extraction and speak the language perfectly. If I could get on one of those to Holland I should be safe, and later on I could get a message back to Cathy and have her brought over to me.

'I hid all Sunday in some woods not far from the city. In the morning I had ventured out to some cottages and stole a newspaper from a letter-box. I was convinced from what I read in it that I must get away. When the night came again I worked my way back into the city, keeping to all the back roads and side lanes, and made a reconnaissance along Riverside. There I found the *Zjytze*. I knew her well – also, she was empty, which meant that she would soon be on her way home. So I crept round into the timber-yard and got aboard her.'

The super slashed parallel lines across a pattern he was building up on his pad. 'You realize, of course, the immediate construction we were obliged to place on your actions?' he asked.

Peter's hand opened appealingly. 'I know . . . I know . . . but what else could I have done? It was not my life that was wanted . . . yet who would believe that?'

'We were bound to catch you in the long run. It would have been best to come to us straight away.'

'I don't know . . . one must try to save one's life.'

Hansom said: 'Was it true that Hoochzjy didn't know you were on the vessel?'

'I could not risk letting him know, not until we were clear of England. I know him well and I don't think he would have given me up; but I was not going to risk it.'

Gently said: 'I'd like to go back a little bit. You said just now that "the quarrel must have been heard by everyone in the house". Whom did you have in mind?'

'There was Susan and my sister . . . perhaps others.'

'Did you see your sister?'

'No, but Susan told me that she was there.'

'Who were the others?'

'Other servants, perhaps . . .'

'Did you see anyone else at all besides Susan and your father?'

'No.'

'Or hear anything, or see any signs of anyone else?'

'Not . . . really.'

'What do you mean by that?'

'I can't tell you anything definite, but while I was talking to Susan in the hall I had the impression that there was somebody upstairs on the landing.'

'You saw them?'

'It is very dark in the hall. I can't be certain.'

'Did you actually look in that direction?'

'Yes, but I didn't see anything. It may be I thought I heard a movement up there, or perhaps I actually did catch sight of somebody out of the corner of my eye; anyway, they had gone when I looked.'

'And you proceeded with the impression that there was another person in the house besides yourself, your father and Susan?'

'If I thought about it at all, I thought it was Gretchen.'

'But you did proceed with that impression?'

'Yes, I did.'

'Coming now to your interview with your father. Whereabouts did you stand during that interview?'

'Oh, by the table most of the time.'

'You are speaking of the large table that stands roughly in the centre of the room, not far from the safe?'

'Yes.'

'You were on the near side and your father on the far side?'

'Yes.'

'Then you had your back to the inside door?'

'Most of the time.'

'During that interview, did you hear anything that might lead you to believe there was somebody outside that door?'

'I can't think of anything.'

'Would you have noticed, for instance, if your father looked at it in a particular way, suggesting that he had heard or seen something?'

'I wouldn't have noticed.'

Gently paused for a moment. 'From where you were standing, you could see through the outer door into the garden, also the outer gate, also part of the summer-house through the small window?'

'I suppose I could, but I didn't notice them much.'

'Can you say whether the outer gate was open or closed?'

'It seemed to be closed, but when I went out I found it was slightly ajar.'

'You saw nobody in the garden at any time?'

'No.'

'Nor in the summer-house?'

'No.'

'You would not have noticed if the summer-house door was opened or closed?'

'Yes, I did. It was standing half-open.'

'Was there anybody in the timber-yard when you went through it?'

'Nobody.'

'Or any vehicle?'

'None.'

Gently spread out his stubby fingers and placed the tips together in strict sequence. 'Your sister,' he said, 'she does not appear to have many acquaintances.'

Peter shrugged and shook his head. 'It is my father's fault . . . she does not know anybody except a few people she meets at church.'

'What sort of people are they?'

'Oh . . . elderly, not very interesting.'

'Has your sister any admirers to your knowledge?'

Peter's long face twisted in a wry smile. 'There was a young fellow once. He was called Deacon . . . he worked in a solicitor's office. But my father soon put a stop to that. It happened several years back.'

'Your father had a plan for marrying you to a Dutch girl. Had he any such plan for Gretchen?'

'No! That would have cost money . . . in Holland she would have required a dot. With me, of course, it was different.'

'If she had a lover, would you expect to be in her confidence?'

'Well . . . that's hard to say. Gretchen is very strange and very religious. She tells me most things, but not all. If it were anything serious I think she would tell me.'

'Have you ever had any suspicions, say of members of the household . . . or the staff?'

'None at all. But I have been away two years.'

'Would you be surprised to hear that Gretchen had, in fact, a lover?'

Peter stared hard at Gently. 'No,' he said, 'I don't think so. Her religion . . . it is the sort that would easily turn to something else . . . a substitution for it.'

'Would you say it was true that she was very much afraid of her father?'

'Everybody was afraid of my father.'

'But Gretchen, perhaps, especially?'

'In her position, I suppose she was . . .'

The shorthand constable closed his notebook and Gently, unable to smoke in the super's office and out of peppermint creams to boot, stretched himself and sighed largely.

'He's clever,' said Hansom, 'he's dead clever. And he can tell a story.'

The super tore off his sheet of doodlings. 'It's the sort of statement an innocent man might make if he were honest . . . and a guilty man if he were clever. It doesn't seem to have helped you much, Gently.'

'I wouldn't say that.' Gently permitted himself the ghost of a smile. 'At least we've got an indication that there was some other person in the house, besides those we know of.'

'But that's all you've got, and you've been hammering away at it all through the questioning. The really important point, that somebody was at hand during the quarrel, you've drawn a blank on.'

'There's the chair-marks and the finger-prints,' mused Gently.

The super made impatient noises. 'You know how much that's going to impress a jury. As part of a chain of evidence it would stand up, but taken on its own it would only furnish an opportunity for sonic forensic fireworks by the counsel. Look here, Gently' – the superintendent adopted a friendly tone – 'let's have young Huysmann back and charge him properly, and forget all this other business. I know you think he's innocent, but he's got himself into a mess and it's up to his counsel to get him out of it, not us. We're just here to get the facts and we've got them . . .'

Slowly Gently shook his head. 'We haven't got them . . . not all of them. For one thing there's the money, and for another there's the gentleman who tried to bounce masonry on my head . . .'

The super's jaw moved out a good half-inch. 'Very well, Gently, have it your way,' he snapped, 'but by God, you'd better be right! I'm giving you forty-eight hours before I charge young Huysmann: after that, you're on your own.'

Gently met the super's eye with a look of mild reproof. 'I do wish you people would realize that I'm on your side,' he said.

CHAPTER NINE

EVEN HIS OWN Chief seemed just a little bit against him, thought Gently, dropping the receiver on a long telephone consultation. Chiefy had seen the papers and left instructions for Gently to ring him. 'I know I can trust you, Gently,' he had said, 'and you can't tell me anything about the attitude of provincial superintendents. But for heaven's sake bear in mind that you're unofficial and don't stir up trouble. If the local gendarmerie think they've got a case, well, just let them keep right on thinking – if they haven't, they'll find out soon enough when it gets to court.'

Which is as good as telling me to drop it, thought Gently . . .

He looked down at the dusky city with its ten thousand lights, with the moving jewels that were cars and the sauntering shop-windows that were buses. In the market place they were busy packing up, flowers and vegetables were being dispatched on hand-carts to the subterranean vaults under the Corn Hall. Down London Street came a news-boy with the Late Night Finals: No Murder Charge in Huysmann Case, Final!

Final! The day was over, the business was done. Now it was time to pack up, to have tea, to slacken the tireding wheels of commerce. And then there was the pictures or the Hippodrome . . .

Gently walked down by the Guildhall and crossed over to the brightly lit foyer of a small café, the Princess. It had a bowl of fruit in one window and a dish of cakes in the other, and both seemed, to a hungry Gently, well up to chief inspectorial standards. He went in. It was a pleasant, intimate place with oak beams and nooks and a large fireplace in which slumbered a mature fire and a wireless turned down low spoke of football in the midlands. He selected a small, nooky table within fire-range and glanced down the menu.

A tall pretty waitress came to him.

'Mixed grill,' said Gently, 'with two helpings of fried onion. What are the sweets like?'

'The fruit salad is very good, sir, and there's clotted cream today.'

'Cow cream?' asked Gently cautiously.

'Oh yes, sir.'

'Ah!' said Gently, 'well, have it all ready. And I'll finish up with biscuits and Stilton and white coffee. And by the way, I like a *lot* of Stilton . . .'

The wireless programme had changed to music, South American, with subtle, nostalgic rhythms. Gently expanded himself towards the benevolence of the fire. Forty-eight hours and then he was on his own . . . with full police non-co-operation. Of course, the break might come sooner. The fact that Peter hadn't been charged right away might set things moving. It would certainly worry somebody. But if it didn't, what then?

It didn't need the super to point out that Gently was butting his head against a wall. The wall was only too obvious. It loomed up everywhere. Try as he might, he always came across it at last, solid and indestructible, surrounding the blank on the map with unswerving determination. But the very fact that it was there, that it kept occurring, was significant: if Gently couldn't get beyond it, at least he had become familiar with its direction and extent.

And the key-stone in the wall was Fisher. It was Fisher who had to crack. Take away Fisher, and the whole obstinate construction would collapse and reveal its secrets, whatever they were. All Gently's mature instincts told him that – break Fisher, and the rest would fall into place. But if Fisher kept his nerve and did nothing foolish . . .

The waitress came back smiling with an interesting-looking tray. Gently called for rolls and went stolidly to work on his mixed grill. He ate seriously and with enjoyment. Food was one of those dependable pleasures, like smoking.

He thought of Gretchen. Had he been right with that shot in the dark, about her being pregnant? It had shaken Fisher, at all events, and confirmed Gently's belief that he was her lover. But why should he have expressed fear? If it was his plan now to marry Gretchen and succeed to the old man, surely to have got her pregnant would have been a step in the right direction? But he was afraid that it was so, and that Gently should know it . . . why? Was there something in Hansom's far-fetched notion after all – had the murder of Nicholas Huysmann been the concerted act of his daughter and his chauffeur?

Gretchen, he thought again. Gretchen. Perhaps his best chance lay there. But Gretchen wouldn't talk any more than Fisher . . . and in her present situation, to bring any sort of pressure to bear on her was distasteful. Yet . . . could Hansom have hit it?

The music lilted some far-off tune of Gently's youth, something connected with people and places unspeakably remote. He laid down his knife and fork. The waitress, who had been watching, came forward directly and removed the plate, wondering why Gently shook his head. Several people came in at that moment and stood looking for tables. Secure in his nook, Gently looked them over. Townspeople going to a show and having tea out . . . and then his eyebrows lifted the merest shade. One of the newcomers was Susan.

But Susan was on her own. Also, she seemed to be in a little 'state' about something. She ignored the waitress who wanted to fit her in a large table and with a toss of her sweeping blonde locks made for a smaller one near Gently's own.

'But we are keeping that table for two of our regulars, madam . . .'

'There's no "reserved" notice on it, is there?'

'It is their usual table, madam . . .'

'A pot of tea and some cakes.'

The waitress shrugged and moved away. Gently indulged in a smile. Someone had let Susan down, he thought, she's all dressed up with nowhere to go . . . is Mr Leaming the culprit? He took delivery of his fruit salad and ate it thoughtfully. How much did Susan know about Fisher and Gretchen? She seemed to be a good deal in Gretchen's confidence, one way or another . . . in fact, most of the clandestine comings and goings in the Huysmann house revolved round Susan. Gently eyed her interestedly over his peaches and cherries. She was dressed to go somewhere, without a doubt. She wore a rather expensive black creation that clung to her challengingly, nylons and a red swagger coat which also looked expensive. Her face was made-up heavily but with taste. She wore a silver bracelet, pearls and a diamond ring which might have been genuine. She was quite something, if the sulky expression of her face hadn't spoiled it all.

Gently ate on through his cheese and biscuits and drank his coffee. Why had Leaming turned Susan up – if it was Leaming, and it was unlikely to have been anyone else? Lover's quarrel, perhaps? Susan trying to exceed her market value? Or was it something more interesting and relevant?

He lit his pipe and moved over to Susan's table.

'Good evening, Miss Stibbons. Are you expecting someone?' he asked paternally.

Susan looked up from an eclair. 'Oh! Good evening, Inspector . . . no, I'm not expecting anybody.'

Gently sat down in the vacant chair. 'I like this restaurant,' he said, 'it's comfortable and friendly. Is this your evening off, Miss Stibbons?'

Susan gave a little shrug. 'I get most evenings,' she said.

'You don't know how fortunate you are. In my business we're supposed to be on duty twenty-four hours a day . . . though of course, there'd be a riot if anyone tried to enforce it. But we get enough dumped on us at one time or another. Were you going to the pictures?'

'I *was*,' said Susan, aggrievedly.

'I believe the picture at the Regent is quite good. I heard one of the men talking about it.'

'That's the one I was going to see.'

Gently took out his watch. 'You've still time, if you hurry.'

Susan shrugged again. 'I'm not going, now . . .'

Gently puffed a few smoke-rings. 'I should,' he said. 'It'll cheer you up no end.'

'I don't want to be cheered up.'

'Oh come, now, it can't be so bad as that. What happened, Miss Stibbons?' Gently leaned forward like a tender father preparing to make all well.

'I don't know what happened. It wasn't anything I said.' She looked up at him, her blue eyes charged with injured innocence. 'He just told me he'd finished with me – just like that!'

Gently tut-tutted. 'But there must have been a reason?'

'There wasn't, Inspector, no reason at all. He picked me up like he always does and we came up here to have a drink at Backs. He was quiet-like, but I didn't take much notice – he's often like that.'

'What happened then?'

'When we came out there he suddenly went all stiff – you know – but I hadn't said anything at all! He stood there for a bit by the car and then he suddenly said, "It's been nice knowing you, Susan, but it's all over now. We're through," he said, "this has got to end right here." And then he got in the car and went off, and left me flat!'

Gently shook his head sympathetically. 'Perhaps he

didn't mean it. Mr Leaming's got a lot on his mind just now.'

'But he *did* mean it! He knows I wouldn't stand for that sort of treatment – and I'm not going to!' She forked viciously at a meringue.

'He may have had an appointment.'

'He didn't say anything about appointments.'

'Well . . . these things happen. I wouldn't take it to heart. There's always someone else round the corner, you know.'

'He may find that out before long.'

Gently smiled encouragingly. 'This business has upset a lot of things, my dear, and affected a lot of people. Take Miss Gretchen, for example.'

Susan mangled a section of meringue and thrust it into her mouth. 'Miss Gretchen's all right,' she said, creamily.

'From a material point of view, I suppose she is.'

'It turned out just right for her. I don't know what she'd have done if it hadn't happened, and that's a fact.'

Gently turned the less-attacked side of the dish of cakes towards the waiting fork. 'How do you mean?' he asked casually.

'Well . . . she was always kept at home . . . she didn't understand.'

'What didn't she understand?'

'You know how it is.'

Gently puffed some smoke at a bulb which gleamed dully behind its mock-parchment. 'In trouble, is she?'

'You'll see, if you're here long enough.'

'How long is that?'

Susan frowned prettily over some green marzipan.

''Bout October, I shouldn't be surprised. Somewhere about then. I warned her, you know, but it was too late then – I didn't know about the first once or twice. After that, of course, there wasn't much point in being careful.'

'Is she really in love with him?'

'What – with Fisher?' Susan sniffed scornfully. 'I shouldn't think so. He goes around with anybody – he tried to get me, but I wasn't having any . . . she was just having him because she couldn't get anybody else.'

'Has this business made any difference?'

'Oh, she won't speak to him now. She won't have anything to do with him. If you ask me, he isn't going to be chauffeur at our place much longer.'

'How does he take it?'

'He doesn't care.'

'I wondered if he'd started getting ideas.'

Susan grinned, cat-like. 'I daresay he had some, but they won't be coming off. Miss Gretchen can pick and choose now . . . even though she is in trouble.'

'Ah well . . . it's a strange world.' Gently thumbed the bowl of his defunct pipe and relit it. 'When was the last time they saw each other?'

'You mean the last time they . . .?' queried Susan innocently.

'Yes.'

'Wednesday.'

'Wednesday, eh?' Gently brooded.

'That's the night Mrs Turner goes to the pictures. She doesn't know anything about it, of course. Miss Gretchen went to bed early and I was there to let him in through the kitchen.'

'Saturday one of his days?'

'Afternoons on a Saturday – I'm out myself after tea.'

'I don't suppose you saw anything of him last Saturday?'

Susan wrinkled her brow. 'I thought maybe he'd slipped in while I was out of the kitchen . . . I felt sure he'd be up there with her. But then, you see, she'd gone out on her own and he stopped at home . . . well, I suppose they had a row. Anyway, she's finished with him now.'

The cakes were finished and the coffee drunk. Susan eased back into her chair and explored her painted lips with the tip of an angelic tongue. 'I like to have a talk,' she said confidentially, 'it makes you feel better.'

Gently said: 'What are you going to do now?'

'Oh . . . I don't know.'

'I was thinking of going to the pictures myself. There's still time.'

Susan unfolded herself another peg and embraced him with a liquid smile. 'I've never been out with a policeman before,' she said.

'It's quite safe,' said Gently.

'We-ell!' She inclined her head coyly.

Poker-faced, Gently paid their two bills and helped Susan on with her flaming red coat. Across the way was a taxi rank. Gently shepherded her through the traffic and handed her into the first car. 'Regent,' he said to the driver, then paused. Over by the Princess foyer stood somebody, watching them, a tall, broad-shouldered figure in an American-cut jacket. Gently shrugged and got in.

'Who was that?' asked Susan.

'Could have been one of our men.'

'I thought it looked like Fisher.'

'Could have been him, too.'

Susan laughed and snuggled against him silkily. 'I've never been out with a policeman before,' she repeated.

At Charlie's the proprietor was in the back helping Elsie with the washing-up. The snack-bar had a sordid, end-of-the-day atmosphere, with dirty cups on the tables and litter on the floor. Its only occupants were the tug-skipper and his mate, who sat talking interminably in low tones, and Fisher, who sat by himself with a cup of tea before him. Outside the street was deserted and silent. Inside there was an occasional clink of cup and saucer from the back and the drone of the conversation, on and on, like an audition from another world. A coffee-stained evening paper carrying Peter Huysmann's photograph shared a table with a half-eaten bun.

Fisher played with the spoon in his saucer. His mouth was small and tight, his dark eyes angry and furtive. They glanced at the two tug-men, at the door, at the clock, which showed eleven. He pulled over the paper, limp and dirty, and stared at it. Why had Charlie looked at him like that when he came in? Why had he said: 'What – *you*?' in that sort of way? Charlie was in with the police, he knew that. Suppose they'd dropped something to him – something about Fisher? But he was safe there, as long as he kept his trap shut . . . they might suspect, but they couldn't prove anything.

Fisher crumpled the paper and threw it into a corner, done and finished with. He looked across at the two tug-men. They were completely absorbed in their conversation . . . or was it that they didn't want to speak to him? Had Charlie said something to them? He could imagine Charlie bending over and whispering: 'Stay clear of Fisher – the police have got something on him!' And so they talked and talked and pretended he wasn't there. He got up and went over to them. They stopped talking and looked round. A movement from the back suggested that Charlie had put his head round the door.

'I'm Fisher,' he said defiantly.

The tug-skipper shrugged his lean shoulders. 'What about it, mate?' he retorted.

'I'm Huysmann's chauffeur.'

'Well . . . what are we supposed to do . . . clap?'

'I could tell them a few things they don't know, if I'd a mind to . . . things they're never going to find out without me.'

Charlie said from the door: 'Well – why don't you tell them? What are you afraid of?'

Fisher swung round to face him. 'I'm not afraid of nothing – see? They can't pin anything on me, whatever they think – and whatever they say they think!'

'What do they think, mate?' put in the tug-skipper.

'Never you mind . . . it isn't your business.'

'Then why come barging in with it?'

Fisher clenched his fists and looked ugly. 'Here . . . stop that!' exclaimed Charlie, coming round from behind the bar.

'Let him be,' said the tug-skipper, 'I know how to handle his type . . .'

'I won't have fighting here.'

Fisher turned furiously on Charlie. 'Policeman!' he burst out, 'bloody policeman! I'm not a policeman, whatever else I am. And you watch out for yourself, that's what I say. Things are going to change round here . . . you may not be so high and mighty, for one!'

Charlie took him by the sleeve. 'What do you mean by that?' he demanded.

'Get your hands off me – get them off!'

'I'm asking you what you mean by what you just said.'

Fisher wrenched himself away. 'You'll find out, don't worry! You'll find out that you can't treat some people like dirt . . .!'

The doorbell tinkled and the bulky figure of Gently entered. He glanced at Fisher with mild surprise. 'We seem to be following each other about . . .' he said.

'Rotten cop!' shouted Fisher, 'coming here trying to find out things . . . but there's nothing you can find out. Ask your pal Charlie, here!'

Gently ignored him and went over to the counter. 'A cup of coffee,' he said. Charlie, with a dangerous glance at Fisher, went to serve him. 'Look at him!' cried Fisher, trying to include the tug-men, 'a bloody know-all cop! A rotten sneaking policeman! Treating us as though we were something out of a drain!'

The second tug-man shifted uneasily. 'If he's a policeman you'd better button your mouth up, chum,' he said. But Fisher would not be silenced. 'You'd think he was clever to look at him – he thinks he's clever himself! But he isn't – not really! There's as clever people as he is about and they aren't chief inspectors . . .' Encouraged by Gently's passive acceptance of his taunts, Fisher moved closer to the counter. 'You took Susan to the pictures, didn't you? I know – I was watching you! And what did you get out of her, I'd like to know? How much do you think she knows?'

Gently turned about and surveyed him expressionlessly. 'Why did Leaming turn her up tonight?' he asked.

'Leaming!' Fisher spat on the floor. 'How should I know why he did it? What's it got to do with me?'

'I was just asking . . .' replied Gently smoothly.

'Bloody coppers – always asking questions! But you won't get anything out of me. And if you've got any sense you won't listen to Susan's lies . . . dirty little bitch!'

Gently turned his back and stirred his coffee. Charlie looked at him questioningly, but Gently's lips framed a negative.

'What's she been saying about me?' blustered Fisher, pushing up and trying to make Gently look at him. 'She's been lying . . . I've a right to know!'

Gently placed his spoon in the saucer and drank some coffee.

'If it's anything about me and Gretchen, it's a bloody lie!'

Gently put his cup down.

'Listen!' shouted Fisher, 'I've got a right to know – you're going to tell me!' and he laid his hand on Gently's shoulder. He didn't realize how big a mistake this was . . .

Unfortunately, the memory of a fragment of masonry bouncing along the pavement came into Gently's mind at the critical moment and he put plenty of pull into the movement. Fisher lay on his back, completely stunned.

'My God!' exclaimed the tug-skipper, 'I didn't even see it happen!'

Gently dusted his hands modestly. 'It's something they teach you at police college . . .' he said. He motioned to Charlie. 'Put him outside while he's quiet.' He looked at the two tug-men thoughtfully. 'I saw you come up this morning. You dropped a barge at the other side of Railway Bridge. Who was that for?' he enquired.

The two tug-men looked at each other and the skipper ran his tongue over his lips. 'It was sawn-out stuff – we drop it there to save time,' he said.

'Does that quay belong to Huysmann's?'

'Well, no . . . it don't. But they handle the stuff there for us.'

'Who handles it?'

'I reckon it's the firm we supply it to.'

'And who are they?'

The skipper paused reluctantly, then shrugged his shoulders. 'They call themselves "The Straight Grain Timber Merchants".'

Gently smiled at the distant reaches of the night. 'It's the first time I've heard of that particular firm,' he said.

CHAPTER TEN

THE HUYSMANN AFFAIR had turned stale by Tuesday. The fun and games were over with the arrest of Peter and although the failure to charge him with the murder was still good for a minor headline, feeling was that time would take care of that . . . as, indeed, it would. More current now was the pulled muscle of the City's centre-forward. The situation was very keen at the top of the third division south.

Impatient Hansom, having slept on it, ventured a suggestion that the super should reverse his decision and charge Peter forthwith. It was Hansom's first chance of getting an unaided homicide conviction . . . it might easily be his last. But the super, also having slept on it, was convinced that his decision had been wise. He had known Gently longer than had Hansom. He had also begun to be affected by a little of Gently's doubt about the case. So he trailed a convenient smoke-screen before the powers that be and went about his superintendental duties with a thoughtful mien.

Mrs Peter Huysmann had seen her husband at police headquarters. In the presence of a curious constable there had been very little said on either side. Such hopes as had been raised in Mrs Huysmann by the delay in charging Peter were quickly shaken – Peter himself had very few. 'But it must mean something . . .' she said. He shook his head. 'It means they're waiting until they've got everything ready.' 'But did you see Chief Inspector Gently, Peter? He *knows* you didn't do it . . . he told me so!' 'He doesn't belong here. Cathy, it won't make any difference.'

'Fancy!' said Mrs Turner to Susan, 'going out with a policeman – and that one too, who's old enough to be your grandfather! I knew you weren't particular, my girl, but I didn't know you'd come as low as that.' Susan sniffed infuriatingly. 'He's a nice man,' she said, 'I like him . . . he's got good taste.' 'He must have been after something or he wouldn't have taken you out!' 'You're completely wrong,' said Susan, 'he wasn't after anything. He was just being sympathetic and nice and manny . . .'

Gretchen's bedroom was small, almost an attic, with a narrow window looking across the river to the willow trees down Riverside. The floor was stained and naked; the walls, distempered grey, bore nothing but a carved wood crucifix and a narrow iron bed, a white-painted deal wash-stand and a cane-bottom chair comprised all the furniture. Gretchen knelt for long periods on the bare floor in front of the crucifix. Her lips murmured over and over: O my God, I am sorry for my sins . . . let me be forgiven and show me the way.

There came a tap at the bolted door. 'Just a minute!' Gretchen called, and rose, rubbing her painful knees. At the door was Susan. 'It's the Chief Inspector, miss – he wants to know if you can see him.' Gretchen hesitated. 'Which – which one is the Chief Inspector?' 'He's the one from Scotland Yard, miss . . . the quiet one who's always nice to you.' 'Very well . . . tell him that I shall be down directly.'

Susan went, and Gretchen moved across to the white-painted wash-stand, which had a small mirror. She patted her straight black hair with plump fingers, turned sideways and examined herself critically. Then she looked back into her dark eyes, large, heavy, betraying nothing except that they had something to betray.

Gently was waiting in the hall. He came forward, smiling sunnily, and took her plump, limp hand. 'I hope I haven't broken in on you too early,' he said. Gretchen shook her neat head. 'I am usually up at six o'clock . . . we have always been early risers.'

Gently said: 'I'd like to have a little chat in the study, if you are agreeable.'

'In the study?' She looked at him in some dismay.

'I want to glance through the papers in your father's desk . . . of course, we can talk elsewhere if you prefer it. I only wanted to kill two birds with one stone.'

Gretchen took two quick little breaths. 'It does not matter . . . one must grow used to these things.' Gently led the way to the study.

The study had a forlorn, removed look, shaken out of its familiar self by the absence of the carpet, which the local police had taken away, and the slight redistribution of the furniture which this had occa-sioned. Gently dusted off a chair with his handkerchief

148

and placed it for Gretchen. He himself sat down at the desk and began a leisurely examination of the contents of the drawers.

'Your brother is bearing up well,' he observed, aside. 'I asked him if he had any message for you, and he said to tell you that you mustn't worry, because somehow it would come out what really happened.'

Gretchen said: 'I would like to see him, when I may.'

Gently nodded, peering into a file of advice notes. 'There won't be any difficulty made about that. You can come along with me, if you like. I suppose you didn't know much about your father's business affairs, my dear?'

'Oh no . . . he did not think that a woman had any part in business.'

'He was one of the old school . . . I'm just a child at business matters myself. I spent a couple of hours looking through the firm's books on Sunday, but I might just as well have had a nap. Why doesn't somebody think out a way of making book-keeping intelligible?'

Gretchen kept her dark eyes riveted upon him, on edge, trying to gather something of what would come. But Gently seemed to be in no hurry. He prodded and poked, drawer by drawer, sometimes musing over bits and pieces with raised eyebrows, as though he had forgotten Gretchen's existence. Occasionally he made a remark of no particular significance and once or twice he asked questions about things. For the rest, Gretchen might just as well not have been there and towards the end of Gently's investigating she began to get impatient.

At last he appeared to have finished. He replaced

everything which had been removed except a green card and closed the drawers. The card he handed to Gretchen. 'Have you seen this before?' he asked.

She nodded. 'It is an advice card from his suppliers in Holland . . . this is perhaps the last one.'

'Do you remember it being received?'

'I think it came one day my father went to London on business. He picked up his mail as he went out.'

'There is something scribbled across one of the margins. Would that be your father's handwriting?'

'Oh yes. He often made little notes like this.'

'Have you ever heard that name before – "The Straight Grain Timber Merchants"?'

'I know nothing of his business . . .'

'The name is entirely unfamiliar to you?'

'Yes . . . entirely unfamiliar.'

Gently received back the card and put it carefully away in his wallet. He took out a large new bag of peppermint creams. 'Have one?' he invited. Gretchen refused. Gently placed half a dozen of them on the desk in line-of-battle and stowed the bag back in his pocket again.

He said: 'Miss Gretchen, I think it's time you told me the truth about last Saturday.'

Gretchen started back in her chair. 'Inspector . . . what is it you mean? I've told you everything!'

Gently shook his head sadly and removed the first of the peppermint creams. He said nothing.

'But you took it down . . . everything I said! What more can there be?'

'First,' said Gently, swallowing, 'you didn't go to the pictures, Miss Gretchen.'

150

'But I did . . . to the Carlton . . . it was *Meet Me in Rio!*'

'Secondly,' continued Gently, unheeding, 'the chauffeur, Fisher, was in the habit of visiting you on Saturday afternoons, here, in this house.'

'You cannot say that, oh no . . .!'

'And thirdly,' proceeded Gently, 'Fisher did not spend the afternoon at his flat, as he would have us believe. He left it at about two o'clock and returned again at four twenty-two and a half p.m. exactly. In addition to this somebody – and I suggest it was either Fisher or yourself – was seen by your brother at the head of the main stairway when he entered.'

'But this is . . . impossible!'

'There are supplementary facts, Miss Gretchen. Fisher has been your lover since January. You are with child by Fisher. You have refused to see Fisher since the discovery of the crime. Fisher has been hinting that he may soon be boss here. He has also hinted that he has knowledge of the crime unknown to the police. When you have added all that together, Miss Gretchen, you will come to the irresistible conclusion that both you and he spent the Saturday afternoon in this house.'

Gretchen gave a low moan and buried her face in her two plump hands.

'I can appreciate your feelings,' said Gently kindly, 'and believe me, I hate this side of the business almost as much as yourself. But there are some important things which must take the place of personal consider-ations or there could be no human society. Miss Gretchen, if your brother is to receive justice you must tell the truth. His life is very nearly in your hands.'

'It isn't true,' moaned Gretchen, 'I can't help him . . . it isn't true!' and her shoulders heaved with sobbing.

Gently took the second peppermint cream. 'If you won't speak,' he said, 'you are leaving me with only one possible conclusion. I shall have to think that you are shielding your lover at the expense of your brother's life and that you are doing it because you can only save his life by accusing your lover . . . is that what you want me to think?'

Gretchen sprang upright, staring at him. 'No, no! That is not so – he didn't do it!'

'But what else can I think, if you will not tell me the truth?'

'I tell you he did not do it!'

Gently shrugged and shook his head, made a pattern with the four remaining peppermint creams. Into the comparative quiet of the room broke the distant shriek of a circular saw biting at oak. The sound was mirrored by a quiver that ran through Gretchen's body. 'Look!' she said, 'I tell you – I tell you the truth about myself!'

Gently's eyebrows lifted slightly. 'I would like the truth about everything you can tell me, Miss Gretchen.'

'It is about everything . . . it is the truth . . .' She stared at him with wide open eyes, as though she would compel him to believe her by the naked will. 'You are right, I did not go to the pictures . . . at least, I did not go in. I just go there to find out about it so I can pretend, that is all.'

'At what time was this, Miss Gretchen?'

'I don't know . . . about half-past four.'

'It would be about the time that Fisher returned to his flat . . . or a little longer, to enable you to reach the Carlton?'

'He – was – not – there!' She beat on her knees with her clenched hands. 'I do not know where he is – if he go out, he go out, but it is not to me. I am the one who was there, in the house . . . it is me that Peter sees . . .'

'Just a moment,' Gently interrupted, 'let's begin at the beginning, shall we? What did you do after lunch?'

'I told you, I have a wash, then I fetch my coffee from the kitchen and take it to my room.'

'Was Susan in the kitchen when you fetched your coffee?'

'But of course.'

'Did you have any conversation with Susan at that time?'

'No doubt . . . we said something.'

'Did she ask you, for instance, whether you were expecting a visit from Fisher that afternoon?'

'It may be that she did.'

'And what did you reply?'

'Oh . . . nothing special. I just shrug my shoulders and let her think what she like.'

'You gave her the impression that he was coming?'

'I do not know.'

'It was the afternoon on which he customarily visited you, Miss Gretchen. If you gave Susan the impression that he was not coming, then surely she would have commented on it and perhaps enquired why that was so. Did she do this?'

'No . . . I think perhaps she thought he was coming.'

'Why was it, in fact, that he did not come?'

Gretchen twisted her hands together. 'How should I know . . .?'

'Then you were expecting him?'

'No! I knew he would not come . . . I think he told me that the last time, but I forget why.'

'Had there been a quarrel?'

'Perhaps it was that.'

'Had it come to your knowledge that Fisher associated with other women besides yourself?'

The clenched hands pulled apart. 'I do not know that!'

'Then why did you quarrel?'

'Perhaps it was not a quarrel. Maybe I told him it was too dangerous for him to keep coming like that.'

'And he agreed straight away not to come any more?'

'Well . . . he agreed.'

'Had you some reason why it should be more dangerous than it had been in the past?'

'I don't know . . . it was never safe that he should come.'

'And he was quite agreeable to give it up immediately on your suggestion?'

'. . . yes!'

Gently picked up the third peppermint cream and ate it solemnly. 'Miss Gretchen,' he said, 'would you consider it as being an unusual coincidence that this should happen immediately before your father was murdered?'

Gretchen bit her lip, but said nothing. Gently swallowed the peppermint cream and arranged the remaining three in a triangle. 'Ah well . . .' he sighed, 'you took your coffee to your room. What did you do then?'

'I . . . prayed.'

'And how long were you occupied with prayer?'

'That I do not know. Sometimes one is taken away and the prayer is very long. It may have been an hour, or less.'

'You would not be aware of anything that was taking place in the house while you were praying?'

'Oh no! I am not in the house, then. It is like a far country where everything is . . . changed.'

'And you do not know precisely when your praying ended?'

'I think it was when Peter came. I heard him and got up.'

'But you have just said that you would not have been aware of anything which was taking place in the house while you were praying, Miss Gretchen.'

The hands twisted again, finger over finger. 'Perhaps I got up before that . . . just before.'

'And then you came out on the landing to see if it was Peter?'

'I thought it would be him . . . I did not know.'

'He says that you withdrew immediately he looked towards you. Why was that?'

'Oh . . . my father would have been angry . . . he might have come out to see who it was.'

'But surely there was no need to have hidden away from him – you might have smiled to him or greeted him with a few words from the landing and still have been in a position to withdraw if your father should have appeared?'

'I don't know . . . I thought it was best not to see him.'

'Tell me what happened after that.'

'I stayed up there on the landing to hear how my

155

father would receive Peter. At first I heard nothing, but later on they raised their voices and I knew it was not going well for him. I heard Peter call my father some names and my father say things which I could not make out. So I crept down the stairs and along the passage in order to hear them better.'

'Between the time when Peter went in and the time when you went down, did you see anybody in the hall?'

'There was nobody there.'

'You're quite sure of that?'

'Oh yes.'

'Then you did not see Susan pass through from the dining-room to the kitchen?'

'Susan? Of course! I thought you meant somebody else . . .'

'Continue with your account, please.'

'I could not hear anything when I went down the stairs . . . they had stopped talking. I stood close to the door, but they had finished, so I thought that Peter must have gone. I was just going to go back again, then . . .'

Gretchen broke off, shaking her head stupidly.

'Then?' prompted Gently.

'. . . then I heard my father . . . scream.'

'What sort of scream?'

'Oh, dreadful . . . terrible! . . . as one screams at a terrible injury . . .'

'What did you do?'

Her head continued to shake, senselessly, like the head of a mechanical doll. 'I stood still . . . I daren't move . . . I could not move at all. I don't know how long it was that I was like that.'

'But afterwards?'

'Afterwards . . . I got the door open and he lay there with the knife in his back . . . by the safe, where you found him.'

Gently said: 'Nobody had passed you in the passage and there was nobody else in the study . . . is that so?'

'Yes . . . nobody.'

'And you heard no movements that suggested the presence of some other person?'

'I heard movements in the study directly after the scream, but nothing else.'

'What sort of movements?'

'First, a thud . . . then the safe door, which squeaks . . . after that it was somebody moving across the room.'

'Nothing else?'

'No.'

'Not after you had entered the study?'

'I heard nothing then . . . I was not listening.'

'What did you do?'

Gretchen spread her hands over her knees and took a deep breath. 'I went and got the knife,' she said.

'What was your object?'

'It was a throwing knife, and Peter could throw knives . . . also, it would have his fingerprints on it.'

'Did you notice if the side door was open?'

'Yes, it was.'

'And the garden gate?'

'I did not notice that.'

'What did you do when you had got the knife?'

'I wiped the handle of it with the hem of my skirt and hid it in the chest . . . then I went up to my room again. All the time it was quiet, there was no sign of

Susan. I say to myself: "She does not know if I am here or if I am not, and I could easily have slipped out earlier on . . . if she sees me come in, she will believe it when I say I went out after lunch." So I put on my coat and creep out through the study. Then of course I went up to the Carlton to find out everything that was on . . . I came back a little while after Mrs Turner.'

Gently removed another peppermint cream from his shrinking battalion. 'Doesn't it occur to you, Miss Gretchen,' he said, 'that it would have been considerably wiser to have left the knife where it was, and to have phoned the police immediately?'

Gretchen stared at him with wide-open eyes. 'But my brother . . . I had to do something to help him!'

'And what in effect did you do?' asked Gently. 'Your brother was bound to be the principal suspect, with or without the knife. Furthermore, the prints on the knife may not have been his. Didn't that occur to you, Miss Gretchen?'

'I don't know . . . I didn't think . . .'

'In which case you will have destroyed the one piece of evidence which would have cleared your brother on the spot. But apart from that, why did you take the trouble of establishing an alibi for yourself? It hardly seems worth the trouble. Once you had satisfied yourself about the knife there was no reason why you should not have contacted the police . . . at least, nothing that appears in the account you have given.'

'My brother . . . it give him time to get away.'

'What connection is there between that and your alibi? Why did you *want* an alibi, Miss Gretchen? It was a difficult thing to establish and it was bound to bring suspicion on you . . . quite unnecessarily, by your account.'

Gretchen twisted herself in her chair. 'I just think it best if you think I have nothing to do with it . . .'

Gently shook his head. 'It doesn't seem worthwhile to me. People in murder cases who can prove their innocence are usually very keen to tell the truth.'

'But it was as I say!'

'It was not to shield someone other than your brother?'

'No!'

'It was not because Fisher was with you?'

'I tell you he is not!'

'Not because he might be suspected of having been here, unless you could prove you were somewhere else?'

Gretchen covered her face with her hands again and sobbed.

'And not,' continued Gently remorselessly, 'because you knew him to be the murderer?'

'No, no! It is not so! Oh why are you asking these things . . . why . . . why . . .?'

Gently sighed and reached for the penultimate peppermint cream. The saws in the yard screamed savagely, two, three, four of them. In his mind's eye Gently saw the blades tearing into the ponderous trunks, cruel and merciless, ripping them into the geometrical shapes of man.

'Do you intend to marry Fisher?' he asked.

Gretchen sobbed on.

'I understand that you have been refusing to see him.'

She looked at him for a moment, tear-wet. 'I shall not see him any more.'

Gently shrugged. 'I don't blame you,' he said, 'he's not the sort of man to make a good husband . . .'

Gretchen sobbed.

'Still, I'm surprised to find him thrown over so quickly.'

'It is to do with me!' she burst out. 'Why have I to tell you about this? Leave me alone!'

'I was wondering if it had to do with me.'

'I tell you nothing more . . . nothing more at all!'

Gently rose, went over to the small window and stood for a moment looking out at the neat little garden with its high walls and quaint summer-house. 'You haven't told me the truth, Miss Gretchen,' he said.

There was no answer but her sobbing.

'I'm going now, but I shall be coming back. In the meantime I would like you to think over your situation very, very seriously.' He moved back into the room. 'Your brother's life is in danger and it may be only by your telling us everything you know that his innocence can be established. I want you to think about that during the next few hours.'

She looked up suddenly. 'I'd like to . . .' she began, her hands gripping each other convulsively.

'Yes . . .?'

'Please, I'd like to . . .' She broke off as a brisk tap sounded at the door. Gently's lips compressed and he strode across and opened it. Leaming stood in the doorway.

'Hullo, Inspector!' he said, 'I didn't realize you were here . . . I've come to fetch a check-list.' He glanced at Gretchen in surprise. 'Why, Miss Huysmann . . . you've been crying!' he said.

160

CHAPTER ELEVEN

LEAMING'S VERMILION PASHLEY slid out of the yard with a surge of conscious power and rode superbly down Queen Street towards Railway Bridge. Gently adjusted himself in the well-padded seat and lit a hand-made cigarette. 'I hope your housekeeper isn't going to mind my coming to lunch . . .' he said. Leaming smiled handsomely. 'Don't worry about that. She always cooks for half a dozen.' 'If I took home someone on spec my housekeeper would go on strike . . .'

The Pashley swept over the bridge and into Railway Road. On the right reared the long, high, windowless back of the football-ground stands. Leaming indicated it with a movement of his head. 'That's it,' he said, 'one of the best grounds outside the First Division. They've got another home match on Saturday . . . the Cobblers . . . usually a hard game. Going to see them?'

'I might,' said Gently. 'Are you?'

Leaming made a face. 'This business is meaning a lot of extra work . . . we've got the accountants in next week. I shall have to spend the weekend preparing for them.'

'You'll have to make sure of your pink'un.'

Leaming dashed away some cigarette ash and was silent. The Pashley sped on through the narrow, smoke-visaged streets adjacent to the marshalling yards and out to the east-bound road. Here it went through Earton, a residential suburb built round a village, and the narrow, twisted road packed with traffic gave Leaming plenty of opportunity to display both his car and his skill. They passed Earton Green, a narrow, tree-shaded strip bounded by the Yar, where rivercraft, spick and span from their winter grooming, lay fresh-launched and naked at boat-yard quays. Past the Green the road widened, still going through suburbs, hesitating before it shook off the last straggling cottages and plunged into the country beyond.

Here Leaming gunned the Pashley till it was leaping eastwards in the eighties. He would probably have gone faster, but the road wasn't built for really high speeds and there was a good deal of outgoing traffic to be passed.

'Like it?' he jerked at Gently.

'Not really,' admitted Gently frankly.

'I can get a hundred and fifteen out of her on the Newmarket road – going down to London I reached Hatfield one hour dead out of Norchester.'

'You must miss an awful lot that way.'

'I've missed everything so far!'

Gently's ordeal did not last long. Three miles beyond Norchester they came to the side turning which led to Haswick. Monk's Thatch, Leaming's house, stood at the nearer end. It was a beautiful modern riverside dwelling standing amongst trees, hidden from the road by a shrubbery. The verandaed front looked over a terraced lawn to the river and a thatched boat-house, standing apart, suggested that Leaming had other interests as well as cars.

Gently said: 'All this must have cost you a penny.'

Leaming shrugged. 'My father left me a little money, you know . . .'

He led the way into the house and showed Gently where he could wash. The indoor appointments matched the outdoor ones in opulence. By the time he was sat down to lunch on a Chippendale dining-room chair, one of a suite, Gently had formed quite a respect for Leaming's father.

Leaming said: 'Of course, you must have guessed that I had a double motive in asking you to lunch. I very much want to hear what's happening with young Peter.'

'Ah . . .!' Gently said, and helped himself to new potatoes.

'I was flabbergasted when he wasn't charged. It seemed more than we could hope for . . . at the same time, it set me wondering what was at the back of it.'

Gently crunched a piece of pork crackling. 'Just means there's some doubt,' he said.

'You mean you're on to something else?'

'Could mean that.'

'And is it likely that young Peter will be cleared, without it ever going into court?'

'That depends on a lot of things.'

'But there's a good chance of that? I know I'm asking you rather a lot, Inspector, but you can't know how much this business means to me. Peter has been – well, almost a nephew to me, if you can understand that, and

I've committed myself to stand by him now, whatever the cost. So if you can give me a little information – strictly off the record – I shall be extremely grateful.' He glanced at Gently winningly.

Gently laid down his knife and took a thoughtful mouthful of beer. 'There's a lot of things to be cleared up,' he said. 'Until they are, I wouldn't be too hopeful.'

'Is Fisher one of those things?'

'I think Fisher could give us some interesting information, if he had a mind to.'

'You know, Inspector, if I had to put my finger on one particular person and say "that's him", I should put it on Fisher.'

'You would?' mused Gently.

'Yes, I would.'

'Have you any especial reason for saying that?'

'He just seems to me the one person who would do it. Isn't that your opinion?'

Gently drank some more beer. 'I suppose he's quite a likely customer,' he said.

'Ah! I thought you would agree.' Leaming returned to his plate for a moment, then said, through the tail-end of a mouthful: 'I believe there's something in that business about him and Gretchen, after all.'

Gently elevated an eyebrow.

'Yes, I know I pooh-poohed it when you suggested it the other day, but I've heard a bit of gossip about it since then.'

'Where?' said Gently, eating.

'I was in that snack-bar across the street from the yard – I heard it mentioned there. Quite confidently, you know, as though there was no doubt about it.'

'Could be just gossip,' said Gently.

'You think there's nothing in it? But there could be some connection there, when you think about it. Just suppose he'd got her into trouble . . . they'd be in a mess, wouldn't they? Both of them . . .'

'You've got a theory about that . . .?'

'Well . . . somebody did the old man in . . . and there must have been a reason for it.'

'Yes, there must have been a reason . . .'

'Of course, there's the money to think of. If Fisher did for the old man with the idea of clearing the way to marry Gretchen, there'd be no point in his pinching it.'

'There's a great temptation in ready money.'

'You're right, of course . . . do you think he did it?'

Gently smiled at the river-side willows. 'I may have an answer to that one shortly.'

Leaming ate and was silent for a short spell. Gently plied himself appreciatively with pork, and added a few more potatoes to his plate . . . after all, what does one's figure matter when one is the wrong side of fifty?

Leaming said: 'When I was talking to you about the money turning up, I didn't know that one note was going to turn up so quickly . . . and right in the wrong place, too.'

Gently said: 'Mmp.'

'But it's still a good angle, don't you think? That money's got to turn up some time.'

'It's not all that easy to trace when it does turn up . . . it may have gone through a lot of hands.'

'There's that, of course . . . but once it starts turning up you're pretty sure that Peter's in the clear.'

'Could be,' said Gently.

Leaming laughed. 'For all I know, of course, that's what's happened . . . maybe that's why Peter wasn't charged. Well, if that's the case, you may well say you'll have an answer shortly.' He glanced at Gently interrogatively.

'And if, in addition, someone cracked . . .'

'You mean Fisher?'

'Perhaps.'

Leaming went back to his eating.

Gently said: 'There's a time in every case that I've had anything to do with when you suddenly find yourself over the top of the hill . . . usually, there's no good reason for it. You just keep pushing and pushing, never seeming to get anywhere, and then some time you find you don't have to push any longer . . . the thing you've been pushing starts to carry you along with it. It's odd, isn't it?'

Leaming said: 'And you've reached that stage in this case?'

Gently shrugged. 'I've got that feeling . . .'

Leaming studied his plate without expression, making small, deliberate movements with his knife. Gently chewed a piece of roll and washed it down with beer. Across the lawn he could see a dinghy, a class-boat, tacking wistfully against the tide, long, painfully slow tacks amongst the trees, with scarcely enough breeze to give it headway. Back and forth it went, its helmsman, patient and determined, moving across with each new tack . . . it seemed like a machine which had lost its raison d'être, still obstinately performing its functions but going nowhere. Gently returned his eyes to the table and found that Leaming was staring at him.

'You do any sailing?' asked Gently.

'I've got a one-design in the boat-house.'

'What do they fetch these days?'

'You might pick one up for two-fifty.'

'That lets me out . . . I'm only a policeman.'

The housekeeper took their plates and served the sweet, which was rhubarb pie and cream. Gently went to work with unabated gusto. 'You've a good cook,' he said, between mouthfuls. Leaming smiled and picked up his fork and spoon. 'I have to do entertaining sometimes . . .'

The dinghy had made the next bend at last and Gently, outside the rhubarb and cream, was looking round for the coffee coming in. 'By the way,' he said, licking his lips, 'I knew there was something I meant to ask you about . . .' He got out his wallet and extracted the green card from it. 'Know anything about these people?' he asked.

Leaming took the card while Gently made room for his cup of coffee. 'That's Huysmann's writing . . .' said Leaming. Gently took three lumps of sugar and began stirring them. The housekeeper retired with her tray.

'I found it in Huysmann's desk this morning,' said Gently helpfully. 'I thought I'd heard the name before somewhere . . .'

Leaming looked from the card to Gently and back at the card again. Then he turned the card over and appeared to study the verso. Gently seemed not to watch him.

'It's one of his notes all right,' said Leaming at length, 'he was for ever scribbling things down . . .'

Gently took it back from him. 'Miss Gretchen

167

verified the handwriting . . . it is the firm I should like to know about.'

Leaming eyed him intently. 'It's a firm we do business with,' he said evenly.

'What sort of business?'

'We supply them with sawn-out timber.'

'And have you been connected with them very long?'

'Oh . . . quite a few years.'

'Ten years, say?'

'Not so long as that.'

Gently reinserted the card in his wallet and tucked it into his pocket. 'I wonder why Mr Huysmann made a note of the firm's name . . . as though it were unfamiliar?' he pondered.

Leaming shrugged slightly. 'It may have been to jog his memory about a contract.'

'But why write out the name in full? . . . Also, I don't remember coming across it when I went through the books.'

Leaming stared straight ahead of him. 'We keep separate books for that firm,' he said.

'Separate books? Why is that?'

'We supply them with sawn-out stuff that hasn't been through the mill . . . we simply act as middlemen. The stuff is processed at Starmouth and we bring it up for them. We take about fifteen per cent on it.'

'Isn't it unusual for a milling firm to supply timber which has been milled elsewhere? I should have thought it would have been more profitable to have supplied timber from one's own mill.'

'You have to do it sometimes, when the mill is working at capacity.'

'But this has been going on over a number of years.'

Leaming bit his lip. 'I imagine Huysmann is the only one who could give you an answer to that . . . and he won't answer any more questions.'

'I thought that perhaps his manager could have told me.' Gently drank his coffee, looking at Leaming across the cup. 'It's an interesting problem . . . I should like to know more about it. Have you got these people's address?'

'Actually, I don't think we have.'

Gently's eyebrows lifted. 'But surely you must have . . .?'

'No.' Leaming put down his cup and faced Gently. 'You see, Inspector, they pay cash on delivery. We simply bring the wood up and they collect it and pay. And that's all we know about them.'

Gently shook his head puzzledly. 'I never did know much about business . . .' he said. 'All the same, I'd like to look over the books. Was it a very large turn-over?'

'About twelve thousand a year . . . but we only took fifteen per cent on that.'

Leaming rose, producing his gold cigarette case as he did so. Gently accepted a cigarette. 'I shall have to be getting back,' Leaming said, 'sorry if I have to rush you.' Gently followed him out to the Pashley and settled his bulky figure in the seat. 'It was a very good lunch . . . you must ask me again some time.' Leaming smiled automatically and sent the Pashley bounding down the drive. 'I like having a chat over lunch,' he said, 'I think it helps to keep you in perspective . . . don't you?'

★　★　★

Queen Street was somnolent in a warm afternoon. The mild, sun-in-cloud sky produced no shadows, only a pervading brightness, and the few vehicles making their way to and from the city seemed to move drowsily, as though the machines themselves were infected by the atmosphere. Even the sawmill seemed subdued, and the bundling and clanking noises from the breweries sounded sleepy and far away. Gently stood on the pavement feeling stupid. He had overeaten rather at lunch.

He pulled himself together and went into Charlie's. Two of the inevitable transport drivers sat at a table eating rolls and drinking tea, one of them wearily turning the pages of a ragged *Picture Post*. The girl Elsie was at the counter. She sniffed as Gently entered and poked her head round the curtain, then disappeared through it. A moment later, Charlie himself came out.

'I was hoping you'd look in,' he said, a gleam of satisfaction in his eye.

'You've got something to tell me?'

'Something what happened about half an hour ago.' He darted a quick glance at the two transport drivers and another at Gently. Gently leaned across the zinc-topped counter. 'He was in here having his lunch,' proceeded Charlie in a lowered tone, 'and he'd got the girl Susan with him – right friendly they was together – having a long talk about something or other . . . they was over there in the corner.'

Gently leaned forward a little further.

'I brought their stuff out for them, and I got to hear a little bit of what they was saying. It was about you asking Miss Gretchen questions, Inspector, how you'd been there a long time this morning, and how she'd listened to it and how it was all about Mr Fisher. And they was that friendly together, you'd hardly believe it. He give her some sort of trinket – a bracelet, I think it was, anyway it was something what pleased her – and when I take their tea over, I heard him arranging to take her out.'

Gently's lips formed a soundless whistle. 'You're sure about that?'

'Heard it with my own ears!'

'And she agreed?'

'That she did, first time of asking.'

Gently slowly shook his head. 'Fisher seems to have got a very long way in a very short time . . . a very long way.'

'That's how it struck me, sir. And I couldn't help bringing to mind how he's been talking this last day or two about how things was going to change and all that. Well, they seem to have changed now all right, and that's a fact.'

Gently said: 'There's only one thing that has any weight with Susan . . .'

'But that isn't all, sir. Fisher, he come back here a few minutes later, seems like he was looking for somebody. "What've you lost?" I say, a bit sharp-like. "Never you mind," he say, "but if that b— Inspector Gently comes snooping around here, just you tell him I want to see him, see?" And out he stalks again. So what do you make of that?'

Gently shook his head again. 'He didn't say where I could find him, I suppose?'

'Well, no, he didn't . . .'

'Never mind, Charlie – you're doing well. Keep your eye on him.'

Gently went out of Charlie's with slightly more zest than when he had entered it. Things were undoubtedly whipping up a bit, he told himself. Something was beginning to move ... He glanced up and down Queen Street for a sight of the familiar figure in the American-style jacket, then ambled slowly away in the direction of the city. At Mariner's Lane he came to a standstill. Had Fisher gone back to his flat? But it was a long climb up there ... and Gently had overeaten at lunch. Moreover, he could still see the fragment of masonry lying at the side of the pavement where he had placed it ... and Fisher might be quieter when he dropped the next piece. So Gently continued to promenade along Queen Street.

He passed the Huysmann house, aloof and with-drawn, its great street-ward gables almost windowless, wended round thick-legged women pushing decrepit prams, stopped to light his pipe in a yard-way. He had just completed this operation when the American-style jacket loomed up beside him. He turned his head in mild surprise. 'You do it better than a policeman ...' he said.

Fisher's dark eyes glared at him. 'You been looking for me?' he asked smoulderingly.

'I thought you were looking for me,' said Gently.

'I got something to say to you.'

'So I gathered, one way or another.'

Fisher indicated the yard from which he had emerged. 'Come up here, Mr Inspector Gently ... I'm not telling it to half Norchester.'

Gently moved into the derelict yard, glancing round quickly at the disintegrating walls, at rotted flooring from which the nettles sprang, at falling plaster chalked on by children. Fisher sneered: 'You don't need to be afraid . . . nobody's going to jump on you.' Gently shrugged and puffed complacently at his pipe.

'You been trying to get Miss Gretchen to say I was up at the house on Saturday,' began Fisher challengingly.

Gently removed his pipe. 'Well – weren't you?' he asked.

'That's what you'd like to know, isn't it? That's what you've been getting at all the while?'

'It's one of the things,' admitted Gently.

'And now you're going to hear about it – straight – just like it happened!'

Gently blew an opulent smoke-ring. 'You wouldn't like to step into headquarters for this little scene, I suppose?' he enquired.

'What – and have it all taken down and twisted about by you blokes? What a hope!' Fisher laughed raucously. 'You just listen to it here, if you want to listen.'

Gently nodded gravely. 'There's just one thing I'd like to know first . . . why are you telling me this now, when you took such pains to hide it before?'

Fisher glowered at him. 'It's on account of you getting at Miss Gretchen.'

'I didn't think you worried a great deal about Miss Gretchen these days.'

'I aren't worried about her – but if she's going to tell her tale then I'm going to tell mine . . . see?'

'Sort of getting it in first . . .' murmured Gently.

'Never you mind.' Fisher came a little closer to Gently, but getting into the line of fire of the smoke-rings he moved back again. 'Listen,' he said, 'just suppose I was there that afternoon – suppose he was there – suppose we were in her room together all the time that was going on – that don't make us murderers, does it?'

'It makes you liars,' said Gently affably.

'But it don't make us murderers . . . that's the thing. Naturally, you weren't going to expect us to be mixed up in it if we could help it.'

'Not even with a man's life at stake?'

'Well, how could us being mixed up in it help him?'

'You're telling me,' said Gently. 'Just keep right on.'

'All right, then, so I was there. I got in through the kitchen while there wasn't no one there and went up into her room.'

'What time was that?'

'How the hell should I know what time it was? It was after lunch, that's all I know about it. She come up a little bit later on.'

'With a cup of coffee?'

'All right – she'd got a cup of coffee! And I suppose you'd like to know what we was doing up there, as well?'

'No,' said Gently, 'no, it might amuse the jury, but it isn't strictly relevant . . . pass on to the next bit.'

'Well, then, during the afternoon there was some-body come to the door, and I go out on the landing to see who it is . . . like you know, it was Mr Peter. Miss Gretchen, she come out too. We stood there listening to what was going on . . . you could hear some of it up on the landing. Then the old man shrieked, and Miss Gretchen she go rushing down to see what had happened.'

'Why didn't you go?' asked Gently.

'I wasn't bloody well supposed to be there, was I? We didn't know the old boy was done for . . . anyway, back she come and tell me what it is, so I say: "You and me is outside this – we'll go out and make it look like we haven't been here this afternoon," and that's what we did, Mr Inspector Gently, so now you know.'

Gently puffed three rings, one inside the other. 'You went out through the study,' he said, 'so you saw the body. Where was it lying?'

'It was by the safe. You don't think we moved it, do you?'

'How was it lying?'

'It was face down with the legs shoved up a bit.'

'Was the knife there?'

'. . . I can't remember every squitting little thing!'

'But this isn't a squitting little thing, and it's not one you're likely to have missed. Was it there?'

'I tell you I can't remember . . .!'

'Was it because you didn't look very closely . . . because it wasn't, in fact, the first time you had seen the body?'

Fisher's eyes blazed at him. 'All bloody right! It was there – stuck in up to the hilt. Now are you satisfied?'

Gently smiled up towards Burgh Street. 'I'm beginning to be . . .' he said.

'You're still trying to get me to say I see it done – that's what you're at!'

Gently shrugged and puffed smoke.

'You may try – but it isn't going to get you anywhere, see? I've told you what happened that afternoon, just like it was, and I'll swear to it in court if need be. But that's all you're getting out of me!'

'Even if Peter Huysmann hangs?'

'If he got into trouble that's his look-out – not mine.'

Gently sighed, and turned to regard a blue-chalk mannequin which leered surrealistically from an obstinate patch of plaster. He poked it tentatively. It came crashing down amongst the nettles. 'That girl Susan . . . she certainly gets around,' he said.

'What do you mean by that?' growled Fisher.

'Oh . . . it was just a passing thought. Aren't you taking her out tonight?'

'Suppose I am – what's it got to do with you?'

'It just set me wondering . . . that's all.'

Fisher towered above the Chief Inspector in stupid rage. 'And so you may bloody well wonder!' he burst out, 'you and all the other coppers with you . . . if I want to take her out, I take her out . . . and you can wonder till the bloody sky drops on you!'

Gently clicked his tongue disappointedly. 'I thought you were going to say till a bit of wall dropped on me,' he said.

CHAPTER TWELVE

MRS TURNER ANSWERED the door when Gently knocked at the Huysmann house. She eyed him inimically with her small mean eyes – she had had her knife into him since the questioning. 'So *you're* here again,' she said. Gently admitted it gracefully. 'A fine one you are, coming and upsetting people with your silly questions – don't even belong here, either. What do you want this time?'

'I want to see Miss Gretchen again.'

'Oh, you do? Well, I'm afraid you're going to be disappointed. Miss Gretchen's gone out.'

'Where's she gone?'

'How should I know where she's gone?'

'It's rather important that I should see her just now.'

Mrs Turner snorted and tilted her chin. 'Strikes me it's always important when *you* want to see somebody – leastways, that's your idea. And it's on account of you she's gone out . . . upsetting her like that!'

'Have you any idea where she might be?'

'I told you I hadn't . . . might be the Castle, or Earton Park . . . she used to go there sometimes.'

'Thank you,' said Gently, and the door was promptly slammed. Shaking his head, he plodded off towards the city. The Castle . . . or Earton Park. Or anywhere else in a city of rising a hundred and fifty thou. He took the Castle first because it lay in his way. Stretching halfway round the base of the Castle's prehistoric mound was the Garden, where once had been the ditch, a crescenting walk, deep-sunken, bisected by the slanting stone bridge which connected the Castle with the cattle market. Here were people enough, strolling amongst the long, sweet-scented beds of wallflowers and beneath the carnival blossom of the Japanese cherry-trees. But there was no Gretchen. Gently glanced up through the elms at the sleepy-faced Castle . . . but one didn't seek consolation amongst stuffed birds and man-traps. He went out to the Paddock and sought a bus for Earton Park.

It was a nice park, but a very large one. Its extent and complexity brought a pout to Gently's lips. But having come, he set about the matter methodically and plodded away across the rose parterre to the avenue of chestnuts, on either side of which old gentlemen were playing interminable games of bowls. Beyond these were the tennis-courts, on which Gently wasted no more than a passing glance. Coming to the Circus with its cupola'd bandstand he paused in indecision. North? South? Long, frequented vistas stretched to the four cardinal points. He took a chief inspectorial sniff and went south.

It was a good sniff. He found Gretchen huddled on a seat beside the great lily pond, staring large-eyed at the shallow water. Gently lifted his brown trilby politely and seated himself at a suitable distance.

Gretchen said: 'I did not know that you would find me here.'

'I didn't know myself until I found you,' Gently replied, feeling about for his pipe.

'Please do not think that I came here specially to avoid you . . . it was just that I had to get away . . . I could not think in the house.'

'I think you were wise . . . a change of venue is helpful.'

Gently went slowly and carefully through the business of filling and lighting his pipe, tamped it down with his thumb and took one or two inaugurating puffs. 'Have you come to any decision?' he asked.

Gretchen turned towards him pitifully. 'It is very difficult . . . I do not know.'

'Perhaps I can help you. I've just been having a very interesting chat with our friend Fisher.'

'. . . Fisher?'

'Yes.'

'And he has said something?'

Gently nodded.

She studied him for a moment in silence, Gently puffing away unconcernedly. 'I do not know . . .' she said.

'You'll have to take my word for it, of course. He admitted that he spent the afternoon with you, that he was there when you discovered the murder, and that it was at his suggestion that you went out and got yourself alibis. Is that correct?'

'He said all . . . that?' Gretchen stared at him incredulously.

'That was the gist of it, though I'm not quite satisfied.'

She looked away from him, her hands beginning to clutch together. 'I cannot understand . . . why should he tell you that?'

'Oh, there's no mystery about why he told me. He's rather thick with Susan these days and she told him how I'd been questioning you this morning . . . I gather she was listening at the door. This seems to have worried Mr Fisher and he hastened to put his story on record.'

'. . . Susan?'

'She seems to be Fisher's latest acquisition.'

'It is not true – you must not speak about him like that!'

Gently shrugged. 'I think you foster a somewhat idealistic opinion of Fisher, Miss Gretchen . . . however, that's why he told his story. Perhaps he will verify it if you ask him.'

'No!' She shook her head vigorously. 'I do not want to speak to him . . . not ever again. Later, I will get a new chauffeur.'

Gently regarded his pipe-smoke rising tenuously in the still, warm air. 'Were you ever really in love with him, Miss Gretchen?' he asked.

Gretchen turned her head away. 'I think that I was, once upon a time.'

'You knew what sort of character he had – I mean, with women?'

'Oh yes . . . I must have known that. It is as you say, I had an idealistic opinion. In my situation such things happen easily . . . we can believe when we want to.'

'And yet now, when the way is clear, you have turned completely against him.'

Gretchen hung her head and said nothing.

'Did you ever think of marrying him?' Gently asked.

'Oh yes, I used to think of that. I thought perhaps, when my father died . . . but that is a very terrible thing to say.'

'And did Fisher know that?'

'We used to talk about it.'

'He knew, then, that once your father was out of the way he could expect to be your husband?'

Gretchen wrenched her hands viciously, one from the other. 'But we did not think of this – we did not think of this!'

'Are you quite certain in your own mind that Fisher did not think of this?'

'No – no! he did not!' A shudder ran through her body, and she crouched away from Gently, over the arm of the seat.

'Miss Gretchen, I am asking you again: why is it that you have now turned against Fisher?'

'I don't know . . . I don't believe in him any longer.'

'Then what has shaken your faith in him so suddenly . . . precisely at this juncture?'

Gretchen moaned but made no answer.

'Let me ask you another question. Whose finger-prints did you suppose you wiped from the handle of the knife – your brother's, or Fisher's?'

'I have told you . . . my brother's!'

Gently leaned away, shaking his head. 'Miss Gretchen, I have still to learn the truth of your and Fisher's actions on Saturday afternoon.'

There was a long pause, broken by nothing but the distant calls from the tennis-courts and the dull murmur of traffic from behind trees. Above the low hedge at the bottom moved a white triangle. It was the sail of a model yacht on the second pond, further down. The triangle shuddered, stopped, wagged a moment, then slowly sank from sight as the model slid away on its new course. Gently watched the little performance impassively. 'They've opened the refreshment bar . . .' he said. 'Let's go and have a cup of tea.'

He sat Gretchen down at one of the little tile-topped tables by a french window and fetched tea from the counter in large, thick cups. Gretchen stirred her tea at some length. Just outside a foursome was being played, a young and a middle-aged couple: other tennis-players sat in groups round the larger tables, chattering and drinking soft drinks from bottles.

Gently sipped his tea and then leaned forward, chin in hand. Gretchen gave him a frightened glance. He said: 'It will have to be told some time . . . why not tell me now?'

'But . . . how can I?'

'Is it so damning, what you know?'

'To you it may seem so . . .'

Gently felt down for his tea-cup. 'At least, you ought to warn Susan what sort of person she's taking on.'

'Susan!' The waxen cheeks flushed.

'She's going out with him tonight.'

'What do I care about that?'

'Well, having done it once and got away with it . . .'

He took another sip of tea and appeared to be watching the foursome through the french window. Gretchen laid a trembling teaspoon in her saucer.

'He told you so much . . . of his own accord?'

Gently shrugged imperceptibly. 'Nobody forced him . . . he buttonholed me in the street.'

'It was because he thinks I have spoken . . .?'

Gently said nothing, continued to watch the four-some fumble its way through another service. There was a burst of laughter from the party at the higher table: 'Harry wouldn't do a thing like that . . . no, no, we can't believe it!' 'But he did, I tell you!' 'Johnny, you're only saying that because Vera's here . . .' They clattered their bottles together and trooped out.

'How about it?' mused Gently.

'Must it be . . . now?'

'It will help me, and you'll feel better to have done with it.'

'Yes . . . I shall feel better.' She gave a deep sigh and faced him. 'Very well . . . it is as you say. I wiped the prints off the knife because I think he did it.'

'And why did you think that?'

'He was not with me then . . . at the time my father was killed.'

'Where was he?'

She shook her head. 'He went down as soon as my brother had gone to the study.'

'Where – into the passage?'

'That is so, but I remained on the landing. I heard the quarrel. After it is over, I expect him to come back up, but he did not come . . . and then there is the scream.'

'About how long would it be between the time the quarrel ended and the time you heard the scream?'

'Two, three minutes.'

'And you went down immediately on hearing the scream?'

'Oh no! It was frightening to hear that . . . I did not dare to go down then. It was another minute or two

183

before I had courage to go. Then it was as I told you . . . I found him near the safe.'

'And you saw nobody?'

'Nobody . . . except my father.'

'About how long were you in the room?'

'It seemed a long time, but it was just a little while.'

'And during that time you heard nothing?'

'I should not have heard . . . once, everything went black and I thought I would fall. Then I came to myself again, and I knew I must do something . . . something to stop people thinking that it was him.'

'You had no doubt in your mind then that Fisher was the murderer?'

'. . . no, I had no doubt.'

'Have you had any doubt since that time?'

'. . . no.'

'Where did you next see him?'

'He was waiting in the bedroom when I got back. He asked me where I had been . . . when I told him that my father was killed he pretended to be surprised.'

'And it was he who suggested establishing alibis?'

'Oh yes . . . he said that I might have gone out through the kitchen, just as he had come in . . . there was nothing to prove that we had ever been there. He told me to find out about the programme at a cinema and it would be all right.'

'And you left by the study and the timber-yard?'

'That is so.'

'As you were passing through the study, did Fisher stop to examine the body?'

'No . . . he went straight through . . . I do not think he looked at it.'

184

Gently brooded over his cooling tea. 'All this . . .' he said, 'you know, it's your word against Fisher's.'

'But it is the truth!'

Gently smiled at a part-submerged tea-leaf. 'I believe you . . . what you tell me fits every fact it touches. But I wish there was some proof, just a little bit. Because without it, one could even make a case against you, Miss Gretchen . . . and it wouldn't be a bad one at that.'

There was a tea-time air about headquarters – against the run of the play, because nothing at headquarters was ever quite normal; but the human touch had its occasional triumphs, and this was one. Gently sniffed as he passed the canteen. They were serving toast and its cosy, inviting smell warned him that even the best of lunches wears off by five o'clock. The toast smell carried over to the superintendent's office, where the great man was sitting ingesting a plateful, a far-away look in his eyes. The look became present and immediate when Gently entered.

'I was just thinking about you,' he said.

Gently acknowledged the thought with the ghost of a bow, moved over and abstracted half a round of toast from the super's plate. 'Of course, if you're hungry . . .' observed the super bitterly. Gently disclaimed the imputation through his first mouthful.

The super said: 'Well?'

'I'm almost home,' returned Gently, butteredly.

'You've got a case made out?'

'It's made out, but it won't stand up yet. All the same, I think I've got enough to let young Peter out . . . so it's a good thing you held back on him.'

The super ate some toast nastily. 'Give,' he said.

Gently crunched a moment. 'First, I've had a statement from Fisher to the effect that he was in the house that afternoon.'

The super's eyes opened wide. 'You mean he's talked?' he fired.

'He's talked, but he hasn't talked enough – not yet. That's the main problem ahead, and I think it's going to be solved without a great deal of difficulty.'

'What do you mean by that?'

'I mean I've persuaded Miss Gretchen to fill in some of the gaps. According to her testimony, Fisher must either have seen it done or done it himself, one or the other. Of course, it's her word against Fisher's, but Fisher is getting to be rather worried, and if you make a pass at him with a murder charge I fancy he'll talk both loud and clear.'

The super brandished a piece of toast. 'Wait a minute!' he exclaimed. 'Do I understand that both of them were in the house at the time of the murder? They've both admitted that?'

Gently nodded pontifically. 'Fisher made a voluntary statement. I had to spend some time on Miss Gretchen. At first she insisted that she was there alone, but after I got Fisher's statement she came across with it. She has been positive that Fisher did it from the first – it was she who wiped the knife and hid it. She's in trouble, by the way. Fisher became her lover a month or two ago and Saturday afternoon was his regular visiting time.'

'Give me time!' pleaded the super. 'I'm still holding Peter Huysmann – doesn't he fit into this thing anywhere?'

'Well, he was there, and his quarrel with his father may have suggested to the murderer that the time was ripe. Otherwise, I don't think he has much to do with the business.'

'You're saying that Fisher got the girl into trouble and then bumped off the old man so that he could marry her . . . is that it?'

'Could be,' admitted Gently cautiously, 'but there's another angle to it . . .'

'Never mind the other angle! Let's get this one straightened out first. You say the girl was sure that Fisher did it?'

Gently finished his piece of toast and licked his fingers. 'Fisher came in through the kitchen just after lunch and went upstairs to Gretchen's room. There was nobody in the kitchen and nobody saw him enter. Gretchen went up with her coffee and stayed there with him. When Peter arrived they went out on the landing to see who it was – Fisher was the person Peter caught sight of – and directly he had gone to the study Fisher left Gretchen on the landing and went into the passage. Gretchen heard the quarrel from the landing. It ended, and she waited two or three minutes for Fisher to come back, but he didn't come back, and at the end of that two or three minutes she heard the old man's death scream.

'By the time she pulled herself together and went down the murderer had gone. She met nobody in the passage and saw nobody in the study, and feeling certain that Fisher was the man, she took away the knife and wiped the prints off the handle. When she got back to the bedroom Fisher was already there. He expressed surprise when she told him what she had found, and suggested going out and establishing the alibis. They went out by the study and the timber-yard. Fisher exhibited no interest in the body when he passed it. I discovered by questioning that he was not even aware that the knife had been removed. Fisher's version differs inasmuch as he claims that he never left the landing, otherwise they pretty well agree.'

'Then he *was* the person in the drawing-room?' interrupted the super, biting mechanically at a fresh piece of toast.

'Unquestionably. Otherwise, he could not have got back to the bedroom without being seen by Gretchen. Of course, we don't know at what point he entered. He may have gone in straight away, watched the quarrel, seen the murder, seen Gretchen go in and then slipped back to the bedroom . . . or he may not.'

'You're telling me he may not! But what about the money?'

'I'm not sure about that. If Fisher was the murderer I think he must have come back for it, after he'd got rid of Gretchen. He might have come back for it anyway, though I don't think it's likely. At all events there was too much of it to carry about his person. There is, incidentally, some indication that Fisher has come into money just recently.'

'And that's one of the seven deadly sins in criminal investigation.' The super's eyes glistened. 'By God, Gently, you certainly get results. I'll let this be a lesson to me.'

Gently shook his head. 'It's mostly one witness against another at the moment. We've got to have proof.'

'We'll get proof. I'll get a warrant and take his flat apart, brick by brick, and if the money's there we'll find it. And I'll make him talk, if I have to question him from now to Christmas.'

'He won't talk if he's the murderer.'

'Then if he doesn't talk I'll charge him with it.'

'I shouldn't be too hasty about that . . .' began Gently, and broke off. Hansom came striding into the room, followed by Police Constable Letts. 'Look at this!' boomed Hansom, 'look at this!' And he waved a limp piece of paper under the super's nose. The super stared at it. 'What is it?' he asked. 'What is it!' 'It's another of the Huysmann notes – it's just been turned in by the bank!'

The super grabbed it as though it were a rare visitant from another world. 'Where did they get it?' he exclaimed.

'It was paid in this afternoon by "The Doll's Hospital".'

'By the *what*?'

' "The Doll's Hospital".'

The super goggled at Hansom. 'And what the blazing blue hell is "The Doll's Hospital" . . .?'

'Excuse me, sir . . .' Constable Letts slid round the mass that was Hansom. ' "The Doll's Hospital" is a toy-shop in St Benedict's, sir.'

'And what the devil has that got to do with the Huysmann case?'

Gently said: 'What sort of toy-shop is it?'

'It's one of those that goes in for Meccano sets and that sort of thing, sir.'

'Does it sell scale model aeroplanes?'

189

'Yes, sir. It's got a window full of them.'

'Fisher!' yipped Hansom, catching on with commendable suddenness. 'He told us he built scale models in his spare time.'

The super shot a meaningful glance at Gently. 'You wanted proof, by golly . . .!' He turned to Hansom. 'We're pulling in Fisher right away. Wait here till I get warrants – I'm in on this party – and send a patrol car round to his flat.'

Ten minutes later the super's Humber bumbled over the ruts of Paradise Alley and pulled up beside the patrol car. A police sergeant ran round and saluted. 'There doesn't seem to be anybody at home, sir,' he said.

'Is the door locked?' snapped the super.

'Yes, sir.'

'Smash it in, then.'

'Very good, sir.'

The super, Gently and Hansom climbed out and watched the sergeant direct smashing operations. It was not the best of doors. It yielded easily to one constable-power. The super, eager to draw blood, went bounding up the narrow stairs, Hansom in close pursuit. Gently followed at a more sedate pace. 'He's not here!' bawled Hansom, emerging from the bedroom. 'Try the lounge,' suggested Gently, 'it's a bit before his bedtime . . .' He wandered into the kitchen after the super, who was making great play with a wall-cupboard full of junk. 'Hell's . . . *bells*!' came from Hansom. 'Chiefy – for God's sake come and look at this lot!' 'What have you found, Hansom?' barked the super. 'Just come and look at it!' The super bounced across the dingy landing, Gently following. Hansom stood back, tallow-faced.

Sprawled on the floor of the sitting-room, mouth open, eyes staring, was Fisher. His throat was cut down from the ear on the right side. A blood-stained razor, which Gently recognized, lay near his right hand and on the couch near him, neatly stacked, stood a fabulous pile of treasury notes.

CHAPTER THIRTEEN

G ENTLY, HAVING SEEN enough, went out and sat in the Humber while the police medico made his examination. After him came the photographer, whose flash-bulbs could be seen popping through the unmasked window. Hansom and the super came out in conference with the medico. '. . . Naturally, it's always possible,' said the medico, 'any self-inflicted wound *may* have been the result of an attack . . . we can only offer proof the other way round, viz., that a certain wound could *not* have been self-inflicted. But there is no suggestion of that here. I am perfectly satisfied that this is a bona fide case of suicide.'

'I wasn't querying the present case,' grunted the super. 'I could see that for myself with half an eye.'

Hansom said: 'And Gently recognizes the razor . . . it's the one he cut out the models with.'

They came up to the car and Gently got out. 'You might well say that Fisher was getting worried,' said the super to him, a trifle grimly.

'He didn't seem so terribly worried when I last saw him . . . just a bit on edge.'

The super shook his head. 'You must put the fear of the Lord into people without realizing it. Well . . . I suppose it's saved a deal of trouble and expense, though personally I should have got a lot of satisfaction out of putting him in dock. We can let young Huysmann go now.'

Hansom said: 'I still can't quite get this straight . . . I feel like a kid who's got his sums wrong. But I hand it to you, Gently. You were right and I was wrong . . . I reckon they don't put you in the Central Office at the Yard for nothing.'

'You weren't the only one who was wrong,' growled the super. 'It just goes to show . . . you need specialists when it comes to homicide.' He glanced at Gently, half-admiring, half-jealous. 'I suppose it gets to be an instinct when someone's been on the job as long as you have.'

Gently shrugged. 'I started with an advantage . . . I saw young Huysmann riding on the Wall. One doesn't do that sort of thing straight after murdering one's father.'

'All the same . . . it was a top-grade job.'

Gently smiled wanly at them. 'I'm glad you're pleased with me, just this once,' he said, 'because you're not going to be pleased with me for very long.'

'What? How do you mean, Gently?' The super glanced at him quickly.

'I mean that unlike yourselves, I do *not* regard the death of Fisher as being suicide.'

'*What!*'

'On the contrary, I am as positive as my specialization and acquired instinct can make me that it's murder.'

193

There was a pause, fraught and ominous. Three pairs of eyes stared at Gently as though he had suddenly touched their owners with three red-hot pokers.

'You're off your chump!' bawled Hansom, finding his voice. 'You – you've got murder on the brain!'

'It's utterly preposterous!' snapped the police doctor. 'Really, Gently, I completely fail to understand—!'

Gently bowed and let the storm pass over his head. 'I don't expect you to agree with me until you've heard my reasons . . . but that is my conviction.'

'But there is nothing – nothing whatever to suggest an attack!'

'It's the stupidest thing I ever heard!'

Gently turned to the furious little police doctor. 'Were you able to form an opinion as to the direction in which the cut was made?' he enquired mildly.

'Direction? What in the world has that got to do with it?'

'I'd like to have your opinion.'

'As far as I can say it was made upwards, from the base of the throat to the ear. But—!'

'If the cut were self-inflicted, isn't it more likely to have been made in the other direction . . . from the ear downwards?'

The little man fumed at him. 'It could be made in either direction – it is only slightly more likely to have been made downwards.'

'And wouldn't you say it was still more likely to have been made on the left side of the throat . . . bearing in mind that the razor was ostensibly held in his right hand?'

'I think this is all highly irrelevant, Gently!' broke in

the super. 'It's ridiculous to suppose that you can deduce murder from such trivial considerations.'

'I'm not deducing murder from them . . . I'm simply demonstrating that the cut was made in the least likely of three ways.'

'But there is no guarantee that a suicide will choose the likeliest way! If you had seen as many suicides as I have . . .!' The medico, his professional skill called to question, fairly chattered with rage. 'And how likely would it be for an attacker to make the cut upwards? You tell me that! How do you attack a man and cut his throat in that direction?'

Gently extended a disclaiming palm. 'Suppose you had to cut Fisher's throat . . . how would you do it?'

'It is not a question of how I would do it!'

'But suppose you did?'

The little man glared at him. 'I should do it – like this!' And he made a downward slash that whistled past Gently's neck.

Gently shook his head gravely. 'You'd be a very brave man to do that,' he said, 'much braver than I should be . . . also, you'd have to be lucky. Now if I wanted to cut Fisher's throat . . . neatly, and without noise and personal danger . . . I should wait till he was bending over something . . . something like a bag containing forty thousand pounds, and then I'd do it – like this!' And he spun the little doctor round, pushed him into a bending position, and drew his right hand smartly across his struggling victim's throat.

'I should also be in a good position to avoid the subsequent rush of blood,' he added, thoughtfully.

'All right, Gently, you've shown us that it could be

done!' snapped the super, 'and where precisely do we go from there?'

'That's right,' echoed Hansom, 'who's it going to be this time – the housekeeper?'

Gently said: 'The person who killed Fisher was the same person whom Fisher saw killing Huysmann. He killed Fisher for three reasons. First, Fisher was blackmailing him. Second, there was a risk that the money he paid Fisher would be traced back to Fisher, and thus to himself. Third, he knew that I had discovered his motive for killing Huysmann, and that he would have to make some sort of move to draw the police off. Unfortunately, I didn't realize he would make it quite so soon.'

'And who is this mythical person, Gently?'

'He is Leaming, Huysmann's manager.'

Hansom set up a howl. 'What – Leaming kill the old man? You're bats – completely bats! Why, Leaming had the one alibi that stood the steam-test – he's fire-proof!'

'It was a good alibi,' Gently admitted reluctantly, 'but that's all it was – an alibi. He probably parked his car at the ground, where no doubt it was known to the attendants. There was then nothing to prevent him from making his way through the crowd back to the yard. I am not certain of his exact movements, but I imagine that he watched the quarrel from the summer-house and emerged from it soon after Peter Huysmann left. With regard to the alibi, I questioned him about the football match on the Saturday evening before he had time to gen up on it. He had three things to tell me about it and they formed the three headlines in the pink'un, in exactly the same sequence. On the follow-

196

ing day he had the match at his fingertips – he even knew the precise minutes when the scores were made, a detail which a man on the terrace is never aware of.

'Also on Saturday evening – and later during the questioning – he introduced obliquely every point which would tell against Peter. Under cover of a pretended solicitude he suggested things which were absolutely damning – such things as Huysmann's resolution to cut Peter out of his will, which he represented as being of recent origin. In addition to this . . .'

'Hold hard!' broke in the super, 'you're making my head spin, Gently. There doesn't seem to be any end to you. When you made your report in the office an hour ago it was Fisher, Fisher, Fisher. So we go out, and find it was Fisher. And immediately you turn the record over and begin on Leaming. If this isn't a sudden spasm of madness, would you mind telling me why you didn't mention Leaming in the office, but only now when the case has cancelled itself out?'

Gently sighed deeply, and felt around for the support of a peppermint cream. 'I was going to tell you about Leaming,' he said, 'but I didn't get a chance. You're all so impulsive round here. I'd just got through telling you what I knew about Fisher when Hansom came in with the note and you straightway jumped to the conclusion that Fisher was the man. *I* didn't say he was . . . in fact, I was pretty certain that he wasn't, and what we've found up there convinces me to the hilt. Fisher was an extrovert if ever there was one – he would no more have cut his throat than spoken English. But you got so sold on the idea, and I wanted Fisher picked up for

197

questioning . . . so I let the rest of it ride till we'd laid hands on him.'

'Then you're not just hanging out this case for the fun of it?'

Gently looked shocked. 'Really, superintendent!'

'All right, all right! Now – you say Leaming killed Huysmann. Why?'

'Because Huysmann had discovered how Leaming bought his cars and his houses and his hand-made cigarettes.'

'And how did he do that?'

'He was flogging timber on the side, about one-fifth of the entire intake . . . twelve thousand pounds' worth a year. That was the leak which Peter said his father suspected, and it had been going on quite a few years. Mind you, Leaming didn't scoop the entire twelve thousand. The tug-skipper and his mate were in it, though I don't think they knew much, and there was a mysterious firm called "The Straight Grain Timber Merchants" who took the stuff away. I imagine they're dissolved as from today, but we might get a line on them . . . the tug-men may talk, with a little persuasion. There's another angle in the books. I went through the Huysmann books on Sunday, so I knew the "Straight Grain" outfit was not in the regular line of business with them. Leaming has got a very thin excuse that they kept separate books for the "Straight Grain" transactions and he's prepared to produce them: I think an expert comparison between the two sets of books will give us an opening.'

The super said: 'Granted that you're right about Leaming's fiddling, how do you know that Huysmann had found out about it?'

Gently drew out his wallet and produced the green postcard. 'I found this in Huysmann's desk. According to Miss Gretchen it is the most recently received card – it is postmarked on the twentieth – and Huysmann took it with the rest of his mail on his last trip to London. Ostensibly it was during this trip that he got scent of the "Straight Grain" set-up, and though he may not have tumbled to the significance of it straight away, his suspicions were aroused and he made this note of the name. That gives us a further angle. If we trace Huysmann's movements on that trip we may find the source of his information . . . though the trail has got a little sketchy now Fisher's dead.

'When he got back off his trip I imagine Huysmann began to make some guarded enquiries about "Straight Grain". He apparently found out enough, and it's my conjecture that his visit to Leaming's office last thing on Saturday morning was to summon Leaming to produce an immediate explanation. It isn't difficult to imagine Leaming's reaction to that. He might be able to satisfy other people with his twin set of books, but there was no prospect of satisfying Huysmann. He faced a long term of imprisonment, plus utter ruination – you will remember in conjunction with this that the last firm he managed went bankrupt, though he got clear from that one – and Leaming was not the sort of man to let that happen if there was a loop-hole. And there was a loop-hole. He could silence Huysmann.

'Consider for a moment how favourable the circumstances were for such a step. First, it was well known that Leaming spent his Saturday afternoons at the football. Second, it was known that he proposed to spend that Saturday afternoon at the football – he would have warned his housekeeper that he wanted lunch promptly, and his gardener was expecting to get a lift down with him. Third, nobody knew that Huysmann had summoned him to his study. Fourth, the study was isolated from the rest of the house, and fifth, it could be entered quite secretly by way of the yard.

'Everything, then, favoured the attempt. I don't know whether the theft of the money was premeditated, because he didn't know that the safe was going to be open. It may have been an afterthought when he saw Peter given one of the notes, or to suggest an outside job if Peter got off, or simply from greed. With regard to weapons, you will notice that in both murders he used the weapon on the spot, that they were the same class of weapon, and that they were used from the same position – behind. The knives in the study he had always known about. You will remember how well they were placed for an attacker entering from the garden – especially a tall attacker. The razor he had undoubtedly seen on his previous visit to the flat . . . I am conjecturing that he went to the flat previously for his first deal with Fisher.

'Huysmann, then, was disposed of, with the un-looked-for piece of luck of Peter being on the spot to collect the blame. Leaming's alibi was fire-proof, he made a good impression on the police, and a little annoyance of myself asking to see the books could be attributed to a policeman's officiousness. Everything was going swimmingly . . . until Monday morning. On Monday morning Fisher visited Leaming's office – I saw him – and Leaming made the spine-chilling discovery that the murder had been witnessed. And it had not been witnessed by his best friend.

'The bone of contention between Leaming and Fisher was the maid, Susan. Fisher had always had a fancy for her, but he was never in the running – it took money to get Susan – and he bore Leaming a deep grudge about her. Naturally, with Leaming completely in his power, his first demand was for Susan . . . with a small cut in the forty thou, to be going on with. And he got her. That same evening Leaming picked her up and brought her into town, told her abruptly that everything was over and left her flat. The deal then was for Fisher to take up the running, but he was a little late on cue. Susan, reacting to a crisis like most women, went in search of a cup of tea, and while she was getting it she bumped into me. She told me the story without much prompting – also, she told me about Fisher's affair with Gretchen and about Gretchen's pregnancy. I kept her by me the rest of the evening . . . when we left the café Fisher was there, watching. Later in the evening I met him at Charlie's, in Queen Street, and he tried to find out what Susan had told me.

'Fisher was beginning to get worried by then. I had been up to his flat in the morning and he had seen me interrogating a little boy who makes a playground of the ruins up there, and probably guessed – which was a fact – that I had obtained an account of his movements on Saturday afternoon which did not tally with the one he'd put on record. Also, I hinted to him that I knew of his affair with Gretchen. This upset him so much that he made his clumsy attempt at inspectorcide . . . I was beginning to know far too much.'

'Then it was Fisher who tried to drop the masonry on you?' broke in the super. 'Why didn't you tell me that yesterday?'

Gently's shoulders rose a fraction. 'There wasn't any proof . . . it just happened that the masonry was dropped on me immediately after I had interviewed him, from a vantage point familiar to him and which he could have attained in the interval.

'With Fisher worried but nowhere near cracking, I decided that Gretchen was my best move, so this morning I interviewed her and got part of her story. I might have got the rest of it then and there, but oddly enough, just as she was working up to it, we were interrupted by Leaming, who hung around with a blanket of small talk until Gretchen cooled off and wouldn't come across. You can imagine that if Fisher was worried, Leaming had got the feeling that he was living on the edge of a volcano, and one that was beginning to rumble ominously. Quite apart from the notes turning up, Fisher was behaving in a way that drew attention to himself – boasting of the changes that were going to take place, and the things he could tell the police if he wanted to – and there was no telling when he would start throwing the money about, thus raising immediate suspicion. In addition to this something had gone wrong about Peter – he hadn't been charged. And there was myself, working on Gretchen, and Gretchen just about to spill the beans.

'All in all, things seemed to be going to pieces in an alarming manner and he invited me to lunch to get from me, if he could, the precise state of affairs. He certainly got value for money. I showed him the card, which I had just found, and showed a good deal of scepticism for his explanation of the "Straight Grain" business . . . especially when he admitted himself unable to produce their address. He knew then that I'd seen past Fisher, that I understood his motive. It only remained for me to crack Fisher – and I could do that fairly easily by getting Gretchen to talk – actually, it became easier still, because Fisher made a partial statement which was instrumental in making Gretchen talk.

'Thus it was merely a question of time and routine before Leaming stood revealed . . . and not very much of either. Somehow he had to break the chain that was forging round him and break it in such a way that it would never come together again. And there was only one way to do that – to get rid of Fisher. With Fisher gone, all direct evidence was swept away . . . and if it could be made to look like suicide, with the money carefully planted, then the trail would come to a dead end. Suspicion of embezzlement might remain, but that would be all.

'I don't know whether he had an arrangement to deliver the rest of the money to Fisher this afternoon, but that is what happened, and the murder took place as I described it . . . I am certain of that because there is some blood on the notes, which there would not have been unless they were closer to Fisher when his throat was cut than when we found them. The evidence to look for in that connection will be the bag in which the notes were brought, which is bound to have extensive blood-stains. We can print the notes, of course, but my feeling is that Leaming is too careful a man not to have used gloves.'

Gently broke off, glancing at the three silent men in the lengthening twilight. 'Well . . . that's my case,' he said, 'it hasn't become any easier with the loss of Fisher, but as far as I'm concerned, it's become absolutely positive.'

The super took a long breath and bored into Gently with his sharp, authoritative eyes. 'So that's your case, is it?' he enquired icily.

Gently nodded without expression. There was a moment or two's silence, emphasized by the distant rumble of traffic, below them in Queen Street and above them in Burgh Street.

Hansom said: 'It stinks, if you ask me.'

'It's childish!' snapped the little doctor. 'I stake my reputation on suicide.'

'You could put that alibi through a rolling mill.'

The super frowned, still boring at Gently. 'You realize that I have a very high opinion of you . . . especially after what you've achieved so far,' he said, 'and I admit that I am to a certain extent impressed with what you have been telling us. I believe that you believe it, and I believe that you've got something about Leaming and the "Straight Grain" business. But really, Gently, have you got anything else? I mean, look at it from my point of view. Three parts of this case of yours is conjecture and for the rest you offer no vital proof. It's ingenious and not improbable, but what else can you say for it?'

Gently said, woodenly: 'We can get the proofs . . . if we work at it.'

'But proofs of what? If we follow up the lines you indicate we may be able to show that Leaming was a large-scale embezzler and we may be able to show that Huysmann found out about it, but how does that make Leaming the murderer? You say yourself that with Fisher gone, the trail has come to a dead end. If there is anything in what you suspect, Fisher's evidence was the lynch-pin, and we've lost it. What else is there that a counsel wouldn't shoot to fragments? You say that Fisher was blackmailing Leaming. Where's the proof? You say that Fisher got the maid off him – but isn't it just as likely that Leaming broke with her because he had ideas about Gretchen? You say that Leaming's information about the football match was derived from the pink'un . . . well, how are you going to make that stand up?'

'I haven't done with that one yet . . .'

'You've got thirty thousand interrogations ahead of you!' jeered Hansom.

The super cocked his head on one side. 'It's no good, Gently, you haven't got a case, not even the makings of one. If it's as you say, it can never be proved. And in the meanwhile, there's nothing in Fisher's behaviour in conflict with the view that he was the murderer and the thief.'

'Except that he wasn't the suicide type.'

'There isn't any suicide type!' broke in the little doctor. 'Anybody will commit suicide under certain conditions.'

'Fisher would have stood trial . . . he was too stupid to want to have avoided it.'

'That's quite ridiculous!'

The super said: 'Even there you've only shown that murder was possible, and it's possible in the majority of suicide cases. You cannot show that murder was likely.'

Gently brooded, felt for another peppermint cream. 'You've searched the flat?' he asked absently.

'Of course we've searched the flat.'

'You've been through his pockets?'

'Naturally.'

'And you found the key?'

The super stared at Gently uncomprehendingly. 'What key?'

'The door-key of the flat . . . it wasn't in the door.'

'What are you getting at, Gently?'

Gently ate the peppermint cream slowly and irritatingly. 'The door was locked,' he mumbled, 'if Fisher locked it, you should be able to find the key.'

Hansom said: 'He'd got a key-ring in his pocket.'

'One doesn't keep door-keys on key-rings.'

'Blast you, Gently!' exploded the super. He turned on Hansom viciously. 'What sort of a bloody policeman are you? Go in there and find that key – and don't come out till you've got it!' He turned back to Gently. 'All right – so if it isn't there you've made a point – but you haven't proved your case or anything like it. Meantime I'm giving the Coroner's Court the OK and this case is going in on its merits. I'm satisfied with what I've got. If you want more, you'd better go after it – only you won't be getting any help from me. Is that clear?'

Gently felt sadly in his pocket and brought out an empty bag. 'Quite clear,' he said, screwing it into a ball, 'quite clear.'

CHAPTER FOURTEEN

THE CORONER'S COURT sat on the day following and returned on Nicholas Huysmann a verdict of death resulting from a stab wound inflicted by his chauffeur, James Fisher, and on his chauffeur a verdict of *felo de se*. Chief Inspector Gently, Central Office, CID, gave immaculate evidence and was publicly congratulated by the Coroner both for this and for his ready assistance, although on holiday. Superintendent Walker and the Norchester Police, CID, also came in for congratulations.

The super muttered grimly as they left the court: 'You given up this Leaming business then?'

Gently smiled and shook his head.

'Thanks for letting it ride, anyway.'

Gently shrugged, but as he turned away the super caught his arm. 'I didn't mean quite all I said last night . . . I'd like you to keep me posted. And if you need any help – within reason, of course.'

Peter Huysmann had been released the evening before, the charge against him dropped out of hand. He had been at court, slightly dazed by his sudden return to the world, but had only been required to testify to the accuracy of his statement, which was then read for him. For the time being he was continuing to live at the caravan, where he had been received with much rejoicing and congratulation by his late boss and by the fair community in general. It was considered a signal victory over the auld enemy . . .

Rejoicing there was also at Charlie's, for Charlie had come to look on the 'getting' of Fisher as almost a personal issue. 'I knew it was him from the start,' he told a group of lorry-drivers, 'right from the time Chief Inspector Gently first come in here, I could smell what was in the wind. Ah, he's a foxy one, he is! He just let the City Police go on thinking it was young Huysmann and then when they got their hands on him, "No," he says, "you let young Huysmann be. Just give me twenty-four hours," he says, "and I'll have the one you want!" Ah, he played with Fisher like a cat with a mouse. Fisher, he thinks he's this and he thinks he's that . . . but all the time the Chief Inspector was getting nearer and nearer to him, taking his time, never in a hurry, till last of all even Fisher can see that the game is up . . . well, there you are. There was only two ways out, and he took the handiest . . .'

Gretchen, subdued, bowed, dressed entirely in black, with a veil which hid any expression in her waxen face, had also made a statement which was read for her in court. It had been drafted by Gently and was exquisite in its restraint. At the point where the hiding of the knife was described the Coroner was moved to raise his glasses and deliver a look of reproof, but a closer view of the dark-clad figure decided him to let the matter rest. With Susan, on the other hand, he was positively genial.

Late final editions carried a full report of the inquest, were scanned perfunctorily in cafés and snack-bars and on the crowded buses carrying city workers back to the suburbs. It was a satisfactory but tame dénouement. The affair had raised expectations of a hard-fought trial with all the exciting trappings of judicial slaying . . . quite a fair stretch of innocent entertainment. As the clerk at Simmonds said to Miss Jones (blouses), 'You can't get really worked up over a thing like that. But if it had been the son, now . . .' 'Bloody flash in the pan *that* was,' said a news-vendor, 'thank God for the football, that's what I say.'

Inspector Hansom went about his duties, a wounded soul. He hadn't had much sleep. Into the small hours of the morning he had been at Fisher's flat and, at the super's suggestion, all the area within a key's throw of the flat, searching for the blasted key that had to be there and wasn't . . . as dawn had begun to show far off down the Yar valley he had been assailed by un-policemanlike thoughts. There was a firm in the city who would turn out an identical key for a couple of bob . . . and wasn't it worth a couple of bob to get one's head down? At the same time, if that key really was missing . . . and you had to admit that Gently was a clever bastard . . . Hansom lit a bad-tasting cigar and breathed expensively towards the dawn.

Leaming, well-dressed and impressive, had given his brief evidence to the court with precision and convic-tion. One felt that here was a man of ability, a man who could handle affairs of moment: a man to be trusted implicitly. The Coroner treated him with deference. As he concluded his short statement he glanced round the court and catching Gently's eye, smiled to him winningly. Gently smiled also, but it would have been more difficult to categorize Gently's smile.

A police car still stood in Paradise Alley, lone and smart amongst the derelict houses and blank, shabby walls. Gently nodded to the constable who stood by it.

'Have they had any luck?'

'Not so far, sir, but they're just taking the floor up.'

Gently clicked his tongue. 'They won't find it there.'

'There's a crack where it might have slipped through, sir . . . they've found the head off an old hammer and a threepenny bit.'

'Well . . . tell them not to spend it all at once.'

'Ha, ha! Yes, sir.'

Gently turned away to the row of empty windows opposite. No fierce little head bobbed up to greet him, but then, it was probably Superman's bedtime. He shoved open a yawing door and went through. The floor above had caved in long since, leaving a rusty fireplace hanging on the wall in heartless nakedness. The back of the house was a collapsed pile of rubble. Gently climbed over it and looked down at the desolation below. Walls disintegrating, sagging roofs, piles of rubble surmounted by nettles and ragwort . . . right down to Queen Street, where the shabby thoroughfare arrested the ruins with a narrow bulwark of vitality. He shook his head and picked his way cautiously through a fragment-strewn yard.

'Gotcher!' rang out a triumphant shout behind him.

Gently put up his hands and came to a standstill. 'Turn around!' commanded the voice, 'and don't try any funny stuff on the Cactus Kid!' Gently turned around. 'Oh . . . it's you, mister . . .'

Gently nodded. 'Yes, it's me . . . can I put my hands down?'

Superman, alias the Cactus Kid, wrinkled his nose in a frown. 'Guess you can, mister . . . though you look mighty like Bad Dan from behind. He's the worsest rustler that ever hit these parts, and I'm sure going to get him one of these days!'

'It's time you hit the hay,' said Gently, lowering his hands, 'there's a sheriff's posse up the alley. They'll keep watch out for Bad Dan till you get on the trail again. You come along back to the ranch with me.' He took the Cactus Kid's grimy paw and led the way round a lurching segment of wall towards Mariner's Lane. 'This is heap bad country, pardner,' he added, 'you should find up a better range somewhere . . .'

The Cactus Kid trotted along beside him happily. 'Mister, they got on to Red Hawk at last . . . I knew about him a long time ago. Did they find all the gold he'd got hidden away?'

'Guess they did, kid.'

'Gee, mister, that must've been exciting!'

'Waal . . . it had its moments.'

'I sure do wish I'd been around about then.'

Gently looked down at his small companion. 'Weren't you up here yesterday?' he asked.

'No, mister, not me.'

'How come, pardner?'

'Someone gave me two bob to spend on the fair . . .

but it wasn't going in the afternoon. So I went round Woolies instead. That's where I bought my six-shooter, mister – see here!' He withdrew his hand from Gently's and held up a new toy gun. Gently examined it gravely, spinning the magazine with a stubby finger. 'Clean, bright and lightly oiled,' he murmured, 'that's a pretty little shooting-iron, pardner . . . here's half a buck to buy it some ammo.'

'Gee . . . mister!' The Cactus Kid's eyes gleamed as he felt the heavy coin with its rough milled edge. Then he tugged back on Gently's hand. 'Mister . . . would you mind if I spent some of it on a special belt with a holster?'

They came down Mariner's Lane, Gently instinctively steering outwards at the spot where the masonry had been aimed at him. Queen Street was lit dully in the twilight. Across the way the Huysmann house reared more blankly and detachedly than ever, white and looming in the blueness of a mercury lamp. 'Whereabouts is your bunk-house, pardner?' enquired Gently.

'Just here, mister – one of those in the row.'

Gently paused in the act of dismissing him. 'Who gave you the two bob yesterday?' he queried.

'Oh, it was a man.'

'Somebody you know?'

'No . . . he wasn't anybody. He came down the Lane when I was keeping watch on Red Hawk.'

'When was that?'

'I don't know . . . it wasn't tea-time.'

'Coming *down* the lane, was he?'

'That's right, mister. I was just on the corner there,

212

keeping watch down the alley. He give me the two bob to go on the fair . . . only it wasn't going in the afternoon.'

Gently bent closer to the little freckled face. 'This man, what was he like?'

'He was just a man . . .'

'Did you notice if he was carrying a bag?'

'That's right, mister – he'd got a bag, one of those bulgy ones.'

'And did he go up the alley?'

'I don't know . . . he might have done.'

Gently stood back again, brooding, gazing into the far distance towards Railway Bridge. The Cactus Kid fidgeted from one foot to the other. 'It wasn't anyone, mister . . . it was just a man.'

'Which way did you go to the fairground?' asked Gently abruptly.

'I went up the lane and along the top . . . but it wasn't going.'

'Did you see a racing car standing at the top – a real fast one, painted red?'

'One that could go a hundred miles an hour?'

'About that . . . maybe faster.'

'Oh yes, I saw that one, mister – it had got an aeroplane on the front – I blew the propeller round!'

A slow smile spread over Gently's face and he felt in his pocket for his bag of peppermint creams. 'Here,' he said, 'take the lot . . . but don't eat them all tonight or you'll have nightmares. There's just one other thing before you go . . . I suppose you haven't found a key up there round the alley?'

The Cactus Kid shook his head vigorously.

'Ah!' sighed Gently, 'we mustn't strain providence too far, must we, pardner?'

The front doorbell of the Huysmann house was engulfed afar off, giving back to the ringer not the faintest vibration to encourage him in his practices: one rang, and waited unhopefully. Eventually Gently heard the soft pad of feet down the hall and the shooting of the bolt. It was Susan who melted in the doorway.

'Oh, Inspector . . .!'

Gently remained on the step. 'I just want some information,' he said.

Susan's blue eyes chided him softly. 'Won't you come in, Inspector? Miss Gretchen has gone to bed, and Mrs Turner has gone to tell her sister about everything . . . it's lonely in here, on your own.'

'I don't think I'll come in at the moment . . .'

'Inspector, I thought you were *wonderful* in court . . . absolutely *wonderful*.'

'Thank you, my dear . . . I've had considerable experience.'

'The way you stood up there in front of them all – so cool and strong – ohh! It just *did* something to me!'

'I hope it was nothing irremediable. Now, my dear—'

'You're sure you won't come in . . . just for a little while?'

Gently sighed. 'I'm *busy*,' he said.

'Oh . . . I see.' Susan's face fell. 'We-ell . . . what did you want to know?'

'I want to know where I'm likely to find Mr Leaming.'

'Him! I s'pose he's gone home.'

'He didn't strike me as the home-loving kind . . . I thought he might be around in the city.'

'Well, he might have gone to a show . . . or he might be at the Venetian. He used to go there a lot.'

'Is that the place near the Castle?'

'That's right. It's a classy sort of place with an orchestra. He was always one to flash his money about.'

'Thank you, my dear . . . you've always been a great help.'

Susan's eyes swam up to him. 'It'd be so nice to have someone to talk to for a bit.'

But Gently had gone.

The Venetian Club was underground, beneath one of the larger and more expensive hotels. One reached it by a long, wide, sweeping stairway with a rail supported on criss-cross steel rods, painted maroon and ivory. Below was a large floor, open in the centre for dancing, carpeted at the sides with deep-pile carpet, also maroon. At the far end was the orchestra rostrum, and on the right the bar. Down each side and along the top ran the tables, glass tops on criss-cross ivory legs, spaced out with tubs of ferns and an occasional settee upholstered in ivory leather. The lighting was soft and diffused. There was an atmosphere of leisured peace and timelessness.

Gently left his coat and trilby upstairs, went jerkily down the stairway, aware of the out-of-placeness of his rather shabbily dressed, heavy figure. He knew Leaming was there. He had seen the vermilion Pashley parked just over the way. Near the foot of the stairs he

215

paused to run his eye over the floor, table by table. Leaming was seated by himself not far from the bar, eating, a bottle of champagne in ice beside him, his back half-turned to the stairs. Gently continued down the stairs.

'A single table, sir?' The head waiter looked down his nose at the incongruous arrival.

'I'll take that one over there,' said Gently, pointing to a table near the wall at the side opposite to where Leaming sat. The head waiter ushered him across and he seated himself heavily in a padded, criss-cross chair. Another waiter slid into position at his elbow. Gently grabbed the menu and examined it, frowning. 'Bring me a coffee,' he said.

There was a pregnant interval. '. . . *only* a coffee, sir?' queried the waiter.

Gently turned slowly about and faced him. '*Only* a coffee,' he said.

The waiter wilted. 'Very good, sir . . . a coffee.'

Gently lapsed back into his chair and tossed the menu aside. The orchestra was playing its pale, emasculated semblance of music, obviously not to be listened to, and two or three couples on the floor were obviously not listening to it: the rhythm alone guiding their sauntered steps. On Gently's right an elderly man in evening dress sat with his wife. They were silently eating asparagus and drinking white wine. On his left, partly obscured by a tub of ferns, sat a party of four, rather noisy, busily attended by two waiters.

'My dear, I thought it was because Gerald wasn't coming . . .'

'Did you really think he wouldn't come . . . I mean, did you?'

'Well, I mean, under the circs . . .'

'Tony sounds as though he knows more about it than we do . . . my dear, it's just possible that he *does*!'

Followed by laughter.

Gently received his coffee in a small, exquisite cup. Across the way a waiter was pouring out Leaming's champagne. Leaming seemed to be cracking a joke with him about something, and they both laughed as Leaming took the filled glass and the waiter returned the bottle to its ice. Leaming was having a little celebration, no doubt. As he lifted the glass, Gently caught his eye. Leaming hesitated a brief second, the glass poised and winking: then he drank it off, turning again to the waiter and laughing.

Gently stirred several lumps of sugar into his inadequate cup. Leaming didn't look his way again. Handsome, smiling, polished, well-dressed, the manager of Huysmann's fitted the picture as though he were made to measure. The waiters admired him, the management rejoiced in his patronage . . . and 'He was always one to flash his money about.' Yes, there was no doubt that Leaming fitted the picture.

He had got to his cigar now. As the waiter lit it for him, Leaming took the waiter's pad and scribbled something on it and sent him off with a motion of his head. Gently watched the waiter threading his way through the tables with bland indifference.

'Well?' he demanded.

The waiter made a slight bow. 'The gentleman at table seven sends you this note, sir.'

Gently took it. It read: 'Join me in celebrating your success.' He took out his wallet and ostentatiously folded the note into it. 'Give my regrets to the gentleman at table seven and tell him I'm here on business,' he said.

The waiter bowed again and departed. Out of the corner of his eye Gently watched him gliding back between the tables. Leaming received his message with a shrug of his elegant shoulders, laughed, and pushed forward his glass for more champagne. But the sparkle had gone out of him now. The laughs were a little forced and came between intervals of brooding over his cigar, over his glass. Once or twice he tried to catch Gently's eye, but each time Gently was resolutely looking in some other direction, or drinking his coffee. He never seemed to be looking at Leaming. He was just there, a dark, remorseless presence.

Leaming called for the evening paper and read it, frowning. It contained a full account of the inquest. There, with complete finality, the Huysmann case was dissected, analysed, judged and put away . . . solved and dismissed. Everyone had been satisfied. Yet there sat Gently like the Old Man of the Sea, clinging, watching, unshakable in his obstinacy, a ratiocinating limpet who refused to be given the slip. What did the stupid little man think he could do now?

The band was playing a popular hit tune of the moment. Several couples got up to dance. A woman Leaming knew came over to his table, gushing, looking for a partner.

'Darling! I didn't know you were here all alone . . .'

'I just looked in for a bite to eat . . .'

'Oh, but you simply must dance this one with me!'

'I couldn't, Laura . . . too soon after dinner.'

'Just the teeniest weeniest hop, darling?'

'Look – there's Geoffrey Davis over there . . . rouse him out for a dance.'

He was staring at Gently more directly now, trying to catch him out. But Gently was not to be caught. The only indication he gave that he was interested in Leaming was that he never looked at him. Now, he was ordering another cup of coffee. With the waiter standing before him, his eyes had only to slip a fraction to one side for a glance at Leaming, yet they firmly refused to make that slip. It was silly, childish . . . like a schoolboy game. He became suddenly furious with Gently. If the man was there to watch him, why didn't he watch him, instead of playing the fool like this? How much longer would he sit there, drinking coffee at one-and-six a cup?

Gently was beginning to wonder about that himself, though with such small cups it represented no hardship, and the coffee was quite good. He was getting hungry, of course . . . but the Venetian's menu had been drawn up for Chief Constables rather than Chief Inspectors. So he toyed with an empty pipe instead. Dancing had become more general now and there was a steady trickle of new arrivals. Supper was being served to the tables all round him. A younger and more romantic couple had taken the table previously occupied by the asparagus-eaters, a callow young man cutting loose with his boss's secretary, perhaps.

At eleven fifteen Leaming paid his bill with two five-pound notes, waiving the change. Gently made no move as he left his table and sauntered casually towards the foot of the stairs. There he paused to light a cigarette. The gold cigarette case opened and closed with a distant snap, and a waiter appeared from nowhere with a lighter. Leaming stood with his head bowed, apparently in thought. Then, as though remembering something, he raised his head with a smile and slipped across to the table where Gently was sitting.

'You run to late hours in your business?' he said brightly.

Gently eyed him without expression. 'It depends on our clients . . . some of them never go to bed.'

Leaming took the seat opposite. 'I thought you were down here on holiday . . . naturally, since our business was cleared up, I didn't expect to find you engaged in something fresh.'

'I'm not.'

'Not on something fresh?'

'No.'

Leaming looked at him uncomprehendingly. 'But I thought this thing came to an end at the inquest . . . there doesn't seem much left to explain.'

'Some things come to an end at inquests, but this isn't one of them.'

'Well . . . if I can assist you in any way, don't be afraid to ask. If it's some silly little complication to do with the firm I dare say I can put you straight.'

Gently rocked a little in his chair. 'It concerns the main issue,' he said, 'the person Fisher saw stabbing Huysmann . . . and the person who cut Fisher's throat subsequently.' His green eyes fixed on Leaming, still completely without expression.

Leaming remained silent, taut, cigarette angled from the corner of his mouth.

'That doesn't surprise you?' enquired Gently, with a trace of sarcasm.

'Yes . . . it does.'

'You'd like to make a statement about it?'

Leaming's eyes met his, brown and powerful, cautious as a wild animal's: they broke into a smile. 'Why should I make a statement about it?'

Gently shook his head, as though acknowledging the point. 'Would you like to tell me how you spent yesterday afternoon?'

'I'd love to . . . where do you want me to start?'

'Start where you dropped me after lunch.'

'Very well. I went to the office and looked through the afternoon mail . . . then I dictated some letters . . . then I took some specifications over to Sainty's the contractors.' Leaming paused, mockingly. 'I was gone about an hour,' he added.

'And the time?'

'Ah . . . the time. I felt that would be important. Well, I left the office at half-past three and re-entered it at twenty-six and a half minutes to five.'

'And you were at Sainty's during all that time?'

'Dear me, no – only for about twenty minutes.'

'Where were you during the remainder of that time?'

Leaming's smile came back, strong, confident, almost reproving. 'Oh, just driving around, you know. I've got a nice car. I get a kick out of negotiating the traffic with it.'

'And that's your official story?'

'Yes, I think so . . . unless somebody can give me a reason for putting out a better one.'

Gently nodded, keeping his eyes fixed on Leaming's.

'Suppose I say that the little boy to whom you gave two shillings saw your car parked in Burgh Street . . . would that be reason enough?'

'There's a lot of cars get parked in Burgh Street.'

'But this one was a red sports car . . . it had an aeroplane mascot. The little boy blew the propeller round. Also, it was parked near Mariner's Lane.'

There was a pause, charged and vibrant. The smile still flickered in Leaming's eyes. 'No,' he said at last, 'I don't think it is. Somehow, I've never relied very much on little boys as witnesses . . . have you? They forget things so easily . . . they rarely make a convincing impression. No, I'll stick to my story.'

Gently said: 'Then there's the bag . . .'

Leaming made no response.

'The gladstone bag that had the money in it, the bag that Fisher was bending over when his throat was cut.' He leaned forward, his eyes boring at Leaming's compellingly. But Leaming met them, hard and impenetrable. There was no give in him at all.

'So it was a gladstone bag?'

'Yes, a gladstone bag. And during the murder it got bloodied . . . so did some of the notes which were lying on top. The blood was wiped off the bag temporarily, but one can't get rid of blood as easily as that – not so that it becomes undetectable in laboratory tests – so the bag had to be destroyed.'

'Go on,' said Leaming, 'you're interesting me.'

'This evening, just before I came up here, I stepped into the timber-yard for a moment.'

'Well . . . I hope everything was in order . . .'

'I noticed a fire smouldering in a corner near the

222

quays, so I went over and had a look at it. It was the remains of a large, sawdust-rubbish fire, apparently one that is kept burning there almost continuously . . .'

'You make a good detective.'

'. . . and after stirring it about a little I came across two interesting items. One of them was the handle-frame of a gladstone bag . . . and the other was the key to Fisher's flat. They were both together in one part of the fire, which suggested to me that the key had been in the bag at the time it was introduced into the fire. The murderer, it seems, had forgotten to take it out . . . which was certainly a mistake, don't you think?'

The stare of Leaming's eyes never wavered. 'It could have been chucked in the river, I suppose.'

'I think that would have been safer.'

'At the same time, there's nothing to connect it with any one person.'

'Oh yes . . . there's the maker's name on the handle-frame, and what may be a serial number on the lock. A little routine work should indicate the owner to us.'

Leaming shook his head slowly. 'It won't do, you know, it isn't a clincher. There've been dozens of those bags sold, and the number on the lock is merely a convenience, in case you lose the key. Nobody keeps a record correlating it with the purchaser.'

'Nevertheless, it will be useful to show that a certain person was the owner of such a bag. It's surprising how points like that increase in significance when taken with other points.'

The smile glided back into Leaming's eyes. 'They might, if you could arrange them convincingly . . . but you've first to convince the authorities that Fisher was murdered at all. At the moment their considered opinion is that he wasn't . . . we mustn't forget that, must we? If you go to them saying, "There's a case against A for murdering Fisher," they will simply look blank and say, "But Fisher wasn't murdered." And what have you got to say to that?'

Leaming leaned back in his chair, his eyes lit and triumphant. Gently sat still and unmoved, one stubby hand clasped in the other.

'Of course, you could talk about finding the handle-frame and the key,' continued Leaming, 'you could tell them all about your imaginative idea of somebody taking Fisher the money in that bag, of how Fisher was murdered over it and how the bag would then have to be destroyed. But how would you set about proving it? And as for the key, they might want to know if there couldn't have been two of them – there usually is, isn't there? – and how can you be sure that the one you found was the one that a murderer locked the flat with? Well, I don't know what you could say to that, but if they asked me . . .'

'Yes,' breathed Gently, 'and if they asked you?'

'. . . I should say that the key was most probably Fisher's spare, and that the bag was an old one that I had given him at some time.'

Leaming broke off, pleasantly, as though intrigued by an interesting speculation.

'And how about the key which wasn't Fisher's spare?'

Leaming shrugged his shoulders gracefully. 'It's a little puzzling, of course. But the fact that it was missing didn't seem to affect things much at the inquest . . . it was such a small point, after all, when the rest of the evidence was so irresistible.' He leaned right back, tilting the chair, quizzing Gently.

Gently twisted his one hand in the other. 'You seem to have given this matter a lot of thought . . .' he said.

'I try to help the police to the best of my ability.'

'There's just one thing, though.'

Leaming's eyebrows lifted, almost negligently. 'Something I've overlooked?'

'You may not have overlooked it, but at the same time you may not have realized its full significance.'

'Go on,' said Leaming.

Gently spread his clumsy hands wide open on the top of the table. 'The case that's building up against Fisher's murderer may be good, may be bad . . . that's something we shall both find out. But if anything should turn up to suggest that Fisher may not have been the one to kill Huysmann, then that case is going to spring to life overnight.'

Leaming leaned forward off his chair. 'Such as?' he demanded.

'Such as somebody's alibi springing a leak.'

Leaming went back again, slowly, thoughtfully, the smile grown thin on his face. 'There's that, of course . . .' he admitted softly, 'there's always a possibility of an alibi being cracked.'

Gently rose to his feet and beckoned to a waiter. 'It's getting late . . . I suppose you're just going?'

Leaming looked up at him lazily. 'I may go – I may stay on.'

'I'll pay my bill at all events . . . then I'll be ready, whichever you decide to do.'

CHAPTER FIFTEEN

GENTLY HAD RARELY felt so checkmated as he did during the next two days. It was true that the super's interest had been well and truly roused by the discovery of the key and the handle-frame, but cautious as ever, he had scented all the difficulties that still remained before a credible case could be made out. The main weakness, he pointed out, was Gently's inability to prove a motive. He could produce no evidence to show that Fisher had been blackmailing Leaming. Without such evidence, there was no logical connection between the handle-frame and Fisher's death, and hence with Leaming. He agreed that Gently was being very convincing and that he appeared to be on a trail. But Gently had to remember that their own medico ruled out the possibility of murder and he, the super, still felt most inclined to support that viewpoint.

In other words, he thought that Gently had a bee in his bonnet.

Glumly Gently went back over the trail, checking and re-checking, asking the same questions again and getting substantially the same answers. He cornered the tug-skipper in Charlie's and gave him a grilling, but he would scarcely open his mouth. The 'Straight Grain' people had packed up, he said, they weren't taking any more deliveries. No, he didn't know where their place had been. No, they didn't own the quay . . . it was derelict. Anybody could use it.

Pursuing this line, Gently went down to the quay itself. There was no doubt about its dereliction. Sited between tumble-down warehouses, its rotting piles formed just enough staithe to moor a single barge. Once there had been a shallow pent roof over it, but of this there remained only a couple of beams, dangerous, decorated with willow-herb, and on each side of the run-in to the quay nettles and ragwort cropped hectically. The place was deserted. Gently hailed an old fellow who was tinkering with a hauled-out rowing boat further down the bank. 'Hi! . . . do you know who owns this place?'

The old man put down a can of varnish and came limping along to the dividing fence. He looked Gently over without interest. 'There int nobody what own it,' he said.

Gently pointed to the piling. 'Somebody must have owned it at some time.'

'Well, there was old Thrower had it . . . thirty odd year ago. But he never owned it neither. He just come and built that there staithe, and nobody said nothin' to him, but he never rightly owned it.'

'And where is Thrower now?'

'Dead . . . thirty odd year ago.'

Gently sighed. 'I suppose you don't know anything about the people who've been using it lately?'

'No, I don't know nothin' about them.'

Of course, if the super would put a fraud man on the books and use his resources for a general check-up, thought Gently bitterly . . . but then again, suppose they *could* bring it home to Leaming – there was still nothing to tie Leaming to the main issue. Works managers have feathered their nests before today without necessarily bumping off the proprietor. No: it was no use chasing side-issues. Once a charge was laid, the details would be ferreted out by routine work. And if the charge wasn't laid, then the details might just as well be forgotten.

Leaving nothing to chance, he plodded across to the Railway Road Football Ground. The car park was as Leaming had described it, between the south end of the ground and the river. There was no direct entry from the park to the ground. One had to return to the road and enter by the turnstiles or by the stand. The surface of the park was cinder-dirt, worn rather thin – dry now, but with plenty of clayey depressions where puddles had been not so long since. Gently came out and went into the ground through the main stand entrance. Nobody enquired his business. Two groundsmen were working in one of the goal-mouths, a third was driving a motor-roller, while three or four City players in tracksuits jog-trotted round the running track. Gently strolled out on to the pitch to where the groundsmen were working. 'Do you know where I can find the car park attendants?' he asked.

One of the groundsmen straightened up and surveyed him coolly. 'Who wants to know?' he countered.

'Police.'

'Why – what's wrong now?'

Gently shook his head sadly. 'I just want some information . . . that's all.'

'What do you want to know?'

'Are you one of the attendants?'

The groundsman twisted his mouth and spat. 'I could be,' he said.

'Were you on the park last Saturday?'

'Suppose I was?'

Gently held out his hand in a gesture of non-aggression. 'I'm not trying to pinch anyone . . . I just want to know something. Do you remember a red Pashley sports with an aeroplane mascot being parked there?'

'You mean Mr Leaming's car?'

'That's right – do you know him?'

'I should do. He's there often enough.'

'And his car was there?'

'Yep.'

Gently paused, comfortably. 'Whenabouts did it check in?' he proceeded.

'I dunno . . . just before the match.'

'Did Mr Leaming say or do anything that he didn't usually say or do?'

'Well . . .' The groundsman looked puzzledly at Gently, trying to decide what was behind it all. 'He talked to me about the team changes and such-like. He don't do that as a rule, I suppose, and then again, it was just on kick-off.'

'Did you see him enter the ground?'

'I'd got other things to do besides watch him.'

'Were you there when he collected his car?'

'Yep.'

'About when was that?'

'Same time as all the others.'

'He wasn't there a little early, by any chance?'

'Not so's you'd notice it . . . he may've been ahead of the rush.'

'Thank you,' said Gently, 'that seems to be everything.'

Outside in Railway Road he stood looking back at the ground. There lay the secret, the missing link . . . if only he could get his hands on it. Someone in there, or someone who had been in there on Saturday, could supply it. Someone who knew Leaming. Someone who could testify that he hadn't been at the match . . . even someone who had seen him double back over Railway Bridge. But how did one separate that someone from the other twenty-nine thousand, nine hundred and ninety-nine?

His eye fell on the little glass box perched on the side of Railway Bridge. The bridge-keeper! A gleam came into Gently's eye. Was it his lucky day . . . was his detective's guardian angel keeping this one up his sleeve for him?

'Police,' he said simply. 'Were you on duty here last Saturday afternoon?'

The bridge-keeper stared at him. 'W'yes . . .' he said.

'Do you know Huysmann's manager, Leaming, by sight?'

'Mr Leaming? Yes, I know him.'

'Did you see him crossing the bridge in this direction just about the time the match started on Saturday?'

The bridge-keeper frowned and rubbed the side of

his chin. 'There was a powerful crowd of people going over the bridge about then . . . I don't suppose I'd have seen him anyway.'

'Later on . . . between four and five . . . did you see him come back again?'

The bridge-keeper brightened up. 'Oh no, sir – I couldn't have done. We close down here at half-past three on a Saturday . . . the bridge don't open again till Monday morning.'

It was the same wherever he went. There was plenty of fuel for his moral certainty, but the cold, hard proof eluded every enquiry. Grudgingly, he had to admire the manager of Huysmann's for his crisp, sure performance. It had needed luck, and Leaming had had luck . . . but, with Sempronius, he had deserved it.

Dispirited, Gently made his way down Queen Street to Charlie's. He had no real purpose in going there. It was rather a piece of conditioned behaviour – Charlie's had been useful before, so he turned to it now when he was at a loose end. Outside stood the usual trucks and vans, and from the yard across the way came the familiar accompaniment of screaming and whining. Leaming's world, going full tilt.

But Leaming himself was in Charlie's. He was standing at the bar eating a sandwich, nonchalant, aware of himself as being of a different creation from his surroundings. He smiled brightly as Gently entered.

'Still busy?' he remarked, tentatively.

Gently glanced at him and grunted. Then he pushed to the bar, ignoring him, and called for a cup of tea. The ghost of a frown appeared on Leaming's brow. He turned towards Gently confidentially, as though expecting a conversation to start. But Gently, having received his tea, went away to a table and began sipping it as though Leaming didn't exist. Charlie watched this little by-play with interest; leant across, and whispered: 'He's on to something – you mark my words!'

Leaming lifted a patronizing eyebrow. 'How do you know?'

'I seen him like that before . . . and you know what happened that time.'

Leaming shrugged contemptuously. 'Don't judge strangers so hastily . . . the Inspector is merely feeling tired.' He went over to where Gently sat. 'You look fed up,' he said, 'haven't things turned out as well as you hoped for?'

Still Gently refused to look at him. The slight, lacing edge of anxiety in Leaming's tone was like music. It reassured Gently. It told him that Leaming was getting worried, that the strain was beginning to tell on him. The heat should have been off by now . . . and it wasn't. Gently was still after him. And though he could tell himself that he held the trump cards, yet always there must be that little element of doubt, that tiny risk of something turning up . . . Even the fed-up look of Gently's was suspect. It might be assumed to lull Leaming into a deceptive sense of security.

Gently sensed this, and smiled inwardly. His labours had not been completely in vain. Leaming was tough and cool and clever, but there was a limit to him: Gently could feel the initiative beginning to pass into his hands.

'I've just come from the football ground,' he said to his tea-cup.

Leaming laughed, but his laugh betrayed no nervousness. 'I hope they're getting into good trim for the match tomorrow.'

'I was talking to the car park attendant.'

'Which one – the red-haired fellow?'

'This one had brown hair and grey eyes and small ears that stuck out.'

'Oh, you mean Dusty.' Leaming grinned, as though to excuse his familiarity. 'He's quite knowledgeable on football matters – I had a chat with him myself the other day.'

'So he was telling me.'

'Indeed?'

'Just as the match was starting, too. I think it surprised him that you should stop to talk football, when you were already late.' Gently turned slowly and fixed his green eyes on Leaming's.

'Oh, he's probably exaggerating. On Saturday, I only had a couple of words with him.'

'It sounded like more than that, the way he told it.'

'Well . . . with a policeman chivvying him and putting ideas into his head . . . but it's quite true that I chatted to him as he was sticking a chit under my windscreen-wiper.'

Gently nodded with a sort of vague satisfaction, as though the answer was just what he wished. 'And as I was coming over the bridge I spoke to the bridge-keeper.'

'You mean . . . Railway Bridge?'

'That's right. I don't know which one, but he knows you . . . by sight.'

The tenseness now was visible in Leaming's face. He

233

stared into Gently's eyes as though he would reach down and pluck out the knowledge that might be lurking there. 'You mean the one with glasses,' he said quickly, 'he's so short-sighted that he can scarcely read his time-sheets . . . he ought not to be on that job at all.'

'He didn't complain of short-sightedness to me.'

'Naturally – he doesn't want to lose his post.'

'I don't even remember the glasses.'

'He tries not to wear them when there's anybody about.'

Gently picked up his cup and took a long, reflective sip. 'What makes you think it was the short-sighted one I was talking to?' he enquired affably.

Leaming hesitated. 'I noticed he was on as I came by after lunch . . . in any case, he's the only one who knows me.'

'Would you say he was the one who was on duty last Saturday?'

'God knows – didn't you ask him?'

Gently shrugged and said nothing.

'Did he tell you that they packed up at half-past three on Saturdays?'

'He might have done.'

Leaming leaned back, away from the table. Gently could see one brown hand tighten till there was whiteness about the knuckles. Then slowly it relaxed, the long, sensitive fingers uncurling, the thumb pointing outwards as Leaming forced calmness on himself. 'You should be on that bridge when a match is on . . . there can be several hundred people a minute going over it.'

'That's a lot of people . . . all going one way.'

'And the boys selling programmes and football

publications, all crowded round with their customers
. . . just in front of the bridge-keeper's box.'

'You're making it sound quite busy.'

'If you don't believe me – tomorrow's Saturday – go
and look for yourself.'

Gently puckered his mouth ruminatively. 'I may do
that,' he said, 'yes . . . I may do that. I hear it's going to
be a good match, against the Cobblers.'

Norchester on a football Saturday woke up from the
even tenor of its week-days. Soon after eleven o'clock
the coaches began to stream into the city, coaches from
the distantmost parts of Northshire – for the City had a
big county following – and even from further afield.
Out of the brooding depths of Thorne Station poured
crowds of supporters with their rattles and gay favours
of yellow and green, and the streets were thronged at
lunch-time with factory-workers. The little cheap cafés
and snack-bars did a roaring trade. Charlie's, for
instance, took on two extra hands for football Saturdays.

Riverside and Queen Street were the two main
arteries from the city. Riverside, wide, tree-lined, with
a long, broad flank between itself and the river, took the
coach traffic: it had brightly painted vehicles parked
three or four deep, so close to the edge of the quay that
passengers were obliged to dismount from one side
only. Queen Street, narrow and close-set, took the
crowds from the city centre. Also it took the cyclists –
for whom, at the far end, an insistent body of Queen
Streeters touted their cycle-parks. At Railway Bridge
the seething current from the city was joined by the
rushing stream from Brackendale and together they

poured over the bridge, a bridge that trembled beneath their thousand feet. Small wonder that Leaming was sceptical about being seen by the bridge-keeper, thought Gently.

He himself passed over quite close to the little glass box, staring hard at its inmate as he went by. But the bridge-keeper was apparently bored by football crowds. He sat with his back to them, reading the midday paper.

On the other side of the bridge the crush was again augmented by the disemboguing of Riverside. Gently was hustled down like a cork. He barely had time to glance across at the car park with its tangle of moving and stationary vehicles when he was swept past and left high and dry on the end of a turnstile queue. How could one man be singled out in all that turmoil . . .? One had enough to do looking after oneself. If this had been last Saturday, would he, Gently, have noticed which way Leaming had gone when he left the car park . . . or even if Leaming was there at all?

The queue behind thrust him through the absurdly narrow little turnstile like a pip coming out of an orange, his one-and-nine snatched from his hand. He found himself amongst the loose, running crowd at the back of the terraces. Already the terraces seemed full, thronged with a dark, mass of humanity, a strange livid weal. But they were not full yet, because the armies still marched over Railway Bridge, still hurried down Queen Street, Riverside, and at the far end, down Railway Road. Thirty thousand people, perhaps more. Gently made his way round to the far side, the popular side, and forgetting he was no longer a uniform man, shouldered his way pretty well to the front.

Opposite him stretched the grandstand, all the length of the pitch, in front the packed enclosure, behind the close-banked tiers of seats, rising into the interior gloom, fully fledged with their human freight. On his right reared the Barclay stand, not seated, airier and less boxed-in than the other. Ice-cream boys marched along the naming-track. They caught sixpences with unerring hands and hurled their wares far up into the murmuring crowd. In the centre of the pitch tossed a bunch of balloons in the opposing colours ... the City's flag hung palely after nearly a season's rains.

Gently leaned on the corner of a crush-rail and took it in, section by section. It was here, if he could find it, there was something here that would give Leaming's alibi the lie ... something. But what was it, that something? How could he abstract it from a pattern so large and overwhelming? The loud-speaker music broke out in a strident, remorseless march, overriding his thought and concentration, compelling him to accept it, to accept the occasion, to accept the mood of the crowd ... he shook his head and went on searching. It was here, he repeated to himself, almost like a spell.

The match went well for the City. Not always immaculate before their own crowd, they took command of the game from the kick-off and rarely let it out of their grasp till the final whistle. Yet there was very little excitement. The score, two-one, indicated a hard-fought battle, whereas if the City had taken all their chances they might have gone near double figures. The crowd was correspondingly apathetic, seeing their team so near a resounding victory and still unable to force it home.

'We ought to have had Cullis here today . . . he'd've shown them where the goal was. Alfie wants to have everything laid on for him.'

'Lord knows how Noel missed that last one.'

'I reckon Ken is standing in the goal there, laughing at them.'

A particularly glaring miss was acknowledged by a slow hand-clap from one section of the crowd. When the final whistle went there was very little ovation for either side. Immediately the spectators turned and began their shuffle towards the exits, dissatisfied, feeling it might have been much better than it was.

'Well,' said one pundit to his mate, 'at least it was a *clean* game . . . they weren't like that lot we had here last week. I reckon Robson is still feeling the effects of that foul.'

'Anyway, it got us a goal.'

Gently pushed his way past them grimly, intent now only on getting out. He hadn't found it. He was going away empty-handed. And he had been so sure, so completely positive . . .! His whole instinct, buoyed on the pattern of the case, had told him that the trail would end that afternoon at Railway Road.

He felt, as Hansom had phrased it, like a kid who'd got his sums wrong. And it was a bitter pill for Gently to swallow. 'Yesterday, the thing had begun to move, it was on its way. It had only needed one more stroke . . . this one, and every nerve in his body had told him that he would find it that afternoon at Railway Road. But he'd been wrong, and he hadn't found it . . . the instinct that had carried him through so many cases had failed him.

Despairingly he thrust his way through the tight-packed crowd, looking at no one, caring for no one. He couldn't quite believe it had happened to him. Always before the luck that smiles on good detectives had smiled on him at the crucial moment ... he felt suddenly that he must be getting old and past it. He was falling down on a case.

At the city end of Queen Street was a small, cheap café, nearly on the corner of Prince's Street. Gently went in, bought himself a cup of tea and some rolls, then sat down with them at a marble-topped table. He'd got to get himself straightened out, to get his thoughts in order. At the moment they were tumbling over each other in a wild commotion, refusing to come together in a coherent picture: while through them all wound the insidious echo – it was there, if you could have found it.

He bit the end off a roll that wasn't fresh and washed it down with some over-brewed tea. His mind was balking, it wouldn't settle down. Stupidly he began to fight his way back into the afternoon, beginning with his walk down Queen Street and adding to it, piece by piece, the people who went in front, the people who went behind, the cars that hooted, the programme-sellers using a sand-hopper for a stall. There was the bridge and the bridge-keeper, who wouldn't have noticed his own brother going by, and the bedlam of the car park with its entrance almost flush opposite the artery of Riverside.

Slowly the picture came into focus, the turnstile, the crowd running loose round the backs, the shove down into the terraces, the music of the loud-speakers. And the game with its end-of-the-season looseness, and the comments of the crowd round about. It came back now, sharp and incisive, even tiny details like the worn paint and patches of rust on the crush-rail. Gently munched on down the roll, the distant look came back into his eye. What had they said about the goalkeeper? Ken was standing in the goal and laughing at them. Well, he looked as though he might have been, up there, watching his team-mates make one glaring miss after another – 'Lord knows how Noel missed that last one.' But the championship was virtually settled: it was time to laugh at one's mistakes. 'At least it was a clean game . . . not like the lot last week.' That was true, there had been very few fouls. 'I reckon Robson is still feeling the effects of that foul.' 'Anyway, it got us a goal.'

Gently paused, the tail-end of the roll halfway between his plate and his mouth. The words echoed back through his mind: Robson . . . foul . . . goal. What was it there that struck a chord, that reached out towards some mental pigeon-hole with a faint, but definite persistence? He took a deep breath and put down the end of the roll. 'Have you got a phone I can use?' he asked the woman who was serving.

'You can use the one in the hall,' she replied, reluctantly.

Gently dialled and waited impatiently. 'Chief Inspector Gently . . . Is the super there?' They put him through to the super's office, but it was Hansom who answered the phone. Gently said: 'Look, Hansom, are the reports of those interrogations where you can lay hands on them?' Hansom snorted down the phone.

'Haven't you turned that job in yet . . .?' Gently said: 'This is important. I want you to read me over the first few questions and answers of the report on Leaming.'

There was a long pause while the phone recorded nothing but vague noises and shifts of sound. Then came the sound of Hansom picking up the instrument again. 'I've got the report here,' he said. 'What do you want to know?'

'Just start reading it.'

'It starts with some junk about football.'

'That's what I'm after . . . don't miss out a word.'

Hansom read in a sing-song voice: 'Chief Inspector Gently you'll be able to tell me who got the City's first goal yesterday was it Robson. Leaming it was Smethick actually he scored from a free kick after a foul on Jones S. Chief Inspector Gently ah yes in the twenty-second—'

'Wait!' interrupted Gently, 'let's have that bit again.'

'What – all of it?'

'The Leaming bit.'

Hansom repeated: Leaming it was Smethick actually he scored from a free kick after a foul on Jones S.'

'Ah!' murmured Gently, 'Jones S.!'

There came an impatient rustle from the other end. 'Say!' bawled Hansom, 'what the hell is this?'

Gently smiled cherubically. 'Never mind now . . . just keep that record where it won't get lost. Oh, and Hansom—'

'I'm still connected.'

'You might get on to the super and warn him that things could get exciting later on.'

'How do you mean – exciting?'

'Oh . . . you know . . . just exciting.' Gently pressed the instrument firmly down in its cradle, then lifted it and dialled again. 'Press office? I want the sports editor . . . no, I don't care if he is busy getting out the football – this is the police.' There was a short, busy pause, then a brisk hand seized the other instrument. 'Sports editor – who's that?'

'Chief Inspector Gently. I want some information about the report printed last week of the match at Railway Road.'

'Well . . . what is it?'

'Your account said that the City's first goal was scored by Smethick after a foul on Jones S., whereas I understand that the foul was on Robson. Can you corroborate that?'

'Yes – it was on Robson. Our reporter misread his notes when he was telephoning . . . we have to work at considerable speed to make the deadline.'

'That's all right,' said Gently genially, 'there's no need to apologize. A slip like that won't worry many people.'

CHAPTER SIXTEEN

LEAMING'S CAR STOOD stood in the corner of the timber-yard, a crouched glowing presence in the gathering dusk. One of the sliding doors of the machine shop stood ajar, sufficient to show a gleam of light in the office at the far end, and Gently, who was long-sighted, could make out the dark figure of the manager bent over his desk. Gently was in no hurry. He ambled over to the car and examined the doors, which were locked. Then he quietly raised the bonnet and removed a small item from the engine.

Leaming was so intent on his work that he failed to notice Gently's approach until warned by the creak of an opening door. But then he spun round and to his feet in one crisp movement. 'You!' he exclaimed, his dark eyes sharp and thrusting, 'what do you want?'

Gently shrugged and closed the glass-panelled door behind him. 'I've been to the football match,' he said, 'I thought you might like to hear about it.' He moved round from the door to Leaming's desk and peered disinterestedly at the open ledger. Leaming watched him closely. Gently felt in his pocket and produced two peppermint creams, which he placed on the desk, pushing one towards Leaming with a stubby finger. 'Have one,' he said.

Leaming remained tense, watching.

Gently pulled up a little chair and sat down weightily. 'It wasn't a very good match. It was a bit end-of-the-season. And the *people*! I think it must have been near the ground record . . . forty-two thousand, isn't it?' His green eyes rose questioningly.

'A little more than that.'

'A little more?' Gently looked disappointed. 'I thought you would have been able to give me the exact figure . . . I know how precise you are about football matters.'

Leaming bit his lip. 'What does it matter, anyhow?'

'Oh, it doesn't, not really . . . but I thought you would have known.'

'It's forty-three thousand one hundred and twenty-one.'

'Ah!' Gently beamed at him. 'I was sure you could tell me. And wasn't that at the cup-tie with Pompey a couple of seasons ago . . . when Pompey won two-nought?'

Leaming came a step forward. 'See here,' he snapped, 'I don't know what you're after, and I don't care. But I've got work to do . . . we've got the accountants coming on Monday.'

'And you've got the "Straight Grain" books to prepare and make plausible before then . . . haven't you?'

Leaming seized the ledger on the desk, jerked it round and shoved it across to Gently. 'There!' he jeered. 'Have a look at it – see what you can find out.'

Gently shook his head. 'It isn't my job. We'll get a fraud man down to go through it.'

'A fraud man? Who's charging me with fraud?'

'Nobody . . . and as a matter of fact, I don't think anybody will.'

'Then what's this talk of getting a fraud man down?'

Gently continued to shake his head, slowly, woodenly. 'They'll want to know all about it in court, you know . . . the prosecution for the Crown will go into it with great thoroughness.'

There was a dead silence. Leaming stood immobile, his handsome face drained of all colour. Against the unnatural paleness his dark eyes seemed larger, darker, more penetrating than ever. 'What do you mean by that?' he asked huskily.

Gently turned away and said, speaking quickly: 'I've got the last piece of evidence I needed against you. There was a mistake in the account of the match which appeared in the *Football News* last Saturday. The same mistake appears in an answer you gave to one of my questions on Sunday . . . a record of it is in the files at police headquarters.'

'You found that out . . . today?'

'A short time ago. I overheard a scrap of conversation at the match this afternoon which led me to check with the Press office. I also checked your account in the police files.'

Leaming went back a pace, his hands grasping involuntarily. 'You're not lying?' he demanded suddenly.

'No, I'm not lying . . . why should I?'

'Suppose I said I wasn't at the match, but I was somewhere else?'

'No.' Gently shook his head again. 'It won't do. You'd have to prove it . . . and you can't prove it.'

'But you can't base a murder charge on that alone!'

Gently reached out for his peppermint cream, slow and deliberate. 'I can show that you had the motive,' he said. 'I can show that you could have hidden in the summer-house while Peter and his father were quarrelling. I can show that Fisher was watching what took place. I can show that Fisher blackmailed you first for Susan and then for the money. I can show that Fisher was murdered and he was murdered just when I had got sufficient evidence to make him speak – which you had grounds to suspect. I can show points of similarity between the two murders. I can show that you can prove no alibi at the time of Fisher's murder. I can show you were seen at the scene of the crime carrying a bag which subsequently became blood-stained and was destroyed here, where it is logical to suppose you would destroy it. I can show that the key which locked the door of Fisher's flat after the murder was found with it. And finally, I can now show that the alibi you gave for the time of the Huysmann murder was deliberately fabricated and completely false.'

'It's not enough – I'll get a defence to tear it to tatters!'

Gently bit into the peppermint cream. 'You might have done before today,' he said smoothly.

'It can't make all that difference . . . I won't believe it!'

'It was the one thing necessary.'

Leaming came forward again and leaned on the desk with both hands. 'Listen, Gently, listen – you can't go through with this. I'm talking to you now as a man, not as a police officer. All right, I admit it – I killed them both, Huysmann and Fisher, and you'll say I should be punished for it. But think a minute – there's a difference! Huysmann died, never knowing what had happened, and so did Fisher, instantaneously. They were both killed in hot blood, Gently. They were killed in the way of life, by their enemy, one man killing another to survive, Huysmann a vicious old man, Fisher a rat who asked for what he got. But you are after something different with me. If you go through with this, I shan't be killed that way. I'll be taken in cold blood, taken bound, taken with every man's hand against me, not a fight, not a chance, just taken and slaughtered in that death-pit of yours. That's the difference – that's what it amounts to! And I say to you as a man that you can't do it. You wouldn't match a killing of that sort with a killing of my sort, and clear your conscience by calling it justice!'

Gently stirred uneasily in his chair. 'I didn't make the laws – you knew the penalty that went with killing.'

'But it only goes with killing when a man's convicted – and I'm not convicted, and except for you I never would be!'

'I'm sorry, Leaming . . . it doesn't rest with me.'

'But it does rest with you – the local police are satisfied to let it go at the inquest verdict. They must know what you know . . . you work together. And they're satisfied, so why aren't you?'

'They don't know I've broken your alibi yet.'

'But they know the rest – and they're doing nothing about it.'

Gently turned away from him, his face looking tired. 'It's no good, Leaming . . . I've got to do it. When a man begins to kill it gets easier and easier for him, and it has to be stopped. I'm the person whose duty it is to stop him. And I've got to stop you.'

'Even if you have to deliver me to a state killing party?'

'I'm a policeman, not a lawgiver.'

'But you're a man as well!'

'Not while I'm a policeman . . . we're not permitted to have thoughts like that. The law allows me only one way to stop killing . . . it's not my way, but it's the only way.'

'Then you're going through with it?'

'Yes, I'm going through with it.'

Leaming drew back from the desk, as far as the closed door. 'Then you leave me no option but to kill you too, Gently,' he said.

Gently looked up at him with unmoved green eyes. 'I realized it would come to that, of course . . . but it won't be easy for you.'

Leaming felt casually in his pocket and produced a small automatic. 'It will be as easy as this,' he said. The colour had come back into his cheeks now and something of the old jauntiness to his manner. 'I'm sorry it's come to this, Gently. I didn't want to do any more killing . . . whatever you may think about killing getting easier, I assure you it's something one would rather not do. And I don't want to kill you, because I admire you. But I have a duty to myself, just as you have a duty to the state.'

Gently said: 'It won't help you to kill me. They'll come straight to you for it.'

Leaming said: 'But they won't find anything . . . and I don't care what they suspect. I shall tip your body into the incinerator at Hellston Tofts and the gun after you. It isn't traceable . . . I bought it on the black market.'

'What about the noise of the shot?'

Leaming smiled frostily. 'Nobody's going to hear that. I shall shoot you here, in the shop.'

'But it's perfectly quiet?'

'It won't be when I shoot you. I shall have all the saws running – the people round here are used to hearing that. We sometimes run them after hours for test purposes.'

Gently reached out for the second peppermint cream. 'When I'm missing they'll come straight to you,' he repeated. 'Hansom knows there's something vital in that answer of yours in the records. He doesn't know what it is, but he'll find out, and the fact that I'm missing will clinch the case for him. Suppose you stop killing and start thinking about your defence?'

Leaming shook his head briefly. 'I'll risk that,' he said, 'now come along with me while I switch the saws on.' He made a movement with his gun.

Gently hung on, mechanically chewing at the peppermint cream. If he refused to go, Leaming was faced with the prospect of shooting him where he sat and thus rousing the neighbourhood. But the rousing of the neighbourhood would be ill-appreciated by a dead Gently. He got up and shambled over to the door.

Leaming switched on the lights as they passed them, flooding the huge, wide sheds with fluorescent glare. He kept Gently walking three paces ahead. The first of the saws broke into life with a snatching whirr, quickly rising, becoming a loud, shuddering drone. Leaming said: 'We must find one with a piece of timber in the feed . . . if I put that through at the appropriate moment I should be all right.' Saw by saw they worked round the shop. The still air became virulent with the high, pulsating drone, throbbing and writhing in waves of vicious power, naked and potential. It made Gently feel sick. It was as though a vast, anti-human power were building up, as though it were rising towards a peak at which his organism would disintegrate, would tear apart, smashed into its component atoms. Leaming set off some band-saws. Their whining shriek imposed itself on the roar of the circulars like a theme of madness twisting through chaos, a sharp, demonic ecstasy of destruction. 'How's that?' bawled Leaming. 'Do you think they'll hear a shot through this lot?' Gently said nothing, would not look back at him.

They went to the centre saws now, moving back towards the sliding doors. Near the further end was a little wooden booth, perhaps for a time-keeper, glass-panelled at the top. Gently kept his eye on it. Slowly they drew closer, moving between pauses while Leaming set going the saws at each side. They drew abreast of it, Leaming going first to the saw on his left, then stepping across to the one on his right.

The noise in the shop was so deafening that the crash of the falling booth was scarcely audible. But Gently heard the riposte of the gun. He didn't stay to argue. A second shot followed the first like an echo and a whiff of white dust sprang up at his feet. He leaped sideways, bending low to get cover from the saws, and made towards the gaping doorway. But Leaming had anticipated the move and sprinted like the wind to cut him off. A bullet out of nowhere warned Gently that he wouldn't get out of the doors.

Zig-zagging, still keeping cover behind the saws, Gently worked back towards the office and the switch-board. If he could put the lights out for a moment . . . But once again Leaming sensed his objective and rushed to cut him off. A fourth bullet smacked into a baulk of wood a couple of feet away. He dodged away behind the tearing saws.

He was getting cornered now, driven back towards the band-saws. Up there it was a dead-end, no door, no windows, and the band-saws didn't give cover like the circulars did. Desperately he tried to double out of the trap, but the agile Leaming beat him each time. He wasn't shooting now at every glimpse – he was holding his last two bullets. And slowly, almost leisurely, he was herding Gently towards the dead-end, where the outcome was inevitable.

With the scream of the band-saws ripping at his ear-drums Gently hung on behind the last circular. Leaming was coming across diagonally towards it, gun low, stooping, like a predatory animal moving in to the kill. Gently saw him past the rippling steel blade, intent, remorseless, moving in. He also saw something else. It was a jack-wrench lying on the saw-bench. His clumsy hand rose up over the edge of the bench and fastened on the handle. On came Leaming, aware of his presence, gun at the ready now. Gently crouched further back along the saw. He saw the face loom up with the look of the kill in its dark eyes, the arm move from the shoulder to fire over the saw-bench . . . then he hurled the jack-wrench squarely into the thundering circle of burnished steel.

Flat on the floor, he never knew quite what happened after that. His next coherent impression was of a sudden slackening of the fearful noise, a dying away, combined with complete darkness and the sickening smell of burned-out cable. Trembling, he got to his feet and fumbled for his lighter. Its tiny flame snapped dazzlingly before his eyes. The first thing he saw was Leaming's gun, lying quite close to him. Instinctively he checked a movement to grab it, pulled out his handkerchief, picked up the gun by the end of its still-warm muzzle.

With ears buzzing he picked his way towards the office and the phone. He put out his lighter and dialled by touch. 'Super there? Put me through to him . . . Chief Inspector Gently.' There was practically no pause at all before the super's voice came on with a barrage of questions. Gently covered the receiver wearily. 'Listen,' he said. There was a silence and presumably the super was listening. 'I'm in the office of Huysmann's yard. I'd like you to come along now for a bit of routine work . . . you'll need an ambulance amongst other things, and bring plenty of torches because I've wrecked the electrics hereabouts . . .' He paused and held the instrument away from him while the super reacted. 'Yes, I have got Leaming here . . . I broke his alibi and he confessed . . . then he pulled a gun and took a few shots at me, but he isn't all that good at shooting . . . he's a bit off-colour just now, though he should be in shape for a trial by the autumn.'

Gently clamped down the receiver and sat quite still

for a moment or two. His ears still buzzed with the pounding they had taken, his hands were still trembling and he felt unutterably tired. Outside in the shop a great silence prevailed, a thick, dark silence, like the inside of the pyramids. Somewhere on the surface of it he could hear a car passing down Queen Street, very distant, a sound from another world. And then came the far-away clamour of a bell which was the ambulance, probably as it shot the lights at Grove Lane.

CHAPTER SEVENTEEN

THERE WASN'T A lot to be made out of the news that the manager of Huysmann's had been injured at the yard and taken to hospital, even though the police did wait at his bedside until he regained consciousness. The Norchester Press, for instance, was very restrained and non-committal. But the Norchester Press was like that anyway. It didn't deceive Charlie for one moment. Charlie knew, if nobody else did, that Chief Inspector Gently had been 'after' Leaming. Hadn't he seen Gently there, with his own eyes, playing with Leaming just as, formerly, he had played with Fisher? Then it was Leaming after all who'd knocked the old man off . . . a man like Gently wasn't going to be fooled by Fisher cutting his throat. Charlie's only anxiety was that Leaming wouldn't pull round. Unless there was a trial, nobody would really know how right Charlie had been.

But he needn't have worried. They took good care of Leaming at the Norchester and County Hospital and lavished a small fortune of drugs and surgical talent on him. A man must look his best when he's likely to be hung . . . also, the trial that followed was magnificent, even by Charlie's standards.

Peter Huysmann returned home to take over the management of the yard himself, bringing with him his wife and the good wishes of the fair community. Cathy was a little nervous of Gretchen, but Gretchen was only too pleased to have a companion to liven up the gloom of the Huysmann house. Mrs Turner improved the occasion by reading a homily to Susan on taking up with men, especially the managerial classes. It fell a little flat. Susan had already ceased to mourn the loss of Leaming and was viewing with interest the attentions of the brewery executive from up the road.

Hansom's generosity was rather strained when it came to congratulating Gently a second time. In his private opinion, Gently was an exponent of art for art's sake. There had been no need to take things further than Fisher . . . they had ended there very neatly. If Fisher wasn't exactly responsible for Huysmann's death, he was as near to it as made no difference, and to go on after that was untidy and a little precious . . . especially with so little in the way of evidence. But he was a nice type really, was Hansom. At parting, he gave Gently one of his best cigars.

The super said snappishly: 'I can't think why the devil you went after him alone, when you might have taken the entire City Police with you. Surely you realized he might be tempted to add you to his other victims?'

Gently shook his head in his wooden way. 'I had to give him enough rope. If we'd simply pulled him in he'd still have had a pretty good case to argue . . . he had to be made to do something silly. Of course, I didn't know he'd got a gun.'

'Oh! So you didn't know he'd got a gun! And would it have made any difference if you had known?'

'No . . . not really.'

'Well, it would have done to me – I can tell you that!' The super sniffed in an aggrieved sort of way. 'I've given up trying to understand you people,' he said. 'As far as I can see, you're either born to homicide or you aren't, and if you aren't, you might just as well keep your big mouth shut and pretend your corpses aren't there. When did you start suspecting Leaming?'

Gently applied a light to his waning pipe. 'I didn't suspect anyone. I just kept finding things out till I'd got a pattern.'

'And why didn't the pattern fit Fisher?'

'Oh . . . I don't know. He wasn't clever enough. If he'd done murder and stolen forty thousand he'd have run off with it, not hung around.'

'And Peter Huysmann?'

'I saw him riding the Wall of Death . . . I knew he hadn't done it.'

'How about the girl Gretchen – and the maid?'

'Gretchen wasn't strong enough to strike the blow that killed Huysmann, and as for the maid—!' Gently smiled lazily. 'I had my fun, too . . . I took Susan to the pictures one night.'

The super's eyes glinted. 'That wasn't professional of you, Gently!'

Gently sighed, and knocked out his pipe.

★　★　★

256

There were two yachtsmen on the river that summer who were very keen photographers. They took photographs of almost everything that came their way. One of these photographs won first prize in the Norchester Press Summer Snaps Competition and was duly published on the front page, right opposite a screed about the manager of a timber-yard being charged with double murder. It was entitled 'Tomorrow *may* be Friday' and depicted a bulky individual sitting asleep on the river-bank, his fishing-rod trailing in the water, his hands clasped on his stomach and a bag of sweets open beside him.

Inspector Hansom saw this photograph. He bought three copies of it and pinned one up on the cupboard door at his office. It kept him happy for weeks.

Gently by the Shore

CHAPTER ONE

EVEN THE SEA which lapped the August beaches of Starmouth looked grey at that hour of the morning. There was something mournful about it – it seemed to be grieving for the thronged crowds of noonday. Northwards it was embraced by the sprawl of the Albion Pier, much destroyed, much reconstructed, south-wards by the elegant iron-work of the Wellesley with its Winter Gardens, while facing it, across the wide promenade, lay the hectic holiday face of the town, a Victorian foundation in evil, dark-red brick with overlays of modern Marine Baroque. And the prevailing note was sadness. The dawn refused to ratify what man called gay. At this solemn hour, when PC Lubbock was observing his regulation speed between pier and pier, the Seaside Of The Midlands looked like a sleeping drunk stretched by the disapproving main.

He stopped, did PC Lubbock: he checked his well-regulated 2mph and conducted a survey of the morning scene. All was quiet, and most was still. On the pale-looking beach below him two or three figures were moving, slow, intent, each with a stick with

261

which he occasionally stirred the marble-cold sand. Beyond them some sandpipers worked along the tide-line, further out some terns, and further still the gulls. Scavengers all were they, men and birds. PC Lubbock marked them with a permitting eye. He had seen them upon their lawful occasions for many a long year now and he gave them a favouring nod as he turned to pursue his jaunt.

But before he could get under way a change took place in the peaceful scene. A movement occurred, quite other than those he had come to expect from the deliberate trade of beach-combing. Towards him came leaping and capering, more animal than human, a strange, chattering figure, a figure that flailed its arms, a figure from whose splaying heels the sand shot up in clouds. PC Lubbock hesitated in his stride. There was something mindless and rather horrible about this bounding creature. Although he recognized it as Nits, a local halfwit, he couldn't help falling back a pace as it vaulted over the balustrade and dropped crouching at his feet.

'Well . . . and what d'you want, m'lad?' he demanded sternly, fixing his gaze on the halfwit's protruding green eyes.

They stared at him silently, seeming to strain towards him: the rest of the face sank backwards towards a toothy gape.

'What is it?' reiterated the Police Constable, raising his voice a degree.

Nits sucked in his lips as though preparing them for articulation. 'He . . . don't wake up,' he blurted in his slurring pipe.

'Eh? Who doesn't wake up?' asked the constable.

'The man . . . he don't wake up.'

Nits made an orang-outang-like gesture towards the direction from which he had come. 'All wet!' he whimpered, 'no clothes on . . . don't wake up.'

There was a pause while the trained mind arranged this information.

'You say it's *a man?*' PC Lubbock demanded suspiciously.

'A man – a man – a man!' Nits nodded his head with astonishing rapidity.

'You mean one like me?'

The head bobbed on as though worked by a piston.

With a stately cock of his leg, PC Lubbock stormed the balustrade and descended to the beach below. Through sand and through shingle went his boots, through shells and through seaweed, till he stood at last where the low slack water played old Harry with his spit and polish. And there he saw him, the man who didn't wake up, the man without clothes, the man who was all wet.

He had stood about five feet ten. He had weighed about 185. His hair had been pale brown, his eyes blue, his eyebrows slanting, his heavy features decidedly un-English. And he had acquired, probably rather late in life, a feature of the keenest police interest: a collection of four stab-wounds in the thorax.

PC Lubbock remarked a high percentage of these details. He glanced sharply at Nits, and sharply at the sea. Then, drawing his whistle with a flourish of professional adroitness, he blew a wailful blast to wake the morning air.

'There seems,' said Chief Inspector Gently, Central Office, CID, sagely, 'to be some as-yet-undiscovered connection between coastal resorts and homicide, Dutt. Have you noticed it?'

Detective Sergeant Dutt nodded dutifully, but without really listening to his senior. It had been hot in the train coming up. It was still hot in the train. Their third-class compartment was a little oven, and its atmosphere wasn't improved by the haze contributed by Gently's pipe.

'You've only to go back to the 'twenties,' continued Gently, with a damaging puff. 'There were the Crumbles murders – Field and Gray in '20, and Mahon in '24. Both classics, Dutt. Especially Mahon.'

'I was bashing me first beat in '24,' said Dutt reminiscently.

'Then there was Smith and the Brides in the Baths – Blackpool and Herne Bay were two of his spots – and coming the other way there's the Brighton Trunk Murders and Sidney Fox at Margate, and that other Starmouth business – slaughter in all shapes and sizes, and all of it going on by the sea. There's a link there somewhere, Dutt, you mark my words. The sea has a bad influence on potential homicides, whether it's recognized or not.'

'Dare say you're right, sir,' replied Dutt, staring out of the window.

'When I retire I shall write a monograph on it,' added Gently. 'There may be some implications which would help a good defence.'

He sank back into his seat and puffed away in silence.

The train clattered on, wearying, somnolent. They were nearing the end of the run, four sun-beating hours of it, and both of them felt jaded and grimy. Outside stretched the marshes of East Northshire, very wide, very flat, their distance broken by nothing except the brick towers of windmills and the white handkerchief sails of yachts. Inside there was Gently's pipe and the sooty smell of third-class cushions . . .

'Well, it won't be so bad, sir,' said Dutt, trying to cheer himself up, 'it can't be worse than Southend or Margate.'

Gently smiled at a distant cow. 'It isn't,' he said, 'there's parts of it one grows to like.'

'You know the place, sir – you've been there before?'

'When I was ten,' admitted Gently, 'and that's further back than I like to remember.'

He thought about it, nevertheless. He could see himself now as he was then, a thoughtful child with sunburn and freckles, and those damned knickerbockers. A solitary child he had been, a bad mixer. It may have been the knickerbockers that made him antisocial.

'There isn't much difference between criminals and policemen,' he said, surprising Detective Sergeant Dutt.

They pulled in at Starmouth Ranelagh, a gloomy terminus where the smell of fish blended into a neat olfactory cocktail with the smell of soot, steam and engine oil.

'It hasn't changed,' mused Gently, 'that's just the smell it used to have.'

He reached down a battered leather suitcase and deposited himself and it upon the platform. Sergeant Dutt followed, carrying a similar case, while in his other hand he clasped the 'murder bag' with which a careful Central Office had equipped the expedition. Outside in the station yard the afternoon sun burned down stunningly. There was a taxi rank, and co-passengers clad in summer dresses and open-necked shirts were streaming towards it. Sergeant Dutt looked longingly, but Gently shook his head.

'It isn't far,' he said, 'they've got their headquarters just off the quay.'

'Don't know what they've gone and packed in the bag,' said Sergeant Dutt reprovingly, 'it's like a ton weight.'

'Probably a ball and chain for when we make the pinch,' replied his senior unfeelingly.

They left the station and plodded over a lift-bridge which carried the main road into the town. Below them a cloudy muddy-banked stream flowed pacifically, bearing on its bosom tugs with barges and smaller traffic. Further down two torpedo boats were moored at the quays, opposite them a lightship undergoing a refit, and one or two stream-drifters. Above the bridge was the yacht station, its staithe packed three-deep with visiting holiday-craft.

'It's a ruddy port!' exclaimed Sergeant Dutt, dropping his bags gratefully as Gently paused to admire the scene.

'Of course it's a port,' said Gently, 'where do you think your breakfast bloater hails from, Dutt?'

'Yus, but I thought it was like Margate — not like flipping Pompey!'

Gently grinned. 'There's a Margate side to it too,' he said. 'Look, Dutt — a ship-chandler's. Have you ever seen a ship being chandled?'

'Can't say as how I have, sir, come to think of it.'

'You should,' said Gently, 'your education is lacking. It's the duty of every intelligent citizen to see a ship being chandled, at least once . . .'

They proceeded across the bridge and down into the sun-baked street leading along the quays. Ahead of them now was the Town Hall, a handsome red-brick building in a style that was purely Dutch. In fact, the whole thing might have been Dutch, thought Gently, there was a strong Continental atmosphere. Coming in, now, through all those marshes with their cattle and windmills and sails . . . And then again it was full of overtones which kept him in a strange frame of mind. He couldn't settle himself to the idea of being out on a case. It was having been here so long ago that upset him, perhaps, the having known the place as a child his mind was baulking and refusing to come to grips with what he was doing. It showed itself in his facetiousness, in the way he twitted Dutt.

But it was no good: he was here on business only. Nostalgic memories didn't mix successfully with homicide, and he just had to shake himself into an alert and receptive state of mind.

'There's a cafe over there,' he said to Dutt, 'let's drop in for a cup of tea before we check in.'

'I was just going to mention it, sir,' panted the sweating Dutt, 'only you seemed to be in such a hurry!'

Gently clicked his tongue. 'I'm not in any hurry,' he said. 'There's nobody as patient as corpses, Dutt, especially when they've come out in a rash of stab-wounds . . .'

★ ★ ★

267

Superintendent Symms of the Starmouth Borough Police paced his office with military stride, a tall, spare man with close grey hair and a little clipped moustache. Inspector Copping, his man of parts, was being strong and silent in a corner.

'And that's it, gentlemen,' said the super, in tones as clipped as his moustache, 'we know nothing – we can find out nothing. We've got a corpse, and absolutely nothing else. There were no clothes and hence no laundry marks. You've had the prints and they're not on record. We've checked the Missing Persons' list for months without getting a lead and we've shown a slide at all the cinemas in town with no better result. In fact, gentlemen, it's a sticky sort of business, and I feel I ought to apologize for calling you in at all. But you understand how I'm placed. There are people above me who pretend to believe in miracles.'

Gently nodded gravely. 'It's our principal business to carry the can.'

'And you were specifically asked for, Gently – after that Norchester case of yours Central Office means only one person around here.'

'It was one of my luckier cases,' agreed Gently modestly.

'So you see, it was out of my hands.' The super paused, both in stride and speech. He was genuinely grieved at having to pass on such a stinker.

'It's a job for the file,' put in Inspector Copping from his corner, 'there's just no angle to it. He might have been jettisoned from a ship, or dumped there, or dumped somewhere else and washed up there. He might even have been shoved out of an aircraft and finished up there. There's no end to the ways he might've come – I've put in hours thinking up new ones.'

Gently nodded a mandarin nod and stuffed a clumsy hand into his pocket. They had some peppermint creams in that cafe, and he had bought a whole pound.

'The body was even *discovered* by a halfwit . . . so far as we can make out he chivvied it around trying to wake it up.'

Gently made sympathetic noises over a peppermint cream.

'And then this blasted Lubbock got the seconds on him and tried three methods of artificial respiration.'

'He's been reprimanded,' said the super grimly, 'there'll be no more of that sort of thing from Lubbock.'

'And all the beachcombers for miles jamming around . . . it was like Bertram Mills'.'

There was a silence, during which the only sound was a sugary chewing from Gently.

'So you see that calling you in is simply a face-saver,' went on the super, recommencing to stalk. 'The lads higher up know there's no chance, but the thing got too much publicity. They daren't just sit tight and let it fade away.'

Gently shuffled a foot. 'Well, as long as you aren't expecting too much . . .'

'We aren't.' Inspector Copping laughed with a little conscious bitterness.

Gently laid a peppermint cream on the super's desk and appeared to study it, as though seeking inspiration. 'This halfwit who found him . . .' he began vaguely.

'They call him Nits,' supplied Copping. 'He's

cracked all right – ought to be in a home. Real name's Gibson. Lives with his mother in one of the Grids.'

'And you checked up on him?'

'Naturally.'

'He wouldn't have been carrying a knife of any sort?'

Inspector Copping hesitated a moment and then plucked something from his pocket and threw it down on the desk in front of Gently. It was a cheap one-bladed penknife, and its one blade was broken. Gently poked it with a stubby finger.

'Of course there's no connection . . .?'

'None,' rapped Inspector Copping.

Gently picked it up. 'I'd like to keep it for the moment, all the same . . .' He opened and closed the little blade with a naïve curiosity. 'Did you find out anything else about him?' he asked. 'Has he got any friends – does anybody employ him?'

Inspector Copping grunted. 'He isn't employable. He hangs around the beach and people give him money, that's all. He spends it in the cinemas and amusement arcades. Everybody knows him, but nobody wants anything to do with him.'

'Has he ever given any trouble?'

'A visitor made a fuss about him once and we pinched him for begging. It took three men to bring him in. He's stronger than he looks.'

Gently revolved the peppermint cream with care. 'About the deceased,' he said, 'when did he die?'

'The report says between eleven and twelve p.m. on Tuesday.'

'When did you find him?'

'Lubbock saw him at five-ten a.m. on Wednesday.'

'So he'd only taken five hours to get where he was . . . it isn't very long. What was the state of the tide?'

'Low slack water. If he came in on the tide he must have grounded at about four.'

'That cuts it down another hour . . .' Gently stared at his white sugar tablet with elevated brows. 'The local currents . . . the ones just off-shore . . . what's their direction?'

Copping glanced at his superior.

'There's nothing just off-shore,' supplied the super, 'it's a perfectly safe beach at all states of the tide. There's a north–south current further out, about half a mile. It accounts for a few damn fools every season.'

'Do you know the speed of it?'

'Not precisely. Maybe six or seven knots.'

'So you give him an hour to get into the current and another hour to come back ashore he might have been put in eighteen miles north.'

'No.' The super shook his head. 'If he was put in from the shore it couldn't be more than five or six. The shore starts in westward just north of the town, and six miles up the coast is Summerness, beyond which it recedes very sharply. At Summerness the current would be two miles off-shore.'

'Two miles . . .' mused Gently. 'He wouldn't drift out that far in the time. It'd have to be lower down. What's up there in that direction?'

The super shrugged. 'It's a wide sand beach all the way, backed with marram hills and freshwater marshes. There are three villages and a lot of bungalows. A little way out of town there's the racecourse.'

'Has there been racing lately?'

271

'No. It's not due till next Tuesday.'

'I suppose you didn't do any checking up there?'

'What's the use?' interrupted Inspector Copping. 'It's a hundred to one against him having been put in there, and even if he was, what would we be looking for?'

'Someone might have seen something,' suggested Gently mildly, 'there's never any harm in asking questions.'

Inspector Copping's heavyish features flushed. 'The case has had publicity,' he said, 'we've asked for information both in the cinemas and the press. If anyone knew anything we should have heard by now – we've looked into everything that's come our way.'

'Please don't get the impression that we've been asleep,' said the super snappily, 'we may not be homicide experts, but at least we carry out our police duties with strict care and attention. You have made the suggestion that the body of the deceased was put into the sea somewhere between here and Summerness, but the suggestion rests merely on the fact that there is a north–south current. And the current may have brought it from some point at sea, and then again it may never have been in the current at all. It could even have drifted up from a southerly direction inside the current.'

Gently hunched his shoulders chastenedly and made a chessmove with the peppermint cream. 'It could even have been dropped off the pier,' he murmured.

'My guess is it came off a ship,' said Copping. 'There's no doubt about the fellow being a foreigner. Anyone could see that at a glance. The ethnologist who saw him reckoned he was a Slav of some sort, Central European. He could have gone overboard in the Wash somewhere and hooked on to that current.'

'And that would mean trying to pinpoint a ship of some or any nationality which was in the Wash about midnight on Tuesday,' said the super, 'and just suppose we found it, what good would it do us?'

'It'd be outside our jurisdiction,' said Copping brightly.

'Unless it was a British ship,' hazarded Gently.

'In which case we would have heard something before now,' said the super with a note of finality. 'No, Gently. I appreciate your attitude. It's your business to see that no stone is unturned and I can see that you propose to carry it out. But I think you'll have to agree in the long run that everything that can be done has been done. Where there's no identity, no apparent motive and no hopeful line of inquiry, then to proceed with a case is simply a formality. You must do it – that's your business: but I'm afraid that in this instance it will be a very thankless task.'

'And yet this man was murdered,' said Gently slowly. 'Somewhere there's someone who will kill more readily another time if we don't put a finger on him . . .'

'I know, I know!' snapped the super, 'but idealism is no use if there's no prospect of implementing it.'

Gently sighed and heaved himself out of the rather bleak chair which was maintained for visitors. 'There's nothing else you want to tell me?' he inquired.

'I've told you everything that we know.' The super paused, frowning. Then he looked at Gently a little more kindly. 'Don't think we're against you . . . I assure you it isn't that. If you can do anything with this affair I shall be the first to congratulate you, and Copping here will be the second.'

'Hear, hear,' responded Copping, though perhaps more from duty than conviction.

'I've arranged lodgings for you and the Sergeant in Nelson Street. There's a private office here you can use for interrogations. If you need a car you have only to ask for it, and any other assistance we can give.' The super stalked round his desk and held out his hand. 'The best of luck, Gently,' he said warmly, 'I only wish it had been someone with no reputation to lose.'

Gently shook the extended hand woodenly. 'I'd like to see the body,' he said.

'I've a full set of photographs and a copy of the pathologist's report for you,' replied the super. 'Copping will give them to you along with his own report.'

'I still want to see the body,' said Gently.

The super shrugged. 'Very well, then. Copping will take you round.'

They filed out in strict order of rank, Gently, Copping and Dutt, the latter having been a silent and respectful auditor of the conference in the office.

'We'll take a car,' said Copping, 'it isn't far to the mortuary, but you can put your bags in and I'll drop you at your lodgings.' He dodged into his office and came out with a file. 'These are the reports and the photographs – for what they're worth.'

Gently took them with a solemn nod.

The mortuary was a neat modern building of pastel-tone brick and had double doors of a reddish wood with lavish chromium-plated fitments. But it smelled exactly like all other mortuaries. Copping explained their errand to the sad-faced attendant. They were ushered into the dim and odoriferous interior.

'He's had company,' observed the attendant, indicating a second draped form, 'they pulled her out of the river up by the yacht-station.'

'You'd better watch they don't get into mischief,' said Copping callously.

The attendant laughed a ghoulish laugh and twitched the sheet from corpse number one.

'*Voilà*,' said Copping, 'the cause of all the trouble.'

Gently stepped forward and conducted a stolid examination of the wax-like body. It had no humanity now. There was nothing about it to suggest the warmth of life, the kindling of a soul. And the attentions of the pathologist had done little to help matters, though he had tidied up afterwards with needle and gut.

Sergeant Dutt made a hissing sound. 'No doubt about him being a foreigner, sir,' he said, 'there's a bit of the old Eyetye about him, if you ask me.'

'Age?' demanded Gently through his teeth.

'Early forties is their guess,' returned Copping.

'Much force?'

'One stab busted a rib. There's three in the lung and one in the heart. Penetration about four inches. Double-edged blade about three-quarters of an inch wide. And his wrists had been tied.'

'Poor beggar!' exclaimed the warm-hearted Dutt, 'they never give him a chance.'

'And those?' jerked Gently, indicating a group of brownish marks just above the pathologist's neat stitches.

'Burns,' said Copping, 'that's what the report says.'

Sergeant Dutt caught his breath. 'I've seen burns like that before, sir . . . during the war when I was in France . . .'

275

'I know,' said Gently, 'I've seen them too.'

He turned away from the slab and stood looking at the narrow window with its bar and pebble-glass pane.

'They didn't just want his life, they wanted something else too. I wonder what it was . . . I wonder why it was so important?'

Copping laughed harshly. 'When you know that you'll have solved the case,' he said. 'Let's get out of here. The smell gets on my stomach. You've done me out of my tea, bringing me to this place just before I knock off.'

CHAPTER TWO

B ODY ON THE BEACH: YARD CALLED IN, ran the
headline of the evening paper, Chief Inspector
Gently To Take Charge, New Move In Riddle Of The
Sands. It continued: 'There were fresh developments
today in the murder mystery which has come to be
known as "The Body On The Beach Murder". The
Starmouth Borough Police acknowledged the gravity
with which they view the case by calling upon the
services of Scotland Yard. Chief Inspector Gently, well
known in Northshire for his handling of the Sawmill
Murders, has been assigned the task and this afternoon
he arrived in Starmouth to take over the investigation.
Superintendent Symms told our reporter in an interview today that sensational developments in the near
future are not expected and that the arrival of Chief
Inspector Gently was purely a routine step.'

There was also a photograph of Gently which the
Norchester Evening News had kept in cold storage from
his last visit, but fortunately it wasn't recognizable . . .

All along the Front they were talking about it, from
the bowling greens in the north to the funfair in the

south. It was really making the week for them, holidaymakers and residents alike. Publicity it was, Publicity with a capital P — it dragged in excursionists to be plucked and made the holidaymakers feel that their stay would be truly memorable. For how often does a first-class murder turn up on one's doorstep during a holiday? A classic murder with stabbing, mystery, the Yard, and all that? They even had the spot marked X for them, thought Gently, as he turned away from the crowd which still milled excitedly on the beach: the Starmouth Borough Police, nothing if not thorough, had set up a ponderous post to mark the site of the discovery. Nobody took it seriously, that was the trouble . . . the police had already written it off as unsolvable, and everybody else looked on it as a bigger and better side-show. Even Gently himself was being infected by the feeling. He had been practically tipped off that he didn't have to exert himself.

And yet it was still there, up in the mortuary. That shrunken husk of what had once been a man. A foreigner, they all said, as though it were something subhuman — a foreigner whom they couldn't really care about, though he had been tortured, killed in cold blood and thrown into the sea, to be washed up, troublesome and unwanted, on their holiday shore . . . just a foreigner: one didn't bother too much about him.

But suppose one did bother, thought Gently, where did one begin on such an impossible business? He had taken the only step that suggested itself. He had got Dutt to phone headquarters to have the prints transmitted to Paris. Where did one go from there — what was one to try that the so-efficient Starmouth BP hadn't tried already? He sighed, and sat down heavily in a deckchair which still remained on the evening sand. He was still baulking, and he knew it. He still couldn't get his shoulder under the thing. There was something about just being in Starmouth, quite apart from anything else, that sapped his power of concentration. Those tight-fitting knickerbockers, for instance . . . And where were the donkeys . . .?

Behind him the lights blazed and jewelled as far as the eye could see, outlining buildings, flashing on signs, revolving on the sails of the windmill which reared further down. The two piers presented a strong contrast. The virile Albion seemed to burn and throb with illumination, to assert itself by sheer candlepower; the Wellesley contented itself with graceful and glittering outlines, making it appear, with its Winter Gardens, like an iced-cake shored-up above the sea. And there was the great evening medley of the Front, the undertone of the traffic, the beat of ten thousand feet, the shrieks and cries of ragamuffin children, the tinkle and soughing roar of mechanical music and the intermittent spang and crash of a shooting saloon not far away.

And then, of course, there was the sea, the sea that knew the secret, the heavy-looking evening sea that hissed and chuckled near that solitary post.

Gently took out his pipe and lit it. There had to be something, he told himself obstinately. After all, that man must necessarily have been murdered not very far away and murder under the best conditions is apt to leave traces. He blew out the match in a gust of smoke and held it poised in the air beside him. Except if it were done at sea, of course . . . but one mustn't begin by assuming that.

Suddenly, the match disappeared from his fingers. It went so quickly and so silently that for a moment Gently simply sat still in surprise. Then he jerked his head round to see by what agency the match had taken flight. But there was nothing to be seen. There was nobody within yards of the back of his chair. The nearest people to him were two uniformed Americans with their inamoratas and they were patently occupied with quite other things. Puzzled, he returned to his meditations. He puffed at his pipe, his empty fingers taking up the same position as before. And then, just as suddenly, with the lightest of twitches, the match reappeared in its former situation.

This time Gently got up. He got up with an alacrity unexpected in a bulky man of fifty summers. But his haste was quite needless, because the worker of these miracles was merely crouching behind the chair and it made no attempt at flight when Gently pulled away the chair and exposed it.

'And who may you be?' demanded Gently, realizing then whom it could be no other.

'I'm Nits – I'm Nits!' piped the halfwit, staring up painfully with his bulbous eyes. 'I know who you are, they told me who you are! I know – I know!'

Gently released the chair slowly and reseated himself, this time with his back to the sea. 'So you do, do you?' he said, 'and who did they tell you I am?'

'You're a policeman!' chattered Nits, 'you're a policeman, though you haven't got a hat. I know! They told me! You want to know about my man who wouldn't wake up.'

Gently nodded profoundly, keeping his eyes fixed on the halfwit's. 'And what else did they tell you about me?' he queried.

'They said I mustn't talk to you – ha, ha! – they said you might take me away and lock me up. But' – Nits assumed an expression of exaggerated cunning – 'I know you won't do that.'

'And how do you know I won't do that, Nits?'

'Because I haven't asked for any money. That's why they locked me up!'

Gently puffed at his pipe, still keeping the staring green eyes engaged. This was it, the solitary link – an idiot who ought to be in a home. Not even a rational creature, however stupid. Just an idiot, someone who couldn't testify anyway. As he sat there, smoking and brooding and watching the ragged Caliban crouched in the sand, he seemed to hear a mockery in the tinkled outburst of music and a laughter in the shuffling of feet on the promenade. What was the use of it? And who cared two hoots, really?

'So you found the man who wouldn't wake up . . .' he murmured.

Nits nodded in energetic glee.

'Just there, where they've put the post.'

Nits's head bobbed ceaselessly.

'And you tried to wake him up . . . then you went and told a policeman . . . and the policeman tried waking him up too.'

The head never wavered.

'You've no idea how he got there?'

The head changed direction agreeably.

'You didn't see anybody around before you found him?'

'My part,' said Nits, his features twisting into an absurd mask of aggression, 'nobody come on my part of the beach.'

It was just what was in Copping's report. The efficient Inspector had covered the ground admirably. Nits had told what he knew, and he didn't know anything: it just so happened that the corpse had been washed up on 'his' part of the beach.

'You were told not to talk to me,' said Gently wearily, 'who was it told you that?'

Nits grinned and chattered but made no intelligible reply.

'And why *did* you talk to me, after being warned not to?'

The halfwit frowned ferociously and turned his trouser-pockets inside-out. 'The other man – he took it away!'

'Took *what* away?'

'My knife – he took it!'

Gently smiled and felt for the little broken-bladed penknife. Nits gabbled with joy and snatched for it with the speed of a striking snake. But Gently had already experienced a sample of the halfwit's snatching and he held the knife carefully out of range.

'Who was it told you not to talk to me?' he demanded.

Nits chattered and tried another sudden grab.

'You get it when you tell me, not until.'

Nits made all sorts of fierce faces, but Gently merely made as if to return the knife to his own pocket.

'Jeff!' piped the halfwit suddenly, 'it was Jeff and Bonce – they told me.'

'And who are they?'

'I don't know – I don't know!'

'You know their names – you must know something else about them.'

'I just see them, that's all.'

'See them *where*?' persisted Gently, 'see them here – on the beach?'

But the halfwit relapsed into a mewing and gabbling, and refused to make himself any further intelligible. Gently sighed and tossed him the knife. It was plucked out of the air as though by the lash of a whip and Nits capered off, clutching it to his bosom, his two trouser-pockets still turned inside-out.

'Whoa – wait a minute!' called Gently, rising to his feet.

He produced a florin and held it out between thumb and finger. The halfwit paused in his flight, hesitated, and then came sidling back, spaniel-like, his chin tucked in until there seemed nothing of his face below the two bulging eyes. He didn't snatch at it, as Gently expected: he reached up and took the coin quietly from Gently's hand. Then he crept closer still, crouching, cringing almost, and stared up with his faceless eyes.

'The man who wouldn't wake up!' he piped, but in a sort of whisper.

Gently nodded silently.

'Different . . . different!'

'Different from . . . what?' murmured Gently.

'From when he was awake.'

'From when he was awake!'

Nits went into one of his fits of nodding.

'Hold it!' exclaimed Gently, feeling his universe beginning to rock, 'did you know him, Nits – did you know him when he was awake?'

'I knew him – I knew him!'

'But when did you know him – and where?'

Nits screwed his face up into an expression of rage and shook his head. Then he pointed to the tip of his almost non-existent chin.

'Hair!' he chattered, 'hair – when he was awake!'

The next moment he was capering over the beach again, leaving Gently with his eyebrows hoisted in almost comical surprise.

Twilight had become dusk and the lights which had sparkled like fugitive jewellery were now glowing and full. The blazing Front had a strange glamour about it, as though it belonged to a different world, and the holidaymakers too seemed to partake of the strangeness. Perhaps it was simply the multiplicity of lights destroying the shadows, perhaps only the sense of anonymity and freedom . . . they felt changed and in some way abnormal.

Gently picked his way through the promenade crowds and paused at the edge of the carriage-way. He felt changed also, though his changedness was due to something quite different. He'd got a lead, that was it. He'd found something to hang on to in this slippery orphan of a case.

Almost jauntily he crossed the carriage-way and directed his steps to a phone-box on the other side.

'Chief Inspector Gently . . . is Inspector Copping in, by any chance?'

The switchboard girl thought he might be if Gently would kindly hang on. Gently grunted and wedged himself into a supportable position in the corner of the box. Outside he could see the front of the amusement arcade from which blared much of the canned music which disturbed that part of the promenade – a striking blaze of light in the shape of three feathers, with a lurid red arrow snapping backwards and forwards as though working up to burst in through the door. And there was some jutting neonry which said LICENSED BAR . . . a ritzy sort of touch for an amusement arcade, thought Gently.

'Inspector Copping,' said the switchboard girl.

Gently jammed the door yet tighter-shut on the racket without. 'Gently here . . . I want something done,' he said. 'Look, Copping, can you get on to the pathologist who did the post-mortem? I want him to have another check.'

'Can't see what that's going to buy,' came Copping's voice plaintively, 'he didn't die of asthma.'

'I'm not interested in the way he died. I want a thorough examination of the skin of the face for spirit gum.'

'Spirit gum!'

'Or any other mucilage that may be present,' added Gently generously.

There was a pause at the other end, and then Copping came back: 'But what's he supposed to be now – a member of a touring company?'

Gently smiled at the leaping red arrow. 'Your guess is as good as mine . . .'

'And where did you dig up the idea, anyway?'

'Oh . . . it was a present for a good Central Office

man. And by the way, Copping, you wouldn't know anything of two characters called Jeff and Bonce, would you?'

'Not to my knowledge. Are they hooked up to this business?'

'Could be,' admitted Gently, 'it's an even chance . . .'

There was a noise like a snort at the other end. 'But how do you *do* it? I've been three days on this case!'

'Just luck, you know . . . you need it in homicide.'

'It looks like all the breaks were being saved up till you came. Are there any other small ways I can help?'

Gently brooded a moment. 'There's an amusement arcade down here . . . it's called "The Feathers" and it sports a licensed bar. What do you know about that?'

'Is that in the case too, or are you just being curious?'

'I've been tailing Nits . . . when he's finished collecting he makes for "The Feathers" like a homing pigeon.'

'Well, it's got a clean record. The proprietor is a man called Hooker – Louey Hooker. He lives in a flat at the back of the building, and he runs a bookie's business too. The office is under the flat and fronts on Botolph Street, which runs parallel with the Front.'

'A bookie's business.'

'That's right. They're still legal in this year of grace.'

Gently nodded at the undiscourageable arrow. 'Well . . . send me Dutt along, will you? And drag that pathologist away from whatever he's doing and put him to work.'

'You mean tonight?' inquired Copping in surprise.

'We're working, aren't we?' retorted Gently heartlessly.

He hung up and levered open the door of the phone-box. The year's hit-tune, mildly interruptive till then, leaped to meet him with a vengeful roar. Gently frowned and felt in his pocket for a peppermint cream. Mr Edison, he felt, hadn't been an unmixed blessing to mankind.

The interior of the amusement arcade was as aggressive as the exterior had promised. It was lit with a farrago of fluorescent tubes and popping bulbs, and the walls were panelled in a gooey pink plastic relieved by insets of 'teinte de boiled cabbage'. And there was a vigorous use of chromium plate in all departments. The décor man had obviously had a flair for it. Left and right of a central aisle the machines were deployed – all the latest attractions, space-flights, atom-bombing and the rest, with a few tried favourites still making a stand against the march of science. There was the crane that picked up a prize and dropped it down a shoot, Gently noticed . . . at least, it picked up a prize when Nits was operating it. The halfwit had apparently got the low-down.

Stationed behind a punchball machine, Gently watched the crouched, ragged figure insert coin after coin. Each time the descending grab would seize on one of the more substantial pieces of trash in the glass case. Sometimes it failed to grasp securely and nothing would rattle down the shoot except a few gaudy-coloured sweets, but always the grab dropped plumb on a prize in the first instance.

Gently lit his pipe and continued to watch. All round him machines were ringing and clattering. Any two of that crowd could be the two in question . . . at any moment they might spot Nits, or Nits them. And what then? he asked himself. Suppose he was lucky and stumbled on them? What they had said to Nits might have been no more than a joke, the sort of silly thing to be said to a halfwit. Of course it was odd that they had known him, Gently, on sight . . . but then, the picture in the evening paper might have jogged their memories. There had been bigger and better pictures of him in the same paper the year before.

No, he told himself, it wasn't much better than a hunch, after all . . .

The music changed to something plaintive and caressing, and as though it were a signal Nits crammed his collection of ballpoints and flash jewellery into his pockets and darted to the door. Gently moved forward also, but the halfwit came to a standstill short of the entrance, so he slid back again into the cover of the punch-ball machine. Was Nits expecting someone? It rather seemed like it. He stood by the door, apparently trembling, and strained his protruding eyes in the direction of the Wellesley Pier. Several people came in, but these were ignored. Nits didn't even glance at them as they pushed past. Then he gave a little whimper and a skip, like a dog sighting its master, and a moment later the object of his vigil appeared.

She was a blonde, a tall, big-bodied blonde. She didn't have to broadcast her vocation, either to Gently or the world. She wore a sleeveless green silk blouse, high-heels and a black hobble skirt, and walked with a flaunt that looked vaguely expensive.

'Geddart,' she said to Nits in the husky voice of sin, 'keep away from me, you dirty liddle so-and-so – how many more times must I tell you?'

288

'I've been a good boy!' piped Nits, frisking and cringing beside her as she hipped down the arcade.

'I don'd care – jusd keep away from me.'

'I got something – I got something! Look for you!' Nits pulled out his hoard of swag and tried to thrust it into the blonde's hands, but she snatched them away and the stuff tinkled on to the floor.

'I don't wand it!' she yelped, 'keep your dirdy muck to yourself! Don'd ever come near me again!' And she bustled away through the grinning crowd, leaving Nits to scrabble amongst the feet for his scattered treasure.

'That's my gal, Frenchy!' shouted someone, 'don't you have him if you don't fancy him!'

The blonde turned back and said something so filthy that even Gently was taken aback, then she swaggered through the swing-doors of the bar.

'Whoo-*whoo!*' was the cry, 'Frenchy's got the answer, don't you forget it!'

On the floor Nits chattered and sobbed with rage. 'I'll kill you – I'll kill you!' he babbled, 'I've been a good boy – I have – I have!'

Gently stooped and rescued a plastic ballpoint from under the heel of a bystander. 'Here,' he said, 'one you missed.'

Nits seized it and stuffed it into his pocket after the others. 'I'll kill you!' he whispered in an ecstasy of passion.

'Did she know him?' asked Gently, 'did she know the man who wouldn't wake up?'

Nits's green eyes burned at him like two malignant lamps and Gently, moving swiftly, moved only just in time. As it was the leaping halfwit sent his trilby flying.

Then, recovering himself, Nits dived for the door and his turn of speed was something that Gently could only have sighed for in his palmiest days . . .

CHAPTER THREE

T HE BAR WAS rather a contrast to the rest of the
establishment. It had got missed out when the
wielder of plastic and chromium-plate had gone his
merry way. It was quite a large place and its dim,
parchmented lighting made it seem larger still. It was
also irregular in shape. There were corners of it that
tucked away, and other corners which had been given
an inglenook treatment. Opposite the swing-doors ran
the bar counter, its supporting shelves well fledged
with opulent looking bottles, and to the left of the
counter was a door marked 'Private'. Further left again
was a small exit door, leading probably into a side-
street.

Gently eased himself through the swing-doors and
stood still for a moment, adjusting his vision to the drop
in candle-power. It seemed a fairly well-patronized
place. Most of the tables and nookeries were occupied,
and there were several customers perched on high stools
at the counter. Also it seemed quiet in there, but that
may have been due only to comparison with the racket
going on outside the swing-doors.

He strolled across to the counter, where the blonde was taking charge of a noggin of straight gin.

'Chalk id up, Artie,' she crooned, 'and no chiselling, mind.'

'Who shall I chalk it up to?' asked the ferrety bartender with a wink.

'Don'd be cheeky, Artie – Louey don'd like it!'

She slunk away from the counter, and her eye fell on Gently for the first time. She recognized him, he knew – there was just that much of alert interrogation in her glance – and for a moment he thought she would say something. Then she shrugged a scantily-clad shoulder, gave her head a little toss, and swung away across the room to one of the nookeries.

Gently seated himself on a high stool and ordered an orange-squash.

'Who is she, Artie?' he asked the ferrety bartender.

Artie gave the squash-bottle a practised twist. 'Don't ask me – ask her,' he retorted sullenly.

'But I am asking you. What's her name?'

'It's Frenchy – and I'm not her boyfriend.'

'Her other name, Artie.'

'I'm telling you I don't know!'

'She mentioned a Louey . . .'

'What's that got to do with me?'

'She spoke as though you knew him . . .'

'Well, I don't. He must be someone new.'

Gently drank a mouthful of orange-squash and appeared to be losing himself in contemplation of the fruit-scum collected at the mouth of his glass.

'That'll be a bob,' said Artie, '*if* you don't mind.'

Gently drank some more and was still interested in

the fruit-scum. 'You know, it's amazing,' he said casually, 'the number of people round here who know me without me knowing them . . . you seem to be the fifth, Artie, by my computation.'

The ferrety one stiffened. 'Don't know what you mean by that . . .'

'Never mind, never mind,' said Gently soothingly, 'we'll go into it some other time, shall we?' He slid off his stool and picked up the part-drunk glass of orange-squash.

'Hey!' clamoured Artie, 'that's still got to be paid for . . .!'

'Chalk it up,' returned Gently, 'and no chiselling, mind. Louey don'd like it . . .'

He ambled over to a small table by the wall and pulled up a seat with better padding than the high stool. There were other eyes on him besides Artie's; several customers at the counter had heard the conversation, and now turned to watch the bulky figure cramming itself into its chair. Not only at the counter either . . . out of the corner of his eye Gently could see Frenchy in her nookery, and two other figures near her. They were all giving him their attention . . .

''Ere!' whispered a sporty-looking individual to Artie, 'is that geezer a busy?'

'Yard,' clipped Artie from the corner of his mouth.

The sporty-looking type favoured Gently with a bloodshot leer. 'Nice bleedin' company we get here these days . . .'

Gently quaffed on imperturbably. He might have been entirely alone in the bar, so oblivious did he seem. He took out his pipe and emptied it with care into the ashtray; then he took out his tobacco and stuffed the bowl with equal care.

''E's set in for the night,' said the sporty-looking individual, 'blimey, you'll have to look sharp with them shutters at closing-time . . .'

'Why don't you offer him a light?' quipped his neighbour.

'What, *me* – and him a busy? Give us another nip, Artie . . . there's a smell round here I don't like . . .'

Gently, however, lit his own pipe, and having lit it he entertained his audience with a scintillating display of smoke-rings. He could blow them single, double and treble, with combinations and variations. He had infinite patience, too. If one of his airy designs went wrong he had all the time in the world to try it out again . . .

The private door beside the bar opened and a man in seedy evening-dress appeared. He was a heavily built type of about forty with dark hair, a parrot-shaped face, and little pale eyes set very close together, and he smoked a cigarette in a gold-plated holder about as long as his arm. Gently surveyed him with mild interest through a pyramid of smoke. Faces of that shape must at all times be rarities, he thought.

'Oi – Peachey!' yipped the sporty-looking individual, and made a cautionary face while he thumbed over his shoulder in Gently's direction. Artie also hastened to breathe a word in the newcomer's ear. The man's two pale eyes reached Gently, paused and strayed uneasily away again. Gently's own slipped round to Frenchy. She was sitting up straight and shaking her peroxide head.

'Louey wants a fresh bottle,' said the newcomer hoarsely, 'gimme a white-label.'

Artie produced one from under the counter and handed it to him. He dived clumsily back through the door. Artie returned to his business of serving drinks without a further glance at Gently; there was an expression of satisfied malice on his face . . .

'You loog lonely for a big man,' said a voice at Gently's elbow, and he turned his head to see that Frenchy had slunk over to his table. She was smiling, at least with her mouth. Higher up it didn't show so much – by the time one got to her rather pretty warm-brown eyes it had gone completely. But she was smiling with her mouth.

Gently smiled too, somewhere between the South Lightship and Scurby Sands.

'I'm not lonely,' he said, 'there's too many people around who know me.'

Frenchy laughed, a throaty little gurgle. 'Thad's because the big man is famous . . . he geds his picture in the paper.'

'You think that makes people notice? Such a bad picture?'

'But of course . . . nobody talks about anything else except whad the police are doing.'

She pulled up another chair and sat down, not opposite Gently but to the side, where the table didn't hide anything. She slid forward and crossed her legs. They weren't terribly attractive, he noticed. The skin was a trifle coarse and the contours inclined to be knobbly – they were designed for strength rather than quality. But she managed them well, they were crossed with great competence. And the hobble skirt contrived to lose itself somewhere above the knee.

'Id musd be exciding,' she crooned, 'hunding down a murderer . . .'

Gently breathed an unambitious little smoke-ring.

'And difficuld too . . . especially one like this.'

Gently breathed two more, one exactly inside the other.

'I mean,' she continued, 'where does one begin to loog if one doesn'd know his name . . .?'

'What's *your* name?' inquired Gently suddenly; 'all they call you round here is Frenchy.'

The brown eyes opened wide and the smile tailed off: but it was back again in a moment, and wider than ever.

'Surely you don'd suspecd me, Inspecdor . . .'

'I'm just asking your name.'

'Bud why should you wand to know thad . . .?'

'I'm curious, like all policemen.'

Frenchy seemed to consider the matter between half-closed lids. Gently stared at the table and smoked a few more puffs.

'If you wand to ask questions . . .' she began.

Gently favoured her with a glance.

'There are bedder places than this to ask them . . .'

She leaned forward over the table and balanced her chin in the palm of her hand. In effect the green silk blouse became an open peep-show.

'Afder all, it's your dudy,' she melted, 'and you know when girls dalk the besd . . .'

Gently sighed and felt in his pocket for a match. 'You're not local,' he said, 'you've had West End training . . . who brought you down here?'

For a moment he thought her scarlet nails were going to leap at his face. They angled for a strike, and the brown eyes burned with the merciless ferocity of a cat's. Then the fingers relaxed and the eyes narrowed.

'You filthy b— cop!' she hissed, all accent spent, 'I wouldn't let you touch me if you were the last bloody screw on God's earth, and that's the stinking truth!'

Gently shrugged and struck himself a fresh light. 'Where do you live?' he asked.

'Bloody well find out!'

'Tut, tut, my dear . . . it would save unnecessary police-work if you told me.'

'Well I'm not going to . . .!'

Gently held up a restraining hand. 'It doesn't really matter . . . now about our friend with the beard.'

She stopped in mid-flow, though whether on account of his casual remark or not Gently wasn't able to decide.

'Where did you meet him – here or in London?'

'Who?' she demanded sullenly.

'The deceased – the man who was stabbed.'

'Me!' she burst out, 'what have I got to do with it?'

'I don't know,' murmured Gently, 'I thought perhaps that was what you came across to tell me . . .'

Frenchy riposted with a stream of adjectives that fairly blistered the woodwork.

'Still, you might like to tell me about your movements on Tuesday night . . .' added Gently thoughtfully.

There was a pause, pregnant but not silent – silence was a strictly comparative term when only a pair of swing-doors separated them from the uproar without –

and Gently occupied it usefully by prodding around in his pipe, which wasn't on its best behaviour. Over at the counter, he noticed, they were straining their ears to catch a word of what was taking place. And in Frenchy's nook two figures in the shadows leaned intently in his direction . . .

'You can't drag me into this, and you bloody well know it!' seethed Frenchy, with the aid of two other words. 'I never knew him – I didn't do nothing – I don't know nothing!'

Gently tapped his refractory pipe in the ashtray and drew on it tentatively.

'It's true!' she spat, 'why do you pick on me – who's been lying about me?'

'Who *might* lie about you?' inquired Gently absently.

'How should I know? – anyone! A girl's got enemies. And I've got a right to know, haven't I? If someone's been making accusations—!'

'Nobody has accused anybody . . . yet.'

'Then what's it all about?'

Gently shrugged and forked about in his pipe again. 'If you're so far in the clear you shouldn't be afraid to tell me what you were doing on Tuesday night . . .'

'It's got nothing to do with it – I can't tell you plainer than that, can I?'

'Of course, if it's something you'd rather not officially acknowledge . . .'

Again the scarlet nails flexed and a flicker went over the brown eyes. But once more Frenchy controlled herself.

'I haven't got to tell you, flattie . . . you've got nothing on me!'

Gently nodded and turned out the fragments from his pipe. 'Between nine, say . . . and midnight . . .'

'All right, you bleeding copper!' Frenchy jumped to her feet and raised her voice to a scream. 'So he wants to know . . . he wants to know what I was doing on Tuesday night when someone was doing-in the bloke they found on the beach . . . I'm a naughty girl, and of course he picks on me!'

'That's right!' bawled the sporty-looking individual, sliding off his stool, 'you tell him, Frenchy, you tell him where to get off!'

'He doesn't know anything . . . he's just picking on me . . . maybe he's after something else too, the dirty so-and-so!'

'He wouldn't be the first, either!'

'And now he's looking for a chance to run me in . . . that's what it is . . .'

'Shame!' welled up from all over the bar.

'He comes from tarn just to pinch our Frenchy!' yapped the sporty-looking individual.

'They're a dirty lot . . . there isn't a man I'd call one amongst them . . . they're sent down here to find a murderer and all they can do is make trouble for girls like me.'

'It's all they're good for, chasing-up women!'

Gently looked up mildly from the refilling of his pipe. 'We don't seem to be getting very far with what you were doing on Tuesday night . . .' he murmured.

Frenchy rocked on her heels, fuming at him. 'I'll *tell* you!' she screamed. 'I'll tell everybody, and they can bear me out. I was right here, that's where I was. I didn't shift an inch from this bar, and God help me!'

'It's the truth!' barked the sporty-looking individual, coming up, 'we saw her here, didn't we, boys?'

There was a unanimous chorus of assent.

'And after half past ten?' proceeded Gently.

'I was outside playing with the machines.'

'And after that?'

'Christ, can't a girl have any private life these days?'

'What was his name?' asked Gently amid laughter and jeering.

'Jeff!' shouted Frenchy, 'come and shake hands with a chief inspector.'

Gently glanced sharply at Frenchy's nook, where one of the two shadowy figures was getting reluctantly to his feet. He was a tall, well-made youth of sixteen or seventeen, not unhandsome of feature but with a weak, wide, thin-lipped mouth. He wore a Teddy boy ensemble of all one colour – plum red. It began with his bow tie and collar, descended through a straight-cut narrow-sleeved jacket and reached the ground via drain-pipe trousers and spats – a red of the ripest and fruitiest.

Gently eyed this vision curiously. It hovered uncertainly at some little distance.

'It was him?' inquired Gently, a shade of incredulity in his tone.

'Of course it was bloody well him . . . they all have to make a start, don't they?'

Gently beckoned to Jeff. 'Don't be frightened,' he said, 'it wasn't indictable . . .'

The Teddy boy came forward, flushing.

'Can you confirm what this woman says about Tuesday night?'

'I suppose so.'

'Would you care to describe it . . . I mean, the relevant parts?'

'There isn't anything to describe!' scowled Frenchy, 'he met me in the bar, that's all.'

Gently glanced at Jeff interrogatively.

'That's right . . . in the bar,' he said.

'And then?'

'And then we went to her . . . place.'

'Where is that?'

'It's a flat in Dulford Street.'

'And you spent the night?'

'I . . . actually . . . you see . . .'

'Of course he didn't!' Frenchy broke in, 'did you think I wanted his old man on my barrow? I turned him out at half past twelve . . . he'd done enough by then, anyway!'

There was a roar of laughter.

'And who is his old man?' inquired Gently smoothly.

'He's Wylie of Wylie-Marine.'

'You mean that big factory on the quays near the station . . .?'

'That's right, copper,' Frenchy sneered, 'you're good, aren't you?'

Gently drew a few slow puffs from his newly-filled pipe. Most of the occupants of the bar seemed to have drawn closer to a centre of such absorbing interest. But the second figure in Frenchy's nook wasn't joining in the general enthusiasm. On the contrary, he had shrunk back almost out of sight.

'And Bonce?' inquired Gently, inclining his head towards the nook.

'Bonce?' queried the Teddy boy. He had stuck his hands in his jacket pockets and seemed to be screwing himself up to an air of toughness.

'If you're Jeff, I take it that your shy friend is Bonce. What was he doing while you were getting off with Frenchy here?'

'Bonce!' shouted Frenchy, 'stop hiding yourself . . . the big noise is on to you too.'

All eyes turned towards the nook, where there was an uneasy stirring. Then there ventured forth a second version of the plum ensemble, shorter, clumsier and even more youthful looking than its predecessor. Bonce was no beauty. He had carroty hair, round cheeks, a snub nose and an inherent awkwardness. But he was sartorially correct. His outfit matched Jeff's down to the tie of the shoes.

'And what's *your* name when you're at home?' queried Gently.

Bonce licked his lips and stared agonizedly. 'B-Baines, sir,' he brought out, 'Robert B-Baines.' He spoke with a Starmouth accent.

'And where do you live?'

'S-seventeen Kittle Witches Grid, sir.'

'Well, Baines, you've heard the account of Tuesday night your friend has given . . . I take it that you can endorse it?'

'Oh yes, sir!'

'You came here with him, in fact?'

'Yes, sir!'

'And you were with him until he departed with this woman here?'

'Yes, sir!'

'All the time?'

'Yes, sir!'

'Even when he was ingratiating himself with her?'

Bonce stared at him round-eyed.

'When he was getting off, I mean?'

'Oh yes, sir! . . . I mean . . . no, sir . . .'

'Well . . . which is it to be?'

'I . . . I . . .!' stuttered Bonce, completely floored.

'And when they had gone,' pursued Gently affably, 'what did you do then . . . when you were left on your own?'

'Don't you tell him!' screamed Frenchy before Bonce could flounder into a reply, 'it's all a have – you don't need to tell him nothing.'

'No, we haven't done anything,' blurted Jeff, trying to swagger, 'you keep quiet, Bonce.'

'He just comes in here trying to stir something up, trying to get people to say something he can pinch them for . . . that's how they work, the bleedin' Yard! I—!'

'CLOSING TIME!!!' roared a stentorian voice, a voice which drowned Frenchy, drowned the jazz and rattled empty glasses on some of the tables.

Every head spun round as though jerked by a string. It was as though a bomb had exploded over by the counter.

'FINISH YOUR DRINKS!!!' continued the voice, 'IT'S HALF PAST TEN!!!'

Gently peered round Frenchy's shapely form, which was hiding the owner of the voice from his view.

'DRINK UP, LADIES AND GENTS. YOU WOULDN'T WANT ME TO LOSE MY LICENCE!!!'

He was an enormous man, not so much in height,

303

though he topped six feet, but enormous in sheer, Herculean bulk. His head was bald and seemed to rise to a point. His features were coarse and heavy, but powerful. There was a fleck in the pupil of one of his grey eyes and he had, clearly visible because of the sag of his lip, a gold tooth of proportions to match the rest of his person.

'BREAK IT UP NOW, LADIES AND GENTS. YOU CAN STILL AMUSE YOURSELVES WITH THE MACHINES!!!'

About fifty, thought Gently, and still in good fighting trim.

The owner of the voice moved ponderously across to Gently's table. He glowered at Frenchy and nodded towards the door.

'Get out!' he rumbled, 'you know I don't encourage your sort.'

Frenchy glared back defiantly for a moment, but she waggled off all the same; her parting shot was at Gently, not the gold-toothed one. It was unprintable.

'GET OUT!!!' detonated the big man, and Frenchy got.

His next target was Bonce.

'*How* old do you say you are?'

'Eight-eighteen!' burbled Bonce.

'When was that – next Easter? Don't let me find you in this bar again.'

'B-But Louey, you never said anything before!'

'GET OUT!!!'

Bonce faded like a cock-crowed ghost.

Louey sighed draughtily. He picked up Gently's empty orange-squash glass and gave it his sad attention. Gently looked also. The hands that held the glass were like two hairy grappling-irons. On one of his crooked fingers Louey wore an out-size solitaire, on another a plain gold ring engraved with a bisected circle.

''Night, Louey,' leered the sporty-looking individual, passing by on his way to the door, 'watch your company – it ain't so healthy as it might be!'

Louey rumbled ominously and set down the glass again. 'Can't help it,' he said, turning apologetically to Gently, 'this time of the year you're bound to get some riff-raff . . . the best you can do is to keep kicking it out.'

Gently nodded sympathetically. He found Louey's gold tooth fascinating.

'There's girls like Frenchy . . . we know some of them, but there's fresh ones come up every summer. If they don't solicit you can't make too much of a fuss.'

Louey permitted himself a searching glance at Gently.

'And those kids . . . I suppose it's asking for trouble to have an arcade next to a bar.'

Gently rose to his feet and felt in his pocket for a coin.

'Here,' he said, 'I haven't paid for my drink.'

'Oh, never mind that!' Louey laughed comfortably, easily, as though he felt Gently to be an equal. 'Only too pleased to see you in here, Inspector . . . sorry if anything happened that shouldn't have done . . .'

'You needn't worry about that – it was nothing to do with you.' Gently paused and looked into Louey's deep-set eyes. They wore a deferential smile, but because of the fleck breaking into one of them the smile had a strangely hard quality, almost a sinisterness.

'There's only one thing bothers me,' mused Gently, picking up his shilling and re-pocketing it.

'And what is that, Inspector?'

'The way everyone around here knows me on sight . . . you, Mr Hooker, amongst the others.'

There was a rowdiness now along the promenade. There were drunks and near-drunks, quarrelsome and loutish roisterers. Alcohol had been added to the heady mixture of humanity about its annual purgation . . . the beer had begun to sing, and the whisky to argue. And they were largely youngsters, Gently noticed, it was the teenagers who did the shouting and singing. Banded together in threes and fours they swaggered about the Front, stupid with Dutch courage: lords of a pint, princelings of Red Biddy. Did nobody spank their children these days?

A burly figure shouldered across the carriage-way and joined him on the pavement.

'Have any luck, Dutt?' inquired Gently with interest.

'Yes, sir, I did, as a matter of fact.'

'Well, go on . . . don't spoil a good story.'

'I stood where you told me, sir, and kept an eye on the bookie's joint at the back. There wasn't no lights on there, but about quarter of an hour after you went in again the door opens and out hops a bloke in a dark suit.'

'Oh, he did, did he? I suppose he wasn't a freakish-looking cove with a parroty face?'

'No, sir, not this one. I got a good look at him under a street-lamp. He was about middling-size, dark hair, sort of slanty-eyed, and he'd got a long, straight conk. And there was a scar of some sort on his right cheek – knife or razor, I should say, sir.'

'Hmm,' mused Gently, 'interesting. And did you tail him?'

'Yes, sir — at least, I stuck to him all along the prom going south. But then he goes into the funfair and there was such a ruddy crowd there I didn't stand a chance. So after a bit I gives it up.'

'Ah well . . . we do our best,' sighed Gently.

'Do you think there's a hook-up there, sir — have we got something definite?'

Gently shook his head sombrely. 'I don't know, Dutt, and that's the truth. There's some racket goes on there, I'm pretty sure, but whether it connects with ours is beyond me for the moment. Anyway, I threw a scare into them . . . I'll tip off Copping to keep an eye lifting.'

'The bloke I was tailing looked a right sort,' said Dutt sagely.

'There's a lot of right sorts in there, Dutt,' agreed his senior, 'they'd keep the average policeman happy for weeks.'

CHAPTER FOUR

GENTLY WAS DREAMING what seemed to be a circular dream. It began at the stab wounds in the man who wouldn't wake up, took in all the principal characters at 'The Feathers' and wound up again with that stabbed torso. And it continued like that for round after round. Or was it all going on simultaneously? His dream-self found time to wonder this. There seemed to be two of him in the dream: he was both actor and producer. First (if there was a first), came the chest of the corpse, caught in a sort of golden glow, and he noticed with surprise that, although the stab-wounds were present, the pathologist's carvings were not. Next, his dream-camera lifted to take in Jeff, or rather the top part of Jeff: the rest of him dissolved into the haze which surrounded the corpse. He was shrugging his shoulders and saying something. Gently didn't know what it was he was saying, but he was acutely aware of the implication. Jeff *wasn't* responsible. He might have done it, of course, that was beside the point. But he wasn't responsible. You couldn't possibly blame him.

As though to make it more emphatic the camera shifted to Bonce, who was blubbing and stuttering his innocence in the background. They couldn't help it. Gently fully agreed. They had done it at the behest of some irrevocable Fate, which was curious but in no way blameable. It was just how things were . . . And then Bonce shrank and his blubbing mouth disappeared. He had become Nits, and Nits had become nothing but two protruding green eyes, painfully straining. Gently knew what *he* was saying. The halfwit's words piped clearly in his brain. 'I've been *a good* boy,' they echoed, 'I've been *a good* boy,' and Gently tried to ruffle his hair good-naturedly, but the head sank away under his hand . . .

Then it was Frenchy's rather knobbly knees trying hard to make themselves look attractive: the camera wouldn't lift to her face, it just kept focussed on those unfortunate knees. We aren't bad, they seemed to be pleading (and Gently heard a twang of Frenchy's croon, though there weren't any words): you'll see a lot worse than us on the beach. Of course, you've got to make allowances, but it's the same with everyone . . . honestly now, we aren't bad at all . . . you must admit it. And Gently admitted it. What was the use of struggling? He'd been round before and knew the rules of the game . . .

So the camera faded across to the parrot-faced man and Artie. They'd got a lot of empty bottles, squash-bottles, and Gently only had to see the bottles to know that he was the one who had emptied them. Not that they were being nasty about it, those two. On the contrary, they seemed to be almost sympathetic, in a sad sort of way. Gently had blotted his copy-book. He'd drunk through all those bottles of squash without paying for them. They knew he couldn't help it, but all the same . . . a man of his reputation . . . Gently felt in his pocket for some money. They shook their heads. It wasn't just paying for it that counted. It was the fact that he'd *done* it at all . . .

And now Louey's gold tooth filled all the screen, a huge, glowing tooth with (and it seemed so natural that Gently realized he was expecting it) a glittering solitaire diamond set in the top and a bisected circle engraved underneath it. It doesn't matter, the tooth was saying, the inspector can do what he likes, he's always welcome. It's not the same with the inspector, he's an old friend of mine. Yes, he can do what he likes . . . he can do what he likes . . . it's not the same with the inspector . . . And then the glowing tooth became the glowing chest of the corpse again, and the dream was off anew. Or was it, after all? Wasn't it really simultaneous, flashing on and off like the arrow outside the arcade . . .?

Either way, the dreaming Gently perceived at last a change coming o'er the spirit of his dream. There was a word that kept getting interjected into the mechanism, and for some reason or none he didn't want to hear that word, he kept struggling not to hear it. But he did hear it. It persisted. It paid no attention either to himself or his characters, who were showing similar disapproval.

'Raouls! Otraouls!'

It was making Frenchy's knees jiffle and the empty bottles fall off the counter.

'Raouls! Raouls!'

Gently held Frenchy's knees still with one hand and tried to pick up bottles with the other, but he didn't seem to be getting anywhere.

'Raouls! Otraouls! Raouls!'

He made a final effort to shore-up his collapsing world, to ward off that frightful trump of doom. It was no use. Frenchy kicked the bottles from under his arm. There was a crash of glass which he knew to be the descent of every bottle in the bar and he was dragged back out of the dark or red-lit tunnel in the nick of time . . .

'Raouls! Otraouls!'

Gently snorted and rubbed his eyes. There really *was* a sound like that. It was coming through his bedroom window, and getting louder every minute. He jumped out of bed and went to have a look. And then he remembered . . . over how many years? It was the boy with the hot rolls, that wandering voice of the morning . . . his very accent had been handed down intact.

Gently hammered on the communicating door. 'Dutt! Aren't you up?'

'Yessir. Been hup half an hour.'

'Half an hour!' Gently glanced at the watch propped up on his dressing-table. 'You're late, Dutt. You should have been up before.'

'Yessir.'

'We aren't on holiday, Dutt, when we're out in the country.'

'No, sir.'

'Discipline,' said Gently, shoving his feet into his bedroom slippers, 'that's the key to success, Dutt. Discipline and luck, but mostly discipline. Is Mrs Davis providing hot rolls for breakfast?'

'Well, sir, I really don't know . . .'

'Then find out, Dutt, find out, and if she isn't go down and buy half a dozen off that expert out there.'

Twenty minutes later a shining morning Gently put in his appearance at the breakfast table. The papers he had ordered lay fragrant on his plate and he turned them over as he stowed butter into his first roll. The case was still making front-page in the local. They had found a bigger and better photograph, one of which Gently was just a little proud. And they were up-to-date on his visit to the mortuary, and especially up-to-date on his calling out of the pathologist.

PATHOLOGIST RECALLED IN BODY-ON-THE-BEACH CASE, ran the local. GENTLY MOVES – PATHOLOGIST RECALLED – SENSATIONAL MIDNIGHT DEVELOPMENT, ran a London paper.

Gently shoved them across to Dutt. 'Nice press,' he said laconically.

'We'll have 'em round our necks today,' grumbled the sergeant.

Gently clipped the top off a boiled egg and took another bite from his roll. 'They make it seem so exciting,' he mumbled, 'as though we were shifting heaven and earth. I wonder what people would think if they knew how simple it all was?'

They were still finishing breakfast when Inspector Copping was ushered in. He bore an envelope in his hand and an almost reverential expression on his face.

'You were right!' he exclaimed, 'my God – and how! There wasn't only traces of gum on the face, there was crêpe hair too, and quite a bit of it considering. The super's blown up the pathy for not finding it the first time and the pathy's as sniffy as hell.'

'Wasn't his fault,' grunted Gently stickily, 'his job is finding out how they died . . .'

He wiped his hands on his serviette and thumbed open Copping's envelope. It contained the pathologist's report. He glanced over it.

'Must have been a full beard,' he mused, 'I'm glad he found some of the hair . . . it might have been a different colour.'

'You were even right about it not being spirit gum. He's going to do a thorough analysis when he's had some shut-eye.'

Gently shrugged. 'Don't wake him up specially. Have you got any artists down at headquarters?'

'Artists?' Copping stared.

'Somebody who can put a beard on some photographs.'

'Oh – *that!* Our camera bloke can do it for you.'

'Then I'll want some copies of the Missing Persons' list and anybody you can spare to help Dutt go the rounds.'

'I'll have them laid on. But' – Copping looked doubtfully at the marmalade Gently was lavishing on his toast – 'what makes you so positive he came from the town?'

'I'm not,' grunted Gently, poising the piece of toast, 'it just seems to fit the picture, that's all.'

'What picture?' queried Copping.

'Mine,' retorted Gently, and he bit largely and well into the marmalady toast.

★   ★   ★

The super seemed a little off-hand that morning. He didn't seem as pleased as he ought to be with the progress being made. He congratulated Gently briefly on his discovery of the beard and asked some terse questions about what he proposed to do. Gently told him.

'You can have a couple of men,' said the super.

'There's something else . . . I mentioned it to Copping.'

'If it means more men, Gently, I'm afraid I can't spare them just now.'

'No hurry,' murmured Gently, 'I daresay it will keep. But it might be worth keeping an eye on the amusement arcade called "The Feathers".'

The super frowned. 'Well?' he snapped.

'I don't know quite what . . . vice, perhaps, for a start.'

'In that case it will have to wait. Vice is too common during the season in towns like this.'

'Could be something else . . . I thought it was worthwhile mentioning it.'

'I'll make a note of it, Gently. Is there anything else you want?'

'Not just at the moment.'

'Then I won't take up any more of your time.'

Outside the super's office Gently shook his head. 'Of course,' he said to Copping, 'I don't expect gratitude . . .'

'Oh, don't let the Old Man worry you,' returned Copping. 'He's got something else on his plate now, as well as homicide.'

'It must be fascinating, whatever it is.'

'It's forgery – a faked hundred-dollar bill. The super's

panicking in case he has to run to the Central Office again. He's trying like mad to trace it to some American Forces personnel.'

Gently clicked his tongue. 'Why should American Forces personnel forge hundred-dollar bills to work off in Starmouth?'

'Search me – but if the super can get back to one of them he's in the clear.'

'Of course, I appreciate his point.'

Copping led the way to the photographer's shop, where Sergeant Dutt was watching the technician apply the final beard to half a dozen postcard prints. He had made two sets, profile and full-face, and the difference between the face bearded and the face unbearded was certainly striking.

Copping whistled when he saw them. 'No wonder we drew a blank the first time round . . . why do you think he dolled himself up that way?'

Gently shrugged. 'The usual reason – he didn't want somebody to recognize him.'

'But that's fantastic when you come to think of it. Nobody does that sort of thing outside spy thrillers.'

'Could be a spy thriller we're working on,' suggested Gently, dead-panned.

'Could be,' agreed Copping seriously.

It was a Saturday, a day of coming and going. As Gently plodded down Duke Street, which led from the dock side of the town to the Front, he was obliged to thread his way through a stream of parties and individuals lugging bags and suitcases, all of them in a hurry, all of them going one way. He surveyed them lugubriously.

They were all good potential witnesses – any one of them might hold the clue he wanted, the unsuspected information. And now they were departing in their hundreds and thousands. They were splitting up and scattering to the four quarters of the Midlands.

On the Front it was the same. The beach had a patchy and unsettled look. Up and down the promenade chased laden cars, taxis and coaches, while the touts stood about in disconsolate groups, their function in abeyance. Everything had stopped. For a few hours the Pleasure Machine stood still. There were those who stayed on, but nobody paid them much attention: they were only there on sufferance, it seemed, until a new lot arrived and the machine began to turn again.

Gently crossed over by the Albion Pier and leaned on the balustrade overlooking the beach. In his breast pocket he could feel the stiff pasteboard of the two doctored photographs, and in the distance he could see the post set up by the Borough Police. If Nits knew him when he was alive, thought Gently, it was at least an even chance he met him here, on the Front . . . and if he met him on the Front it was ten to one he met him on this stretch, between the two piers. Because that was where 'his' part was, and beachcombers were jealous of their territories.

What next . . . where was the best prospect after that?

Did he drink, this false-bearded fugitive? Did he play bowls, or tennis, or eat a sandwich at one of the tea-shacks that prospered along the golden mile? Or buy himself a straw hat or sunglasses? Or an ice-cream?

Sunglasses, mused Gently, rummaging in his pocket for a peppermint cream – he'd want some sunglasses if he were playing hard-to-find. At least, he would if he hadn't bought them earlier, about the same time as he was buying crepe hair and adhesives. But it was no use making difficulties. There was a beach-gear stall only a dozen yards away. Gently swallowed the peppermint cream and presented himself at the counter.

'Police,' he said tonelessly, 'can you remember having seen this man during the last week or ten days?'

By lunchtime he'd got the usual mixed bag of possibles and improbables. There were people who thought they had, and those who weren't quite sure: there were numbers who were determined to recognize nothing shown them by a policeman. One gentleman, indeed, was completely positive. The deceased had been to his stall two days running – he'd bought some sun-tan lotion and a pair of frog-man flippers. 'When was that?' asked Gently eagerly. 'Yesterday and the day before,' responded the helpful one . . .

It was a dispiriting business. He'd been through it before many a time, and with similar results. But here and today it seemed particularly dejecting, as though the whole prospects of the case were tied up with his good or ill success that morning . . .

They weren't, of course. He was only probing a little of the surface. Elsewhere Dutt and his colleagues were at work on the lines of strongest probability. He glanced at his wristwatch and made for a phone-box. By now they ought to have made some progress.

He dialled, and got the switchboard girl.

'Chief Inspector Gently. Give me the desk.'

She gave him the desk and the duty sergeant answered slickly.

317

'Gently here . . . has Sergeant Dutt reported back yet?'

There was a buzz and a faraway question and answer.

'No, sir,' returned the duty sergeant, 'Bryce and Williams have come in – they're in the canteen having their lunch. I don't think they had much luck, sir. Shall I get them to speak to you?'

'No . . . don't bother them.' Gently made a rapid survey of the terrain without. 'When Dutt comes in get him to phone me at the Beachside Cafe . . . you got that?'

'The Beachside Cafe . . . what is the number, sir?'

'Find out,' retorted Gently peevishly, 'I'm a policeman, not the local directory.'

He hung up frowning and shouldered his way out of the box. So Bryce and Williams had drawn a blank also. Like himself. Like Dutt, probably. And there couldn't be so many chances left on that list . . .

He directed his steps to the Beachside Cafe. It was one of the smaller of the cafes on that part of the Front, a green-painted wooden structure with a sort of veranda that faced the sea. Gently sat himself at one of the veranda tables and ordered a *table d'hôte* lunch. Three out of the four of them had drawn a blank . . . three out of four. Was it going to fold up on him, that little streak of luck – his 'dramatic midnight move', as the paper called it? But he'd been right . . . the man *had* been wearing a false beard. And Nits had known about it, so the man must have been in Starmouth . . .

'Your soup, sir,' said the waiter at his elbow. Gently grunted and made room for the plate.

'Excuse me, sir, but aren't you Chief Inspector

Gently?' faltered the waiter, hovering at a respectful distance.

Gently eyed him without enthusiasm. 'I might be,' he said.

'I recognized you from your picture in the paper, sir.'

'You're good at it,' said Gently, 'my mother wouldn't have done.'

'Naturally we're interested, sir, it all happening so close . . .'

Gently sighed and gave the waiter the benefit of a prolonged stare. 'You wouldn't like to be helpful, I suppose?' he asked.

'Of course, sir . . .' The waiter sounded as though he were conscious of being about to buy something.

'Really helpful?'

'If there's anything I can do . . .'

Gently produced his two doctored prints and shoved them under the waiter's nose. 'What did he have for lunch last time he was here, or don't you remember?'

The waiter gulped like a guilty schoolboy. 'Dover sole and chips, sir, and fruit salad to follow.'

'He had *what*—!'

'Dover sole and chips, sir. I remember because it was on the Tuesday, which is the only day we have it.'

There was a razor-edged pause while Gently clutched at his chair to prevent it revolving quite so fast. The waiter flinched and edged back a pace.

'Now let's be calm about this,' said Gently sternly, 'it was Dover sole *and* chips – not just Dover sole?'

'No, sir . . . it was always chips. He was very fond of them.'

319

'You mean he'd been here *before*?'

'Of course, sir. He came here regular.'

'*Regular!* How long does it take someone to become a regular?'

The waiter looked worried. 'I think it was Thursday last week . . . might have been Wednesday. Anyway, he came every day after that, including Sunday . . . he sat at this table, sir. I thought perhaps you knew him.'

Gently laughed with a certain amount of hollowness. 'I do,' he said, 'in a manner of speaking. But I've still a lot to learn. What's your name?'

'Withers, sir.'

'Well, take that other chair, Withers.'

'Y–yes, sir.'

'Don't be nervous – I'll square you with your boss. And you can fetch in the roast beef when I'm ready for it – even Central Office men have to eat.'

'Yes, sir. Of course, sir!'

Withers pulled out the chair and lowered himself dubiously on to the edge of it. He had the unhappy air of someone who had bitten off more than he could chew. Gently crumbled some roll into his Brown Windsor and tested a mouthful. It seemed up to a fairish standard in provincial Brown Windsors.

'So he came here first on Thursday, Withers. Or it might have been Wednesday.'

'That's right, sir.'

'You haven't any preference.'

'N–no, sir . . . I just don't remember.'

Gently nodded intelligently and tried another spoonful of soup. 'Did he have any name that chanced to leak out?'

'He said to call him Max, sir.'

'Max, eh?' Gently rolled the word round his tongue. Now he'd even got a name for the fellow! 'Max anything or just Max?' he asked hopefully.

'Just Max, sir.'

Gently sighed. 'I felt it had to be. He had an accent, though, this Max?'

'Oh yes, sir.'

'What sort of an accent . . . did you recognize it?'

The waiter stirred tormentedly. 'Foreign, I'd say, sir.'

'Was it French, for instance?'

'Yes, sir, it might have been.'

'Or German?'

'No, I don't think so, sir.'

'Russian, maybe?'

'I wouldn't like to say it wasn't, sir.'

'You couldn't imitate something he said?'

The waiter shook his head and sent a haunted look towards the rear of the cafe. Gently shook his head also and reapplied himself to his soup. But why should he complain, he asked himself, why look such a regal gift-horse in the mouth? Ten minutes ago he had begun to despair and now he actually knew the dead man's name . . .!

'Describe it,' he said, 'describe Max coming in here and having lunch.'

'H-how do you mean, sir?' faltered the waiter.

'Tell me, man! Tell it as though he were just coming in at the door.'

The waiter twisted his hands together agonizedly and cleared his throat. 'H-he'd come in . . .' he began, 'he'd stand for a moment looking about . . . as though he expected to see somebody he knew . . .'

'Did he ever see that somebody?'

'No, I d–don't think so, sir.'

'What was he wearing?'

'He'd got a light grey suit, sir. On Sunday he wore a darker one, but the other days it was the light grey. And he had a blue bow tie.'

'Go on.'

'He carried an attaché case, sir, he had it with him every day except the last day . . . then there was his beard, that struck me as being funny . . . and the way he spoke . . .'

'What did he say?'

'When he first came in he asked me my name, sir. Then he sort of laughed and told me to call him Max.'

'Was there any reason for that?'

'It was because I called him "sir," sir. He said they didn't call people "sir" where he came from, and then he laughed again and patted me on the arm.'

'He was a friendly type, was he?'

'Oh yes, sir, quite a gent.'

'So he patted you on the arm. What happened then?'

'He ordered the chicken, sir, and sent me out for a bottle of wine . . . we aren't on the licence here, sir.'

'And what day were you serving chicken last week?'

'Wednesday, sir.'

'Ah!' said Gently with satisfaction. He laid down his spoon. 'We'll pause for a moment on that happy note . . . just pop along and see what the roast beef is doing.'

'Certainly, sir!'

'And fetch me a lager, Withers. The occasion seems to justify it.'

The waiter slipped from the chair and resumed his function with obvious relief. Gently smiled distantly at a paddling child. Another time Withers wouldn't be quite so forward in accosting chief inspectors who got their pictures in the papers . . .

And the name was Max. Max, in a light grey suit with a blue bow tie. Max, who came from somewhere where they didn't 'sir' people. Max, who was friendly. Max, who was quite a gent. Max, who had sat at that same table from Wednesday till Tuesday, eating his chicken, his Dover sole and chips, and drinking the wine Withers brought him from over the road . . . and Max, who had finished up as Exhibit A on the mortuary slab exactly a week after his first appearance. He was getting into focus, that one. Gently was beginning to see him, to fit him in. And over all there was his foreign-ness, pervasive and misty, his Franco-German-Russo-what-have-you foreign-ness . . .

Withers returned with Gently's roast beef and the lager. He seemed to have been gone a good deal longer than was strictly necessary, even allowing for the trip across the road. Gently raised his eyebrows to the unhappy man.

'Talked it over with the boss, Withers?' he inquired affably.

'I–I beg your pardon, sir!' stammered Withers, spilling some lager.

'Never mind, Withers . . . and don't be well-bred about the vegetables.'

The waiter served, and Gently picked up his knife and fork. It was odd, but he hadn't been feeling hungry when he came into the cafe . . .

'Sit down,' he mumbled to Withers, 'you'll give me indigestion, jiffling about like that.'

'I b–beg your pardon, sir, but really I ought to be getting on with my work . . . there isn't n–nothing I haven't told you, honest . . .'

Gently beamed at him over a mouthful of lager. 'Nonsense, Withers, we've only just begun . . .'

'It's making extra work for the others, sir,' persisted Withers, encouraged by the beam.

'Sit down!' retorted Gently with a slight touch of Bogartesque.

Withers sat down at great speed.

'. . . Now,' continued Gently, after a certain amount of plate-work, 'we got to him ordering the chicken and sending out for some wine. What sort of wine did he send for?'

'Just red wine, sir. I got him a brand they specialize in over the road.'

'I don't doubt it for a moment. Did he express his satisfaction?'

'N–no sir, not really.'

'Did he order the same wine the next day?'

'He asked if they hadn't got another brand . . . I couldn't understand the name he gave it.'

'What did it sound like?'

'It just sounded foreign, sir . . .'

'Like what sort of foreign?'

'I d–don't know . . . just gibberish.'

'Did you ask if they'd got it?'

'No, sir. I couldn't say the name.'

'So what did he have?'

'I got him Burgundy, sir, when he wanted a red, and Sauternes when he wanted a white.'

'And that was satisfactory?'

'He seemed a bit surprised at the price, sir.'

'He was a foreigner, Withers.'

'Yes, sir, I dare say that had something to do with it.'

Gently brooded a moment over a roast potato. Then he halved it meticulously and transported one half, suitably garnished with gravy, to a meditative mouth. 'What did he have for sweet, Withers?' he asked through the potato.

'Ice-cream, sir.'

'Not much to be deduced from that . . . was his coffee black?'

'Yes, sir.'

'Did he smoke . . .? Cigarettes . . .?'

'He bought a box, sir.'

'A box, Withers?'

'Twenty-five Sobranie, sir.'

Gently raised an eyebrow. 'And what particular variety?'

'Just Balkan Sobranie, sir. He bought a box every day after that . . .'

'He seems to have been a well-heeled foreigner, Withers.'

'Yes, sir. He never tipped less than half a crown.'

Gently finished his roast beef and motioned to have his plate removed. Withers took it adroitly and produced a cold sweet from a side-table. It was a trifle, a robustly constructed affair involving sliced pineapple, and Gently inserted a spoon in it with unabated gusto.

'Of course, he asked a few questions,' volunteered Withers, beginning to feel that Gently wasn't so bad after all. 'He wanted to know if we got many foreigners in Starmouth.'

'Mmph?' grunted Gently, 'what did you tell him?'

'I told him we scarcely saw one — not a right foreigner . . . just midlanders and such-like.'

'Yanks,' mumbled Gently.

'Well there . . . we don't count them.'

'Was he happy about the situation?'

'It didn't seem to worry him, sir. He said we might have him around for a bit . . . and later on, of course, he picked up with a woman . . .'

Gently made a choking noise over a segment of pineapple. 'What was that, Withers . . .!'

'He picked up with a fern, sir. Brought her in to lunch here on the Tuesday.'

Gently got rid of the pineapple with a struggle. 'So he did . . . did he! Just like that! Why the flaming hell didn't you say so sooner?'

'You never asked me, sir!' exclaimed Withers, surprised and apprehensive, 'it wasn't nobody really, sir . . . just one of the girls you get around here during the season . . .'

'Just one of the girls!' Gently gazed at the wilting waiter. Then he took himself firmly in hand and counted ten before firing the next question. 'You know her name? It wouldn't be Yvette, by any chance?'

'No, sir! I don't know her name! I've never had nothing to do with women of that class . . .'

'She's the little dark one with long slinky hair.'

'But this one's a blonde, sir — quite well set-up. And her hair is short.'

'Nice legs — smooth, rounded knees.'

'I d–didn't notice, sir . . .'

'Don't lie at this stage, Withers!'

'I thought they were bony, sir – I did, honest I did!'

'She speaks with an educated accent.'

'Not this one, sir – she's terribly common!'

'You'd recognize her again?'

'Of course, sir. Anywhere!'

A telephone began pealing at the counter inside the cafe and Gently relaxed his hypnotic attention from the freshly-shattered Withers. 'Go and take it,' he purred, 'it's probably for me.'

Withers departed like greased lightning. He was back inside seven seconds.

'A S-sergeant Dutt, sir, asking for you . . .'

Gently made the phone in even better time than Withers.

'Gently . . .!' he rapped, 'what's new with you, Dutt?'

'We've placed him, sir!' echoed Dutt's voice excitedly, 'he was missing from a lodging in Blantyre Road – disappeared on Tuesday evening and nothing heard since. The woman who let the room identified him straight away. His name was Max something – she didn't know what.'

A faraway look came into Gently's eyes. It was directed at the ceiling, but in reality it plumbed sidereal space and lodged betwixt two spiral nebulae.

'Get a car, Dutt,' he said, 'come straight down here and pick me up . . .'

'Yessir!' rattled Dutt, 'I'll be with you in ten minutes.'

'Ten minutes,' mused Gently, 'that'll just give me time to drink my coffee . . . won't it, Withers?'

CHAPTER FIVE

BLANTYRE ROAD WAS a shabby-genteel thoroughfare which began at the top of Duke Street and meandered vaguely in a diagonal direction until it joined the Front a good way south, where hotels had already begun to thin out. It was at its best at the top end. Just there it skirted a small park or garden, and the houses which faced it, Edwardian Rococo, had a wistful air of having known better times and more civilized people.

Outside one of these a crowd had collected. It spread along the pavement in both directions and was a model of quietness and patient expectancy. On the steps behind them the careful Copping had stationed a uniform-man, but his authority was somewhat vitiated by the presence of three gentlemen with cameras supported by four gentlemen without cameras – a contingent possessed of far more glamour than a mere police constable.

'Blimey!' exclaimed Dutt, as he, Gently and Copping came dramatically on the scene in the back of a police Wolseley, 'there wasn't a soul about here half an hour ago.'

'That woman must have blabbed,' snapped Copping, 'I sent Jennings down to try and stop it . . . blast her tattling tongue!'

'Of course, she's got a perfect right to . . .' murmured Gently.

The Wolseley made a three-point landing opposite the door and the police constable marched down to give them his official greeting.

'Sorry about this here, sir,' he apologized to Copping, 'that was all done before I arrived . . .'

'Never mind – never mind!' barked Copping, 'just keep those wolves there out of the house, that's all.'

He strode up the steps, an impressive figure. Gently followed with Dutt at a more sedate pace. The flash-bulbs popped and the crowd rippled.

'How about a statement!' demanded a reporter, pushing up, notebook at the ready.

'Nothing about a statement!' boomed Copping, 'if you want a statement, come to headquarters for it.'

'A statement from you, then,' said the reporter, turning to Gently.

Gently shrugged and shook his head. 'Did you get one from Mrs Watts?' he inquired.

'We were actually getting one when the constable interfered . . .!'

'Then you probably know more than I do just at the moment . . .'

He pushed past and up the steps.

The interior of the house was as pleasingly period as the outside. Inside the front door was a long, narrow, but lofty hall, a good deal of it occupied by a disproportionately wide staircase. At the far end another door led into the back garden, a door equipped with panes of red and blue glass. There was a certain amount of upheaval apparent, quite incidental to the main theme – it was a lodging-house Saturday, one set of guests departed, the other not yet arrived. At the foot of the stairs lay a bundle of dirty sheets, in the dining-room, its door ajar, a heap of tablecloths and napkins . . . *Entr'acte,* thought Gently. The phrase epitomized Starmouth on a Saturday.

Copping had marched ahead into Mrs Watt's private parlour, from whence could be heard issuing the landlady's strident and aggressive tones.

'I don't know why you're making all this fuss *now*, I'm sure . . . I told the man who called round here on *Wednesday* . . . well, is it my fault if you didn't know about the beard?'

'There must be some mistake, mam,' came the discomfited voice of Copping, 'I'm sure O'Reilly . . .'

'Mistake, Inspector! I should just say there was a mistake. My daughter Deanna and my husband Ted both backed me up about it . . . "Beard or no beard," I says, "the man on that photograph is our number seven" . . . and that was on *Wednesday,* Inspector, yet you come worrying me today of all days, a Saturday, and Race Week – it's too bad, it is really! If it's not making me all behind with my work, it's what my people are going to think with all that lot gawping outside . . .'

Dutt gave Gently a knowing wink. 'Aye, aye! I was waiting for him to run into that lot.'

'Somebody's boobed, Dutt.'

'Yessir . . . and it isn't you and me.'

Gently pushed in at the parlour door. It was a small

but expensive room. The gilt-edge of Mrs Watts's season expended itself on radiograms, television sets, slow-burning stoves, carpets and furniture notable for its areas of glossy veneer. The available floor-space was a trifle restricted by these evidences of wealth. It occurred, where it occurred in small islands of gold mohair. On the largest of these, which adjoined the multi-tile hearth, Mrs Watts was conducting her attack, while a red-faced Copping had got himself wedged into a triangle between a radiogram and a television set.

'What do you send them round for?' continued the stalwart matron, snaking a glance at the new intruder *en passant*. 'What's the idea of wasting our time asking questions when you aren't going to believe us anyway? Is that how you run the police in Starmouth? Is that why they keep putting the rates up?'

'I assure you, mam, if you'll let me explain . . .'

'Oh, I don't doubt, you'll be a wonderful one for explaining. And I dare say your explaining will get the work done by the time my people start coming in. If you ask *me*, Mr Inspector, we need someone in Starmouth who can teach you your job . . . that body on the beach was a show-up for you, wasn't it just . . .?'

'Ahem!' coughed Gently, appropriating some mohair behind the door.

Mrs Watts shook her platinum locks and presented a square chin at him. 'And who's this?' she demanded of Copping, 'how many more have you brought down here to waste my time?'

'This is Chief Inspector Gently, mam!' explained the squirming Copping, 'he's in charge of the case . . . he wants to ask you a few questions.'

There was a pause while Mrs Watts digested this information. Then her expression underwent a change, passing from steely aggressiveness to steely affability. 'Well!' she said more placably, 'well! And aren't you the gentleman they've sent from Scotland Yard to clear up this body-on-the-beach business?'

Gently nodded gravely.

'The same Chief Inspector Gently that did that case at Norchester?'

'The same, Madam.'

'Well!' repeated Mrs Watts, 'of course, if I'd known that . . .' She favoured Gently with a smile in which steeliness was still the principal ingredient. 'Do please sit down, Inspector . . . I shall be pleased to be of any assistance. Deanna!' – her voice rose to a shout – 'Deanna, leave what you're doing and make a pot of tea, do you hear?'

There was a faint acknowledgement from without and Mrs Watts, satisfied, ushered Gently to the room's most dramatic and veneer-lavish chair. He contrived to avoid it, however, and it was Copping who became the victim . . .

'Now,' pursued Mrs Watts, 'I'd like you to know, Inspector—'

'Just a minute,' interrupted Gently, 'has the room been interfered with?'

'The *room*, Inspector . . .?'

'Number seven – the room from which this man disappeared?'

Mrs Watts looked doubtful. 'I don't know what you mean, interfered with. I've changed the sheets and pillow-cases, and Ida (that's the maid) has polished and hoovered, but that's all . . . there's nothing been moved about.'

Gently sighed softly to himself. 'Well . . . we'll look in there later, if you don't mind. Now about the man himself. . .'

'I recognized him directly, Inspector. There was never any doubt.'

'You recognized him without the painted-in beard?'

'As soon as I clapped eyes on the photograph . . . "Yes," I says to the man, "that's our number seven. Only he's got a beard," I says, "a lot of it – all over his face."'

'And that was on Wednesday, the day after your lodger was missing?'

'That's right – Wednesday evening. Naturally, I didn't pay too much attention to him spending the night out . . . you can't be too particular about that sort of thing, Inspector. But when it got near tea-time and still no sign of him . . .'

'You rang the police and were shown the photographs. You acted very properly, Mrs Watts.'

'But the man didn't *believe* me, Inspector – I could see he didn't!'

Copping made a rumbling noise. 'It was O'Reilly,' he brought out, 'he was going on transfer to Liverpool the next day . . . he didn't want to believe it . . .'

Gently nodded comfortably to one and the other. 'Everyone is human . . . even the police. And of course you recognized the touched-up photograph, Mrs Watts?'

'Naturally I did – and so did Deanna – and so did my husband Ted, who was in after his lunch.'

'You'd be prepared to swear to the identity in court?'

'I'd take my Bible oath on it, Inspector . . . and so will *they*.'

Gently nodded again and felt absently in the pocket where he stowed the peppermint creams. 'When was it he arrived?' he asked, struggling with the bag.

'It was last Wednesday week – in the morning, just after breakfast.'

'Go on. Describe what happened.'

'Well, I answered the door, Inspector, and there he stood. "I see you've got a room vacant," he says – only he had a queer way of slurring it, as though he were trying to be funny – "do you think I might see it?" he says. I mean, the cheek of it, Inspector! People are usually glad enough to *get* rooms in the middle of the week at this time of the year, without being awkward about it. And him a foreigner too, and smelling as though he'd just walked off a fishing boat . . .!'

Gently paused in the act of transporting a peppermint cream to his mouth. 'A fishing boat?' he queried.

'Yes – that's just the way he smelt. Mind you, I don't want to accuse him of having been a dirty man. It was something that wore off later and the first thing he did was have a bath. But there's no doubt he had a fishy smell on that particular morning . . . well, I nearly slammed the door in his face!'

Mrs Watts pulled herself up in a way which reminded Gently of a baulking mule.

'How was he dressed . . . can you remember?' he asked.

'He'd got his light grey suit on – he nearly always wore that . . . a bit American, it was, with one of those fancy backs to the jacket.'

'Tie?'

'That was a bow.'

'Hat?'

'He never wore one that I can remember.'

'Did he have some luggage with him . . .?'

'He'd got a couple of cases, one bigger than the other . . . the big one is still in his room.'

'How about the other – what happened to that?'

'I suppose he took it with him, Inspector. He always did when he went out . . . he seemed to think there was something very precious about it.'

'Did you see him leave with it the last time you saw him?'

'No . . . I didn't see him after I'd given him his tea. Deanna saw him go out, perhaps she noticed. Deanna!' – Mrs Watts's voice rose piercingly again – 'come in here – the inspector wants to ask you a question!'

'Coming, Ma!' replied a sugary voice just without the door, and a moment later Deanna made her entrance bearing a chrome-and-plastic tea-tray.

'Put it down here, Deanna – I'll pour it out.' Mrs Watts was obviously proud of her daughter and wanted her to be admired. 'This is Chief Inspector Gently down here about the body on the beach . . . don't be afraid of him, my dear, there's no need to be shy.'

Deanna wasn't shy. She beamed at Gently with a mechanical smile which had haunting overtones of Mrs Watts in it, then seated herself next to him. She had a cat-like grace too studied to be pleasing. She was twenty-one or -two.

'My daughter's on the stage, Inspector,' chattered Mrs Watts, sploshing tea into straight-sided cups with lustred rims, 'she was in the pantomime last season . . . just in the chorus, you know.'

'I understudied the principal boy,' beamed Deanna.

'They're going to give her something bigger this year . . . of course, she's home with me during the summer.'

Gently accepted one of the straight-sided cups and stirred it with a spoon that had a knob of black plastic to its spindly shank. 'Getting back to your lodger . . .' he murmured.

'Of course, Inspector.' Mrs Watts handed a cup of tea to Dutt behind the television. 'Deanna dear, you saw him go out on Tuesday . . . the inspector wants to know if he had his case with him.'

'I don't really remember, Ma . . . I didn't know it was going to be important.'

'But it *is* important, dear . . . you *must* try to think.'

'I *am* trying, Ma, but it isn't any good.'

'What time was it when he went out?' asked Gently.

Deanna curled round in her seat to him. 'I just can't remember, Inspector . . . isn't it awful of me?'

'What were you doing when you saw him?'

'Oh . . . I was going up to my room to get ready for the Tuesday dance at the Wellesley.'

'How long would that have taken you?'

'About an hour . . . aren't I terrible!'

'And then your boyfriend called for you?'

'Well yes, he did, Inspector!'

'And what time was that?'

'It was a quarter past eight . . . he was late.'

'Thank you, Miss Deanna.'

In his veneered throne Copping stirred restlessly.

'How about the visitor's book – what did he put in there?' he asked.

Mrs Watts's chin took on an ominous tilt. 'He didn't put anything in there. They don't, most of them, until they're going.'

'They should,' said Copping stoutly, 'they should make an entry as soon as they arrive.'

'Well, they *don't*, Mr Nosey, and that's all there is to it. And if you're going to make trouble out of it you'll have to make trouble for everybody in Starmouth who lets rooms . . .'

Gently made a pacifying gesture. 'But surely he gave a name, Mrs Watts? Naturally, you would ask for that . . .'

'Of course I did, Inspector. And he gave it to me without any hanky-panky – only it was such a peculiar one that I couldn't even say it after him. So he just laughed in that rather nice way he had and told me to call him Max . . . and that's what we all called him.'

'Didn't you inquire his nationality?'

'He said he was an American but if he was, he hadn't been one for long, not with that accent.'

Gently sipped some tea and looked round for somewhere to put his cup. 'How long was he going to stay?' he asked.

'Just on to the end of this week – I hadn't any room for him after that. I'm usually full up right through, of course, but it just so happened through an illness . . .'

'Quite so, Mrs Watts. And did he pay up till the end of the week?'

'He did – it's one of the rules of this establishment.'

'There seemed to be no shortage of money with him?'

337

'Not him, Inspector. He'd got a whole wad of notes in his wallet – fivers, most of them.'

'Did he ask any questions before he took the room?'

'Well, the usual ones . . . how much it would be, if we'd got a separate bathroom and the like.'

'Did he ask about the other guests, for instance?'

'Yes, he did, now you come to mention it. He asked if they were all English and if they had all arrived the Saturday before.'

'And did that suggest anything to you?'

'He seemed a bit anxious about it . . . I thought he might be expecting to run into somebody he knew.'

'Somebody pleasant or somebody unpleasant?'

'Unpleasant, I suppose . . . if he really is the one you picked up on the beach.'

'Did he suggest that from the way he spoke?'

'Well no, Inspector, he didn't actually . . .'

Gently prized up a peppermint cream from the dwindling stock in his pocket. It induced that faraway look in his eye which Mrs Watts mistook for profound cerebration, but which in reality was connected with his solvency in terms of that important commodity . . . though Starmouth was pretty good peppermint cream country at most hours of the day and night.

'Was he a good mixer?' he asked absently.

'Oh, he got on with everyone, though I wouldn't say he made friends. But he got on with them. They all liked our Max.'

'Was he regular in his habits?' Gently yielded up his cup for a second fill from the hotel-plate teapot.

'I dare say he was . . . as people go when they're on holiday.'

'Tidy . . . a good lodger?'

'Oh yes . . . most of the time.' A frown hovered over the steely eyes as she handed Gently the freshly-filled cup. 'He left his room in a bit of a mess when he went out that last time, but probably he was in a hurry . . . you haven't always time to clear up after you.'

'A mess . . .!' Gently hesitated in the act of plying his plastic-knobbed spoon. 'What sort of a mess?'

'Well, if you ask *me*, Inspector, he'd lost something and was trying to find it quickly, that's what it looked like. The wardrobe was open, the drawers pulled out of the dressing-table – right out, some of them – and if he hadn't up-ended his suitcase on to the floor then he'd given a good imitation of it. And the bed, too, I should say he'd had that apart, not to mention turning up a corner of the carpet. It was a proper mess, you can take it from me!'

Gently drew a long breath. 'But of course,' he said expressionlessly, 'of course you cleared it all up again, Mrs Watts?'

'I did, Inspector,' the regal matron assured him, 'I can't stand untidiness in my house, no matter from whom.'

'Ahh!' sighed Gently, 'I needn't have asked that one, need I . . .?'

The room faced back with a solitary and not-very-large sash window overlooking a small backyard. It was a typical lodging-house 'single', about eight by ten, not much more than a cupboard in which had to be packed the bed, wardrobe, dressing-table, chair and the tiny fitted wash-basin which tried to substantiate the terms

Mrs Watts charged for such accommodation. The walls were papered in an irritable grained brown friezed with orange and green, the floor had a strip of carpet which echoed these colours. The bed and other furniture were of flimsy stained wood, late thirties in vintage, and the light-shade was a contraption of orange-sprayed glass with a golden tassel for the flies to perch on. In essence it bore a generic resemblance to the parlour downstairs, thought Gently. There was the same over-crowding and full-bodied vulgarity. It was only the cash index that varied so considerably.

Beside the bed stood an expensive looking suitcase, a rather jazzy affair styled in some sort of plastic with towelling stripes. Copping bent down to pick it up, but Gently laid a sudden hand on his arm. 'Watch it . . . I want this place printed,' he said.

'Printed?' Copping stared in surprise. 'There can't be much left to print after all this clearing-up . . .'

Gently shrugged. 'If there is, I want it.'

'But what does it matter – we've got three witnesses at least to identify him?'

'It isn't only him that interests us . . .'

He moved to the window, leaving Copping still staring.

The window was part open at the top. Immediately below it were the red pantiles roofing the outside offices, at the end of which could be seen part of a corrugated steel water-butt. The yard itself was no more than twenty yards long by ten wide. It was separated from its neighbours and the alley on which it backed by grimy brick walls. In the far corner a sad laburnum trembled, in the centre rotted a part-buried

Anderson shelter, while close at hand there roosted three dust-bins, one of them with its lid at a rakish angle . . .

Gently produced a not-perfectly-clean handkerchief and closed the window. 'Look,' he said to Copping, pointing to the catch.

Copping looked intelligently. 'It's broken,' he said.

Gently nodded and waited.

'Done from the outside – forced up with a chisel or something . . .'

Gently nodded again.

'Hell's bells – the room's been *burgled!*' exclaimed Copping, suddenly catching on. 'It wasn't the boyo who left it upside-down – it was somebody else – somebody looking for something he left behind here!'

'Which is why I'm printing the place . . .' murmured Gently helpfully.

'It's plain as a pikestaff – I can see the whole thing! He sneaked in up the alley – got in through that broken gate down there – climbed on to the roof by the water-butt and the down-pipe – forced up the catch!'

'Hold it,' interrupted Gently. 'Dutt, step up here a moment.'

Dutt, who had been lingering respectfully in the passage, came quickly to the window. Gently spoke to him without turning his head.

'Over there – where the coping's knocked off the wall . . . don't make it too obvious you're looking.'

'I can see him, sir,' muttered Dutt, 'if he'd just turn his loaf a fraction . . .'

'But who is it!' interrupted Copping, shoving in, 'is it someone you know—?'

341

'Back!' rapped Gently, 'keep away till Dutt has had a good look . . . there, you've scared him . . . he's off like a hare!'

Dutt raised himself from the stooping position he had taken up. 'It was him, sir,' he asserted positively, 'I saw the scar as he turned to run . . . you can't mistake a face like that.'

'I saw it too, Dutt, right down his cheek.'

'He must have copped a fair packet somewhere . . .'

'Also he has a strange interest in what goes on . . .'

'But who is he?' yapped Copping again, 'what's it all about, this I–spy stuff?'

Gently smiled at some spot that was miles behind Copping's head. 'It's just a little thing between Dutt and me,' he said, 'don't let it bother you . . . it's all over now. Suppose we do what you wanted and take a look in the suitcase?'

They retired from the window and a disgruntled Copping demonstrated how to open a suitcase before it had been printed. It was a charmingly well–filled suitcase. It contained an abundance of shirts and socks and underwear, besides some hairbrushes and toilet accessories which the tidy Mrs Watts had garnered from wash–bowl and dressing–table. And the contents were determined to be helpful. There were makers' labels attached to some of the clothes, names and patent numbers stamped on other items . . . even the suitcase itself had a guarantee label tied to the lining with blue silk. Gently had never seen such a helpful lot of evidence . . .

'It's American,' declared Copping brightly, 'look at this one – "Senfgurken Inc., NY" – and that razor – the toothbrush, even. It's all Yank stuff, right through.'

'And all brand new,' mused Gently.

'He must have bought it for the trip and he can't have been over here long. Or maybe he's a service-man on leave and fixed himself up at his P.X. Anyway, we know where to start looking. If his embassy doesn't know about him, the US Army will.'

'I wonder . . .' Gently breathed.

'Eh?' stared Copping.

'Of course, he said he was an American . . .'

Copping's stare became indignant. 'Who else but a Yank could get hold of this stuff? And who would want to fake up some American luggage, here in Starmouth? What's the point?'

Gently shrugged and dug up the last of his peppermint creams. 'That's what I'd like to know,' he said.

'He's a serviceman got in some bad company, you take my word. It's happened before in Starmouth . . . he's a deserter, that's my bet.'

Gently shook his head. 'It doesn't fit in. There's nothing American about Max except his clothes, and even they seem too good to be true. No . . . everything about him is wrong. He just won't add up into a good American.'

'He might add up into a bad one,' quipped Copping, but Gently didn't seem to be listening.

'The suit – his dark suit! What happened to that?'

'His dark suit?' echoed Copping.

'The one he wore on Sunday. Look in the wardrobe, Dutt. It may still be hanging there.'

Obediently Dutt pulled out his handkerchief and unlatched the wardrobe door. Sure enough a dark suit hung there, a shouldery close-waisted number in discreet midnight blue. Dutt turned back a lapel to show the tailor's label. It was of one Klingelschwitz, operating in Baltimore.

'Still American,' commented Copping, a shade triumphant.

'Go through the pockets,' ordered Gently dully.

Dutt went through them. There wasn't even any fluff. But as he was re-folding the trousers something small and bright fell from one of the turn-ups, a little disc of metal. Copping swooped on it and held it up.

'His lucky charm. He ought to have had it with him on Tuesday.'

'A circle with a line through it!' exclaimed Dutt, 'there's something familiar about that, sir – I've seen it before somewhere.'

'So have I.' A gleam came into Gently's eye. 'I saw it last night on the ring of a Mr Louis Hooker. I wonder if Louey has ever been to America . . .?'

CHAPTER SIX

THE SUPER WAS out when they arrived back at headquarters – rather to Gently's disappointment, because he would like to have bounced some of his findings on that sceptical man's desk. But the super was out: he had received a hot tip about his forgery scare, said the desk sergeant, and had departed with Bryce and two uniform men at a high rate of knots.

'He's got a warped sense of value,' pouted Gently to Copping. 'In some places it's homicide that gets top rating . . .'

'You're forgetting he handed that baby on to you,' grinned Copping, 'he's got an alibi now.'

'I still think a little bit of audience reaction is called for.'

They went into the canteen, where Copping did the honours. It was rather a dull place. The walls were distempered in a dingy neutral tint, the inadequate windows both at one end, the paint worn on lino-top tables and the bentwood chairs looking as though they had been rescued from a jumble sale.

'They've talked about refitting it for years,' Copping apologized, 'but somehow the finance committee never quite gets round to it . . . the food's all right, though. We made a stink about that a couple of months back.'

Gently examined a plate of sausages and beans apathetically. 'You have to make a stink at intervals if you want to keep them up to scratch . . .'

'Yes, but you should have seen what it was like before then!'

Gently shrugged and embarked on his sausages.

'We get in touch with the US authorities now?' inquired Copping, after a silence broken only by the incidental noises made by ingesting policemen.

'Nmp.' Gently pursued an errant bean round the rim of his plate.

'The military's got good records . . . they could tell us straight away.'

'Never mind. Some other time.'

'They'd know in town . . .'

'I know, but never mind.' Gently swallowed the tail-end of a sausage and grounded his knife and fork. 'Your print king,' he said, running his tongue round his lips, 'what's his name?'

'Dack's your man. Sergeant.'

'He's reliable . . . really?'

'You trained him, so he'd better be.'

Gently nodded and added a mouthful of strong tea to the sausages. 'Get him on the job. I can't spare Dutt just now. See that he does everything that might give something . . . *inside* drawers as well as out . . . and then in the yard, at the *back* of that down-pipe . . . he'll probably have to dismantle it. Don't wait for me. If you get results, rush some copies to town and check your own files.'

A smile spread over Copping's heavy features. 'What about Mrs W's new lodger?'

'Nothing about Mrs W's new lodger . . . he can sleep under the pier for all I care. When you've finished in there, seal it up and leave a uniform man in charge.'

'I don't pity the poor swine . . .! Where can I get you?'

'Oh . . . I'll look in later, or maybe ring.'

'You've got something else?'

'Could be,' returned Gently evasively, 'and then again, it couldn't.'

He drank some more tea while Copping indulged in speculative ratiocinations. 'It'd be easy to give the US military a ring . . . just to be sure.'

'No,' said Gently, kindly but firmly, 'we'll leave them to concentrate on Western Defence or whatever else it is they do in these parts . . .'

The Front had become its old gay self again by evening. Everybody hadn't arrived yet – there were still momentary appearances of towering coaches hailing from Coventry, Leicester, Wolves and Brum, dusty from long journeying, their passengers lolling and weary – but enough had already arrived, enough had checked in at their lodgings, deployed their belongings, washed, changed, tea'd, and now sallied forth, cash in hand – they really spent with a will on the Saturday night. Remote from it all, the sea looked cold. Nobody wanted the sea on that day of the week. It was there, it was the alleged attraction, but that was all . . . and in the setting sun it looked cold and hard.

More interesting was the local Evening and the two

Londons. They proclaimed the wisdom of having chosen this week for the holiday instead of last week. Last week, of course, the body had been found and the Yard called in, but it was pretty obvious from the way things were going that it would be this week when the mystery was solved, the arrest made . . . BODY IDENTIFIED BY LANDLADY ran the local – Lodger Said to Have Worn False Beard: Missing Suitcase – and there was a photograph showing Gently's back and Copping posed at the top of the steps. The Londons didn't get it early enough to feature. They had to be content with a stop-press and no pics. But they did their best. They whooped it up joyfully. IT WAS ROGER THE LODGER – AND HIS WHISKERS WERE PHONEY, one was captioned, BODY ON THE BEACH – WHY SHAVE IT? asked the other. Yes . . . things were moving. It was obviously the right week to be in Starmouth, quite apart from the races.

'Can't help feeling we've been mucked about, sir,' observed Dutt, as the two of them turned the corner at the end of Duke Street, 'all these new people . . . thahsands of them . . . and we know for a start they haven't got nothink to do with it.'

Gently belched . . . those damned sausages! 'It's the ones who've gone that worry me,' he muttered.

'And then again, there's him we're going to pinch . . . could be any one of them, sir. This bloke coming along here, now, the one with the tasselled hat . . . I wouldn't put it past him.'

Gently clicked his tongue. 'You can't go on that sort of thing, Dutt.'

'I know, sir, but you can't help thinking about it. This isn't like the usual job – as a rule there's one or two to have a go at. But this time there's not a soul, not a blinking sausage' – Gently winced at this unkind reference – 'not a solitary bloke anywheres who you can lay your hand to your heart about. I mean, even that bloke with the scar, sir. What have we got on him, apart from him acting suspicious? I dare say he's up to something he wouldn't like us to know about, but honest now, what connection is that with the deceased? We've often put up pigeons like him on a job.'

Gently sighed, but the sigh was interrupted by a belch. 'This is why we get on so well together, Dutt,' he said bitterly, 'your cockney common sense is the best foil in the world for my forensic intuition . . .'

'Well, there you are, sir. I don't want to look on the black side . . .'

'Of course not, Dutt.'

'But you've got to admit it's still a bit speculative, sir.'

'Highly speculative, Dutt . . . which is why we're keeping firmly on the tail of any pigeons we put up.'

'Yessir. Of course, sir.'

'Including your man with a scar.'

'I wasn't presuming to criticize, sir . . .'

'No, Dutt, please don't . . . at least, not after I've been eating dogs in that damned canteen up there . . .!'

'I'm sorry, sir . . . they was perishing awful dogs.'

They came to a side street running along blankly under the shadow of a Babylonian cinema, a brick vault of Edwardian foundation and contemporary frontage.

'This is me, sir,' said Dutt, halting, 'I can work my way round and come out on the far side of Botolph Street.'

'There's cover there . . . you don't have to lean on a lamp-post?'

'There's a builder's yard with a gate I can get behind.'

'We don't want our pigeon frightened . . . if he's there. I'll give you twenty minutes to get set.'

'That'll be about it, sir.'

'And if he gives any trouble put cuffs on him. My forensic intuition suggests you'll be justified . . .'

Dutt turned off down the side street and Gently, with a dyspeptic grimace, crossed the carriageway and joined the noisy crowd jostling along the promenade. Everything was in full swing again, the lights, the canned music, the windmill sails, the crashing and spanging of the shooting saloon . . . a sort of fey madness, it seemed, a rash of inferno at the verge of the brooding ocean. He turned his back on it and leaned looking out at the cold water.

Dutt was right, of course. There was precious little connection. You could say Frenchy for certain, and that was all . . . and what did Frenchy add up to, even if you could prove it? A friendly foreigner dressed like a Yank and generous with his pound notes . . . he was natural meat for Frenchy. And of course she would lie. Of course she would dig up an alibi. Quite apart from anything else it was bad business for your last boyfriend to wind up a corpse on the beach.

And after Frenchy it was all surmise. There was nobody else who tied in at all, or not in a way that looked impressive when you wrote a report. He had wandered into town, this enigmatical foreigner, he had taken lodgings, he had found a cafe to his taste and a prostitute to his taste; and then he had been, in a short space of time, kidnapped, tortured, murdered and introduced into the sea, his room ransacked and plundered of something of value. There was a ruthlessness about that . . . it bore the stamp of organization. But there was no other handle. The organization persisted in a strict anonymity.

So he was left with his intuition, thought Gently, his intuition that made pictures and tried to fill them in, to make them focus, to eliminate their distressing areas of blankness. One didn't know, one simply felt. With the facts firmly grasped in the right hand one groped in the dark with the left . . . and if you were a good detective, you were lucky. Mere intellect was simply not enough.

He swallowed and grimaced again. If ever he ate another sausage . . .!

There was an air of restraint in the bar of 'The Feathers', as though everybody had been put on their best behaviour. It wasn't too full, either, considering it was Saturday night. The sporty type sat drinking whisky on a high stool, and one or two other less-than-salubrious characters whom Gently remembered from the previous night were scattered about the nearby tables. But there wasn't any Jeff and Bonce, and there wasn't any Frenchy . . . in fact, Gently noticed, there weren't any women in the bar at all, not of any kind.

He went across to the counter and settled himself on a stool, one from the sporty type.

Artie and the latter exchanged a leer, but there was no comment made.

'The usual?' inquired Artie, with a slight sneer in his voice.

Gently quizzed his ferrety features. 'You wouldn't have any milk, by any chance?'

'*Milk!*' Artie almost snorted the word. 'There's a milk-bar just down the road!'

351

'I'm serious . . . I want some milk.'

Artie eyed him balefully for a moment, then shrugged his shoulders and snatched a glass from under the counter. 'Boss's orders,' he sneered, 'got to treat policemen like gentlemen.' He ducked under the counter and disappeared through the adjacent door.

The sporty type tipped up the remains of his whisky. 'If you're looking for your girly, you won't find her here, guv,' he observed spiritously. 'Louey's had a purge – no women, no kids, and nothing out of line from no one . . . getting quite pally towards the coppers is Big Louey.'

Gently lifted his eyebrows. 'It's not a bad thing to be in most lines of business . . . what's yours?'

'What's mine?' The sporty type affected jocularity. 'Ho–ho! I'll keep on drinking what I'm drinking, and thank you very much!'

'I mean your business,' said Gently evenly.

'Oh, me business . . . I was going to say it was the first time a copper ever asked me . . . well, there you are! I'm what you might call a Turf Consultant.'

'You mean a tipster?'

'Now guv, when we're trying to add dignity to the profession . . .'

'And you make a living at it?'

'A bit of that and a bit of working with Louey. You don't run a bookie's business on your own.'

'Well, you seem to do all right at it.'

The sporty type squirmed a little, but was relieved of the necessity of making a reply by the return of Artie with the glass of milk. He slammed it down perilously in front of Gently.

'It's on the house . . . with Louey's compliments.'

Gently nodded and drank it slowly. He really needed that milk. Its soothing coolness flooded into his digestive chaos like a summons to order, nature's answer to a canteen sausage. He drained the last drop and regarded the filmy glass with a dreamy eye. There were just a few things in life . . .

'Louey got company?' he asked Artie.

'Nobody who's worried by policemen.'

'Tut, tut, Artie! I'm sure Louey wouldn't approve of that attitude . . . I was just wondering if he could spare me a few minutes.'

'Why ask?' retorted Artie, 'just walk right in like every other cop.'

Gently shook his head. 'You've got the wrong impression, Artie . . . you must have been rude to a policeman when you were a little boy.' He slid off the stool and went over to the door. Then he paused, hand on the knob. 'I suppose you didn't have sausages for tea, Artie?'

Louey's office was a comfortable room which exhibited a good deal of taste and some quiet expense. The walls were papered in two colours, maroon and grey, the floor was completely carpeted in grey to match and the pebble-grained glass windows, being on grey walls, had maroon curtains relieved by hand-blocked designs in dark blue. The furniture was in keeping. It was of discreet contemporary design showing Scandinavian influence. On the walls hung two coloured prints of race-horses after Toulouse-Lautrec, and under one of the windows stood a jardinière of cream wrought-iron containing a pleasant assortment of indoor plants. There was a short passage separating the office from the bar: it had the effect of reducing the canned crooners in the arcade to a distant, refined murmur.

Louey sat sprawled in a chair by his desk when Gently entered. He was nursing a cat on his knees, a black-and-white tom with a blue ribbon round its neck and a purr like an unoccupied buzzsaw. On another chair was seated the parrot-faced man, still garbed in his dubious evening-dress and still armed with his yard of gold-plated cigarette-holder. Louey greeted Gently with a smile from which his gold tooth shone.

'Pleased to see you, Inspector. I was wondering if you would honour us tonight.'

'Indeed? Then I won't be interrupting any business.'

Louey laughed his comfortable laugh and chivvied the tom with a huge hand. 'No business tonight . . . it's been a bad day for the punters. Not a favourite came home at Wolverhampton. A bad day, eh, Peachey?'

The parrot-faced man mumbled a nervous affirmative. He seemed equally apprehensive of both Gently and Louey. His small pale eyes wandered from one to the other, and he sat in his chair as though it were a penance to him.

'Peachey's my clerk,' explained Louey, seeming to linger on the words, 'he's a good boy . . . very useful . . . aren't you, Peachey? *Very* useful! But sit down, Inspector, make yourself at home . . . as a matter of fact, we've just been talking about you.'

'Really?'

Louey smiled auriferously. 'The evening papers . . . probably exaggerated . . . still, we feel you deserve congratulations. The inspector has got a long way in twenty-four hours, hasn't he, Peachey – eh?'

Gently selected a chair upholstered in blue candy-stripe and swung it round, back to front. Then he seated himself heavily. Louey continued to smile.

'Will you have a drink . . .? Some more milk, if you prefer it?'

'No, thank you. I'll just smoke.'

Louey swept up a silver box from the desk and inclined his gigantic frame towards Gently.

'Try one of these . . . Russian. It's a taste I've acquired.'

'Thanks, but I smoke a pipe.'

'You watch your health, Inspector.'

Such a polite and obliging Louey, thought Gently, as he stuffed his pipe-bowl. Who would have expected such polish from the Goliath who had bawled out the bar last night? There seemed to be two of him . . . one for out there and one for in here, a Jekyll and Hyde Louey. He glanced around the room. Certainly it wasn't furnished by a moron . . .

'You like my office?' Louey leaned forward again with a lighter.

'It's not the usual sort of bookmaker's office.'

The gold tooth appeared. 'Perhaps I'm not the usual sort of bookmaker . . . eh? But most of my business is done in the outer office. I keep this one for myself and my friends.'

His eyes met Gently's, frank, steady, even the sinister effect of the fleck in the pupil seeming softened and modified. We are equals, they were trying to say, you are a man like myself: I recognize you. When we talk together there is no need for subterfuge . . .

'So you don't know that prostitute, Frenchy?' demanded Gently roughly – so roughly, in fact, that Peachey dropped his cigarette brandisher. But the grey eyes remained fixed unwaveringly upon his own.

'I'm afraid not, Inspector . . . apart from warning her to leave the bar once or twice.'

'Does *he* know her?' Gently motioned towards Peachey with his head. Louey turned slowly towards his trembling clerk.

'Go on . . . tell the inspector.'

'I've s–spoken to her once or twice . . .!' Peachey had a whining, high-pitched voice, oddly reminiscent of Nits.

'Nothing else but that?'

'N–no . . . honest I haven't! Just in the bar . . . a joke . . .'

'You've never seen her with this fellow?' Gently whipped out one of the doctored photographs and shoved it under Peachey's nose. The unhappy clerk shot back a foot in his chair.

'Tell him,' rumbled Louey, 'don't waste the inspector's time.'

'No . . . n–never . . . I never seen him at all!'

'Then you know who he is?' snapped Gently.

'I tell you I never seen him!'

'Yet you recognize the photograph?'

'I never . . . I tell you!'

Louey broke in with his comfortable laugh and reached out a great hand to tilt the photograph in his direction.

'I think he can guess, Inspector . . . it isn't difficult, with all this talk of beards in the evening papers.'

'I'm asking Peachey!' Gently snatched the photograph out of Louey's fingers. 'You recognized him –
didn't you? You didn't have to stop to work it out!'

'It's like Louey says!' burst out Peachey in desper-
ation, 'I read about it in the papers . . . just like he says!'

Gently eased back in his candy-striped seat and laid
the photograph on the corner of the desk. Louey
studied it with interest, leaning his massive bald head a
little to one side.

'They've touched it up neatly . . . the beard looks
quite convincing.'

Gently felt for his matches but said nothing.

'No doubt he's a foreigner,' mused Louey, 'what part
of the world would you say he came from . . .
Inspector?'

Gently shrugged and struck a match.

'Of course, he could be a first-generation American
. . . eh?'

Gently puffed a negative stream of smoke.

'Perhaps not. I've a feeling I'm wrong.'

Gently reached out to drop his match in an ashtray.

'Maybe Central European is nearer . . . or further
east. Behind the Curtain, even?' Louey's eyes drifted
slowly back to Gently, strong, assured.

'The Balkans?' suggested Gently quietly.

The grey eyes smiled approval. 'That would be my
guess, too. Or perhaps we could be more definite . . .
after all, the cast of feature is very distinctive. Shall we
say Bulgarian?'

Gently nodded his mandarin nod.

'And – I think – a cultivated man . . . possibly Sofia?'

'As you say . . . possibly.'

Still smiling, Louey fondled the purring tom which continued to loll on his knees. It stretched itself and yawned contentedly. Then it flexed its claws with an exaggerated expression of unconcern, whisked its tail and tucked its head under one of its paws.

'Rain,' said Louey, 'it'll make the going soft . . . eh, Peachey?'

Peachey was sitting with his mouth open and giving an imitation of someone expecting an atomic bomb to explode.

'Then there's the other one . . .' murmured Gently, absently blowing a smoke-ring. 'You were saying, Inspector?'

'The man with the scar, doesn't he strike you as belonging to the same racial group?'

There was a pause broken only by the muted skirl of electronic jazz. Louey's fingers paused halfway along the tom's back. Even Gently's smoke-ring seemed to pause and hover, exactly between the three of them.

'Do I . . . know him, Inspector?' queried Louey in a finely-blended tone of frustrated helpfulness.

'You should do. He was here last night.'

'Last night? You mean here in the bar?'

'I mean here in the office – this one or the outer one.'

There was a further pause while Louey shook his head perplexedly. 'I don't know . . . it's rather puzzling. I'm afraid I'm not acquainted with a man with a scar – it's a conspicuous scar, I suppose, something that stands out?'

'Very conspicuous.'

'And he was here in the office?'

'He left at nine thirty-one.'

'Someone saw him leave?'

'Exactly.'

Louey looked hopelessly blank. 'If I knew his name, Inspector . . .'

'I intended to ask you for it.'

Louey sighed regretfully and reached out for the silver cigarette-box. 'He couldn't have been in here . . . I was here myself the whole evening. And as for the other office—' he hesitated in the act of selecting a primrose-coloured cigarette – 'Peachey!'

Peachey jerked as though yanked by a wire.

'*You* were in the other office at half past nine . . . Peachey!'

'B-but boss—!'

'Now no excuses – you were working there till ten – you didn't leave the place except to fetch me something from the bar. He was getting out accounts, Inspector . . . we do a good deal of postal work.'

'But *boss!*' interrupted the anguished Peachey.

Louey pinned him with an unanswerable eye. 'Who was it, Peachey – who was the man with the scar? The inspector isn't asking these questions out of idle curiosity, you know . . .'

Poor Peachey gaped and gasped like a hooked cod.

'But wait a minute!' boomed Louey, 'half past nine – that must have been about the time I sent you for my whisky. Inspector' – his eye dropped Peachey as a terrier drops a rat – 'you were in the bar yourself just then, I believe. Did you notice Peachey come out, by any chance?'

Gently nodded reluctantly.

'Of course! Perhaps you can tell us at what time?'

'About half past nine . . . more or less.'

'Half past nine! Then it seems that Peachey *wasn't* in the office when this man of yours was alleged to have left. Is that what you wanted to tell me, Peachey – is it?'

Peachey gulped apoplectically. 'That's right, boss! I wasn't there to s–see nobody!'

'And nobody looked in before that . . . none of our regulars about their accounts?'

'No, boss – no one at all!'

Louey extended a gigantic hand towards Gently. 'Sorry, Inspector . . . it doesn't look as though we can help much . . . does it?'

'No,' admitted Gently expressionlessly, 'it doesn't, does it?'

'Of course, this man may have looked in while the office was unoccupied.'

Gently shook his head. 'Let's not bother about that one, shall we?'

The grey eyes smiled approval again and Peachey sagged down into his chair, breathing heavily. Louey lit his cigarette, slowly, thoughtfully.

'You know, I've given this business a certain amount of thought, Inspector . . . one can't be indifferent, with the Press making so much of it . . . and there are certain points which seem to stand out.'

Gently hoisted an inquiring eyebrow, but said nothing.

'I admit in advance that I'm the merest amateur . . . naturally! But it's just possible that being outside it, away from the . . . tactical problems? . . . I'm in a more favourable position to study the strategy.'

'Go on,' grunted Gently.

Louey inhaled deeply and raised his head to blow smoke above Gently's face.

'There's this man . . . what is he doing here? A complete stranger – nobody knows him – the police don't know him (at least, I presume they don't?) – turning up one day at a popular English seaside resort – and disguised. What would bring him here? His motive is past guessing at. Why should anybody kill him when he got here? The motive is just as obscure.'

'Robbery,' suggested Gently, puffing some Navy Cut into a haze of Russian.

'Robbery?' The gold tooth showed lazily for a moment. 'You're forgetting, Inspector, he was reported to have been killed in cold blood. His hands were tied. Does that seem like robbery?'

'It seems like more than one person being involved.'

'Exactly . . . and that's my point! It wasn't the crime of an individual. All the facts are against it. The more you juggle with them, the more emphatic they become. It was an organized killing, an act carried out by a group of some description . . . who knows?'

The grey eyes slid up and fastened on Gently's, holding him, commanding him.

'A political killing, Inspector. The execution of a traitor . . . that's my reading of the situation. Your man was a fugitive. He chose Starmouth for his haven. But the organization he had betrayed found him out and exacted justice . . . doesn't that seem to fit what we know?'

Gently blew an exquisite ring.

'I think it does . . . better than any other

interpretation. I hope I'm wrong – for your sake, Inspector. I believe these political killings are planned with a care which makes detection onerous and arrests unlikely. But the odds seem to lie that way . . . at least to my amateur way of thinking.'

The smile strayed back into the magnetic eyes and Louey part snuffed, part sucked a tremendous inhalation of smoke.

'I'd like you to know I appreciate your difficulties,' he concluded, spilling smoke as he talked. 'My admiration for your abilities won't be lessened, Inspector . . . what can be done by the police in these cases I am sure you will do.'

Gently nodded towards a peak in Darien. Then he reached for the photograph, pulled out his pen and drew on the matt surface a clumsy circle divided by a line. Without looking he handed it to Louey. The big man took it and stared at it.

'Is this something I should know about?' he inquired softly.

Gently lofted a careless shoulder. 'You were wearing it on your ring last night.'

'*My* ring?' Louey extended his hand to display his solitaire.

'The one you were wearing last night.'

Louey hesitated a split second and then laughed. 'No, Inspector, you are mistaken . . . this is the only ring I wear. Tell him, Peachey, tell him . . . I wear this diamond to impress the clients . . . eh?'

The miserable Peachey contrived to nod.

'They like to do business with a man of substance . . . it's paid for itself over and over again.'

Gently turned towards him. There was a glint of excitement in the masterful, smiling eyes.

'So you see, you were mistaken, Inspector . . . you do see that, don't you?'

'Yes,' murmured Gently, 'I see it very plainly indeed.'

He didn't have far to go outside before he was joined by Dutt. The sergeant's cockney visage had a glum expression which told Gently all there was to know . . .

'No pigeon, Dutt . . . the dovecote was empty.'

'That's right, sir. Not a flipping feather.'

'I got the impression it might be. Everyone was so pleased to see me. A pity, Dutt. I get more and more interested in that laddie.'

'We could put out a portrait parley, sir. He shouldn't be difficult to pick up.'

'I wonder, Dutt. My feeling is that he's a bit of a traveller . . . it's the docks and airports that'll need an eye kept on them. On the other hand . . .'

'Yessir?'

'If he's the bird I think him, it's a matter of some curiosity why he's hung around here so long already.'

'You mean you know who he is, sir?'

'I wouldn't put my hand to my heart, Dutt. I'm of a suspicious character, like all good policemen. And then again . . . it doesn't do to overestimate. There's one thing, though: I want a sound sure ruling on the origin of that circle with a line through it.'

'You mean that little charm, sir?' queried Dutt, brightening.

'I do indeed, Dutt – that little charm.'

'Well, sir, I can tell you that right off the cuff . . . it came to me as I was standing there watching, sir. I knew I'd seen it before, like I said when we found it.'

'Go on, man . . . stop beating about the bush!'

'It's the sign of the TSK Party, sir – I come across it when I was attached to the Special.'

Gently halted under the blaze of one of the multi-coloured standards that afforested the Front. 'And what,' he inquired, 'do we know about TSK Parties, Dutt?'

'Not a darn sight, sir,' replied Dutt, 'not if you put it like that. It's a sort of Bolshie outfit – they reckoned it picked up where the old Bolshie boys left off. They didn't even know wevver Joe was backing it or not – sort of freelance it was, if you get me. That Navy sabotage business was TSK. We had some US Federal men attached to us – they've had a lot of trouble with them in the States.'

'The States!' echoed Gently, 'It's always the States. Have you noticed, Dutt, how the American eagle keeps worrying us as we go about our quiet Central Office occasions?'

CHAPTER SEVEN

THE FLAP WAS still on at headquarters, in fact it had stepped up considerably during Gently's absence. There were lights on where they were usually off at such an hour, cars parked that ought to have been garaged and policemen due off duty, still buzzing around like (as Dutt rather coarsely described it) 'blue-arsed flies'. Gently, going down the corridor, was nearly bowled over by an impetuous Copping clutching a file.

'We've picked up the boyo who passed that note!' exclaimed the Borough Police maestro, sorting himself out. 'He's a skipper from up north – he's lousy with them – and what a yarn he's spun! They must think we're cracked, trying to pull gags like that. But the super'll give him a going over he won't forget in a hurry!'

Gently sniffed a little peevishly. 'Don't think I'm frivolous . . . I'm still trying to keep my mind on the crime before the last. Did your man get some prints?'

'Oh, the prints! He got a couple of sets that didn't tally with anything we've got.'

'A couple?'

'That's right . . . one lot on the suitcase and one on the window-frame. They turned up in other places, too, but those were the best impressions.'

'He compared them with Mrs W's and the rest, of course?'

'We know a little bit about the job . . .!'

'And you've sent them to town?'

'Right away, as per instructions.'

Gently fished out his wallet and extracted from it the doctored photograph. 'I want this printed now . . . is your man still around? He'll find mine on it amongst some others, but he needn't bother about them . . .'

Dutt was despatched with the photograph and Gently accompanied Copping to the super's office. That austere abode, always impressive, was now fairly crackling with forensic atmosphere. The super sat behind his desk as stiff as a ramrod. At a discreet distance a sergeant was ensconced at a table, taking down some details. At the same table sat a constable with a shorthand book and three pencils. On the door was a second constable, uneasily at ease. The focus of all this talent, a fresh-complexioned middle-aged man, had been arranged on a chair in the geometrical centre of the office: he sat there with a nervous awkwardness, like a member of an audience suddenly hoicked up on to the stage.

The super nodded to Gently as the latter entered and motioned him to take a seat. 'You'll excuse me, Inspector . . . I'm rather busy. I'd like a conference with you later, if you don't mind waiting.'

Gently inclined his head and sat down at the less

congested end of the office. Copping delivered the file and appended himself to the end of the super's desk.

'Dalhoosie Road,' spelled out the sergeant. 'McKinky & Mucklebrowse Ltd, Potleekie Street, Frazerburgh. I think that's the lot, sir. It checks with the ship's papers.'

The super stiffened himself a few more degrees. 'Now, McParsons . . . I want you to listen very carefully to what I have to say. I'm charging you with being in possession and uttering a counterfeit United States banknote, and also with being in possession of four similar notes. Do you wish to say anything in answer to this charge? You are not obliged to say anything unless you wish to do so, but whatever you say will be taken down in writing and may be used in evidence.'

McParsons screwed up his weather-beaten face. 'But I tellt yer the whorl *lot*, sir – I gi'ed ye all the evidence to prove I'm an honest man . . . what more do yer want noo?'

'It isn't evidence,' snapped the super, 'we didn't take it down and we're prepared to forget it. Think carefully, McParsons. You're in trouble, quite a lot of trouble, and the tale you told me down at the docks won't impress a jury – I can assure you of that. My advice to you is to forget it. The truth will help you a lot more, especially if it enables us to arrest the counterfeiters.'

'But losh, man, it *was* the truth! I canna make up tales out of my heid.'

'Stop!' interrupted the super sharply. 'All you say now is evidence.'

'Then Gordamighty, let it be so – I'll noo complain

o' ye puitin fause words into my mouth. It's jist the way I tellt it, nae more and nae less, so yer may as well scratch it doon on yer paper – it's all the evidence Andy McParsons can gi' ye.'

The super drilled at the same Andy McParsons for ten acetylene-edged seconds before replying . . . quite a feat, thought Gently, who was a connoisseur of superlatives. Then he snapped off a 'Right!' which seemed to suggest every bit of ten years and opened the file Copping had brought. The pages rustled accusingly.

'Starmouth Branch of the City & Provincial Bank . . . US banknote of one hundred dollar denomination, etc, etc . . . paid in by Joseph William Hackett, licensee of the "Ocean Sun" . . . see preceding report. Hackett on being questioned deposed that he changed the note for a seaman, a stranger to him . . . sparely built man, about five feet ten, aged about fifty, dressed in navy-blue suit and cap, fresh complexion etc . . . Scots accent. Detective Sergeant Haynes questioned Andrew Carnegie McParsons, Skipper of the steam-drifter *Harvest Sea*, at the yard of Wylie-Marine, where the said steam-drifter was undergoing a refit . . . denied all knowledge, etc—'

Gently coughed loudly and the super broke off to throw him a sharp stare. 'You had something to say, Inspector?'

'The name of the yard,' murmured Gently apologetically, 'could you repeat it, please?'

'Wylie-Marine, Inspector.'

'Thank you. I thought it sounded familiar.'

The super snorted and returned to his recitation.

'Afternoon of the fifteenth Hackett reported having

seen aforementioned seaman in the neighbourhood of the yard of Wylie-Marine ... proceeded to the same yard ... Hackett picked out McParsons ... McParsons admitted changing the note and was taken into custody ... four similar notes of one hundred dollar denomination found in McParsons's possession.'

The super paused again and smoothed out the nicely typed report sheet.

'*Now*,' he said bitingly, 'we come to your story, McParsons.'

'But ye've had it a'ready,' replied the disconsolate skipper, 'hoo often maun I tell it to yer?'

'What you told us before you were charged will not be used as evidence. If you want to make a statement, now is the time.'

'Och, aye ... ye're all for doing it by the buik, I ken that. Well, jist pit doon I had the notes fra ain Amurrican body ... I see fine yer dinna believe a word of it.'

The super signalled to the shorthand constable. 'Begin at the beginning, McParsons. If this story of yours is to go on record we want the whole of it.'

McParsons sighed feelingly to himself. 'Aweel ... ye'll have your way, there's noo doot. It was on the Tuesday then, the Tuesday last but one ... we'd been in Hull a week, y'ken, wi' the boiler puffin' oot steam fra every crook an cranny ... the engineer had puit in his report lang since, but auld Mucklebrowse is awfu' canny aboot runnin' up bills for repair ... then awa' comes a wire to the agent tellin' us to puit out for Wylie's, me ainsel' to stay wi' the ship and the crew to take train back to Frazer. Sae we jist tuik aboard ain or

369

twa necessaries and hung waitin' there for the evenin' tide. Noo the crew bodies was all ashore takin' their wee drap for the trip and Andy McParsons had jist come awa' fra the agent's, when along happens this Amurrican I tellt ye of . . . "Captain," says he (and morst respectful, the de'il take him!), "is that your ain ship lyin' there with steam up?" "It is," says I, "sae long as the rivets stick in the boiler." "Then ye're aboot goin' to sea," says he. "Aye," says I, "jist as soon as the laddies get back, which'll noo be a great while." "And you'll be goin' a long trip?" says he, gi'en a luik ower his shoulder. "Jist drappin' down the coast," says I, "we'll be sittin' tight in Starmouth before breakfast-time."

'Noo ye maun believe this, Supereentendent, or ye maun not – it's a' ain to the truth – but I hadna been gabbin' five minutes with this smooth-spaken cheil when he was jawin' me into stowin' him awa' in the *Harvest Sea*. "But wit's the trouble?" says I, "is it the police ye have stuck on yer sternsides?" "Naethin' of that, I swear," says he, "it's a private matter, an like to be the dearth of me if I canna get clear of this dock wi'out walkin' back off it. I'll pay ye," says he, "it's noo a question of money – but for the luve of the A'mighty let's gae doon into the cabin," and the puir loon luikit sae anxious I hadna the heart tae refuse.

'Weel, the short and the lang o't was we struck a bargain – twa hundred dollars and nae questions asked. I couldna take less, says I, since the crew maun be squared on tap, and in ony case it was a wee bit inconvenient tae get it in dollar notes, and sich big ains at that. "Och, but the crew mauna ken!" says he, "ain body's ower muckle – I canna bide more." "Then I doot the deal's off," says I, "for de'il a bit can ye be stowed awa' in sich a corckle-shell as this wi'out the crew being privy, not," says I, "unless we pop yer into a herring-bunker, where ye'll be wantin' a stomach lined wi' galvanized sheet to say the least o't." "Let it be sae," says he, "I've sleepit in places as bad or worrse." "Mon," says I, "if ye've nae been jowed around in a herring-bunker on the North Sea ye havena lived up till noo, sae dinna gae boastin'. Take yer ease in the cabin, where yell nose a' the fish ye'll be wantin' if there's a wee swell ootbye."

'But listen he wouldna, sae it was agreed he should ship in a bunker – though had I kent then whit I ken noo it'd been into the dorck wi' him, and nae mair argument – and he paid up his twa hundred dollars . . . not mentioning some wee discount business on three ither notes (I'd ta'n a bodle o' cash fra the agent and it rubbed against the grain tae say nay, ye understand). "Keep an eye lifted for strangers," says he, as I clappit him doon under the hatch, "dinna let a soul aboard ither than the crew bodies." "Dinna fash yersel," says I, "I ken fine how to earn twa hundred dollars."

'Weel, there ye have it, Supereentendent. We drappit down here owernight and fetchit up at Wylie's before the toon was astir. I paid aff the crew bodies and saw them awa' to the station, then I lifted the hatch and huiked out the cargo. He wasna in the best o' shape, ye ken – it gi'es me a deal o' consolation thinkin' o't – but I gar him ha' a wash, whilk he did, and a swig at the borttle, whilk he didna, and betwixt doin' the ain and not doin' t'ither he was sune on his legs agin and

371

marchin' off doon the quay. And that's the spae, evidence or testament of Andy Carnegie McParsons, the truth of whilk is kenned by him on the ain part and his creator in pairpetuity, whatever doots may occur in the more limited minds of his accusers.'

Saying which he folded his arms independently and returned the super some measure of that worthy's police-issue stare.

'And you expect to have this colourful account believed?' fired the latter corrosively.

'Och, noo! It's naethin' but the naked truth,' returned the Scot ironically, 'I dinna expec' the police to believe sich simple things.'

'I see nothing simple about it, McParsons. It has all the marks of being deliberately contrived. First this hypothetical American meets you just as you're about to put to sea – and when you're alone. Then, for reasons the most vague, he elects to spend a night on the North Sea immured in a herring-bunker rather than show himself to the crew. And finally he takes his leave when, once more, there are no witnesses. It's pretty thin, McParsons. It'll be cut to ribbons in court. If I were you I'd stop trying to shield whoever it is behind this racket and try to be helpful – we shall get them in the long run, you can depend on that.'

'Then for Gord's sake get them, Supereentendent, and dinna waste any mair time! Ye're noo the ain half sae anxious aboot it as I am sittin' here.'

'So you're sticking to your story?'

'Aye – onless ye can puit me up tae some lees whilk will suit yer better.'

The super glanced down at the file with something

which might have been a low sigh. 'Very well,' he said dangerously, 'if you insist on having it that way . . . describe the man!'

'The Amurrican body?'

'Precisely, McParsons.'

'Weel, I doot I'm noo a policeman to be forever noticin' the crinks and crankles o' folk . . .'

The super snorted. 'Don't strain your imagination.'

'I willna, Supereentendent . . . it's me memory I'm jowin' the noo.'

'For instance . . . was he clean-shaven?' mumbled Gently, apparently studying his stubby fingernails. The Scot turned quickly towards him.

'Noo yer mention it, he wasna – he had a beard fra the temples doon.'

'He would have, wouldn't he?' demanded the super derisively.

'And his suit . . . Scots tweed?' suggested Gently.

'Na, man, it was ain o' they Yanky-doodle jobs, a' tap and noo bottom.'

'Dark?'

'Na . . . aboot the colour o' pipe-ash.'

'He was a youngish man?'

'Ower forty, ain or twa.'

'And he spoke with an educated accent?'

'Noo this cheil – he was Amurrican by adoption, ye ken . . . he spoke a fair smatterin' o' Sassenach, but he hadna it fra his mither.'

Gently felt once more in his breast-pocket for one of his doctored prints.

'Had he a beard like this one?'

McParsons rose excitedly to his feet. 'But yon's the

man – the verra spittin' image! Sae ye kent him – ye kent him a' the while – it's jist a try-on, a' this chargin' and fulin' – ye've got yer hands on him a' the while!'

Gently's gaze strayed mildly to the thunderstruck super. 'I'd like to get Hull on the wire . . . it may be a longish call.' He turned back to McParsons. 'You wouldn't remember what ships docked at Hull on that Tuesday . . . from the continent, say?'

'Fra the Continent? Och aye! There was that Porlish ship they made a' the fuss aboot aince – we ganged roon to ha' a luik at her. But concairnin' the body on yon photygraph—!'

'Thank you, Skipper,' murmured Gently distantly, 'the body on the photograph is undoubtedly your next port of call.'

They were obliging, the Hull City Police, without being able to do much more than fill in a few details. They knocked up numerous people (including con-stables) from the first and important hours of their slumber. No, they had no record of a man of Max's description. No, their life was not being blighted by an irruption of counterfeit hundred-dollar notes. Yes, the Polish liner *Ortory* had broken her Danzig-New York run at Hull on the Tuesday week last. She had docked at noon and sailed again at 19.30 hours: she had discharged seventy-five crates of Russian canned salmon and picked up a Finnish trade delegation on its way to Washington. Yes, they would get on to the dock police if Gently would hang on for a while.

'So he was a Pole, was he?' brooded the super,

sniffing meanly at the Navy Cut contaminating the aseptic night air of his office.

Gently shook his head. 'A Bulgar from Sofia.'

'You know that for a fact?'

'Not really . . . but I'm prepared to accept it as a working hypothesis.'

'How do you mean?'

'Just a hunch. I don't think someone I know could bear to tell a lie about it . . . provided he wasn't implicating himself.'

'And who is this someone?'

'Oh, it's a bit vague at the moment . . .' returned Gently evasively.

The super grunted and toyed with a retractable ball-point which seemed to be a novelty with him. 'So he was a member of this TSK . . . they were sending him to the States guyed up like a Yank and loaded with counterfeit . . . is that the angle?'

Gently nodded through his smoke.

'What was he supposed to do when he got there?'

'Oh . . . they'd have put him ashore quietly before the ship docked.'

'And then?'

Gently shrugged. 'Sabotage seems to be their line . . . he was probably going over to organize it.'

'He must have been well up in the party,' mused the super, 'it was a position of trust . . . what do you suppose went wrong?'

'That's something we're not likely to know.'

'A double-cross inside the party, maybe.'

'You're probably safe in saying that . . .'

There was a dulled, small-hour silence broken only

by a scratching in the uncoupled phone and a sizzle from Gently's pipe. From the nearby harbour came the mournfully alert toot of a siren, twice repeated.

'Of course you'll get on to the Special,' muttered the super drowsily.

'Dutt's getting them for me . . . he was attached to them a time back.'

'They may know something . . . then there's the US Federal . . . could be something they're looking for.' The super jerked himself to attention. 'Look here . . . there's something that puzzles me. If this fellow was so worried about his health, why didn't he seek political asylum when he skipped the *Ortory?* That would have been his obvious move. There was no need for all this chasing around and stowing-away aboard fishing-boats.'

Gently gave himself a little shake. 'There's the missing suitcase . . . if it were stuffed with hundred-dollar bills it seems a fairish reason for keeping things private.'

'But they were counterfeit!'

'He may not have known that.'

'You mean his party sent him off on this mission without telling him?'

'It would seem to square with what we know about the methods of these parties . . .'

The super nodded sapiently. 'But the person who swiped that suitcase must have known they were phoney, because he hasn't been passing them.'

'You can't bank on that either . . . the TSK weren't planning to spend them in Starmouth. What puzzles me is the way that bedroom was frisked. You don't have to tear a bedroom apart to find a suitcase . . .'

They were interrupted by the entry of a constable with a tray from the canteen. It bore a plate of corned-beef sandwiches and two mugs of hot coffee. Gently gladly grounded his pipe in favour of the more substantial fare – there was an almost psychic quality about corned-beef sandwiches and hot coffee at that hour of the morning. He chewed and swilled largely, and the super kept in strict step with him.

'May have hidden the stuff about the room,' mumbled the super, flipping a crumb from his moustache.

'Then why was he always carting the suitcase about with him? Everyone's agreed about that.'

'Could have been a blind.'

'Why should he bother? . . . the stuff would be safer by him.'

'He seems to have left it behind in the last instance, at all events,' grunted the super beefily.

'There may have been a purely incidental reason for that . . .'

Dutt came in, looking peeked and heavy-eyed. 'Special is going into it, sir,' he said laconically. 'I gave them a p.p. as good as I could remember and all the information we've got to date.'

'What did they say?' asked Gently, shoving him a charitable sandwich.

'Nothink, sir. They never does.'

'Did they confirm the identity of the charm?'

'Only after I'd got on to 'em, sir, and told them it was hanging up the case. You never knew such a lot for keeping their traps shut.'

Gently drank the last of his coffee and looked sadly

into the empty mug before returning it to the tray. 'Maybe they don't know much . . . maybe they aren't going to until the day-shift turns up. Did Sergeant Dack get any results with that photograph?'

'Yessir. A lot of beautiful prints.'

'Any on record?'

'He thought there was, sir – would've sworn blind about one lot. He said they matched up with the prints of a con man who specialized in flogging licences to manufacture Starmouth Rock.'

'And did they, Dutt?'

'No, sir. They was yours.'

Gently shook his head modestly. 'You compared them with the ones out of the bedroom?'

'Yessir. No resemblance.'

'And sent a set off to town?'

'Automatic, sir.'

'Have another sandwich, Dutt.'

'Thank you, sir . . . this night work makes you peckish.'

The telephone scratched its gritty throat and began to emit adenoidal language. Gently picked it up and murmured kindly to it. The dock police had been roused and briefed. They had pulled in, or rather out, the two men who had been on duty at the pier where the *Ortory* had docked on the day in question. No. 1 was applied to the line and upon invitation gave an efficient description of what occurred.

'And no civilian disembarked from the time she docked to the time you went off duty at five?' queried Gently encouragingly.

'Only one, sir, and he came down with three or four

of the ship's officers . . . they seemed to be inspecting the cases of salmon which had been unloaded.'

'The salmon? Would that have been unloaded by the ship's crew?'

'Yes, sir, it was in this instance.'

'Down a separate gangway?'

'That's right, sir.'

'And loaded on to trucks?'

'No, sir, not directly. They built it up on a pile on the pier and it wasn't till the evening when it was taken away.'

('That's it!' whispered the super, listening on an extension, 'he bribed the sailors to get him off . . . they built a hollow pile for him to hide in.')

'This civilian who came to inspect the cases . . . when did he come ashore?'

'Just before I was relieved, sir.'

'What do you mean by "inspected"?'

'Well, sir, they appeared to be counting them . . . they got one or two off the top to see how many were underneath.'

'You noticed nothing unusual take place?'

'No, sir. They just did their check and then stood about talking and looking about them for a minute or two. After that they strolled up the pier to the office and went inside.'

'The civilian too?'

'Yes, sir, the civilian and the officers.'

'Can you describe the civilian?'

'Middle-aged, about five-nine, medium-build, dark, dark-eyed, slanting brows, long, straight nose, small mouth, rather harsh voice.'

379

'Distinguishing marks?'

'I thought he had a scar on one side of his face, sir, but I only caught a glimpse of it as he came down the gangway. The rest of the time it was turned away from me.'

'Ah!' breathed Gently and propped himself up at a better functional angle with the super's desk. 'Now . . . this is important . . . did the civilian return on board with the officers?'

'I don't know, sir. My relief came just then and I went off duty. He's in the office now, sir, if you'd like to speak to him.'

There were some confused ringing sounds at the other end and No. 2 took over. Gently repeated his question.

'Well, sir . . . I regret to say I didn't notice.'

'Didn't notice? Didn't the other fellow tell you there was a civilian ashore?'

'Oh yes, sir, he did. But soon after I got on the pier there was a row amongst some of the Polish seamen and it sort of took my mind off the others.'

'What sort of a row was that?'

'I don't know what it was about, sir. Half a dozen of them came ashore and started shifting some of the cases that had been unloaded. Then all of a sudden a row broke out and a couple of them started a fight. I went up and separated them, but they kept on shouting at each other and making as though they'd let fly again, so I had to stand by and keep an eye on them. In the end one of their officers came up and sent them on board again.'

'And during that little diversion the party in the pier office slipped aboard?'

'I suppose they must have done, sir . . . they weren't there when I checked up later.'

'So if the civilian stayed ashore you wouldn't have noticed?'

'I'm afraid not, sir . . . I'm very sorry . . .'

('Cunning lot of bastards!' interjected the super with reluctant admiration, 'you can see they're professionals!')

Gently took in a few more inches of desktop. 'Give me the other bloke again,' he said. The other bloke was given him. 'What else was going on at the pier while the *Ortory* was there?'

'What sort of thing, sir?'

'Any loading or unloading going on?'

'There was a Swedish vessel unloading timber on the other side, sir.'

'And that meant a bit of traffic up and down the pier?'

'Quite a bit, sir. They were trucking some of it.'

'Was it going past the pile of cases from the *Ortory?*'

'Yes, sir, just behind it. Some of the trucks parked there to wait their turn.'

Gently nodded towards the slow-mantling dawn. 'And the Finnish Delegation?' he asked, 'what time did that embark?'

'Just after lunch, sir . . . might have been half past two.'

They sat drinking a final mug of coffee with the electric light growing thin and fey under its regulation shade. The super was looking sleepily pleased with himself, as though he felt he had a good case to go before the ratepayers, both in forgery and homicide. After all, nobody could hang Special Branch business round his neck . . . concern he might show, when secret agents bumped each other off on Starmouth Sands, but he was only nominally responsible . . .

'I suppose the bloke who did it is miles away by now,' he murmured into his coffee. 'If he shows the same ingenuity getting out of this country as he did getting into it . . .'

Gently shrugged slightly, but he didn't seem to be listening.

'And even if they get him I don't suppose we can make a murder rap stick . . .'

There was a tap on the door and the duty sergeant entered.

'Excuse me, sir,' he said to the super, 'but PC Timms has just turned in this here. It was given to him by the publican of the "Southend Smack". He changed it for a Teddy boy in his bar last night, but later on somebody tells him about some duff ones going about, so he's handed it in to be on the safe side.'

The super extended a nerveless hand. The duty sergeant placed therein a certain bill or note. And from an unexpected backyard at no great distance a cock crowed.

CHAPTER EIGHT

S UNDAY SUN FALLING steadily on the platinum
beaches, on the lazy combers, on the strangely
subdued streets. On the well-spaced, comely mansions
of High Town. On the quaint, huddled rookeries of the
Grids. On the highly-polished bonnet of a police
Wolseley as it halted on the crisp gravel of Christopher
Wylie's retired drive. On the more sober bonnet of PC
Atkins as he knocked on the door of No. 17 Kittle
Witches Grid.

'I knew he won't come to no good, that kid of
Baines's,' said a frowsy matron to the newspaperman as
they watched a goggle-eyed Bonce being marched
away. 'I said so as soon as I saw him in that fancy get-up
of his. Did you ever see such frights as they look? And
then for him to be mixing with that young Wylie . . . I
said it would be his ruination.'

'Going about the town at all hours and taking up
with all sorts,' said the cook at Wylie's, relinquishing
her vantage-point at the larder window, 'they should've
let *me* had the handling of Master Jeff – I'd have let him
mix with riff-raff like the Baineses, *I* would!'

'I dunno,' returned the kitchen-maid dreamily, 'I rather *liked* him in that silly suit of his.'

The cook snorted. 'Well, you can see where it's got him now, my girl!'

In the ill-lit parlour of No. 17 John George Baines, dock labourer, sat in his shirt-sleeves staring sullenly at the *News of the World*. His wife, a bold-faced woman, was slapping together the breakfast plates at a table covered with oil-cloth and two juvenile Baineses were scuffling and screaming on the floor.

'It wouldn't have happened,' snapped Mrs Baines for the twentieth time, 'it wouldn't have happened, not if you'd kept a proper hand on him . . .!'

'Oh, shut your mouth, woman . . . it's your fault if it's anyone's.'

'You've never give him a good hiding in your life!'

'And who was it encouraged him with that bloody suit – trying to be up to His Nibs . . .?'

More silent was the breakfast-room in High Town. No sound fell upon the ears of Christopher Wylie, except the sobbing of his wife Cora. He stood with his back to her, staring out of the expensive oriel window, staring at his cypress and monkey-puzzle trees, his impeccable gravel drive.

'I'll get on to the chief constable,' he muttered at last, 'we'll get it straightened out, Cora . . . there can't be anything in it.'

'Oh, Chris . . . I'm so frightened . . . so frightened!'

'It's all a mistake . . . we'll get it straightened out. The lad's due for his service in October . . .'

Up the long High Street marched PC Atkins, the Sunday-silent High Street with its newspaper-men, milkmen and a few early-stirring visitors in holiday attire. Beside him slouched Bonce, looking neither to right nor left. Behind him frisked Nits, a chattering, excited Nits. Halfway along the High Street PC Atkins paused to address the ragged idiot. 'You run along home, m'lad, and stop making a nuisance of yourself . . . off with you now, off with you!' Nits backed away apprehensively while the constable's eyes were on him, but as soon as the march recommenced he was dancing along in the rear again . . .

The sunshine had renewed Gently's feeling of nostalgia. They had all been sunny days, on that holiday of long ago. He remembered getting sunburned and his nose peeling, and the peculiarly pungent lotion they had put on his arms to stop them blistering (though of course they did blister), and, by association the suave smell of the oiled-paper sunshades which had been fashionable about then.

'We had rooms somewhere about where we've got them now,' he confided to a bleary-eyed Dutt as they set out for headquarters. 'They used to do you awfully well in those days . . . I can remember having chops at breakfast.'

'Don't know as I should think so much of that, sir,' admitted Dutt honestly.

'Nonsense! You've been having these degenerate meals of bacon-and-egg too long.'

'I should think a chop sits a bit heavy on your stomach first thing, sir.'

'It's true I was only a boy, Dutt . . . all the same, I think I could still face one.' He plodded along silently for a space, a little frown gathered on his brow. 'We seemed to be younger in those days, Dutt . . .'

'*Younger*, sir?' inquired Dutt in surprise.

'Yes, Dutt . . . younger.'

'Well, sir, I s'pose we was – in those days!'

But there was no smile on the face of his superior as they turned up the steps at headquarters.

The landlord of the Southend Smack was waiting patiently in the office which the super had assigned to Gently, and Copping, who had got to bed earlier than most, and was consequently his old spry self, officiously performed the introduction.

'You think you can remember the youth who changed the note?' inquired Gently dryly.

'Ho yes, sir – don't you worry about that!' replied the landlord, a red-faced beery individual called Biggers.

'You've seen him before, then?'

'Ah, I have – once or twice.'

'You know his name?'

'No. No, sir. But he's been in the bar once or twice, I can tell you that.'

'It didn't occur to you that he might be a little young to be served in a bar?'

'W'no, sir . . . I mean . . . there you are!' Biggers faltered uneasily, beginning to catch on that he wasn't Gently's blue-eyed boy. 'He *looked* old enough, sir . . . couldn't be far off. You can't ask all of them to pull out their birth-certificates.'

'Was he on his own?'

'Ho yes, sir!'

'Does he always come into your bar on his own?'

'Y-yes, sir, as far as I remember.'

'How do you mean, as far as you remember?'

'Well, sir . . . I wouldn't like to swear he never had no one with him.'

'A woman, perhaps.'

'No, sir – no women!'

'Another youngster dressed like himself?'

'Yes, sir, that's it!'

'Dressed exactly like himself?'

'Yes, sir, exactly!'

'And younger – about a year?'

'Yes, sir . . . I mean . . .!' Biggers trailed away, realizing the trap into which he had been unceremoniously precipitated. Gently eyed him with contempt.

'This hundred-dollar bill . . . didn't it seem odd to you that a young fellow should have one in his possession?'

'Oh, I dunno, sir . . . what with the Yanks about and all . . .'

'And how should he have acquired it from an American?'

'Well, sir, they're master men for playing dice.'

'You thought he'd won it gambling?'

'I never really thought . . . that's the truth!'

'Good,' retorted Gently freezingly, 'I'm glad it's the truth, Biggers. The truth is what we are primarily interested in . . . let's try sticking to it, shall we? How much did you give him for it?'

'I . . . I give him its value.'

'How much?'

'Why, all it was worth to me . . .'

'*How much?*'

Biggers halted sulkily. 'I give him a tenner . . . now

turn round and tell me it wasn't enough, when it was a dud note in the first place!'

Gently turned his back on the sweating publican. 'Is the parade lined up?' he asked Copping.

'They're in the yard – just give me a moment.'

It was a scrupulously fair parade. Copping had wanted to impress Gently by his handling of it, and after witnessing the momentary appearance of the mailed hand lurking beneath the chief inspector's velvet glove he was glad that he had so wanted. There was something almost deceitful about Gently, he thought . . .

Biggers took his time in going down the line, as though wishing to display his helpful care and attention. He paused before several law-abiding youths before making his final selection. He also paused before Bonce, whose wild-eyed guilt proclaimed itself to high heaven, but the pause was a brief one and might even have been involuntary . . . Having done his conscientious best, he carried his findings to Gently.

'That's him . . . fifth from the far end . . . kid in the brown suit.'

Gently nodded briefly. 'And this one . . . the carroty-headed boy?'

'No, sir. Don't know him. Never seen him before!'

'Positive?'

'Ho yes, sir . . . I never forgets a face.'

The same mailed hand which Copping had so judiciously observed fell lightly on Bigger's arm and the astonished publican found himself whirled a matter of three yards in a direction not of his choosing.

'Now see here, Biggers, you've come forward voluntarily and given us some useful information, but there's not much doubt that you're sailing a bit too close to the wind. From now on there'll be an eye on you, so watch your step. Don't change any more money, American or otherwise, and if any of your customers looks a day under fifty – ask for his birth certificate. Is that clear?'

'Y–yes, sir!'

'Quite clear?'

Biggers gulped assent.

'Then get away out of here . . . we've finished with you – for the moment!'

A blue-bottle buzzed in a sunny pane of the office window, a casual, preoccupied buzzing which focussed and concentrated in itself a vision of all fine Sundays from time immemorial. Copping lifted the bottom of the window and let it out. It fizzed skywards in a fine frenzy of indignant release, wavered, scented a canteen dustbin and toppled down again from the height of its Homeric disdain. Copping left the window half-open.

'One at a time?' he asked.

'Yes. Shove the Baines boy into a room by himself where he can do a little quiet thinking.'

Copping nodded and went out. Gently seated himself in awful state behind the bleak steel desk with its virgin blotter, jotting-pad and desk-set. He slid open a drawer. It contained a well-thumbed copy of Moriarty's *Police Law* and some paper-clips. The drawer on the other side contained nothing but ink-stains and punch confetti.

'I wonder who the super turfed out to make room for us?' he mused to Dutt.

Copping returned, prodding Jeff before him. The Teddy boy looked a good deal less exotic in his quieter lounge-suit, but there was still plenty of swagger about him. He stared round him with a sullen defiance, his thin-lipped mouth set tight and trapped.

'Sit down,' said Gently, indicating a chair placed in front but a little to the side of the desk. Jeff sat as though he were conferring a favour. Copping took the chair on the other side and Dutt hovered respectfully in the background.

'Your full name and address?'

'You know that already—'

'Answer the inspector!' snapped Copping.

Jeff glared at him and clenched his hands. 'Jeffery Wylie, Manor House, High Town.'

'Your full name, please.'

'Jeffery . . . Algernon.'

Gently wrote it down on his jotter.

'Now, Wylie . . . you had better understand that you are here on a very serious matter, perhaps more serious than you at first supposed. You have been identified as possessing and uttering counterfeit United States currency – wait a minute!' he exclaimed, as Jeff tried to interrupt, 'You'll have plenty of opportunity to have your say – you've been identified as handling this money and we happen to know the source from which it emanated. Now what I have to say to you is this: you may be able to explain satisfactorily how you came to be in possession of that note, in which case there will be no charge made against you. But you are not obliged to give an explanation and you are not advised to if you think it may implicate you in a graver charge. At the same time, if you take the latter course I shall automatically charge you and you will be held in custody on that charge while further investigations are made. Is the situation quite plain to you?'

Jeff shuffled his feet. 'I can see you're out to get me, one way or the other . . .'

'We're not out to "get" anyone, Wylie, if they happen to be innocent. I'm simply warning you of where you stand. And I'd like to add to that some advice if you help us you'll be helping yourself. But it's up to you entirely. Nobody here is going to use third-degree methods.'

The Teddy boy sniffed derisively and stuck his hands into his pockets. 'I know how you get people to say what you want . . . I've heard what goes on.'

'Then you'd better forget what you've heard and consider your own position.'

'A fat lot of good that'll do me . . .'

'It'll do you more good than trying to be clever with policemen.'

'You say yourself I don't have to tell you anything.'

There was a silence during which Copping, to judge from his expression, was meditating a modified use of the third-degree methods which Gently had disowned.

'It's only his word against mine . . .' began Jeff at last.

Gently cocked an eyebrow. 'Whose word?'

'His – the pub-keeper's.'

'And who told you he was a publican?'

Jeff flushed. 'Isn't that what he looked like?'

'He may have looked like a publican or he may have looked like a barman. What made you think he was one and not the other?'

'I just said the first thing that came into my head, that's what I did!'

Gently nodded a mandarin nod but said nothing.

'He could have been wrong,' continued Jeff, encouraged, 'he might've just picked on me because he couldn't remember and thought you'd jump on him if he didn't find someone. He can't prove it was me.'

'I dare say other people were present . . .'

'There were only two of them and—' Jeff stopped abruptly, glowering.

'And they were busy playing dominoes or something?' suggested Gently helpfully.

Jeff dug deeper into his pockets. 'I won't say any more – you're trying to trap me, that's what it is! You're trying to get me to say things I don't mean . . .!'

'Suppose,' said Gently, beginning to draw pencil-strokes on his pad, 'suppose we go back to the beginning and try a different tack?'

'There isn't any tack to try – it wasn't me and nobody can prove it was.'

'Then you didn't change a dollar bill . . .'

'I never had a hundred–dollar bill in my life.' Gently's pencil paused. 'What size bill?'

Jeff bit his lip and was silent.

'He doesn't even know how to lie . . .' observed Copping disgustedly.

Gently finished off his stroke-pattern with aggravating deliberation. Then he felt in his pocket for the spare photograph and regarded it indifferently for a few moments. Finally he leaned across the desk and shoved it at Jeff.

'Here . . . take a look at this.'

Jeff unpocketed a hand to take it, but Gently was being so clumsy that he knocked it out of the Teddy boy's hand and on to the floor. Sullenly Jeff reached down and scrabbled under his chair for it.

'Was he the man who gave you the note?'

'I told you I never had one.'

'Have you ever seen this man before?'

'I saw his picture on the screen at the Marina, only it didn't have a beard.'

'But you've never seen the man?'

'No.'

Gently retrieved the photograph carefully from fingers that trembled and beckoned to Dutt.

'Take this along to the print department and see if they've got an enlargement, Dutt . . .'

'Print department, sir?' queried Dutt in surprise.

Gently nodded meaningly. 'And check it with the original, Dutt . . . it might bring out some interesting points.'

'Yessir. I get you, sir.' Dutt took the photograph gingerly by the extreme margins and went out with it. Gently picked up his pencil again and began laying out a fresh stroke-pattern. Through the open window could be heard, faint and far-off, Copping's blue-bottle or one of its mates improving the shining hour round the canteen dustbin, while more distantly sounded the hum of excursion traffic coming up the High Street. A perfect day for anything but police business . . .

'You see, Wylie . . . I'll come to the point. The note you are alleged to have had in your possession was one introduced into this country by the man on the photograph. That man, as you are aware, was murdered.'

'I never knew him – it's nothing to do with me!'

'If it's nothing to do with you then it would be a good idea to tell the truth about the note.'

'But I never had any note – it's all a lie . . . I keep telling you.'

Gently shook his head remorselessly. 'All you've told me to date has convinced me of the reverse. Besides, the man who identified you gave a pretty damning description when he handed in the note. That suit of yours is rather distinctive, you know. I don't suppose anybody else in Starmouth wears one excepting Baines . . . and I shall be questioning him in due course.'

'He's seen me before, he could have made it up.'

'He's seen you before? I thought he wasn't supposed to be known to you?'

'He *could* have seen me before . . .'

'And made up the whole story about a complete stranger?' Gently hatched a few of the lines in his pattern.

Copping snorted impatiently. 'You're lying . . . it's too obvious. We know what you got for the note and when we picked you two up this morning you each had five-pound notes on you. What was that – a coincidence?'

'I get pocket-money!' Jeff exclaimed, 'my father isn't a labourer.'

'No, but Baines's father is. Where did *he* get five pounds?'

'He works – he's got a job!'

'That's right – thirty bob a week as an errand boy and pays his mother a pound of it. Do you think we're fools?'

Jeff's breath came fast. 'I tip him a pound now and again . . .'

'And he saves it up?'

'How should I know what he does with it?'

'If you don't, nobody else does. What were you doing at ten to ten last night?'

'I . . . I was on the Front.'

'Alone?'

'I . . .'

'Answer me!' snapped Copping, 'you don't have to think if you're telling the truth. Baines was with you, wasn't he?'

'No! I mean . . .!'

'Yes! Of course he was. Why bother to lie? And you were skint, weren't you? You'd got rid of your precious pocket money and Baines's ten bob with it. All you'd got left was an American note – a note you'd begged, borrowed, stolen and perhaps murdered for—'

'No!'

'—and that was all there was between you and a bleak weekend. So you picked out a quiet-looking pub – one where you knew there wouldn't be many witnesses to the transaction – and slipped in and flogged the note to the publican. He wasn't offering much, was he? Less than a third of what it was worth! But you couldn't stop and argue – it might draw attention – they might ask questions you hadn't got the answers for—'

'It's a lie!' screamed Jeff, as white as a sheet, 'you're making it all up – it's all a lie!'

'Then you can prove you were somewhere else?'

'I was never near that pub!'

'Then what pub were you near?'

'I wasn't near any pub at all!'

'Is the only pub on the Front the one you weren't near?'

'I don't know . . . I didn't notice . . . I didn't go into a pub anywhere last night!'

Gently clicked his tongue. 'It's a pity about that . . . it might have helped you to establish an alibi that doesn't otherwise seem to be forthcoming.'

Copping repeated his snort and seemed, with flaming eyes, about to continue his verbal assault upon the shaking Teddy boy: but at that moment Dutt re-entered.

'Ah!' murmured Gently, 'did you make a comparison, Dutt?'

'Yessir.' The sergeant's eye strayed to Jeff. 'Very like, sir, at a rough check. Sergeant Dack thinks so too, sir. He's going over them proper now.'

Gently nodded and stroked off a square. 'Bring in Baines, Dutt . . . oh, and just a minute . . .'

'Yessir?'

'Take him along to the prints department first, will you?'

Dutt withdrew and Copping looked questioningly at Gently. But Gently was busy with his patterns again.

'Y-you can't go on anything Baines says,' muttered Jeff tremblingly.

'Oh? And why can't we?' barked the ferocious Copping.

'He'll say anything . . . you can make him say what you like.'

'If we can make him tell the truth it'll be the first time we've heard it this morning, my lad. I should button my lip, if I were you.'

Jeff licked dry lips and took the advice. There wasn't an ounce of swagger left in him. He sat sagging back in his chair, his feet at an awkward angle, his hands digging ever deeper into his pockets. Copping got up and went over to the window. The fine weather outside seemed to anger him. He studied it tigerishly for a moment, sniffed at the balmy sea air, then turned to eye the Teddy boy from between half-closed lids.

'A nice day for a picnic,' suggested Gently cautioningly.

'I was going round the links . . . if I'd got away early enough.'

Gently shrugged. 'Something always turns up . . . it's the bright day that brings forth the adder.'

But Copping sniffed and would not be comforted.

Bonce was brought in, as wild-eyed as ever, and scrubbing recently-inked fingers on the seat of his cheap trousers. Jeff pulled himself together a little at the sight of his henchman, as though conscious of a sudden that he was cutting a poor figure. Gently glanced at Dutt, who shook his head.

'Not this one, sir. Nothing like.'

'Are you sure of that?' asked Gently in surprise.

'Positive, sir.'

'Well . . . they're not supposed to lie! Sit down, Baines. You can wash your hands later on.'

Bonce sat down automatically in the chair indicated to him. He had an air of bereftness, as though he had lost all will of his own. His mouth was hanging a little open and his face had a boiled look. His eyes resolutely refused to focus on anything more distant than the blunt tip of his freckled nose.

Gently pondered this woebegone figure without expression.

'Robert Henry Baines of seventeen Kittle Witches Grid?'

Bonce nodded twice as though the question had operated a spring.

Gently cautioned him at some length, though it seemed doubtful if what he was saying penetrated very clearly into Bonce's shocked and bewildered mind.

'I'm going to ask you one question, Baines, and it's entirely up to you whether you answer it or not. You understand me?'

The spring was operated again. Gently paused with his pencil at one corner of his pad.

'I want you to tell me, Baines . . . if you assisted Wylie when, on the night of Tuesday last, he entered a rear bedroom of 52 Blantyre Road and removed from there a suitcase containing United States treasury notes.'

'Don't tell him, Bonce!' screamed Jeff, leaping to his feet, 'don't tell him, you bloody little fool!'

'*Silence!*' thundered Gently in a voice that made even Dutt wince, 'get back in your chair, Wylie!'

'But it's a lie . . . he'll say anything . . .!'

'*Get back in your chair!*'

Copping sent the Teddy boy sprawling into his seat again and held him there struggling and panting.

'Now, Baines . . . have you anything to answer?'

Bonce gaped and gurgled in his throat, his eyes rolling pitiably. Then the spring clicked and his head began to nod. 'I went with him . . . it's true . . . I kept watch in the alley . . .'

'You fool – oh, you bloody little fool!' sobbed Jeff,

'don't you understand it's murder they're after us for – don't you understand it's murder?'

There was a ripping sound as Gently's pencil crossed from one corner of the pad to the other.

The charge was made: burglary on the night of the eleventh. Jeff was in tears as he gave his statement. Of the two of them, it was Bonce who showed the better front. Having shed the intolerable load of conscious guilt he seemed to stiffen up and gain some sort of control of himself, while Jeff, on the other hand, went more and more to pieces. It was from Bonce that Gently received the more coherent picture.

They had been in 'The Feathers' late on the Tuesday evening when the prostitute Frenchy entered. She was well known to them – Jeff claimed to have slept with her and Bonce wasn't sure that Jeff hadn't – and she approached them with the information that a man-friend of hers had left in his bedroom a suitcase containing something of considerable value.

'Was she in the habit of divulging such information?' queried Gently.

Jeff stoutly denied it, but Bonce admitted one or two instances.

'And were you accustomed to act on it?'

Bonce hung his head. 'Once we did . . .'

Frenchy had struck a quick bargain. They would go halves in whatever the loot realized. She gave them the address, explained the situation of the bedroom and guaranteed to keep the man busy for another hour or two at least. When she left they followed her at a discreet distance and saw her meet a man resembling the one in the photograph. He had exchanged a few words with her and then signalled a taxi. The taxi had departed in the direction of the North Shore.

'Where did the taxi pick them up?' asked Gently.

'It was just outside the Marina.'

'What would have been the time?'

Bonce glanced at Jeff. 'About ten, I should think.'

'Would you know the taxi again?'

'N-no, sir, there wan't nothin' special about it.'

'From which direction did it come?'

'From the Pleasure Beach way, sir.'

The owner of the suitcase having been seen on his way, they hastened round to Blantyre Road and identified No. 52. Then they approached it by the back alley and while Bonce kept watch outside, Jeff broke into the rear bedroom.

'Weren't you taking a bit of a risk?' inquired Gently of Jeff. 'The lodger may have been out, but it's pretty certain the landlady wasn't.'

'We could see them down below,' sniffed Jeff, 'they were watching the telly.'

'The television couldn't have had much longer to go by the time you got there.'

'It's the truth, I tell you!'

'All right, all right – just answer my questions! It may have been running late on Tuesday. How long did it take you to do the job?'

'Ten minutes . . . quarter of an hour, perhaps.'

'No longer than that?' Gently glanced at Bonce.

'That's about it, sir.'

'But you had to hunt around for it?'

'Why should I?' sniffed Jeff, 'I knew what I was

looking for . . . a blue suitcase with chromium locks. It was standing with the other one near the wardrobe.'

'Did you look in the other one?'

'No . . . I never touched it.'

'Didn't you go through the drawers or anything of that sort?'

'I tell you I didn't touch anything! I just got what I came for and went. Ask him if I aren't telling the truth.'

Bonce corroborate his leader's statement – he had returned with the blue suitcase and nothing else. They had carried it off to a quiet spot in Blantyre Gardens, forced the locks and discovered the astounding contents. Immediately there was a change of plans. Jeff decided they would tell Frenchy that they had been unable to find the suitcase – a proposition she wasn't situated to contradict – while in reality they would keep it hidden until the hue and cry had died down and then dispose of it by slow and cautious degrees. This they did, and for some reason Frenchy accepted their story without much fuss. When the murder became news and they recognized the pictures which were issued as being of Frenchy's man-friend, they had an additional incentive for keeping the stolen notes under cover. Unfortunately, their patience was soon exhausted. A financial crisis at the end of the week had slackened their caution. Surely, they had thought, there could be no harm in cashing just *one* of that inexhaustible pile of notes . . . just one, to see them comfortably through the weekend . . .

Gently sighed at the end of the recital. 'And the rest of them, where are they now?'

Bonce swallowed and glanced again at Jeff. 'They're under the pier.'

401

'Which pier is that?'

'Albion Pier . . . there's a hole between two girders.'

'You'd better show me . . . Dutt!'

'Yessir?'

'Tell them to bring a car round, will you?' He returned to Bonce. 'That evening . . . in the bar at "The Feathers" . . . were all the usual crowd there?'

Bonce twisted his snub nose perplexedly. 'I – I suppose so, sir.'

'Was Artie serving at the bar?'

'Oh yes, sir.'

'That fellow who wears loud checks and lives on whisky?'

'Yes, sir.'

'Louey?'

'N-no, sir . . . *you* don't often see him in the bar.'

'Peachey?'

'I think he looked in while we were talking to Frenchy . . .'

There was the sound of a car swinging out of the yard and Copping rose to his feet. He looked at Gently questioningly and motioned to the two youths with his head. 'Cuffs on them . . . just to keep on the safe side?'

Gently smiled amongst the nebulae. 'Let's be devils this morning, shall we? Let's take a risk!'

Exceeding Sunday-white lay the Albion Pier under mid-morning sun. Its two square towers, each capped with gold, notched firmly into an azure sky and its peak-roofed pavilion, home of Poppa Pickle's Pierrots, notched equally firmly into a green-and-amethyst sea. Its gates were closed. They were not to open till half past two. The brightly dressed strollers, each infected in some degree by the prevailing Sundayness, were constrained to the languid buying of ice-cream, the indifferent booking of seats or the bored contemplation of Poppa Pickle's Pierrots' pics. They didn't complain. They knew it was their lot. Being English, one was never at a loss for a moral attitude.

Even the arrival of a police car with three obvious plain-clothes men and two obvious wrong-doers didn't seriously upset the moral atmosphere, though it may have intensified it a little.

'Which end?' inquired Gently, shepherding his flock down the steps to the beach.

'This end . . . up here where the pier nearly touches the sand.'

They marched laboriously through soft dry sand, the cynosure for an increasing number of eyes. Dutt led the way, the Teddy boys followed, and Copping and Gently brought up the rear. Under the pier they went, where the sand was cold and grey. A forest of dank and rusty piles enclosed them in an echoing twilight.

'Up there,' snuffled Jeff, indicating a girder which nearly met the sand, 'there's another one joins it behind . . . it's in the gap between them.'

'Get it out,' ordered Gently to Dutt.

The gallant sergeant went down on his stomach and squirmed vigorously till he was under the girder. Then he turned on his back and began feeling in the remote obscurity beyond. He seemed to be prying there for an unconscionable length of time.

'Have you found the hole?' asked Gently, his voice echoing marinely amongst the piles.

'Yessir,' came muffledly from Dutt, 'hole's there, sir
. . . it's what's in it I aren't sure about . . . couldn't get
hold of me legs and pull me out, sir?'

Copping went to the rescue and a grimy Dutt
renewed acquaintance with the light of day. In his arms
he bore a bundle, also grimy. 'This is all there was, sir
. . . ain't no trace of any suitcase.'

'Open it!' snapped Gently.

Copping broke the string and unwrapped the paper.
There lay revealed a crumpled grey suit, a pair of
two-colour shoes, shirt, socks, underclothes, suspenders
and a blue bow tie.

'Sakes alive!' exclaimed Copping. 'Look at this label
– Klingelschwitz – it's the same as in the boyo's suit!'

'And look at this shirt,' added Gently grimly, 'four
nicely grouped stab-holes . . . same as in the boyo's
thorax.'

A sugary thump made them all turn sharply. It was
Jeff going out cold on a sand that was even colder.

CHAPTER NINE

IT WAS A hefty lunch for a hot day and Gently
followed Dutt's example of shedding his jacket and
rolling his sleeves up. There wasn't any frippery about
it. Just straight roast beef and Yorkshire pudding, and
vegetables followed by hot apple turnover with custard.
But either Mrs Davis was a demon cook, or else the
Starmouth ozone had really come into its own that day
. . . there wasn't much in the way of conversation for
quite some time.

'Superintendents!' muttered Gently at last, evaluating
the remains of the turnover with sad resignation.

'Never alters,' agreed Dutt sympathetically, cutting
an absent-minded slice.

'I can't help coming to the conclusion, Dutt . . .'

'Yessir?'

'. . . if it didn't savour of insubordination . . .'

'Aye, aye!' Dutt winked at his superior over a
spoonful of juicy pastry. 'Don't have to say it, sir. I
knows well enough what you mean.'

Gently picked up his plate and placed it at some
distance from himself, as though finally to sever

connections with that beguiling turnover. 'You make a pinch . . . you dig up some evidence . . . it does something to them. They're all the same, Dutt.'

'Yessir. Noticed it.'

'They suddenly turn impatient. It's an occupational disease with superintendents. At a certain stage in the proceedings they get the charge-lust. They want to charge someone. And if there's half a case against anybody it's the devil's own job to head a super off and make him be a good boy . . .'

'Don't we know it, sir?'

Gently drew a deep breath and pulled out his familiar sandblast. 'Of course, you have to admit it . . . there's enough on Baines and Wylie to make the average super sit up and howl blue murder. But at the same time, it only needs the average forensic eye. Baines isn't a liar, for instance, and Wylie's got too scared to lie. No, Dutt, no. Our super is doing himself no good by tearing the bricks apart at the Wylie's. He won't find anything, and he won't improve his standing with anyone.'

Mrs Davis brought in their cuppa, making room for the tray beside Gently. She hesitated on seeing the chief inspector's pipe on the point of being lit and then produced, from nowhere as it seemed, a capacious glass ashtray. Gently nodded a solemn acknowledgement. Mrs Davis beamed at the still-eating Dutt. 'Aren't you going down to the beach now this afternoon, Inspector?'

Gently smiled wanly and unbonneted the teapot.

'Well, sir . . . what do *you* make of them clothes turning up like that?' queried Dutt when the tea was poured and Mrs Davis had retired.

'They were planted deliberately, Dutt. By the person who lifted the suitcase.'

'But how did they know where it was, sir?'

'By deduction and observation – just as we find out things.' Gently doused a match and took one or two comfortable pulls. 'Obviously . . . they wanted that suitcase back. Whether they still intended to use the money or not we don't know, but they feel it's important that a large consignment of it shouldn't be lying around loose . . . it would almost inevitably finish up in our hands. So their first move after settling with Max was to recover the suitcase and I can imagine they were a little upset to find it missing when they got to his lodgings . . .'

'Lord luvvus, sir – that other set of prints! I've been puzzling my loaf about them all the morning.'

'Exactly, Dutt . . . the first little slip our friends seem to have made. But I don't suppose they aimed to be around when those prints came to light. It was just a bit of bad luck that the suitcase had vanished into thin air . . .'

'So it was them who ransacked the room, sir.'

'Undoubtedly.'

'On account of he may have hidden the stuff somewhere.'

'It was a possibility they wouldn't overlook.'

Dutt gave a little chuckle. 'You're right, sir . . . their faces must have dropped a mile when they found the cupboard was bare!'

'A good mile, Dutt, and possibly two. It upset all their calculations. It meant they would have to hang around and look for it instead of getting to hell out of the country . . . and hanging around would get to be more and more dangerous as the investigation went on. At first, I imagine, they hadn't a clue about it. They may have visited the bedroom more than once and they were certainly interested to know what we found when we got there . . . and then, of course, they began to think it out and perhaps make some inquiries. They found out, or possibly they knew, that Max had been consorting with Frenchy . . . that was an obvious lead. No doubt they gave her flat a going-over. They might even have questioned her. But there was no suitcase at the flat, and all that Frenchy could tell them – even if she came clean – was of Jeff and Bonce's allegedly fruitless attempt to get the suitcase . . . Anyway, they got on to Jeff and Bonce somehow. It wouldn't have been too difficult if they checked up on Frenchy.'

'And then they kept them under observation, sir?'

'Just as we would have done, Dutt.'

'And last night they found out where the case was hidden – and left the clothes there for a false scent, sir?'

Gently nodded pontifically. 'A false scent for a charge-happy super.'

Dutt swallowed a mouthful of tea and looked a little dubiously at the remaining shoulder of apple turnover. 'Just one thing, sir . . .'

'Yes, Dutt?'

'I don't want to seem critical, sir . . .'

'Don't be modest, Dutt – just come to the point.'

'Well, sir, what I want to say is, how did they know we was ever going to find them clothes, let alone connect them with the Teddy boys?'

Gently nodded again and smiled around his pipe. 'That's what we want to know, isn't it, Dutt. That's going to be the clincher!'

He rose from the table and went over to Mrs Davis's telephone. The phonebook lay beside it. He flicked through it and traced down a column with a clumsy finger.

'Starmouth 75629 . . . this is Chief Inspector Gently.' He tilted the instrument to one side so that Dutt could hear too. 'Biggers? There's something else I want to ask you, Biggers . . . yes, about last night.'

'Ho yes, sir?' came the publican's anxious voice from the other end.

'You told us in your statement that after you had changed the note you heard there were some counterfeit ones going about. I want to know where you obtained that information.'

'Yes, sir! Certainly, sir! It was a bloke in the bar what told me that.'

'A bloke you know?'

'Ho no, sir. Quite a stranger.'

'He was in the bar at the time of the transaction?'

'No, sir, not as I remember. The first time I noticed him there was when the young feller went out.'

'You mean he came in while the transaction was in progress?'

'Must've done, sir, 'cause he soon ups and tells me to watch my step with regard to Yank money. "Wasn't that a hundred–dollar bill?" he says. "Ah, it was," I says. "Then it's ten to one you've been had," he says, or words to that effect, "there was a sailor got copped with some this afternoon."'

'Oh did he . . .?' Gently exchanged a glance with Dutt.

'Yes, sir . . . God's honest truth!' The voice on the phone sounded panicky. 'I don't have no cause to lie, now do I—!'

'All right, Biggers . . . never mind the trimmings. What else did this man tell you?'

'Well, he told me I could get five years, sir, and that I ought to hand it over to the police . . . naturally, me just having paid ten quid . . .'

'We know about that. Did he say anything else?'

'No, sir . . . not apart from ordering a whisky. It was nearly closing-time.'

'Would you recognize him again?'

'Ho yes, sir! Like I was telling you, I never forget a face.'

'Can you describe him?'

'Well, sir . . . he wasn't English, that I can say.'

'Did you notice a mole on his cheek by any chance?'

'No, sir. No. But he'd got a scar running all down one side . . .'

Gently hung up the instrument and leaned on it ponderingly for a few moments. His eyes were fixed on Mrs Davis's flowered wallpaper, but to a watchful Dutt they seemed to be staring at something a good six feet on the other side of the wall. Then he sighed and straightened his bulky form.

'So there it is, Dutt . . . our clincher. And they even knew about McParsons . . . eh?'

Dutt shook his head ruefully. 'They must have quite an organization, sir . . .'

'An organization!' Gently laughed shortly. 'Well . . .

410

we'd better get our own organization moving, too. Go back to headquarters, Dutt, and tell them to put a man each on the two stations and another on the bus terminus, and to warn the men on the docks to keep their eyes double-skinned. It's an even bet that our scar-faced acquaintance is well clear of Starmouth, but we can't take any risks . . . Then give Special a ring and let them know.'

Dutt nodded intelligently. 'And the clothes, sir . . .?'

'Get them sent to the lab, and the paper and string. Oh, and that cab-driver . . . the one who picked up Max and Frenchy on Tuesday night . . . see if you can get a line on him, Dutt.'

'Yessir. Do my best.'

Gently scratched a match and applied it to his pipe. 'Me, I'm going to pay a little social call in Dulford Street. I think it's time that Frenchy assisted the police by supplying the answers to one or two interesting questions.'

Dulford Street was a shabby thoroughfare adjoining the lower part of the Front. It began as though by accident where some clumsily-placed buildings had left a gap and proceeded narrowly and crookedly until it got lost in a maze of uncomely backstreets. There was a feeling of having-gone-to-seed about it, as though its original inhabitants had given it up in despair and left it to go its own way. From one end to the other it could boast of no fresh paint except the lurid red-and-cream of an odiferous fish and chip shop.

Gently eyed the assemblage moodily and applied to a new bag of peppermint creams for encouragement.

411

Sunday was obviously an off-day in Dulford Street. The signs of life disturbing its charms were few. On the right-hand side was a frowsy little corner-shop with some newspapers in a rack at the door, and at the entry from the Front lurked a furtive and ragged figure . . . Nits, who had been following Gently all the way along the promenade. Gently shrugged his bulky shoulders and pushed open the clanging door of the newspaper shop.

'Chief Inspector Gently . . . I wonder if you can give me some information?'

It was a white-haired old lady with beaming specs and an expression of anxious affability.

'What was it you were wanting?'

'Some information, madam.'

'The newspapers is all outside . . . just take one, sir!'

'I want some information.' Gently raised his voice, but the only effect was to increase the old lady's look of anxiety. He pointed out of the dusty window.

'That apartment over there . . . do you know who lives in it?'

'Oh yes, I do! She isn't nothing to do with me!'

'Is that her permanent address or does she just make use of it?'

'Eh . . . eh?' The old lady peered at him as though she suspected him of having said something rude.

'Is that her permanent address?' began Gently, *fortissimo*, then he shook his head and gave it up. 'Here, how much are these street directories?'

'They're sixpence,' retorted the old lady sharply, 'sixpence – that's what they are!'

Gently put a shilling on her rubber mat and made a noisy exit.

Frenchy's apartment, flat, or whatever other dignity it aspired to was situated above a disused fruiterer's shop. The shop itself had been anciently boarded up, but the degree of paintwork it exhibited matched evenly with that of Frenchy's door and the windows above, leaving no doubt about the contemporaneity of the decoration. Gently tried the door and found it open. It gave directly on to uncarpeted stairs which rose steeply to a narrow landing. At the top were two more doors, one with a transom light which did its best to illumine the shadow of the landing, and at this he knocked with a regular policeman's rhythm.

'Who is id . . .?' came Frenchy's croon.

'It's Chief Inspector Gently. All right if I come in?'

There was a creaking and scuffling, and finally the sound of shuffling footsteps. Then the door opened to display a draggle-haired Frenchy, partly-clad in a green dressing-gown. She glared at Gently.

'What are you after now?'

'I'm after you,' said Gently cheerfully, 'weren't you expecting me to call?'

Her eyes narrowed like the eyes of a cat. 'You've got nothing to pinch me for . . . you bloody well know it! Why can't you leave a girl alone?'

Gently tutted. 'This isn't the attitude, Frenchy. You should try to be co-operative, you know – it pays, in your profession.'

'That's none of your business and you ain't got nothing on me!'

Gently shook his head admonishingly and pressed past her into the room. It wasn't an inviting prospect. The furniture consisted of an iron bedstead, a deal table and three cheap bedroom chairs. The floor was covered with unpolished brown lino, the walls with faded paper. At the window, curtains were drawn to keep out the sun, but in spite of this the room was like a large and unventilated oven, an oven, moreover, that possessed a vigorously compounded odour, part dry rot, part cigarette smoke and part Frenchy. Gently fanned himself thoughtfully with his trilby.

'Doesn't seem a very comfortable digging for a trouper like you, Frenchy,' he observed.

'What's it got to do with you?' spat Frenchy, closing the door with a bang.

'And you're travelling light this season.' He indicated a dress and a white two-piece which hung on hangers from a hook in the wall.

'If you're going to pinch a girl for being short of clothes . . .!'

Gently concluded his unhurried survey with the dishevelled bed, some empty beer-bottles and a chamber-pot. 'And then again, my dear, this place is in the wrong direction . . .'

'Whadyermean – wrong direction?'

'It isn't in the direction the taxi took.'

'What taxi – what are you getting at?' Frenchy whisked round fiercely to confront him.

'Why . . . the taxi you and Max took from outside the Marina at about 10 p.m. last Tuesday. It went off towards the North Shore . . . that's in a diametrically opposite direction, isn't it, Frenchy?'

The sudden pallor of the blonde woman's face showed up the dark wells of her eyes like two pools, but she took a furious grip on herself. 'It's a filthy dirty lie

. . . I didn't take no taxi! I was in "The Feathers" at ten . . . ask anyone who was there . . . ask Jeff Wylie – it was him who came away with me!' She broke off, breathing hard, crouching as though prepared to ward off a physical blow.

Gently's head wagged a measured negative and he felt in his pocket for some carelessly-folded sheets of the copy-paper. 'It won't do, Frenchy . . . it isn't good enough any longer. I've got a couple of statements here which tell a different story.'

'Then some b—'s been lying!' Frenchy tried to snatch the sheets out of Gently's hand.

'Nobody's been lying and you'll get a chance to read these in a couple of minutes. Now sit down like a good girl.'

Frenchy hovered a moment as though still meditating an attempt on the papers. Then she swore an atrocious oath and dumped herself down on the side of the bed, an action which endangered the decency of her sparsely-clad person. Gently turned one of the chairs back-to-front and seated himself also.

'First, I'd better have your name.'

'What's wrong with Frenchy . . . it suits everyone else round here.'

Gently clicked his tongue. 'Let's not be childish, Frenchy. Why make me bother the boys in Records?'

'Trust a bloody copper! So it's Meek, then. Agnes Meek.'

Gently scribbled it in his notebook. 'And where do you hail from, Agnes?'

'I was born and bred in Maida . . . but don't use that filthy bleeding name!'

'And when did you come up here?'

''Bout Whitsun or just before.'

'And whose idea was it?'

'Mine – who the hell's do you think it was?'

'Now Frenchy! I'm only asking a civil question.'

'And I'm telling you I came up on my own! Don't you think a girl needs a holiday?'

Gently shrugged. 'It's up to you . . . So you've been living at this address since Whitsun?'

'That's right.'

'And nowhere else at all?'

Frenchy swore a presumable negative.

'How did you find it? Who's your landlord?'

'Why not ask your pals up at the station – they're supposed to know every bloody thing going on round here!'

Gently sighed sadly. 'You're not being helpful, Frenchy . . . and I had hoped you were going to be.' He served himself a peppermint cream and chewed it sombrely for a moment. 'Well . . . to come to the business. I'm pinching you for conspiracy to burgle, Frenchy—'

Frenchy screeched and shot up off the bed. 'It's a frame-up, that's what it is, a filthy, stinking—!'

'Shh!' murmured Gently, 'I don't have to warn an old-stager like you.'

'They'd say anything in a jam, dirty little bastards!'

Gently handed over his sheets of copy-paper. 'In effect they said this . . . and there's a certain amount of evidence to back them up.'

Frenchy seized the sheets and went over to the window with them, turning her back on Gently. It didn't take her long to extract the gist of them. There was a moment when she discovered how she had been double-crossed that added three distinct new words to Gently's vocabulary.

'It's a filthy bag of lies!' she burst out at last. 'The – little liars – they're trying to pin it all on me!'

'They seem to have made a job of it, too . . .'

'There isn't a word of truth!'

'But there's some evidence that goes with it . . .'

Frenchy stormed up and down the muggy room with perspiration beading on her pasty face. 'You know what it is . . . You know why these pigs have said this. It's because I wouldn't go to bed with them . . . that's what they've wanted! They've wanted to be little men, to go to bed with a woman . . . they've been hanging round me ever since I came up here. But I don't go to bed with children . . . nobody can blame me for that! . . . and now they're in trouble they're trying to blame me – somebody it's easy to get in bad with the police!'

'Whoa!' interrupted Gently pacifically, 'it's no use getting out of breath, my dear. Somebody had to tell them about that suitcase and where to find it . . .'

'It wasn't me! I didn't know nothing about it.'

'Then who did – who else knew about it?'

'How the hell should I know? Perhaps they saw him carting it around and got the idea it was something valuable . . .'

'Who told you he was given to carting it around?'

'Nobody told me—!'

'And how did they know where he lodged – that he was out – that for some reason he'd left it in his room?'

'They could've watched him, couldn't they?'

'They aren't professionals, Frenchy.'

'They're sneaking little swine, that's what they are!'

She flung herself at the bed and disinterred some cigarettes from under the pillow. Gently produced a match and gave her a light, steady brown fingers against her trembling pale ones. She swallowed down the smoke as though it were nectar.

'You know, Frenchy, it isn't burglary you've got to worry about . . . we aren't terribly interested in that. It's the way your customer finished up on the beach the next morning that's the real headache.'

'He wasn't my customer – I never knew him!'

Gently shook his head. 'I've got another witness who saw you with him, quite independent. Do you remember having lunch at the Beachside Cafe?'

'I was never in the place!'

'And now, according to these two statements, you were the last person we know to see Max alive . . .'

A shudder passed through the blonde woman's body and she had to struggle to keep her hold on the jerking cigarette.

'Weight it up, Frenchy . . . it's a nasty position to be in.'

'But mister,' – her voice was hoarse now – 'it wasn't nothing to do with me – nothing – I'll swear to it!'

Gently shrugged and picked up his hat to fan himself again.

'I didn't have no hand in it . . . honest to God!'

Gently fanned himself impassively.

'I didn't – I *didn't* – I *didn't*!' The voice was a scream now and she threw herself on her knees in a fit of anguish. 'You got to believe me . . . mister . . . you *got* to!'

Gently nodded a single, indefinite nod and went on fanning.

'But *you've got to*, mister!'

Gently paused at the end of a stroke. 'If,' he said, 'you *didn't*, Frenchy, then the best thing you can do is to come clean . . .'

'But I can't, mister!' Her face twisted in indescribable torment.

'You can't?' Gently stared at her bleakly and recommenced his fanning.

'I can't – I *can't*! Don't you understand?'

'I understand there's a murder charge being kept on ice for someone.'

Frenchy moaned and sank in a heap on the floor. 'I didn't do it,' she babbled, 'I didn't do it . . . you got to believe me!'

Gently bent over and picked up the cigarette, which was making an oily mark on the dubious lino. 'Listen, Frenchy, if it's any consolation to you, I don't think you knocked off Max, and I'm not personally trying to pin it on you. But you're obviously in it up to your neck, and unless you make yourself useful to us you're going to have a pretty rough passage in court. Now what about it . . . suppose we do a deal?'

'I can't, mister – I daren't!'

'We'll give you protection. You've nothing to be afraid of.'

The dyed-blonde hair shook hopelessly. 'They'd get me . . . they always do. They don't never forget, mister.'

'Nonsense,' said Gently stoutly, 'this is England, Frenchy.'

Her haunted eyes looked up at him, hesitating. Then she gave a hysterical little laugh. 'That's what Max thought, too . . . he'd be safe once he got to England!'

They went down the naked stairway, Frenchy clicking her high heels, Gently clumping in the rear. She had put on her white two-piece with its red piping and split skirt, and there was almost a degree of respectability about her make-up. At the bottom she fished a key out of her handbag and locked the street door. Gently took it from her and slipped it into his pocket.

'And to save a little trouble . . .?'

Frenchy sniffed and tossed her head towards the corner shop. 'Mother Goffin over the way . . . and don't let her kid you up she's deaf.'

'I won't,' murmured Gently, 'at least, not twice in one day.'

They proceeded towards the Front, Gently feeling a trifle self-conscious beside so much window-dressing. At the corner of the street lurked Nits, his bulging eyes fixed upon them. As they drew closer he sidled out to meet them.

'Giddout of the way, you!' snapped Frenchy, angering suddenly. But Nits' attention had focused on Gently.

'You leave her alone – you leave her alone!' he piped, 'she's a good girl, you mustn't take her away!'

'Clear out!' screeched Frenchy, 'I've had enough of you hanging round me!'

Gently put his hand in his pocket for a coin, but as he did so the halfwit came flying at him with flailing arms and legs.

'You shan't take her away – you shan't – I won't let you!'

'Here, here,' said Gently, 'that's no way for a young man to behave——!'

'I'll kill you, I will, I tell you I'll kill you!'

'And I'll bleedin' kill you!' screamed Frenchy, catching Nits such a cuff across the face that he was almost cart-wheeled into the gutter. For a moment he lay there, pop-eyed and gibbering, then he sprang to his feet in a whirl of limbs and darted away down Dulford Street like a bewildered animal.

'Dirty little git!' jeered Frenchy, 'they're all the same – doesn't matter what they are. Men are all one filthy pack together!'

The super wasn't feeling his pluperfect best just then. He'd been butting his head against brick walls all day. He'd disregarded Gently, made an enemy of Christopher Wylie, been torn off a helluva strip by the chief constable, failed to find the merest trace of a suitcase full of hundred-dollar bills and, to cap it all, he was beginning to realize that he'd been wrong anyway. It was this last that really hurt. The rest he was prepared to take in his superintendental stride . . .

'So she won't talk!' he almost snarled, as Gently and he sluiced down canteen tea in the latter's office.

Gently shrugged woodenly. 'You can't really blame her. She's convinced she'd be signing her own death-warrant.'

'Well, if she doesn't sign it I shall – she can bank on that for a start!' yapped the super.

'Oh, I don't know . . .' Gently put down his cup and

421

mopped his forehead with a handkerchief that had been seeing life. 'I've got a couple of men looking for the taxi that picked them up on Tuesday night . . . if we can find that, we shall be getting somewhere.'

'Now look here, Gently!' The super almost choked. 'This woman is the crux of the case. If your guessing is correct she knows everything – where he went to, who picked him up, who was after the money – she may even have been a witness to the murder, for all we know! And all you can tell me is she won't talk. That's all! They've put a scare into her, so she won't talk!'

'It isn't a small size in scares, when you come to think of it.'

'I don't care what size it was!' raved the super. 'I've got a scare up my sleeve, too, quite as big as any of theirs. We'll soon see who's got the biggest!'

Gently looked woodener than ever. 'She's got a perfect right to keep quiet. And you're overestimating your scare. There's nothing you can pin to Frenchy apart from conspiracy to burgle, and she's not such a fool that she doesn't know it.'

'Oh, she isn't, isn't she? We'll soon see about that! I'll make a pass at her with a murder charge that'll put paid to all this nonsense . . .!'

'No.' Gently shook his head. 'I've tried it, anyway. The position is that you *might* get her, but they *certainly* will. They're the ones who are holding a pistol in her back . . . or at least they've made her think so. No . . . Frenchy's our ace in the hole, and for the moment we'll have to leave her there. I've got an impression she'll be a lot more vocal when she sees certain people wearing handcuffs.'

'But how the devil are you going to get handcuffs on them when she won't talk? And the man we want – let's face it, Gently, it's the fellow with the scar who's got high jump written all over him – where will you ever lay hands on him again?'

'He was here last night,' muttered Gently obstinately.

'Last night, last night! But where is he now – today? He isn't just a criminal on the run. He's part of a powerful and ruthless organization, professionals to their fingertips.'

Gently smiled feebly. 'Even organizations are run by human beings ... they're sometimes quite modest concerns when you get to grips with them. Anyway ... about Frenchy. I want to ask a favour.'

The super grunted fiercely, as though indicating it wasn't his day for such things.

'I don't want her kept here ... I'd like her released on bail.'

'On BAIL!!!' erupted the super, his eyes jumping open as though he had been stung.

'Yes ... nothing very heavy. Just a modest little reminder.'

'But good heavens, man – bail! A woman of that character – arrested for a felony – suspected of complicity in murder – and you're asking for bail! What the devil do you think I should put on my report?'

'Just say it was at my request,' murmured Gently soothingly, 'I'll carry the can if she doesn't turn up.'

'But I'm already in bad with the CC over this business—!'

'She'll be in court. You needn't worry about that.'

The super treated Gently to several seconds of his

best three-phase stare. 'All right,' he said at last, 'it's your idea, Gently. You can have her. But God help you if she's missing when we go to court. You'll have her tailed, of course?'

'Oh yes . . . Dutt's one of the best tails in the business. And I'd like someone to check up on the flat in Dulford Street. The rent is paid to a Mrs Goffin who keeps a newsagent's opposite . . . I'm just the wee-ish bit interested to know where it goes after that.'

The telephone rang and the super hooked it wearily to his ear. Gently rose to go, but the super, after a couple of exchanges, motioned for him to wait and grabbed a pencil out of his tray.

'Yes . . . yes . . . d'you mind spelling it? . . . yes . . . as in Mau-Mau . . . got it . . . you'll send his cards . . . right . . . yes . . . thank you!'

He hung up and pushed his desk-pad across for Gently's inspection. 'There you are − for what it's worth!'

Gently glanced at the pad and back at the super.

'The names of our playmates . . . Special *does* work on a Sunday! Olaf Streifer is Scarface − he's an agent of this precious TSK Party's secret police . . . Maulik, it's called. Special want him in connection with some naval sabotage at Portsmouth two years ago. You seem to have got a set of his prints from somewhere, inciden-tally . . .'

Gently nodded. 'And this . . . Stratilesceul?'

'Stephan Stratilesceul − the lad on the slab. He wasn't known over here, but the Sûreté had records. They wanted him in connection with a similar business at Toulon . . . the TSK seems to have a lien on naval

424

naughtiness.' He picked up the pad and held it up ironically. 'So now we know – and how much further does it get us?'

Gently hoisted a neutral shoulder. 'It all helps to fill in the picture . . . you can't know too much about a murder.'

CHAPTER TEN

I T HAD BEEN too fine.

The peerless sky which had filled the beaches yesterday had vanished overnight literally in a clap of thunder and its place was filled by low, yellow-grey cloud which drizzled warmly, as though somewhere that wonderful sun was still trying to filter its way through. Perhaps it was wise of nature. There had been havoc enough wrought by one fine Sunday. In the damp streets plastic-caped holidaymakers went about with a wonderful solicitude for their fiery backs and arms . . .

Now it was the cafes that came into their own. The innumerable little boxes clustered cheek by jowl all the way down Duke Street, empty and forlorn while the sun reigned, filled up now to the last tubular steel chair. After all, it wasn't an unpleasant rain . . . one expected it some time during the holiday. And there were worse things to be done than drinking one's coffee, smoking, writing cards and going through the newspapers . . .

Not that it was front-page today, their own especial murder. The super had kindly released the news of the arrest of Jeff and Bonce and the discovery of the grey suit, but in the face of fierce competition from a Cabinet re-shuffle it hadn't made the grade. It had slipped to page five. Strangely unanimous, the editors of the dailies had each come to the conclusion that the Body on the Beach wasn't going to get anywhere, and they were quietly preparing to forget the whole thing.

Like a certain superintendent, thought Gently, resting his elbows on the low wall bounding the promenade . . . though of course, the man had his reasons.

He hitched up his fawn raincoat and produced his pipe. He couldn't help it . . . this sort of weather always made him moody. To wake up and find it raining induced in him a vein of pessimism, both with himself and with society. He just wanted to turn over and go to sleep again and forget all about them . . .

Well . . . if it *would* rain!

He lit the sizzling pipe, tossed the match on to the sand below and turned abruptly away from the melancholy sea.

Opposite him, across the carriage-way, loomed the garish tiled front of the Marina Cinema. A spare, florid-faced man with a wrinkled brow and a shock of tow hair was polishing the chrome handles of the swing-doors. Gently went across to him.

'You're at it early this morning . . .'

The man paused to throw him a sharp look and then went on with his polishing. 'It's got to be done some time, mate.'

'The sea air can't do them a lot of good.'

'Telling me! It plays the bloody hell with them.'

He rubbed away till he came to the top of the handle, Gently watching patiently the while. At last he straightened out and gave his cloth a shaking.

'What are you – a cop, mate?' he asked briefly.

Gently nodded sadly. 'Only I was hoping it didn't show quite so much . . .'

'Huh! I can always smell a cop a mile away.'

'I shouldn't have stood to windward, should I?'

The tow-haired man took a reef in his cloth and advanced to the next door-handle. 'What do you want here, anyway?'

'The usual thing. Some information.'

'And suppose I haven't got any?'

'Suppose,' said Gently smoothly, 'suppose you be a smart little ex-con and keep a civil tongue when you talk to a policeman?'

'An ex-con . . .! What creeping nark told you that?'

Gently smiled at a diagonal frame filled with Lollobrigida. 'You aren't the only one with a developed sense of smell . . .'

But he didn't get any information from the man. He didn't, or wouldn't, remember anything about people taking taxis on Tuesday night last. Yes, he would have been in the vestibule just before the last house turned out, but he was probably chatting to the cashier or one of the girls . . . no, there wasn't anybody else on late turn that night . . . no, he didn't know Frenchy or anyone like her . . . going straight he was, and he defied anyone to prove different.

Gently left him to his handles and plodded on down the Front, pessimism confirmed in his soul.

'The Feathers' was open, but it seemed rather a waste

of electricity on such a customless morning. Its arrow was darting away with customary vigour, albeit it fizzed a little in the rain, but there were few enough strollers to be pricked into the temporary refuge of the arcade: its music drooled hollowly down empty aisles. Gently went up the steps and through the doors. Not a soul was about except the attendant, who was sweeping the floor at the far end. Through the doors of the bar, which were stood open with two chairs, could be seen a figure similarly engaged and a 'closed' notice hung rakishly on a chair-back. Obviously, they weren't expecting a rush of business.

He turned to the nearest machine and dropped a penny in the slot. It was one of the pre-war 'Stock Exchange' type and a pull on the handle yielded a brisk no-dividends. Gently tried again. He'd got quite a pocket-full of coppers. Absently he yanked the lever and watched the colourful passage of Rubber, Textiles, Railways and Gold . . . it seemed hard that such a well furnished wheel should come up no-dividends twice in a row. But it did. It was clever. It sorted out a solitary white from a whole rainbow of coloured, and stuck to it with an obstinate firmness.

A gigantic hand ornamented with a solitaire diamond suddenly covered the handle and its guard.

'You haven't got the knack, Inspector,' purred Louey's voice behind him, 'let an old professional show you how to beat the book!'

Gently stood back without replying and Louey pressed a coin into the slot. Then he caressed the handle with an even, almost casual pressure and the wheel drifted lazily round to a Gold segment. A second coin brought coppers cascading down the shoot.

'You see, Inspector?' Louey's gold tooth shone its message of innocent goodwill. 'It *is a* matter of skill, after all . . .'

Gently shrugged and repossessed himself of his twopence. 'It needs a safe-breaker's touch . . . the way one tickles a combination lock.'

Louey's smile broadened. 'Some of the kids learn how to play them, though it costs them a few weeks' pocket-money. But I don't mind that . . . there are fifty who never learn for every one who does.'

'Sounds like an expensive accomplishment to me.'

'We have to risk our stakes, Inspector, when we're out to win something.'

Louey picked up the rest of the coins from the shoot and paid them back into the machine, one by one. They flicked up no-dividends as surely as a till flicking up no-sales.

'Skill,' purred Louey, 'you can't really call it gambling, Inspector.'

Gently quizzed the huge man's sack-like raincoat and corduroy cap. 'You were just going out?'

'My morning constitutional,' nodded Louey, 'I always take it, summer and winter.'

'Mind if I come too?'

'Delighted, Inspector! I was hoping for the opportunity of another little chat.'

He ushered Gently out, holding the door obsequiously for him. They crossed the carriage-way and turned southwards along the almost deserted Front. The rain, from being a drizzle, had now become quite steady and gusts of sea-breeze made it cut across their faces as they walked. Louey snuffed the air and looked up at the sky.

'It's set in for the day . . . I shall be a richer man by tomorrow night, Inspector. You remember my pussy? I expect you thought he'd got his lines crossed yesterday, but he never makes a mistake. I suppose we shan't have the pleasure of your company at the races tomorrow?'

Gently grunted. 'I follow my business . . . wherever it takes me.'

'Ah yes . . . and I see by the papers that you're making great strides. Well, well! Those two youngsters in their ridiculous suits! It must be a lesson to me to keep a tighter check on the customers in the bar . . .'

Gently flipped the sodden brim of his trilby. 'I still prefer your first theory, the one about a political organization.'

'You do?' Louey seemed pleasantly surprised. 'I thought you must have forgotten that, Inspector . . . my amateur summing-up of the case! But these new facts explode it, I'm afraid. There wouldn't seem to be much connection between Teddy boys and politics.'

'There isn't,' grunted Gently.

'Then surely we must give up my theory . . .?'

'We could if the Teddy boys killed Stratilesceul, but as it is they only pinched his suitcase.'

Three strides went by in silence. 'Stratilesceul?' echoed Louey, 'is that the name of the murdered man?'

'The man who skipped the *Ortory* at Hull and was chased down here by Streifer.'

'Streifer . . .?' This time Gently lost count of the number of strides. 'I'm sorry, Inspector . . . a lot of this hasn't appeared in the papers, or if it has, I've missed it. Was it from Hull that this unfortunate man came?'

'It was.'

'And he was chased by someone?'

'By Streifer. Olaf Streifer. A member of the Maulik, the TSK secret police. It was just like in your theory, Louey . . . the execution of a traitor by an organization he had betrayed.'

The big man shook his head with an air of bewilderment. 'You must excuse me if I seem a little dense . . . I'm not so familiar with the business as yourself, Inspector. Am I to take it that the case is closed and that you have arrested this . . . Streifer?'

Gently didn't seem to have heard. He was poking in his pocket for a peppermint cream.

Louey gave a little laugh. 'I was saying, Inspector . . . has this Streifer been arrested?'

The peppermint cream was found and Gently nibbled it with deaf composure . . . it might have been the rain which was making him so hard of hearing. Louey shook his head again as though realizing that it was necessary to humour a Yard man. After all, he seemed to be saying, it was a privilege thus to be taken into the great man's confidence at all . . .

They strode on towards South Shore. The rain kept driving in from the sea. There were warm sheets of it now, really wetting, and Gently's experienced brogues were beginning to squelch. Even Louey was constrained to do up his top button, though it meant veiling the glories of a pearl tie-pin stuck in a grey silk tie but there weren't many people to see it in any case.

'Of course, it was Streifer we saw coming out of your office on Friday night,' grunted Gently at last, the peppermint cream being fairly disposed of.

'I thought we had disposed of that point, Inspector.'

Louey sounded justifiably piqued. 'But it was Streifer all right, and it was your office all right.'

'Well, if you say so . . . but I can't imagine what he was doing there. Naturally we had a little check after you'd told us about it, but as far as we were able to discover nothing had been stolen or disturbed.' Louey turned his huge head towards Gently. 'Do you want my opinion, Inspector?'

Gently shrugged, hunched down in a leaky collar.

'My opinion is that *if* it was Streifer and *if* it was my office, he must have ducked in there to avoid running into your man. Doesn't that sound a reasonable explanation?'

'Very reasonable . . . and why did he duck out again?'

'Obviously he would have heard Peachey coming back.'

'Why wasn't he worried by the risk of meeting Peachey when he ducked in?'

'Oh, come now, Inspector, I can't work out the minute details for you . . .!'

'And how did he know the door was unlocked in the first place?'

'One must use one's imagination. Perhaps he took cover in the doorway, and then tried the handle . . .'

'Why, in fact, would he take cover at all? On Friday night he wasn't known to us, and neither was my man known to him.'

Louey chuckled softly. 'There you are, Inspector! My naïve amateur deductions don't hold water for a moment, do they? I'm afraid it's as big a mystery as ever . . . I would never have made a policeman.'

'One other thing,' added Gently evenly, 'how did

you come to know that it was my man who saw Streifer leave your office?'

Louey's chuckle continued. 'How else could you have known about it? You admit that Streifer meant nothing to you on Friday night, so you could hardly have been making inquiries after him, Inspector . . .'

They had passed by the Wellesley, its wrought-iron fantasia washed and gleaming, and were approaching the weirdly incongruous skyline of the Pleasure Beach. High over all reared the Scenic Railway, a miniature Bass Rock fashioned out of painted canvas and paper mache, and under it, like a brood of Easter chicks under a hen, the gay-painted turrets and roofs of side shows, booths and the other mechanical entertainments. Harsh strains of music through the rain suggested that the Pleasure Beachers, like lesser mortals, were assuming a custom though they had it not.

Louey gestured comfortably towards the gateway. 'Rivals of mine . . . but they don't have a licence! Shall we stroll through?'

Gently nodded drippingly. 'I want to see the place. It's where Streifer dropped the man who was tailing him on Friday.'

'Which shows he knew his job, Inspector. Isn't this where you would come to shake off a tail?'

'I can't say I've had much experience . . .'

They passed under the flaunting portal with its electric jewellery. The close-packed attractions within wore a rueful look, unsupported by the crowds. Larger and more expensive pieces were frankly at a standstill – the Caterpillar had postponed its gallop, the Glee Cars their jaunting – while the smaller roundabouts and rides were operating at a profit margin which was doubtful. Booth attendants stood about in each other's stalls. They were drinking tea and staring around them morosely. The owner of the Ghost Train, for want of something to do, was riding round in his own contraption, but all its promised thrills seemed unable to raise the siege of boredom which had invested his countenance.

'Of course there's Frenchy,' brooded Gently, obstinately undiverted by all these diversions.

'Frenchy?' echoed Louey indifferently, 'is she mixed up with the business too? She took a hint the other night, Inspector. She hasn't been near the bar since then.'

'Stratilesceul was a client of hers . . . she went off to the North Shore with him in a taxi just before he was murdered.'

'Ah, that accounts for a rumour I heard that she had been arrested.'

'You heard such a rumour?'

'We're for ever hearing them in our business.'

'Undoubtedly . . . you are very well placed.'

Gently halted to inspect the front of a sideshow. It was an exhibition of methods of execution through the centuries and was advertised by some particularly lurid illustrations. He seemed to be strangely fascinated.

'And she will have given you some useful information?' suggested Louey, moving on a step impatiently.

'She knows a good deal . . . she'll be a devastating witness.'

'There would be some danger in it for her.'

'Danger? With police protection?'

Louey turned his back on the sideshow and busied himself with lighting a cigarette. 'If this murder was the work of an organization – and you don't seem to be in any doubt about it now – then there would be a very real danger for anyone bearing material witness. Men can be hanged, Inspector, but organizations cannot. And my feeling is that a person of Frenchy's kidney wouldn't risk too much for pure love of our excellent police force.'

Gently stooped to get a closer view of a gentleman who had been given too long a drop, with the usual top-secret result. 'You know Frenchy well?' he asked carelessly.

'I? Not apart from running her out of my bar on several occasions.'

'Dulton . . . Dulsome Street is where she lives.'

'Dulford Street, Inspector.'

'That's right. You've been there?'

'Not visiting Frenchy, if that's what you mean.'

'You're sure of that? Not in the last day or two?'

'Quite positive, Inspector. My tastes have never been that way inclined.'

Gently straightened up slowly. 'Odd,' he said, frowning.

'What's odd about that?'

'These two cigarette ends.' Gently felt in his pocket and produced a crumpled envelope. 'There . . . you see? Your blend of Russian. I found them in an ashtray in Frenchy's bedroom yesterday afternoon.'

Louey poked at them with a gigantic finger and nodded heavily. 'You're right, Inspector . . . it is my blend.'

'I was sure of it . . . I was feeling positive you'd been there.'

The grey eyes rested on his firmly, the flecked pupil seeming curiously larger than its neighbour. 'Isn't it a shame, Inspector,' purred Louey, 'I thought my cigarettes were exclusive. And now, in the commission of your duty, you've proved that someone else in Starmouth smokes them too . . . at least, I take it, it was in the commission of your duty?'

Gently shrugged and shoved the envelope back into his pocket.

The Scenic Railway had its shutters up, though someone was tinkering with one of the trolleys. It wasn't quite so impressive on a nearer view. Its cliffs and crags were so palpably props, its tunnels and bridges so contrived. And the rain made it look sorrier still, a great, hollow, sodden mockery. Gently took refuge in a peppermint cream as they squelched past it. If only he'd thought to bring a more reliable pair of shoes . . .!

'I suppose I don't have to ask you to account for your movements last Tuesday night?' he growled, as they got out on to the promenade again.

'But of course!' Louey chuckled, as though he welcomed the inquiry. 'I was having a little party in the back . . . Peachey, Artie, Tizer and some more of the boys. You ask them, Inspector. They'll all remember my party on Tuesday night.'

'I'm sure they will. And of course it went on till late?'

'Not terribly late. I cleared them out at two.'

'Just late enough, in fact.'

'Well . . . it was late enough for me.'

'And that would be your story – supposing you had to have a story?'

'Certainly, Inspector. Why should I tell any other?'

'There's no knowing what Frenchy may say.'

'She's a woman without character.'

'Or Streifer, for example.'

'Streifer?' Louey hung on to the word, as though expecting an explanation.

'And then there's your car,' continued Gently, ignoring him. 'Was that borrowed or something on the Tuesday night?'

'My car . . .?' This time the inquiring tone had an edge of anxiety.

'You lent it to someone – and they went up to North Shore?'

'I don't understand, Inspector. My car would have been in its lock-up in Botolph Street.'

'Even though it was seen somewhere else?'

'That would hardly be possible . . .'

'Then you didn't lend it to anyone?'

'No. It was never out of the garage.'

'So the people who saw it at North Shore would be liars?'

'They were certainly under a misapprehension . . .'

Gently flicked briskly at his over-worked trilby. 'You'll have got rid of the ring, of course . . . that was too much of a coincidence.'

The big features relaxed and there was a glimpse of gold. 'If you don't mind me saying it, Inspector, I think we had better consider that ring to have been an illusion.'

'I'm not subject to illusions, Louey.'

'But just once, perhaps, in a long career?'

'Not even once, and certainly not prophetically. I didn't know the TSK or its secret sign existed when I saw your ring, but I knew where I'd seen it before when it turned up a second time.'

'A trick of the memory, perhaps.'

'The police aren't much subject to them.'

'Well, shall we say rather dubious evidence?'

In a court of law it would be for the jury to decide.'

Louey laughed his low, caressing laugh. 'How we talk, Inspector . . . how we do. But I like these examples of your official approach to a problem. It's comforting to feel that the guardians of our law and order work so efficiently and so intelligently. As I said on a former occasion, I could only wish you had more promising material to deal with in the present instance.'

'I'll make do,' grunted Gently, 'it doesn't seem to be running out on me at the moment.'

Louey shook his head with a sort of playful sympathy. 'I respect your attitude . . . it's the attitude one would expect and look for in such a man as yourself. But honestly, Inspector, when one takes stock of the situation . . . for instance, this Streifer. What can you do about him? You can connect him with the murdered man in a dozen ways, you can show he was the most likely one to have done it – but what's all that worth when you haven't got a scrap of proof that he did it? I don't have to remind you of our careful court procedure. In some countries Streifer would be ex-ecuted out-of-hand on a tenth of the evidence . . . and perhaps you'll allow, without too much injustice. But here you have to convince your jury. Here you are obliged to go to fanatical lengths to show proof and double proof. And you don't seem to have it, Inspector. You are faced with a planned execution, the details of which have been efficiently erased. I've no doubt that a jury would convict Streifer of something – there must be several lesser charges you could bring – but as a betting man, Inspector, I'm willing to give you ten to one they never convict him of murdering Stratilesceul.'

Louey took a farewell puff at his cigarette and seemed about to toss it away. Then he changed his mind and with a gilded smile handed it to Gently.

'Another one for your collection!'

Gently nodded and extinguished it carefully.

'The previous remarks,' continued Louey, watching him, 'supposing you have in fact arrested Streifer . . .?'

Gently tucked away the sodden end without replying. Louey nodded as though that were sufficient answer.

'And I don't think you will, Inspector . . . I don't really think you will. If he was, as you say, a member of the . . . what was it? A secret police? I imagine he will know his way out of a country . . . don't you? Especially with the assistance we must assume he will get from his organization over here.'

Gently stuck his hands in his pockets and plodded on. He seemed completely immersed in something taking place over the pale sea-horizon.

'It's wrong of me,' mused Louey, 'I shouldn't say it . . . but I can't help feeling a little sympathy for the man.'

'Sympathy? For a cold-blooded murderer?'

'Not a murderer, Inspector . . . an executioner, I think you must call him.'

'Stratilesceul's hands were tied – do you sympathize with that?'

'You're forgetting, Inspector, we also tie a man's hands for execution. If killing is the order, one may as well kill efficiently.'

'But we don't torture, Louey. Stratilesceul was burned with cigarettes.'

'Our torture is mental, Inspector . . . it lasts longer, and it isn't done for useful ends, such as eliciting information. No . . . I'm sorry. You must permit me to feel some sympathy for Streifer. He did what he did in the service of an ideal, rightly or wrongly . . . you really mustn't equate him with even the common hangman.'

Gently's shoulders hunched ever higher. 'He was paid, wasn't he . . . just like the common hangman?'

'Naturally, a labourer is worthy of his hire. But the pay wasn't his motive, you know. It wouldn't be an adequate incentive to such risk and responsibility. Your hangman is a mere assassin . . . you hand him his thirty pieces of silver and say Murder; we have bound your victim. And he murders, Inspector. He has your full protection. His crime is written up to humanity and he departs to spend the blood-money. Is this the way of the man you want to hang? Is this the way of any of the men you hang?'

'At least we kill only the killers . . .'

'Is that better than killing for an ideal?'

'It is an ideal – to protect people on their lawful occasions.'

'If only it protected them, Inspector . . . if only it did! But your ideal is a pathetic fallacy, I'm afraid. Of course it's wrong to say this . . . I understand your position.

Your duty is to catch a criminal and judgment is elsewhere. But I want you to understand me when I say I feel a little sympathy with Streifer . . . we can talk together, Inspector. You are a man of intelligence.'

They had come to the end of the town, a straggle of houses on one hand, wasteground and the beach on the other. Louey paused as they came abreast with a decaying pill-box.

'This is as far as I go, fair weather or foul.'

Gently nodded woodenly and gave his trilby a further flick. Then he turned to face the two grey eyes which rested on him confidently, almost affection-ately.

'I'm glad you made the point . . .' The eyes were interrogative. '. . . about my duty. It *is* to catch the criminal.'

Louey's enormous head tilted backwards and for-wards almost imperceptibly.

'And since I'm in betting company, Louey, I'll take you at the odds. Wasn't it ten to one you quoted?'

'At ten to one . . . and Louey always pays.'

'I'll have a pound on. You can open my account.'

The grey eyes flashed and the big man burst into laughter.

'You're on, Inspector . . . the first policeman I ever had on my books!'

Gently quizzed him expressionlessly from the depths of his comfortless collar. 'Let's hope you're lucky,' he said, 'let's hope I'm not the last.'

The lonely phone-box had a tilt in it, due to the subsidence of its sandy foundation. But it was dry inside and Gently took time off to light his pipe before getting down to business. He gave headquarters' number.

'Get me Inspector Copping.'

Copping arrived in fairly prompt switchboard time.

'Gently here . . . are we still entertaining Frenchy?'

'Entertaining's the word!' came Copping's disgusted voice. 'She's been yelling her head off since they brought her back . . . says she wants a lawyer and that we're holding her under false pretences.'

Gently grinned in a cloud of pipe-smoke. 'She's got her bail . . . what more does she want?'

'The cash, apparently . . . you seem to have pinched her at the end of the month.'

'Well . . . keep her nice and cosy. Has anything else come in?'

'Not a darned thing.'

'Have the lab made anything of that paper?'

'They say it's manufactured in Bristol and used for packing mattresses. I've got a man going round the stores trying to match it.'

'No prints worth having?'

'Nothing anybody's heard of.'

'You haven't traced that taxi?'

'Not so's you'd notice it.'

Gently clicked his tongue. 'It's a wet Monday all right, isn't it? Is Dutt anywhere handy?'

'He's hanging about waiting for someone to bail Frenchy.'

'I want him for a job . . . one of your own men will have to watch our Frenchy.'

The phone at the other end was laid down and Gently whiled away the odd moments watching two raindrops making tracks down the ebony panel in the back of the box. Then Dutt's chirpy accents saluted him from the receiver.

'Yessir? You was wanting me?'

'Yes, Dutt . . . I want you to do a little scouting in your old pitch in Botolph Street. There's a lock-up garage there where Louey keeps his car. You might find out if anyone noticed the car being used on Tuesday night . . .'

'Yessir. I think I knows the very garage you're talking about.'

'Stout fellow, Dutt. And don't forget your mac.'

'No, sir! Don't you worry!'

Gently eyed the rain-swept vista outside his box with a jaundiced stare. 'And while we're at it, Dutt, get them to send a car to pick me up at South Shore . . . I've had all the constitutional my constitution will stand for one wet day!'

CHAPTER ELEVEN

T HERE WAS A hiatus in the proceedings and the super, excellent man, had scented it out with his keen, service-minded nostrils. Gently had come to a standstill. His case was bogging down. He had pushed it up the hill with his bulky shoulder until he was in hailing distance of the top and now, with the deceptive vision of arrests and charges dead ahead, he was stuck fast as though he had run into an invisible barrier. It was a sad sight, but not an unexpected one. The super had had a strong intuition all along that this was how it would wind up. Because he knew something about secret agents, did the super. He had come across them before in his long career and he could tell Gently, if Gently was harbouring any illusions, just how slippery these birds inevitably were . . .

'You see, they *plan* their murders . . . that's the vital difference between them and the ordinary homicide. They know what we'll do and they take damn' good care to protect themselves.'

Gently looked up from a large-scale map and smiled with an irony which the super was unable to appreciate.

'In fact we're . . . "faced with a planned execution, the details of which have been efficiently erased".'

'Precisely.' The super cast him a suspicious glance. 'We may as well face it, Gently. We're not infallible. We make use of our skill and technique to the best of our ability, but the people on the other side start with an enormous advantage and if they use it intelligently then we're batting on a pretty sticky wicket.'

'I know, I've heard it once before today. We haven't got Streifer, we can't prove he did it and' − he rustled the map on his desk − 'we don't even know where it was done.'

'Well − those are the facts, Gently, and you'd better add that we've exhausted most of the chances of improving on them. Oh, I don't want to be discouraging, and I'm certainly not disparaging all the sound work you've put in getting this case into perspective, but you are scraping the bottom of the barrel now and getting precious little for it − and every hour that passes makes it less and less likely that we shall lay hands on Streifer. This isn't his first job here, you must remember. The Special have been after him before without finding hide nor hair of him and there's no reason to expect they'll be luckier this time.'

'You think I should write my report?'

The super's grizzled brows knitted in a frown. 'I'm not saying that, Gently. I'll leave you to be the judge of when you can no longer usefully continue the investigation. The point I'm making is that we should look at the thing realistically. For instance, those men of mine at the stations and the bus terminus.'

'You can have them back now,' Gently shrugged.

'And the two men you put on the taxis . . . they've checked and re-checked every hackney-carriage driver in town.'

Gently looked obstinate. 'That taxi must be somewhere.'

'You say it must – but your only evidence is Wylie's and Baines's statements. I wouldn't be inclined to give it too much weight if I were you.'

'They'd no reason to lie.'

'They'd every reason to lie. They wanted to make it seem that Frenchy was the principal . . . it could just be that she's as innocent as she says she is.'

Gently shook his head impatiently. 'Baines wasn't lying. The statements agree except where Wylie is trying to whitewash himself.'

'The fact remains that no taxi driver in town remembers the incident and nobody's got records of such a journey. Of course it's just possible that it was a taxi licensed at Norchester or Lewiston that picked them up . . . you know the distances, you can judge how likely it would be.'

'I'm sorry . . . but that taxi has got to be found.'

'Then what do you suggest – a general check-up of all the taxis in a fifty-mile radius?'

'It may come to that, though first I would like your men to re-check their re-check . . . it's surprising how repetition sometimes jogs people's memories.'

The super gave Gently what from meaner men would have been classed as a dirty look.

'Very well . . . you know your job. But remember that I've got plenty of routine work going begging when you're through with the bottom of the barrel . . .!'

It was a good exit line and the super duly acted upon it. Gently folded up his map with a sigh and stowed it in the drawer with the Moriarty. He didn't blame the super. He would have felt exactly the same in the great man's shoes. Police routine didn't stop because a couple of Yard men were trying to hatch a murder charge . . . it just became more difficult. And when the murder charge didn't look like hatching anyway, well then the Yard men started to become a nuisance about the place. The trouble was that the super hadn't got an incentive any more. He was reasonably happy with the way things had panned out. His corpse was no longer an unsolved mystery, he had pinched a small handful of auxiliaries in the case and if the principal had made tracks for a far country it wasn't through any dereliction of the super's duty . . . All that really concerned the super now was the propitiation of Christopher Wylie and the making of his peace with the chief constable.

Gently sighed again and unhooked his clammy raincoat. There were times when being a Central Office man wasn't all it was cracked up to be.

Accoutred for the fray, he went along to the canteen for a preliminary cup of tea. It was a quiet time there. He had the gloomy room all to himself. Behind the scenes could be heard the chink and clatter of washing-up in progress, but the only other excitement the place afforded was the distant view of someone working on a car under a tilt. Gently sauntered to the window to watch the operation while he sipped. There was something soothing about watching other people grapple with their troubles.

And then, perhaps inspired by the tea, a dreamy

expression crept into his eye. He drew closer to the window. He pulled back one of the blue cotton curtains. At one stage he was even pressing his nose against the pane.

Finally he put down his cup half-finished and let himself out into the yard by the side-door.

It was an elderly car of the high-built and spacious days, and the elderly man who worked on it, though not high built, was spacious also. The dungareed rear end of him which protruded from the bonnet was particularly spacious, and so too was the language which rose in a muttered stream from somewhere in the interior. Gently hooked his fingers in the climb-proof wire fence which surrounded HQ property and conducted a leisurely survey.

'Having a spot of bother?' he inquired affably.

The stream of language faltered and a red, moon-like face disengaged itself from the oily deeps.

'Bother! Can't you hear I'm a-havin' some bother?'

'Well . . . it sounded like a big end gone, to say the least.'

The spacious one heaved himself upright and shored his bulk against the off-side mudguard. 'Jenny!' he observed feelingly, 'that's the bloomin' trouble – Jenny!'

'There's a woman in the case?' queried Gently, who wasn't mechanically minded.

'Woman? Naow – the Jenny! Stuck away there at the bottom till it's nearly draggin' on the ground – an' they must know it's goin' to give trouble – Jennies *allus* give trouble!'

He waved an adjustable at Gently as though daring

him to contradict, but Gently's interest had slipped to some crude white lettering just visible on the uptilted bonnet. It read: 'Henry Artichoke, Hire Car, 76 High Street.'

'This your car?' he asked casually.

''Course it's my car – who's did you think it was?' Mr Artichoke gave the vehicle a glance of mingled affection and exasperation. 'Good now as half your modern tin-lizzies – only thas like me, getting old . . .'

Gently nodded understandingly. 'And how's business with you these days?'

'Business? Well – I don't complain. Though I aren't saying it's like it was in the old days—!'

'Too many charas and coach-trips.'

'An' all these new-fangled cars about . . . still, don't run away with the idea that I'm complainin'.'

'Were you doing much last week?'

'I was out on a trip or two – can't do without me altogether, you know.'

'Last Tuesday, for instance. Did you have a trip that day?'

Mr Artichoke ruminated a moment and dashed away a raindrop which had leaked on to his oily cheek. 'Tuesday . . . that was the day old Hullah was buried. Yes. Yes. I had a couple of trips on the Tuesday . . . in the mornin' I took Sid Shorter over to see his missus at the nursing home. Then last thing they had me out to fetch an old party and her things from Norchester – that's it!'

'What time would that have been?'

'Well, I hadn't got really set down at the "Hoss-shoes" . . . that couldn't have been much after seven.'

'Then you went to Norchester to pick her up?'

'Her'n her things – you'd be surprised what the old gal fetched away with her!'

'Made you late, I dare say . . .'

'Late enough so's I didn't get into the "Hoss–shoes" again . . .'

'It was after ten by the time you'd got her unpacked?'

'As near to it as makes no difference . . . parrot she'd got too – damn' nearly had my finger as I was carting it in!'

'And where did you take her . . . what was her new address?'

'Oh, she was goin' to live with the Parson of St Nicholas.'

'Is that the big church?'

'No – that's St John's. St Nicholas is the one down in Lighthouse Road.'

'You mean down at South Shore?'

'That's right . . . the one with a herrin' stuck up for a weather–vane.'

Gently relinquished his grip on the wire fence and dived his hand into a pocket that rustled. 'The Front – was it very busy when you came back that night?'

'Huh! Usual lot of rowdies – kids, the best part on'm.'

A peppermint cream came to light and lay poised on a stubby thumb. 'Did you have any luck . . . like picking up an odd fare?'

Mr Artichoke raised two round eyes grown suddenly suspicious. 'Here!' he exclaimed, 'come to think of it, I don't like the side of the fence you're standing on – I don't like it at all!'

'It's the honest side, Mr Artichoke . . .'

'That's as may be – I don't think I like it!'

The peppermint cream went into Gently's mouth and was chewed upon thoughtfully. Mr Artichoke watched the operation indignantly, his broad face flushing a deeper shade of red. One would have thought there was something almost indecent about eating a peppermint cream.

'Now look, Mr Artichoke, I think you're in a position to help me in a rather important matter. I know you haven't got a hackney-carriage licence and that it was an offence for you to pick up a fare in the street, but if you picked up the people I think you did, then between you and me there won't be any charges . . . is that quite plain?'

Mr Artichoke nodded non-committally, but kept his mouth tight shut.

'Well then . . . did you or didn't you?'

Mr Artichoke shrugged his heavy shoulders and stared at the adjustable in his hand. 'That depends a bit on who them people was, don't it?' he remarked tentatively.

'I want you to tell me that.'

'But how am I goin' to know if they're the ones I shan't get pinched over?'

Gently returned the shrug. 'I've got a very bad memory except for criminal offences.'

Mr Artichoke brooded some more on the adjustable. 'Just suppose there were two of them – a male and a female. Is that somewhere about the mark?'

'It's right on the target.'

'And suppose this female was a blonde female – one of them there that work up this way during the season . . . am I still going the right way?'

Gently nodded with deliberate slowness.

'And suppose this bloke was a foreigner with a beard, dressed a bit flashy, and answering to the name of Max – and suppose they wanted taking to a house on the cliff which as far as I know has been empty for the last five years. Would I still be heading straight?'

There was the briefest of wavers in Gently's nodding and a smile little short of angelic crept over his face. 'Mr Artichoke . . . you've just answered the sixty-four dollar question, whether you know it or not.'

'Eh?' queried Mr Artichoke.

'The sixty-four dollar question,' repeated Gently. 'Now just stop here. Don't move. Don't go away. I'm going to have a short chat with the superintendent about his man-power problem and after that we'll make a little trip to North Shore together . . . who knows? We may even be lucky enough to find a tenant in that house on the cliff . . .'

Copping made one of the party and Bryce, at Gently's request, was added to the strength. Copping became highly indignant when he heard about Mr Artichoke's activities.

'And after all the ratepayers' money that's been spent trying to find the cabby! What's the use of issuing these licences if a lot of pirates come along and gum up our investigations for us?'

Gently clicked his tongue. 'He was only turning a slightly dishonest penny.'

'We might never have caught up with him . . . you admit it was pure accident.'

'Luck,' said Gently, 'you have to cultivate it in the Central Office . . .'

Copping snorted. 'We shouldn't have needed luck. Routine will catch a criminal if everyone is being completely honest . . .!'

Under Mr Artichoke's directions they proceeded north along the main Norchester road. The dreary suburbs passed by, the expensive splendours of High Town and finally the long, level, white-railed expanse of the race-course, its empty stands lifted gloomily against the rain-pale sea.

'Steady!' warned Mr Artichoke, made uneasy by the driver's reckless and newfangled technique, 'we're turning off here – if you can pull up this side of Barston!'

The driver slowed down to a dangerous thirty.

'There!' exclaimed Mr Artichoke, 'Up that little loke. There's only one house up there, so I shan't have made a mistake.'

'It's "Windy Tops"' muttered Copping, 'it belongs to one of the Thorners of Norchester.'

Gently glanced at him questioningly.

'We had some trouble with them a few years back. The Borough Engineer scheduled it as being unsafe because of cliff erosion and they made a case of it. He won the case, but there hasn't been a cliff-fall in that area from that day to this. Just mention "Windy Tops" if you want to get him in the raw.'

'It's been empty all the time?'

'Naturally. Nobody's allowed to live in it. The B.E. is just living for the day when it goes over the top.'

The narrow road skirted the northern end of the racecourse, crossed the railway line and turned abruptly left. Here the ground rose suddenly to form the first of a line of crumbling gravel cliffs and perched at the top, looking in no-wise conscious of its danger, was a small but well-architected modern house.

'Looks safe enough,' Gently murmured.

'Probably is,' grunted Copping, 'but the B.E. got rapped on the knuckles about a row of cottages that went over . . . he hasn't taken any chances since then.'

The road came to an end at a spacious turning place and the gate to 'Windy Tops'. Bryce was sent round to the back while Gently and Copping advanced on the front. The garden had run to seed and there was grass growing out of the crazy paving, but the house itself seemed in a fair state of preservation and Gently found himself sympathizing with the Thorners in their reluctance to abandon the place. He stooped to inspect the crazy paving.

'Someone's been up here recently all right.'

The grass had been bruised by trampling feet. But Copping was already trying the front-door handle and apparently expressing surprise at finding it locked against him. He ran an eagle eye over the front of the house and thus discovered a partly-open window which Gently had noticed as they got out of the car.

'Easy!' called Gently, 'there may be some interesting prints about.'

Copping whisked up the sash and dumped himself over the low sill. Gently followed him at a more dignified pace. It was a large room and had probably been the lounge, but it was quite empty except for some ashes of burnt paper in the grate. Copping swooped on them, sniffing like a well-trained hound.

'They're fresh!' he exclaimed, 'they haven't been there longer than a few days.'

Gently nodded and applied a speculative finger to the light switch. Pale radiance shone from an unshaded bulb.

'Every modern con . . . and I think I can hear a cistern hissing somewhere.'

'He's been living here!'

'Undoubtedly . . .'

'He might be here now!'

'There's just the remotest chance . . .'

The efficient Copping needed no more. He invaded the house like an unleashed jumping-cracker, pouncing from room to room, poking in cupboards, surprising the backs of doors and generally making life hectic for anything in the shape of a secret agent.

'He slept up here!' came his muffled cry from above-stairs, 'There's a mattress and some blankets . . . cigarette-ash . . . empty matchbox!'

Gently shook his head sadly and went to unlock the kitchen door. The cupboard was bare, he knew it intuitively. There had been that chance, that one chance, that Streifer had decided to lie low until the heat was off, but he had sensed it evaporating the moment he had set foot in this so-silent house. He called to Bryce.

'Any signs of life out there?'

'No sir, nobody – not even on the beach.'

'What about the garage?'

'The door's on the latch – there's nothing in there except a pair of old tyres.'

'Well, come in and give Inspector Copping a hand upstairs. You'll have to get into the loft somehow.'

Bryce came in without much enthusiasm and went

456

up to join his superior. Gently remained below in the kitchen. There were plenty of signs there of recent occupation. On the draining-board stood a plastic cup and plate with a knife and fork, all dirty. A hot-plate was plugged in at the electric switch-point, upon it a tin kettle and nearby an aluminium teapot. In a wall-safe were a tin of condensed milk, tea, sugar, a couple of rolls . . . stale of course, but no staler than Saturday's rolls usually are on Monday afternoon . . . butter and an unopened tin of anchovies. By the wall leaned two cheap folding-stools. Under the sink stood a rusty distemper-tin containing refuse. And there were several newspapers, including Sunday's, and a pile of brown paper. Gently unfolded a *Sunday Express*. It had had a cutting taken from it. He unfolded three others. Each had cuttings taken from them.

'He's hopped it all right.' Copping came in, dusty and aggrieved. 'Bryce is up in the loft now, but he'd have hardly got up there without someone to give him a bunk . . . there's nothing to stand on. I'm afraid we're just too late . . . they always seem one jump ahead, these bastards!'

Gently pointed to the pile of brown paper. 'What do you make of that?'

Copping stared intelligently. 'Looks as though he bought a geyser or something.'

'Was that mattress upstairs a new one?'

'Brand new – and so were the blankets.'

'And what does that suggest to us . . . knowing what we do?'

There was a pause and then the divine spark fell. 'By glory – it's the same paper that was used to wrap the clothes!' Gently nodded approvingly. 'Used to wrap mattresses – and there's the new mattress and you can *see* it's the same paper – it's got that crimp in it, just the same!'

'And it's had a piece torn off it . . . just about the same size.'

Copping's heavy features flushed with excitement. 'We've got him, then – we can tie him in! We've got proof now, good, hard, producible proof – the sort of thing juries love – material proof!'

'Just one thing, though,' murmured Gently.

'Proof!' boomed Copping, 'what more do we need?'

'We need something we haven't got right at this moment and that's the initial proof that Streifer was ever in the house at all.'

Copping faltered in his raptures. 'But good lord . . . it *must* have been him!'

Gently shook an indulgent head. 'Remember that jury and keep your hands to yourself. Don't touch the paper, the taps, the dishes or anything else that's lying about. I suppose it's too late to worry about the doorknobs. As soon as Bryce is through having fun in the loft he'd better light out for your print man. It isn't likely that Streifer was too careful here . . . he expected to be far otherwheres when and if we ever identified the place.'

'And how right he was – how dead bloody right!'

Gently hunched his shoulders soberly. 'He's a man like you and me. People don't become magicians when they join a secret police.'

'It's enough to make you think so, the way this bloke keeps himself lost.'

A dishevelled and wash-prone Bryce was dispatched in the car and Gently, having completed his tour of the house, went out to inspect the grounds. They had nothing relevant to disclose. The tumpy wilderness which had been a lawn, the nettled and willow-herbed flower-beds, these looked as though a full five years had elapsed since a foot had trodden there, or a hand had been raised in their defence. Gently went round to the Achilles heel, the seaward side. Not more than five yards of stony land separated the house from its inevitable tumble to the beach.

'Can't last another winter,' observed Copping knowingly, 'should have gone in the January gales. It was sheer cussedness that made it hang on . . . there were falls everywhere except here.'

Gently approached timidly to the treacherous edge. Seventy feet below the wet sand looked dark and solid. North, south, the sullen lines of slanted combers fretted wearily, told their perpetual lie of harmlessness and non-aggression. Down by the racecourse a lonely path wore its way to the beach.

'That's it,' muttered Gently, 'they carted him down there. How far would you say we were above the Front?'

Copping did some calculations. 'Two miles, about . . . might be a trifle less.'

'It just about tallies . . . I was reckoning on two miles. They dumped him in down there in the ebb, expecting the current to pick him up and carry him right down south. It was just rank bad luck that he finished up on their doorstep again . . .'

'You're positive it was done in the house?'

'Quite positive . . . I can see the whole picture now.'

'There weren't any signs of it – no blood-stains or anything.'

Gently smiled grimly. 'Professionals, Copping. He wasn't hacked about. Didn't you notice how little blood there was on the clothes?'

'And if they'd used violence it wouldn't have shown much, not in an empty house.'

'But they didn't use any . . . they didn't have to. He was delivered right into their hands, unarmed and unsuspecting. My guess is that the first thing he knew about it was an automatic dug into his ribs . . . you don't argue with a thing like that in the first instance. By the time he'd weighed the situation up his hands were tied and he hadn't any option. It's a classic case, Copping. Only our Delilahs come a bit coarser these days.'

'Delilahs!' Copping gave a laugh. 'He must have wanted his brains tested to take up with a mare like Frenchy.'

There was a sound of two cars pulling up and they returned to the front of the house. To their surprise it was the super who came stalking up the crazy-paving. The great man had a taut look, as though primed with high enterprise, and having stalked to the end of the crazy-paving he halted smartly, straddled his legs and quizzed Gently with a sideways look in which were blended both jealousy and admiration.

'All right!' he rapped, 'you're a happy man, Gently. You know your job, and I'm just a blasted ex-infantry officer who's got shoved into a rural police force!'

Gently bowed modestly, as though disclaiming praise

from such high places. The super snorted and directed his gaze at a 'Windy Tops' chimney.

'So they got him!' he jerked from the corner of his mouth, 'laid for him on information – Special and the Limehouse lot – picked him up going aboard a Polish tramp. Nearly shot two men and laid out a third. They're bringing him up now and a big-shot from Special along with them.'

There was a gratifying silence.

'You mean . . . *Streifer*?' gasped Copping.

The super withered him with an acetylene flicker of his eye. 'We're not after Malenkov – nor Senator McCarthy! And just to temper the general glee I may as well add that Special are not the teeniest weeniest bit interested in our lousy little homicide. They couldn't care less. What they're coming for is the whole TSK Party handed to them on a platter and if we can't produce it then they aim to make life irksome in these parts – you understand?'

Gently nodded his mandarin nod. 'I've worked with Special . . .'

'Then you know what's coming – and it'll be here just after tea! So get your facts marshalled, Gently. There's a top-level conference staring you in the face. Amongst other things I've had to pull the CC off a theatre party he's had planned for the last six weeks . . . that's one nasty-minded person who's going to be there, for a start!'

461

CHAPTER TWELVE

ASSUREDLY THERE WAS was an array of formidable talent lined up in the super's office on that grey August evening. It required the impression of seating accommodation from several other departments and it was sad to see so many men of such lustre crammed together like constables at a compulsory lecture. As far as sheer superiority of rank was concerned, the home team had a clear advantage. They were led by the Chief Constable of Northshire, Sir Daynes Broke, CBE, ably supported by his Assistant CC, Colonel Shotover Grout, DSO, MC, with the redoubtable flanks of Superintendent Symms and Inspector Copping. But rank, of course, wasn't everything. There was a matter of quality also, and in this respect, to judge from their attitude, the visiting team felt themselves to have the edge. They were four in number, a sort of Special commando unit. Their ranks comprised Detective Sergeants Drill and Nickman, as dour a pair of bloodhounds as ever signed reports; their lieutenant was Chief Inspector Lasher, a man who had earned the hearty dislike of a select list of international organizations. But it was their No. 1 who really set the seal on the outfit. You could feel his presence through six-inch armour plate. He was a comparatively small man with a large squarish head and blue eyes that glowed hypnotically, as though lit by the perpetual and unfaltering generation of his brain. His name was Chief Superintendent Gish and the date of his retirement had been set aside by the entire world of espionage as one for public holiday and heartfelt rejoicing.

Between these two mighty factions Gently, the lonely representative of the Central Office, felt somewhat in the character of a light skirmisher. He'd got a nuisance value, they would probably concede him that, but otherwise he was merely there as a point of reference. So he squeezed himself into a seat behind Detective Sergeant Nickman, and contented himself with issuing entirely unauthorized smoke-rings.

Chief Superintendent Gish said: 'I want to impress on everybody concerned the urgency and importance of our mission down here. We have sent you a certain amount of information already to assist you in the homicide investigation . . . we've got your man for you and I take it you have prepared a case against him. If you haven't, it doesn't matter because we can put him away ourselves on a certain charge of sabotage. The importance and urgency of this business lies elsewhere and it's that I want to talk about.'

He paused, not so much for comment as to drive home his conviction that comment was superfluous. Gently puffed a sly ring over Detective Sergeant Nickman's right ear. There was a general silence on all fronts.

'Very well, gentlemen,' continued Superintendent Gish, his floor confirmed. 'Now it must certainly have occurred to you, though possibly you have been unable to trace it, that Streifer has received assistance in what he did here. The circumstances of the crime as they are known to me leave no doubt about that. They are typical of the organized killing, the sort that we of the Special Branch are all too familiar with. Now that in itself is an important and urgent matter, but it becomes doubly so in the light of what I am about to tell you.

'The TSK Party came into existence shortly after the war. Officially it has no connection with the authorities on the other side of the Curtain, but I don't have to tell you that it wouldn't have thrived so long as it has done without connivance, and probably assistance, from the gentlemen over the way. It contains a strong Trotskyite element, which no doubt accounts for the nomenclature, but it pursues its aims not by assassination – though it isn't above it – but by extraordinarily well-executed sabotage.

'We first came across it in Yugoslavia. Later on it turned up in Czechoslovakia, Western Germany, France and the Suez Canal Zone. Three years ago the FBI were considerably shaken up to find it active and flourishing in the States – not just one or two agents but a complete organization, with some very dangerous contacts inside two atomic research stations. Fortunately they got on to them in time and pretty well stamped them out, though if this little affair is anything to go by the TSK still have a foot-hold over there. In the suitcase Streifer was carrying there were $1,000,000 in counterfeit bills.

'Over here our first brush with them occurred at about the same time. They suborned a couple of atomic research physicists and when the balloon went up, I regret to say that they succeeded in getting one of them out of the country. After that we had the sabotage trouble down at Portsmouth in which Streifer was identified as the agent. There was nothing else then for some time. But about a year ago, as you may remember, a rash of naval sabotage broke out from Scapa down to Plymouth and it didn't take us long to discover that the TSK were back, this time in some strength. In fact, gentlemen, they had built an organization over here, an organization similar, though perhaps not so extensive, as the one they had built in the States.

'I need hardly mention that we have left no stone unturned to get at grips with this organization. Chief Inspector Lasher and myself were assigned to the task and we have pursued every opening and lead with the not inconsiderable resources at our command. We have had some success. We have arrested and deported or imprisoned a round half-dozen of agents. But we have never been able to locate the centre, the headquarters of the organization – there are never any lines back to it. The men we arrested wouldn't talk, and the impression I received after personal interrogation was that they didn't know anyway.

'Of course, we've had theories about it. We decided early on that it was probably on the east coast. Here there's some little traffic with the other side – cargo-boats trade in and out of the ports, fishing-boats operate off-shore, liners like the *Ortory* touch in on some pretext or another. It seemed logical to give the east coast preference. And knowing the sort of people we were up against, we didn't necessarily expect to find it in an obvious centre such as Newcastle or Hull. We felt it was much more likely to turn up in a smaller place, an innocent-seeming place . . . a holiday resort like Starmouth, gentlemen, with its perpetual comings and goings, its absorption with visitors, its easy-going port and fleet of fishing vessels . . .'

Chief Superintendent Gish dwelt fondly on his theory, as though he enjoyed its sweet reasonableness. But he had got the opposition in a raw spot. There were underground growlings from Colonel Shotover Grout, an aggressive cough from Superintendent Symms and finally the home team found its voice in an exclamation by its illustrious leader:

'But good God, man, there's nothing like that in Starmouth!'

'Indeed, Sir Daynes?' Chief Superintendent Gish looked bored.

'No, sir. Quite impossible! The Borough Police Force is one of the most efficient in the country, including the Metropolitan, and the crime figures for this town, sir, bear comparison with those of any similar town anywhere. We harbour no criminal organizations in Starmouth, political or otherwise. Starmouth is by way of being a model of a respectable popular resort.'

'Here, here!' grumbled Colonel Shotover Grout chestily. 'You are mistaken, sir, gravely mistaken.'

'I'm not prepared to say,' added Sir Daynes generously, 'that Starmouth is completely free from undesirable activity. There are features – ahem! – moral features which we would gladly see removed. But that is an evil common to this sort of town, sir, and under the present limitations forced upon the police of this country we have not the power to stamp it out, though we keep it rigidly in check. Apart from this I may safely say that Starmouth is an unusually orderly and well-policed town. I assure you that nothing of the sort you describe could establish itself here without our knowledge.'

'Quite impossible, sir!' rumbled the colonel, 'you don't know Starmouth.'

Chief Superintendent Gish let play his hypnotic blue eyes from Sir Daynes to the colonel, and back again to Sir Daynes. 'And yet you wake up one morning to find a TSK agent and saboteur lying stabbed on your beach,' he commented steelily.

'It was hardly in our province to have prevented it!' came back Sir Daynes. 'If agents and saboteurs are permitted such easy entry into this country, then responsibility for their misdeeds must lie elsewhere than with the Starmouth Borough Police.'

'I agree, Sir Daynes. My point is that the Starmouth Borough Police knew nothing of their presence until a dead body turned up.'

'And the Special Branch, sir, knew nothing of their presence until informed by the Starmouth Borough Police.'

'With some Central Office assistance.'

'Invoked in the common round of our duty.'

There was a silence-at-arms, each mighty antagonist feeling he had struck an equal blow. Chief Superintendent Gish appeared to be putting the super's desk calendar into a trance. Sir Daynes Broke was giving his best performance of an affronted nobleman. Gently, after waiting politely for the launching of some fresh assault, improved the situation by relighting his pipe and involving Detective Sergeant Nickman in a humanizing haze of Navy Cut.

'You'll have to admit,' continued Chief Superintendent Gish at length, 'that Streifer received assistance in killing Stratilesceul.'

'I admit nothing of the sort,' countered Sir Daynes warily.

'What other interpretation can be put on the facts? Is there any doubt that his hands were tied?'

'One man can tie another's hands, Superintendent.'

'He can if the other will submit to it.'

'Streifer had a gun when he was arrested. Why should he not have threatened Stratilesceul into submission?'

'Have you ever tried tying the hands of a man you are threatening with a gun, Sir Daynes?'

'He could have bludgeoned him.'

'There were no head injuries.'

'Or drugs, perhaps.'

'Where would he obtain such drugs at short notice, supposing he could have induced Stratilesceul to take them? No, Sir Daynes, it won't do. Streifer wasn't on his own. He found help here, in this town, and help for the like of Streifer can only come from one source.'

'That source, sir, need not be in Starmouth. You have offered no certain grounds for your assumption that it is in Starmouth. Since TSK agents proliferate to such an amazing extent in this country I see no reason why Streifer, having followed Stratilesceul to Starmouth, should not have summoned one of them to his assistance. He had time enough. The murder was not committed till almost a week after Stratilesceul arrived.'

'It is possible, Sir Daynes, but that is all one can say for it.'

'As possible as your own hypothesis, and a good deal more probable.'

'I beg to differ. If I thought otherwise I should not be here.'

'Then, sir, there is little doubt that you have made a fruitless journey.'

'We will defer judgment until we see the results, Sir Daynes. I do not propose to be deflected from my object.'

At this point an interruption became a diplomatic necessity and it was fortunate that Colonel Shotover Grout, who had been preparing himself with a great deal of throat work, chose the slight pause which ensued for his cue.

'I suppose we can have the fella in – question him – see what he has to say himself about the business?'

They both turned to regard the colonel with unanimous unamiability.

'I mean he's the one who knows – can't get away from that.'

Chief Superintendent Gish gestured. 'Of course he has been questioned. The results were as anticipated. You'll get nothing out of Streifer.'

'But simply as a formality, y'know—'

'This type of man never talks.'

A light of battle gleamed in Sir Daynes's eye. 'Symms!' he exclaimed, 'be good enough to have our prisoner brought in, will you?'

Superintendent Symms hesitated a moment, catching the Special Branch chief's petrifying glance.

'What are you waiting for, man?' rapped Sir Daynes, 'didn't you hear what I said?'

'I can assure you,' interrupted Chief Superintendent Gish, well below zero, 'that Streifer has been thoroughly and scientifically interrogated without the least success—'

'Superintendent Gish,' cut in Sir Daynes, 'I feel obliged to point out that Streifer is required by this authority to answer a charge of murder and that however high the Special Branch may privately rate sabotage, in the official calendar it is homicide which takes pride of place. Streifer has been brought here primarily to answer such a charge and I propose to make it forthwith. I suppose' – a sudden note of unease crept into his voice – 'I suppose a case has now been made out on which a charge can be based, Symms?'

The super looked at Copping, and Copping looked at Gently. Gently nodded and puffed some smoke at Detective Sergeant Nickman's long-suffering ear.

'Very well, then – have him brought in, Symms!'

Streifer was produced in handcuffs, presumably on the strength of his record – he certainly looked subdued enough, being prodded into the crowded office. He was a man of forty or forty-two, dark hair, dark eyes, slanting brows, a long, straight nose and a small thin-lipped mouth. He wore a well-cut suit of dark grey and had an air of refinement, almost of delicacy, about him. The only thing suggesting something else was the long, crooked scar which stretched lividly down his right cheek, beginning under the temple and trailing away at the angle of the jaw.

Colonel Shotover Grout gave a premonitory rumble. 'Cuffs, sir – take it they're absolutely necessary?'

Chief Superintendent Gish spared him a look of hypnotic pity.

'Remove them,' ordered Sir Daynes crisply. 'There would appear to be sufficient men with police training present to render the step unperilous.'

The cuffs were removed. A chair was drafted in. With a shorthand constable at his elbow Sir Daynes levelled a model charge and caution at the silent Streifer, inasmuch as he had, on the twelfth instant, with malice aforethought, stabbed to death one Stephan Stratilesceul, alias Max.

The baby being passed to Streifer, he simply shook his head.

'You don't wish to make a statement?'

'No.' His voice was harsh but not unpleasant.

'You realize the invariable penalty annexed to a conviction of homicide in this country?'

'I am not . . . unacquainted.'

'It is a capital offence.'

'Ah yes – England hangs.'

'Yet you still do not wish to say anything in your own defence?'

Streifer shrugged his elegant shoulders. 'Have you proof of this thing?'

'We have a very good case.'

'Enough to drop me into your pit?'

'To convict you – yes.'

'Then what should I say? Have you a confession for me to sign?'

The chief constable frowned. 'We don't do things

that way. You may anticipate perfectly fair proceedings in this country. We have a case against you, but you are perfectly free to defend yourself. What you say will be equally considered with what we say in the court in which you will be tried.'

'Then I shall plead that I am innocent. What more will be necessary?'

'It will be necessary to prove it – as we shall seek to prove our contentions.'

Streifer smiled ironically and cast a deliberate glance round the assembled company. 'What pains you take! In my country we are more economical. But let me hear these contentions of yours. I have no doubt that your scrupulous system permits it.'

Sir Daynes signalled to the super, who once more communicated with Gently by the medium of Copping. Gently, however, having produced a crumpled sheet of paper, elected to pass it back to the seat of authority. The super straightened it out hastily and began to read.

'We can show that the accused, Olaf Streifer, is a member of a revolutionary party known as the TSK and that he is a member of the Maulik or secret police appertaining to that party and that previous to the present instance he has illicitly entered this country for the purpose of forwarding the aims of that party by criminal process.

'We can show that the murdered man, Stephan Stratilesceul, was also a member of the TSK party, and that he was similarly engaged in forwarding its aims.

'We can show that, on Tuesday, 5 August, Stephan Stratilesceul entered this country as a fugitive from the

Polish liner *Ortory*, which liner was at that time breaking at Hull a voyage from Danzig to New York, and that he was pursued ashore by Streifer, and that he escaped in the trawler *Harvest Sea*, which brought him to Starmouth where he was landed on the morning of Wednesday, 6 August.

'We can show that Streifer also arrived in Starmouth, date unknown, and that he took up quarters in a deserted house known as "Windy Tops", and that he traced Stratilesceul to lodgings he had taken at 52 Blantyre Road.

'We can show that on Tuesday, 12 August, at or about 22.00 hours, Stratilesceul proceeded in a hired car to "Windy Tops" in the company of a prostitute named Agnes Meek, alias Frenchy, and that he was not again seen alive.

'We can show that his naked body, bearing four stab-wounds of which two would have been instantly fatal, as well as burns made before death, suggesting that he had been subject to torture, was washed ashore between the Albion and Wellesley Piers some time before 05.10 hours on Wednesday, 13 August, and that the time of death was estimated as being five or six hours previous, and that in the state of the tides and the offshore current then prevailing a body introduced into the sea near "Windy Tops" at or about 24.00 hours Tuesday would, with great probability, be washed ashore at the time and place at which Stratilesceul's body was washed ashore.

'We can show that following Stratilesceul's murder, burglary was committed by Streifer at 52 Blantyre Road in the hope of recovering a suitcase containing a quantity of counterfeit United States Treasury notes, but that his purpose was frustrated by a previous burglary committed by Jeffery Algernon Wylie and Robert Henry Baines on information received from Agnes Meek.

'We can show that Streifer eventually traced the suitcase to its hiding-place under the Albion Pier, that he recovered it, that he substituted for it a brown paper package containing the clothes worn by the deceased at the time of his death, and that he caused the attention of the police to be drawn to the part played by Wylie and Baines, presumably in order to mislead the investigations.' (Here the super seemed smitten by a troublesome cough and the chief constable sniffed rather pointedly.)

'We can show, finally, that the piece of brown paper used to wrap the clothes of the deceased is identical in composition with a sheet of brown paper discovered at "Windy Tops", this sheet forming part of the packing of a mattress acquired for his own use by Streifer, also discovered at "Windy Tops", and that the torn edges of the one piece match exactly the torn edges of the other piece.'

The super halted and laid down his sheet of paper.

'Excellent!' chimed in the colonel, aside. 'First-class case – magnificent phrasing!'

Chief Superintendent Gish turned his head sideways, as though he felt it unnecessary to turn it any further. 'What a pity,' he said to Gently behind, 'what a pity you couldn't have made it water-tight.'

Gently issued a quiet ring at Detective Sergeant Nickman's plastic collar-stud.

'When you've done so well . . . not to be able to show that Streifer was in Starmouth at the time of the murder.'

'What's that?' barked Sir Daynes, 'Not here at the time of the murder? I fail to follow you, sir, I completely fail to follow you!'

'Oh, I dare say you'll get a conviction.' The chief superintendent came back off his half-turn. 'The rest of it's so strong that it's almost bound to carry the day. But as I said, it's a pity that you have to admit a phrase like "date unknown" against the important event of Streifer's arrival in Starmouth . . . his defence are bound to be time-wasting and oratorical about it.'

Sir Daynes stared murder, and the chief superintendent stared it back.

'Is this a fact?' snapped the former at Gently. 'We have just heard it read,' chipped in the chief super scathingly.

Gently raised a calculating eyebrow. 'How long,' he mused, 'how long would you say it would take a man – even supposing he was a confirmed anchovy addict – to eat five average-size tins of anchovies?'

'Anchovies!' exploded Sir Daynes, 'what the devil have anchovies got to do with it, man?'

Gently shook his head. 'I was going to ask Streifer that, if he had been feeling more communicative. But there were five empty tins in his waste-bucket at "Windy Tops" and I find it difficult to believe that he consumed one whole tin each tea-time for five days together . . .'

'It isn't proof,' whipped in the chief super, razor-sharp.

'No, it isn't proof . . . just a curious example of devotion to anchovies. On the whole,' added Gently mildly, 'I was rather glad to find that a gentleman named Perkins, an employee at Starmouth Super Furnishings, was able to remember selling the mattress to a person resembling Streifer as early as Wednesday, 6 August . . .'

The dust died down and Sir Daynes, full of beans, returned to the problem of the reluctant Streifer.

'You have heard the case against you. I think it is plain that it requires a better answer than mere silence. In your own interest, Streifer, I advise you to be as helpful as you can.'

'In my own interest?' Streifer gave a little laugh. 'You are very kind people – very kind indeed! But what interest have I left when I am faced with this so-excellent case?'

'You will not find the police ungrateful for any assistance you may be able to give them.'

'Their gratitude would be touching. No doubt I should remember it with pleasure as I stood on your gallows.'

'If you are innocent you can do no better than tell the whole truth. You are probably aware of other charges which will be preferred if you are acquitted on this one and I can say, on certain authority, that those charges will be dropped if you give us the assistance which we know to be in your power.'

'And that would be the names of my associates in this country?'

'Their names and all the information you possess about them.'

476

'To turn traitor, in fact?'

'To assist the ends of justice.'

Streifer laughed again and fixed his coal-black eyes on Sir Daynes. 'Tell me,' he said, 'on this certain authority of yours – would it not be possible to forget Stratilesceul altogether if I gave this information?'

Sir Daynes jiffled impatiently, but the question pinned him down. 'No,' he admitted at last, 'that charge is irrevocable, Streifer.'

'But you could perhaps buy off the judge, or ensure that these quaint jurymen of yours returned a certain verdict?'

'Quite impossible!' rapped Sir Daynes, 'understand once and for all that such courses are not followed in this country.'

'And even if they were – even if I could be sure – even if you were to hand me a free pardon signed and sealed by your Queen herself – I would not betray the humblest comrade who marches with me towards the final liberation of mankind. That is my answer to you, the policemen. That is the only statement I wish to make. If you are just, as you claim you are just, you will take it down in writing and read it at my trial. But I have nothing more to say, excepting that.'

The silence which followed was slightly embarrassed. Sir Daynes seemed to freeze in his stern official look. Colonel Shotover Grout made rumbling noises, as though he thought the whole thing in very bad taste, and Superintendent Symms sniffed repeatedly in his superintendental way. It was the Special Branch Chief who spoke.

'You see, Sir Daynes? This is the sort of thing we are

up against at every turn . . . you may find criminals difficult to deal with, but believe me they are child's play compared with fanatics.'

'I cannot believe he will continue in this – this obstinacy,' returned Sir Daynes, though his non-plussed tone of voice belied him, 'his life is at stake, sir. Men will attempt their defence in however desperate a situation they find themselves.'

'Not once they have become inoculated with creeds of this description,' sneered the chief super. 'They become intoxicated, Sir Daynes. They become tipsy with the most dangerous brand of aggrandizing delusion – political idealism. It means nothing for them to kill, and a triumph for them to die. We know these people. You had better let us handle them.'

Sir Daynes shook his head bewilderedly. 'I must admit that it is something new in my experience . . . I feel somewhat at a loss.' He glanced at the colonel. 'What is your opinion, sir?'

'Preposterous!' grumbled the colonel half-heartedly, 'unstable, sir . . . foreigners . . . unstable.'

'Then, Sir Daynes, I take it you will make no further opposition to my investigations in this town.'

Sir Daynes pursed his lips. 'If you think it is necessary it is my duty to give you every assistance.'

The chief super nodded in the comfortable consciousness of prevailed merit. 'In effect I shall be taking over the present investigations at the point where your men and Chief Inspector Gently have left off. I shall want a full report from everyone engaged on the case and in addition I intend to conduct personal interrogations to bring to light points which may not hitherto have seemed important. Inspector Gently,' – his head turned sideways again – 'I have full authority to release you and your assistant from your duties here. Later on I should like to have a private chat with you and tomorrow you will be free to return to town.'

Gently nodded his mandarin nod and slowly removed his pipe from his mouth. 'I'd like to make a point . . . if it isn't interrupting the proceedings too much.'

The chief super's head remained sideways in indication of his supreme patience.

'One or two side-issues have cropped up in the course of my minor activities . . . I would have liked another day or two to tie them up.'

'Unnecessary, Inspector Gently. They will certainly be taken care of.'

'They concern,' proceeded Gently absently, 'the organization you are interested in disbanding.'

There was a silence in the crowded room. Nine pairs of eyes focussed with one accord on the man from the Central Office.

'Of course . . . it's not for me to suggest the line of further investigation . . . I don't want to deflect the Special Branch from what it conceives to be its duty. But if they care to hold their horses for just a day or two, I feel I may be able to save them a certain amount of frustration.'

'Come to the point, man!' yapped Chief Superintendent Gish, proving for all time that his neck was fully mobile. 'What is it you're trying to say?'

'I'm trying to say,' replied Gently leisurely, 'that I'm fully aware of the identity and whereabouts of the TSK leader in this country and you could arrest him this evening . . . if you thought it would do you any good.'

479

CHAPTER THIRTEEN

T HEY THOUGHT IT would do them some good
for quite a long time together, did the chief super,
Sir Daynes and Colonel Shotover Grout. In the first
flush of enthusiasm they were for leaping into a Black
Maria and descending upon Big Louey with drawn
automatics and a full complement of iron-mongery. It
took time and a certain amount of cold water to correct
their transports. Gently was obliged to apply the latter
in generous doses.

'We've got nothing on him . . . nothing whatever
. . . we couldn't even take his licence away.'

'But good God, sir!' gabbled Sir Daynes, 'that ring –
it's positive evidence – when he denied possession he
practically declared his culpability!'

'We should never find it . . . he's a clever man.'

'And being able to tell you Stratilesceul's nationality
when even Central Records didn't know him –
it's damning, sir, absolutely damning!'

'Just his word against mine . . . or intelligent guessing.'

'We'd better throw a cordon round the place and raid
it,' snarled the chief super, 'he'll have records – names

and addresses – there'll be a short-wave transmitter somewhere.'

Gently shook his head very firmly. 'Not in Louey's place. He's far too fly. If they were ever there – which I doubt – they came out directly this Stratilesceul business got muddled.'

'But how shall we know for sure if we don't raid it?'

'We know for sure now. He would never have behaved so confidently if he'd got anything to hide.'

'There'll be something to give him away.'

'I wouldn't like to bet on it.'

'And we can't just sit around waiting for him to disappear and set up somewhere else.'

'He'll do that all the quicker if he knows you're out gunning for him.'

'I say pull him in!' erupted the colonel from his thoracic deeps. 'Confront him with the other fella – make them see the game is up!'

'I'm afraid it wouldn't have that effect, colonel . . . they're very old hands at this particular game.'

'But damn it, sir, we must do something!'

'Yes!' struck in Sir Daynes irritably, 'you're very good at telling us what we *can't* do, Gently, now suppose for a change you tell us what we *can* do?'

Gently sighed and felt about in his pockets for a peppermint cream that wasn't there.

'There's just one saving grace about this business, as far as I can see . . . and it's up to us to play it for all it's worth. In your previous dealings with the TSK' – he inclined his head deferentially towards the chief super – 'I think you have had to do solely with agents of the party. Is that correct?'

The chief super scowled what was presumably an affirmative.

'They were men like Streifer – men with an ideal – men who would sooner go to the gallows than give the least particle of information about the party. Now in the present instance there is a significant difference. We have here a person involved – deeply involved – who isn't a party member, who has no burning desire to liberate mankind, and who is only being prevented from giving evidence by mortal fear for her personal safety. That person is the prostitute Frenchy. She knows enough, I'm reasonably certain, to put Louey into the dock beside Streifer . . . perhaps somebody else too. But she's been got at. She doesn't dare testify. She's seen how Stratilesceul finished up, and no doubt she's been told that whoever she gives away, there'll always be someone left to take care of her.

'But there she is – somebody who can do our job for us. If we can only find a way to coax her to talk we shall have Louey and possibly his associates in the palm of our hand. Unfortunately it runs in a circle . . . we've got to pull in Louey and company before she'll talk, and before she talks we can't pull in Louey and company . . .'

'In fact it doesn't seem to be getting us very far, does it?' interrupted the chief super jealously.

Gently sucked a moment on his unlit pipe. 'What puzzles me is how they got her to help them in the first place,' he mused. 'I've never been able to see that quite clearly . . .'

'If they're terrorizing her now they could have terrorized her before.'

482

'I don't think so . . . not Frenchy. She isn't one to terrorize easily. I imagine Louey would need a corpse at his back before he could get much change out of her and the job she had to do would be better done in the spirit of co-operation than in the spirit of coercion.'

'Well then – she was paid.'

'But she didn't have any money.'

'Of course not!' snapped the chief super, 'her boyfriend would have had it.'

'She doesn't admit to any boyfriend, not even to get herself bailed.'

The chief super drew a deep and ugly breath. 'It isn't *getting* us anywhere!' he bawled. 'Does it matter two hoots how they got her to do it? The fact is that she did do it, and precious little help it looks like being to us!'

Gently shook his head in respectful admonishment. 'It means there's a link somewhere . . . something we don't know about. There's a link between Louey and Frenchy, and as a result of that link Frenchy was prepared to act the decoy, without pressure and probably without payment . . .'

'Perhaps this Louey fella's the boyfriend himself,' suggested the colonel.

'He's too clever . . . and women aren't his weakness. No. It's something else.'

'I really can't see that it's important, Gently,' weighed in Sir Daynes.

'It isn't!' barked the chief super, 'we simply sit here wasting our time while the chief inspector amuses himself by . . .'

He broke off as a tap came at the door. It was Sergeant Dutt's homely visage that appeared.

'Begging your pardon, sir . . .'

'Yes? What is it?'

'It's something for Chief Inspector Gently, sir . . . he wanted to know directly a certain party left the premises.'

'Well, cough it up – don't stand there like a dummy!'

Dutt transferred his stolid gaze to his superior. 'It's Frenchy, sir . . .'

'Frenchy!' Gently rose slowly to his feet.

'I just arrived back, sir, and they tell me she was bailed aht half an hour ago.'

A faraway look stole into Gently's eye. 'And who was it, Dutt . . . did you get the name?'

'Yessir. It was a Mr Peach, sir.'

The faraway look lengthened till it embraced some islands of the distant Hebrides. 'Peachey!' murmured Gently, 'my old friend Peachey! I always had a feeling we should find him sewn into the lining of this case . . . somewhere!'

It rained still, as though it had never thought of stopping that side of Michaelmas. The picture-houses, theatres and pavilions were packed solid with moist audiences, the cafes had never had such a day, the lessees of dance-halls and amusement arcades were indulging in dreams of a late-autumn holiday at Cannes or Capri . . . Only the beach was having a bad time of it. Only the beach was dark and deserted and desolate to behold. Soft, unnoticed, another flood-tide crept upwards towards the hectic Front. It washed round the piles under the piers, looked up at its auld enemy, the cliffs, and made to list a few more degrees a certain post which some policemen had set up in the shingle.

But there was nobody there to see it, except a crouching halfwit. The rest of Starmouth kept tryst with their bright lights. Rain it might and rain it did, but the electric rash burned on, the music wailed, the rifles spanged, the audiences laughed and the great Till of Starmouth rang its steady chorus.

Artie in the bar was getting quite irritable with his customers, and he could afford to be. They didn't want away once they were there. And it was a gay crowd that night, on the eve of the races. Several old faces had turned up which had been missing for quite a while . . . it was just like it had been before that b. Inspector Gently set foot in the place, as the sporty individual observed. Even Louey seemed in a festive mood. He had been out twice in the course of the evening and each time it had been drinks all round. It was communicative, that mood of Louey's. For better or worse it affected the company in the bar. But now the clouds which had momentarily gathered about the gigantic brow had faded away, the sunshine had returned, the bar was its old happy self again . . .

Or it was till nine-thirty. Nine-thirty-three and a half, to be precise. At that exact moment a bulky figure in a fawn raincoat and a despairing trilby pushed through the swing-doors and looking neither to right nor left, shouldered its way across to the door opposite and disappeared again.

It was done so quickly that it might have been an optical illusion. Ferrety-face Artie had to shake his head to convince himself he wasn't seeing things. The sporty individual, halfway down his eighth Scotch, screwed up his eyes in a search for assurance that he was stone-cold sober.

'That bloke just now . . . it was him, washn't it?'

Artie nodded absently and moved down towards the door, as though hopeful of hearing something above the din outside.

'But whatsh he doing here . . . I thought Louey said it was OK?'

Artie waved him down with his hand and got still closer to the door. The whole bar held its breath in a sort of hushed watchfulness. In the comparative calm a tincased version of 'Cherry Pink' seemed to vibrate the plastic-topped tables with its singeing vehemence.

'I don't undershtand . . .' burbled the sporty individual, 'something's going on, Artie . . . I don't undershtand.'

Artie didn't either, but there wasn't very long to wait. At nine-thirty-seven, or a trifle before, the door reopened with a suddenness that nearly pinned Artie to the wall. Out waddled Peachey, red in the face. Out marched the bulky figure, his hand tucked affectionately under Peachey's arm. Again no time was wasted. Again no looks were cast to right or to left. The brief procession headed forthrightly through the swing-doors and vanished like a dream, though in this case one part of the dream was left standing in the doorway by the bar. It was Big Louey. And his gold tooth wasn't showing at all . . .

Outside Dutt was waiting in a police car. Peachey was bundled in and Gently gave an address to the driver which didn't sound like Headquarters. A short drive brought them to a dark and empty street where but few lamps shone islands of radiance on the gleaming pavement. Dutt alighted and stood by the door.

486

'Get out,' ordered Gently to Peachey.

Peachey gulped and gave a frightened look up and down the street.

'This isn't the police station! I d-demand to be taken to the police station!'

'Get out!' snapped Gently and Peachey scuttled forth like a startled rabbit. Gently followed him and after tossing a word to the driver, slammed the door resoundingly behind them. He indicated the house by which they had stopped.

'In there.'

'B–but I've g-got rights . . . you c–can't do this!'

Gently poked a steely finger into his plump back and Peachey forgot about his rights with great suddenness.

There was nothing alarming about the house, however. The door opened on a well-lit and comfort-able-looking hall containing a hat-stand and an aspidis-tra on a side-table and the room into which Peachey was marshalled bore all the appurtenances of respectable boarding-house practice. Gently took off his hat and raincoat and hung them familiarly on the hat-stand.

'See if Mrs Davis has got the tea on, will you?' he said to Dutt, 'and ask her if she's got some biscuits . . . I like those shortbread ones we had the other night.'

Dutt departed and Gently joined Peachey in the lounge. Gently seemed in no hurry to begin business. An electric fire was glowing in the fireplace and, standing with his back to it, he slowly filled and lit his seasoned briar. Peachey watched every move with pathetic attention. Twice he seemed about to recall his flouted rights, but each time, catching Gently's mild eye, he thought better of it. The horrid ordeal ended when Dutt re-appeared bearing the tea tray. There were three cups and Peachey was even indulged with two lumps of sugar.

'And now . . .' mused Gently, seating himself with his teacup, 'now we can have our little chat in peace and comfort . . . can't we, Peachey?'

'You haven't g-got no right!' broke out the parrot-faced one unhopefully.

Gently clicked his tongue. 'No right, Peachey? Why, we're treating you like an old friend – bringing you to our nice cosy lodgings, instead of that bare old police station! Now sit yourself down on one of Mrs Davis's best chairs, and try to be a bright lad . . . you need to be a bright lad, don't you, Peachey?'

Peachey blinked and swallowed, then lowered himself into a chair. Gently drank a large mouthful of tea and set his cup down near the electric fire.

'You're here for a reason, Peachey. Two reasons, as a matter of fact. The unimportant reason is because there's a pack of wolves down at Headquarters who would just love to tear a little boy like you into small pieces. The important reason is that I want to talk to you off the record – no charges, no taking it down, nothing being used in evidence. Anything you tell me here is in confidence and it won't appear again till you're ready to give it in a sworn statement . . . you get the idea?'

Peachey's close-set eyes seemed to get closer together than ever. 'I-I'm not going to m-make a statement . . . I don't know nothing to make one about!'

Gently shook his head paternally. 'Don't say that, Peachey. You don't know how useful that statement's going to be. At a rough guess I should say it would make eighteen months' difference to you, besides a slimming course with the pick and shovel. You wouldn't be too handy with a pick and shovel, would you, Peachey?'

'I don't know what you're t-talking about!' Peachey gulped, his cup and saucer beginning to chatter.

'Come, come, Peachey! You're amongst friends. There's no need to be bashful. Almost any time now we're going to run you in for living on immoral earnings and I'm sure you know what that means. If you go before a beak, it'll be six months in one of our more comfortable establishments; if you go up with an indictment, it'll be two years with the pick-and-shovel boys.'

'B-but it isn't true!'

'We've got the goods, Peachey.'

'I'm a b-bookmaker's clerk – you know I am!'

'Six witnesses, Peachey, and two of them your neighbours in Sidlow Street.'

'It's a f-frame, I tell you!'

'And three past convictions, all neatly filed at Central Records . . . no, Peachey. You're due for a holiday. And just between us you'll be lucky if it stops there, won't you?'

The parrot-faced one put down his cup, which he was no longer in a condition to support. He made a pitiful effort to get out a cigarette, but the packet fell from his hands and its contents distributed about the floor. Dutt helped him pick them up. They got him lighted at the second attempt.

'As I was saying,' resumed Gently meditatively, 'you'll be lucky, won't you? You'll need all the goodwill that's going if you're not going to be roped in for complicity in the murder of Stephan Stratilesceul . . . did you know his name? At "Windy Tops"?'

He paused for artistic effect and Peachey shrank down in his chair several degrees.

'Of course, it may be that in making a statement you would incriminate yourself . . . there's always that to be thought about. We shall quite understand your keeping silent if you were in fact an accomplice . . .'

The goad was irresistible. Peachey squirmed as though it had galled him physically. 'I didn't know – I swear – it wasn't nothing to do with me!'

'Nothing to do with you? How can you, Peachey! When it was Frenchy who got him out to "Windy Tops" in the first place.'

'I tell you I didn't know . . . they didn't say n-nothing!'

'You mean they didn't tell you they were going to kill him?'

Peachey sucked hard on a cigarette which was coming to pieces between his lips.

'You might as well come clean, Peachey. It's off the record.'

Peachey gulped and sucked, but he had dried up again.

Gently sighed. 'Let me see if I can reconstruct it. They had a conference, didn't they? Streifer had traced Stratilesceul to his lodgings in Blantyre Road, but he was rather at a loss to know how to deal with him. It wasn't just a question of killing the man and recovering the money. Streifer could handle that well enough on his own. No – what was important about Stratilesceul was certain information he could give . . . with a little persuasion, perhaps . . . about other untrustworthy members of the TSK Party. Am I right?'

The cigarette was definitely a spent force, but Peachey kept on working at it.

'That was the problem, then – to get Stratilesceul in a place where he could be duly persuaded, and afterwards, as a mere formality, put to death. It wasn't an easy problem to solve. Stratilesceul wasn't laying himself open to being kidnapped. As far as he knew, he had shaken off the pursuit, but he was still taking precautions – like lodging in a crowded boarding-house and sticking to the frequented parts of the town. I dare say there were several plans made. The length of time it took to do the job suggests it. But they all fell through for that very simple reason – they could never get him where they could lay their hands on him.

'So we come to the final conference – Louey, Streifer and Little Peachey . . . because you were in on it, weren't you, Peachey? And Louey sits on a striped chair behind that very nice desk of his, thinking, thinking. At last he says to Streifer: "You're familiar with Stratilesceul's confidential record?" – And Streifer nods with that quiet little laugh of his. "Is there nothing in it that might serve our turn?" – Streifer shrugs and says: "He's fond of women." "Women!" says Louey, showing some gold, "any particular sort of women, or just women in general?" "Blonde women," says Streifer, "nice big blondes."

'At that Louey really smiles. "We've got the very thing . . . haven't we, Peachey?" he says, "a nice big blonde who'll do just what we ask her! Why, I dare say that if we play it right we can get friend Stephan delivered to the very door . . ." And what did Little Peachey say to that? He said: "Yes, Louey, of course, Louey, anything you say goes with me, Louey—"'

'I didn't know!' shrieked the tormented Peachey, 'they never said anything about killing him in front of me!'

'You didn't guess?' rapped Gently. 'You thought it was just going to be a social evening?'

'They said he'd hidden the money, that's all. They said they wanted to get him to find out what he'd done with it!'

'So you're entirely innocent – and Frenchy's entirely innocent?'

'She didn't know neither!'

'Just a couple of little lambs! And where were you when Frenchy was doing her dirty work?'

'I don't know – I was in the bar!'

'You were in the bar – then you didn't get Louey's car out of the garage?'

'No!'

'Then two witnesses we've got are liars?'

'I wasn't near the garage!'

'And you didn't pick up the reception committee and take them to "Windy Tops"?'

'. . . I was in the bar!'

'And you didn't wait there with them to give a hand tying up Stratilesceul?'

'I didn't – I didn't! When they'd got him in there they sent me back with Frenchy . . . we never knew nothing . . . nothing at all.'

'So it was just one big surprise when you saw it in

the papers.' Gently reached down for his cup of tea and tossed it off fiercely. 'And when you found out, what did you do?'

'I didn't do nothing!' floundered Peachey, his little eyes roving from side to side as though in desperate search for escape.

'Nothing. Nothing! You knew the murderers – you'd been tricked into helping them – unless you spoke up quick you were in it along with them – and yet you did nothing. Is that your tale for the jury?'

'I ain't going before a jury!'

'Oh yes you are, Peachey, somewhere along the line.'

'But you said it wasn't evidence!'

'It will be when you've sworn it.'

'I ain't going to swear it – never – no one can make me.'

'They won't have to, Peachey. You'll do all the swearing that's necessary when you go up on a murder rap.'

'But I never did it – you know I never did it!'

'I shall feel a lot more certain when I've got a statement on paper with your signature underneath.'

Peachey shrivelled up in the chair like a punctured balloon. 'I ain't going to swear,' he whispered, 'I ain't – I ain't!'

'Then it's two years' hard at the very least.'

'I ain't going to swear, not though it was twenty.'

Gently shrugged his bulky shoulders and handed his cup to Dutt, who silently refilled it. Gently drank some and gnawed a shortbread biscuit. 'Of course, you know we've got Streifer,' he muttered casually amongst the crumbs.

'Str-Streifer?' Peachey unshrivelled a little.

Gently nodded and bit another piece.

'But Streifer is g-gone . . .!'

'We took the trouble to bring him back again . . . your grapevine can't be as good as it was.'

Peachey's small eyes fixed on the pattern of Mrs Davis's best carpet, but he made no other contribution for the moment.

'He's safe and sound,' continued Gently, 'you don't have to worry about *him* any longer. And if a certain little bird would sing his song we could put Louey in with him. Louey in jail,' he added helpfully, 'would be just as harmless as the average mortal.'

The pattern still had Peachey fascinated.

'And with a little further assistance, Peachey — all confidential, you understand, no names published, no questions asked about how a certain individual came by his information — we could arrest and imprison or expel quite a fairish bag of unfriendly-minded persons. In fact, we could make this country a healthy place for little Peacheys to come back to after a six-month vacation . . . couldn't we?'

For a moment the small eyes lifted from the carpet and rested just below Gently's chin. Then they sank again, sullenly, and the dry lips bit together.

'Ah well!' sighed Gently, 'we do our best, don't we? We always do our best!' He appropriated another biscuit and crammed it into his mouth. 'Take him home, Dutt . . . take him to his flat in Sidlow Street. I don't suppose he wants to see Louey again tonight.'

Dutt took a step forward and Peachey looked up suddenly, his mouth dropping open.

'B–but aren't you going to p-pinch me . . .?'

Gently shook his head and swallowed some tea.

'B–but you've got a charge – y–you said you had!'

'Can't bother with it just now, Peachey. The local lads will see to it some time.'

'B–but it's true – you've got some witnesses!'

'You just comalongofme like the chief inspector says,' said Dutt, hoisting the parrot-faced one to his feet, 'he's done with you now . . . you're even getting a nice ride home. You don't want us to lock you up, do you?'

If Peachey's expression was anything to go by he did want that very thing, but neither Gently nor Dutt seemed willing to oblige. He was stood firmly in the hall while Dutt was putting on his raincoat and Gently, still ravaging amongst the biscuits, appeared to be forgetting the existence of both of them. But as Dutt reached for his hat, Gently sauntered to the lounge door.

'By the way, Peachey . . .'

Peachey blinked at him hopefully.

'If you were running a short-wave transmitter it would be useful to have a nice high aerial, wouldn't it?'

'T–transmitter . . .?'

'That's right. For sending little gossip-notes to the Continent.'

'But I don't know nothing about it!'

Gently tut-tutted and felt for a scrap of paper. 'Here we are . . . hot from Central Records. They released you from a stretch in '42 to go into the Services; you were trained as a radio-mechanic at Compton Bassett; radar course at Hereford in '44; demobilized as a Sergeant-Radar-mechanic in '46. Quite a distinguished career, Peachey . . . and of course you'd know all about building and working a simple transmitter, wouldn't you?'

Peachey gulped and tried to get some moisture on to his lips.

'And about that aerial? There aren't so many high places in Starmouth. There's the monument, but that's a bit too bare and obvious. And there's the observation tower, but that would be even worse. No . . . what you'd want would be something unobtrusive . . . something where a little private wiring wouldn't notice very much, where perhaps there was an off-season when you could do the job without interruptions. That's what you'd want, isn't it, Peachey?'

'I forgot all that . . . I don't remember nothing about radio!'

Gently shook his head consolingly. 'Never mind, Peachey. I dare say you will. It'll come back to you with a rush one day. Oh, and just one other thing.'

Peachey sucked in breath.

'Tell Louey I'll be in tomorrow some time to settle up a bet, will you? He'll know what I mean . . . just tell him that.'

Dutt hustled him out and the door closed behind them. Gently hesitated a moment till he heard the car pull away, then he returned swiftly to the lounge, uncoupled the phone, dialled a number crisply.

'Chief Inspector Gently . . . oh, hullo, Louey! I thought it was only fair to ring you up . . .'

He smiled pleasantly to himself at the note of tenseness in the voice at the other end.

'Yes, of course you have to know . . . with the races

tomorrow too . . . naturally you'll be stuck if we pinch your head boy. But there's nothing to worry about, Louey . . . no, we came to an agreement. I've just sent him home now, as free as a bird. He's a sensible chap, Louey . . . knows when it's time to do a deal. We all have to play along with the police sometimes . . . eh? Yes . . . yes . . . Sidlow Street . . . yes. I'm glad it's eased your mind, Louey. Have a good day with the gee-gees tomorrow . . . yes . . . good night.'

He pressed the receiver down a moment and then dialled again.

'Gently here. Give me Copping.'

'Hullo?' came Copping's voice, 'have you had any luck? The chief super says that if you haven't—!'

'Never mind the chief super,' interrupted Gently with a grimace. 'Listen, Copping. This is vitally important. I've just sent Peach home to his flat at 27 Sidlow Street with Dutt to keep an eye on him. Now I want Dutt relieved at midnight and your best man sent to replace him. And armed, you understand? Peach has got to be guarded from now on, day and night . . . and heaven help the man who slips up on the assignment!'

CHAPTER FOURTEEN

STARMOUTH RACES – that colourful, money-ful, tax-free event – Starmouth Races, when a town already full to the brim began bursting at the seams. From early in the forenoon the train-loads started to emerge. By lunch-time you could hardly move on the road to the race-course, and as for getting a sit-down meal, you were lucky to pick up a couple of cheese sandwiches. But it was Starmouth Races and nobody cared. You came for the fun and the flutter and the sea-air, and if you went back skint it was all part of the outing.

They'd got a brass band from Norchester, a regular festival-winning affair. It had come out today in a fanfaronade of new grey and pink, with a man on the baton who really knew his business. Dutt was enthralled. He had always had a weakness for brass bands. When they went to town with 'Blaze Away' it touched a chord in his simple cockney heart . . .

'Worst day of the year!' moaned Copping to Gently, 'how can you police this lot with the men we've got? If we arrested all the dips and shysters who come up for the races it'd need a special excursion train to cart them back to town!'

The super was there, looking very spruce and commanding in his best blue with its rainbow of medal ribbons. He sharpened a glance for Gently's baggy tweed. 'I hope you know what you're doing, Gently . . . Gish is out for your blood if anything goes wrong.'

Gently tilted his head accommodatingly and the super passed with a sniff.

As a matter of fact, Gently was beginning to worry himself, just a little bit. The thing wasn't going to pattern at all. There had been no alarums and excursions, no rush for Sidlow Street in the quiet hours . . . Peachey had spent a restful night, said the report, or if not a restful one, at least a peaceful one. In the morning it was the same. The routine of 'The Feathers' had continued undisturbed. Louey had gone for his constitutional, Peachey had reported to the office, at lunch-time they had eaten together at a nearby restaurant and directly afterwards Peachey had fetched the car and driven Louey and two of the bar-regulars to the race-course. It was almost as though Louey were ignoring the situation, as though he were deliberately calling Gently's bluff. Certainly there was no anxiety in his aspect, and if Peachey was looking rather more like a boiled stuffed rabbit than usual it was hardly to be wondered at.

Gently's eye wandered through the busy crowd to the line of bookies' stands. Biggest of all flamed a great orange banner, set up on two poles, and licking across it like scarlet fire ran the legend: LOUEY ALWAYS PAYS! – Not that it was necessary, such a banner. You could

499

hear the voice of Louey like distant thunder, over-topping crowd, band and competitors:

'FIVE TO TWO ON THE FAVOURITE . . . COME ON NOW . . . ONLY LOUEY GIVES IT . . . FIVE TO TWO ON THE FAVOURITE!'

His gold tooth shone, his diamond ring flashed, he loomed over the crowd like a genial Goliath. And they liked Louey. He was an institution on the race-course. Plump Peachey could hardly scribble slips out fast enough to keep pace with the money going into that gaping Gladstone.

'FIVE TO TWO ON THE FAVOURITE . . . TEN BOB TO WIN TWENTY-FIVE . . . HUNDRED TO EIGHT ON CAMBYSES . . . COME ON NOW, THESE ARE THE ODDS YOU'RE LOOKING FOR!'

Up beside him the sporty individual was taking signals from someone across in the stands and chalking up fresh odds on the blackboard. Down below a couple of bar-types were touting recklessly, yanking custom from the very shadow of rival stands.

'COME ON NOW . . . NO LIMIT . . . IF YOU WANT A FORTUNE COME TO LOUEY . . . YOU SEE MY BANNER — IT MEANS WHAT IT SAYS! . . . COME ALONG NOW AND DO THE INCOME-TAX COLLECTOR IN THE EYE!'

It was all so innocent, all so regular. Moral or immoral, book-making was legitimate business and watching Louey up there in all his glory tended to shake one's convictions. He looked so little like a murderous fanatic with the gallows threatening to yawn at his very feet.

But that was the situation and Gently had made sure that Louey knew where he stood. He was counter-bluffing, that was all; doing what Gently would have done himself if the positions had been reversed. But counter-bluff was a temporary measure. There would be a plan behind it, a positive step. What was it cooking now, that calculating mind, when was it going to happen, and where?

Gently moved over to Dutt, who had resumed his role as Peachey's protector.

'Keep your eyes on your man,' he warned him snappily, 'he'll be easy enough to lose in a crowd like this.'

'Yessir . . . of course, sir. But you got to admit it's a smashing bit of brass . . .'

'I don't admit anything – keep your eyes on Peachey.'

Dutt clicked his heels and did as he was ordered.

Gently wandered away with a frown on his brow. He was biting Dutt's head off now! The double strain of a waiting game with Louey and a checking game with Gish was beginning to fray at his nerves. Gish wanted action. He hadn't any faith in Gently. One had a shrewd suspicion that twenty-four hours would be the limit of his patience.

A slinking figure appeared to materialize out of the worn turf in front of him and Nits' pop-eyes strained up to his own. Gently summoned up a smile for the halfwit.

'Hullo! You come to see the races too, my lad?'

Nits gibbered a moment with his invisible mouth.

'You better get over by the rails – there's a race starting in five minutes.'

'You let her come back!' piped the halfwit, 'you let her come back!'

Gently nodded gravely. Nits chittered and gabbled under his staring eyes. Then he turned to cast a glare of hatred at the towering form of Louey.

'Him – he's a very bad man – very bad!'

Gently nodded again.

'He came to see her – frighten her!' Nits hesitated and crept a little closer. 'You take him away! Yes! You take him away!' He laid a hand on Gently's sleeve.

'I'm thinking about it, Nits . . .'

'He's the bad one – yes! You take him away!'

Gently shrugged and slowly released his sleeve. The halfwit gabbled away furiously, darting angry glances, now at Louey, now at Gently. Gently produced a coin and offered it to him.

'Here you are . . . but don't go making bets with Louey.'

'Don't want it – don't want it!'

'Buy yourself an ice-cream or a pint of shrimps.'

The halfwit shook his head violently and knocked the coin out of Gently's hand. 'You take him away!' he reiterated, 'yes – you take him away!' Then he jumped backwards with a sort of frisking motion and dived away through the crowd.

There was a stir now and a general surge towards the rails. The horses had come up to the tapes and were under starter's orders. Out of a grey sky came a mild splash of sun to enliven for a moment the group of animals and riders, the brilliantly coloured shirts, the white breeches, the chestnut, grey and dun of satin flanks. Tense and nervy were the mounts, strung up and preoccupied the jockeys. A line was formed, a jumpy horse coaxed quiet and almost before one realized what

502

was happening the tapes flew up and the field was away. Instantly a shout began to rise from the crowd, commencing near the gate and spreading right down the track. Fifty thousand pairs of eyes were each magnetized by that thundering, flying, galloping body of horse.

Out in front went the favourite, Swifty's Ghost, and following it close came Cambyses and Rockaby, the latter at a hundred to one and scarcely looked at by the punters. Three furlongs, and the field was getting lost. Six furlongs, and you could almost draw your money. Seven furlongs, and Cambyses, a big grey, was making a terrific bid and going neck-and-neck. Eight furlongs, and out of the blue came Rockaby, fairly scorching the turf, a little dun horse with a halting gallop, but moving now like a startled witch. Could Swifty's Ghost hold them? Could Cambyses maintain his challenge? – The roar of the crowd ebbed up to a fever pitch. But Rockaby drew level with a furlong to go, Rockaby slipped through with a hundred-and-fifty yards in hand, Rockaby passed the post two lengths ahead of the grey and the favourite was beaten to a place by another outsider called Watchmego. The roar died away, the roar became a buzz. They'd done it again . . . another race to line the bookies' pockets!

Gently hunched his shoulders and turned away from the rails, and at that precise moment things began to happen. He had only time for a confused impression; it took place like a dream. There was a crash, some angry shouting, a sound like a quantity of coins being shot on the ground, and then somebody or something struck him heavily in the back and he was lying on his face on the bruised turf.

He wasn't hurt. He got up in a hurry. All around him a crowd was milling about a centre of attraction which was otherwheres than himself. Inside this centre a dialogue for four voices was developing with great verve.

'Of course it was on purpose – I bloody saw you do it!'

'I was shoved, I tell you.'

'You can tell it to the coppers!'

'I tell you I was shoved – some bastard tripped me up!'

'Do you think we're blind?'

'Well, you don't look too bloody bright.'

'Now look here, you dirty so-and-so!'

Gently shouldered his way through. The scene enacting was self-explanatory. A bookie's stand lay on its side amid a debris of betting-slips, notes and coins, about it four angry men. Three of the men were obviously allies. The fourth, a burly gentleman in a mackinaw, appeared to be the defendant in the case.

'Police!' snapped Gently, 'you can stop that shouting. One of you tell me what's been going on here.'

The gent in the mackinaw broke off a challenge to the opposition and stared at Gently with aggressive insolence.

'Police, he says! A snouting copper! You keep your big nose out of this, mate, or it'll finish up a different shape from what it started this morning!'

'You hear him?' struck in one of the aggrieved, on his knees and trying to collect the scattered money, 'that's your man, officer – you don't have to ask! Come

504

up and threw down my bleeding stand, he did, never as much as a word offered to him!'

'Mad!' snapped a little man with a big coloured tie, 'mad, I tell you – that's what he is!'

The gent in the mackinaw seemed about to resent this allegation when he was interrupted a second time by a new arrival. This time it was Dutt and he was propelling in front of him no less a person than Artie of the ferret face.

'I got him, sir!' panted Dutt, 'he's the one, sir – saw him wiv me own mince pies! Standing right close-up to you he was, sir, all during the race, and as soon as this lot here started he catched you a right fourpenny one and hooked it . . . all he didn't know was that I was watching him!'

Gently stared at the scowling bartender as though he had seen a ghost. 'Get back!' he thundered at Dutt. 'Good God, man – *don't you understand*? The whole thing's a trick to get us out of the way – get back at the double, or there may be another body on the beach tomorrow!'

The odds were still being called under the orange banner, but it wasn't Louey calling them. The slips were still being scribbled and handed out, but the man with the book wasn't Peachey. It was the sporty individual who had taken over, with one of the touts for his clerk. He welcomed Gently and Dutt derisively as they rushed up to the stand.

'Hullo-ullo! Coupla gents here getting in training for the selling-plate!'

'All right!' rasped Gently, 'where are they – where have they gone?'

'Gone, guv'nor? And who is it that's s'posed to have gone somewhere?'

Gently wasted no time. A brown hand flicked out and fifteen stone of sporty individual was picked off the stand like a pear. 'Now . . .! This may be fun for you, but it's murder to me, and if you don't tell me what I want to know I'll see you in dock for complicity. Where's he taken Peachey?'

'I don't know, guv, honest—!' He broke off with a yell as Gently applied pressure to his arm.

'Where's he taken Peachey?'

'I don't know – we don't none of us know!'

'That's right, guv!' broke in the tout with the book, 'he just said him and Peachey had got some business to see to what he didn't want you to know about.'

'It's the truth!' shrieked the sporty individual, 'oh, my bloody arm!'

Gently threw him down against the stand, where he lay massaging his maltreated limb and moaning. 'Find Copping!' rapped Gently to Dutt, 'tell him what's happened – tell him to issue a description to all his men – send one to "The Feathers" and one to Sidlow Street – the rest fan out and search the area round the race-course. Where's Louey's car parked?' he fired at the sporty individual.

'It's over there – right by the gate!'

'Check and see if it's gone – if it has, alert all stations.'

Dutt hesitated a moment and then turned in the direction of the gate, but before he could set off an animal-like form came darting and swerving through the crowds and threw itself at Gently's feet.

'He went that way – that way! I saw him! I saw him go!'

Gently's eyes flashed. 'Which way, Nits? . . . which way?'

'That way!' The halfwit made a fumbling gesture towards the north end of the enclosure.

'Gorblimey!' exclaimed Dutt, 'it's "Windy Tops" again!'

Gently rounded on him. 'Forget what I've been saying – just tell Copping to bring his men up there. And when you've done that, don't wait for him . . . I shall probably be in need of some help!'

'Yessir!' gasped Dutt, 'yessir – I'll be there with you!'

But by that time Gently was gone.

It was a hummocky bit of paddock separating the race-course from the lane to 'Windy Tops' and Gently, past his best sprint years, found it very heavy going. At the far side was a scrubby thorn fence in which he had to find a gap. Nits, frisking along at his side, went over it like an Olympic hurdler.

'You get back, m'lad!' panted Gently, 'there'll be trouble up there!'

'You going to take him away!' chuckled Nits. 'I want to see you take him away!'

'You stop down here and you'll get a grandstand view!'

'I want to see – I want to see!'

There was no discouraging him. Gently ploughed on up the slope of the cliff. By the time he reached the gates of 'Windy Tops' he was glad of the breather offered by a pause to reconnoitre and Nits, entering into the spirit of the thing, gave up his leaping and frisking, and slid away like an eel behind the cover of some rhododendron bushes. Not a sound had come from the house. Not a vestige of life was to be seen at any of the windows. Only the front door stood half ajar, as though whoever was within didn't mean to be there for very long.

Keeping his breathing in check, Gently moved swiftly across to the threshold. Inside he could hear voices coming from somewhere at the back. Silently he worked his way down the hall towards the baize-covered door of the kitchen, which was shut, and pressed himself close to it, listening . . .

'No, Peachey,' came Louey's voice at its softest and silkiest, 'we don't seem able to find that money anywhere, do we?'

'B-but boss . . . he give me the message,' came Peachey's whine in reply.

There was the sound of a cupboard door being opened and shut, and something else moved.

'Quite empty, Peachey . . . not a dollar-note to be seen.'

'Boss, he t-took it with him . . . you don't think I'd l-lie?'

'Lie, Peachey?' Louey's laugh sounded careless and easy. 'You wouldn't lie to me, now, would you?'

'N-no, boss, of course I wouldn't!'

'And you wouldn't tell tales, Peachey, would you . . . not even to save your own worthless skin?'

A confused noise was Peachey's answer to this sally.

Louey's laugh came again. 'You see, Peachey, we all have our value, looked at from a certain point of view. I have mine. Streifer has his. Stratilesceul had a value too, but unfortunately for himself he lost it. And now the pressing problem of the moment, Peachey, is your value . . . you do see what I'm driving at?'

A strangled sound suggested that Peachey saw it very plainly.

'Yes, Peachey, I thought you would. I don't want to be unkind, you know. I'm prepared to listen to any defence you may have to offer, but it seems to me that there can't be any real doubt about the matter ... doesn't it to you? Here am I, on whom the forces of liberation in this country depend, and there are you, a small and expendable unit. Now I could betray you, Peachey, and that might be wrong. But if you were to betray me, that would be a crime comparable to the crime of Judas. You understand?'

'But boss – I never – I didn't – I told them I wouldn't!'

'SILENCE!' thundered Louey's voice, stripped in a moment of its silky veneer. 'Do you think I didn't know, you miserable worm, do you think you can lift a finger without my knowing it?'

There was a pause and then he continued in his former voice: 'I like to make these matters clear. I tried to make them clear to Stratilesceul. I'm not a criminal, Peachey, in any real sense of the word. There's only one crime and that's the crime against the forces of liberation: when we, the liberators, proceed against that crime, we are guiltless of blood, we are the instruments of true justice. So I am not killing you, Peachey, from hatred or even personal considerations ... I am killing you in the name of Justice, in the name of Society!'

'... No!' came Peachey's terror-stricken cry. 'Boss ... you can't ... you can't!'

'Oh but I can, Peachey.'

'No boss – no! It's a mistake – I never told them nothing!'

'And no more you shall!' came Louey's voice savagely, 'this is it, Peachey – this is the tool for traitors!'

Gently hurled open the door. 'Drop it!' he barked, 'drop that knife, Louey!'

The big man spun round suddenly from the sink, over which he was holding the helpless Peachey. His grey eyes were blazing with a malevolent light, strange, fey. '*You!*' he articulated with a sort of hiss, '. . . you!'

'Yes, Louey – me. Now drop that knife and take your hands off Peach.'

'. . . You!' hissed Louey again, and the light in his eyes seemed to deepen.

'Stop him!' whimpered Peachey, 'oh, God, he's going to do for me!' And with the energy of despair he twisted himself out of Louey's grip and made a dive for the back door, which fortunately for him was only bolted. But Louey made no move to restrain him. His eyes remained fixed on Gently.

'Let him go!' he purred, '*he* won't talk . . . I'm not so sure now he ever would have done, are you, Chief Inspector Gently?'

'He'll talk,' retorted Gently, 'there's a limit to what you can do with a knife. Now drop it and put your hands up. It's time you started thinking of your defence.'

By way of answer Louey let the knife slide down his hand, so that now he was holding it by the tip of the blade. 'My defence, Chief Inspector Gently; you are looking at it now. Isn't it a pity? I've let a miserable parasite like Peachey escape and in his place I must execute a man of your . . . attainments. Isn't – it – a – pity?'

With the last four words he had reached back with his gigantic arm and was now leisurely taking aim at Gently's heart. There was no cover to dive for. There was no prospect of a quick back jump through the door. The knife was poised and on a hair-trigger, it would reach its mark long before Gently could move to evade it. And then, at the crucial split second, the knife disappeared – one instant it was flashing in Louey's hand, the next it was spirited away as though by a supernatural agency.

'You take him!' piped the delirious voice of Nits through the back door, 'ha, ha, ha! You take him – you take him!'

With a roar of anger Louey recovered himself and leaped at Gently, but it was too late. A hand that felt like a steel bar smashed into the side of his throat and he collapsed on the floor, choking and gasping, a pitiful, helpless wreck of humanity. Gently snapped handcuffs on the nerveless wrists.

'It had to come, Louey,' he said grimly, 'there has to be an end to this sort of thing.'

'Ha, ha, ha!' giggled Nits, dancing around them and brandishing Louey's knife, 'we'll take him away now – we'll take him away!'

Gently put out his hand for the knife. It was a curious weapon. The hilt and blade were one piece of steel, the former heavy, the latter relatively light and narrow. On each side of the hilt was engraved the mark of the TSK along with a number of Egyptian hieroglyphics.

'Double-edged, about three-quarters of an inch wide,' mused Gently, 'it couldn't be any other . . . it would have to be this one.'

Louey struggled up into a sitting position. He was still gagging for breath, his face was grey. He stared at Gently, at the knife, at the discreet links shackling his enormous wrists. 'No!' he whispered hoarsely, 'you weren't big enough . . . *you just weren't big enough!*'

Gently nodded sadly and slipped the knife into his pocket. 'It's you who weren't big enough, Louey . . . that was the mistake. We're none of us big enough . . . we're just very little people.'

Half the Starmouth Borough Police Force seemed to be congregating in the garden as Gently led Louey out. There was the super with Copping and three or four plain-clothes men, at least ten constables and the complete Special Branch outfit. Dutt came panting up the steps, relief showing in his face at the sight of the handcuffs and an unmarked Gently.

'You're all right then, sir – he never give you any trouble?'

Gently shrugged faintly. 'About the routine issue . . .'

'And Peachey, sir – you got him away safe and sound?'

'Safe and sound, Dutt . . . all Peachey had was a scare.'

'By thunder, Gently, you've pulled off a splendid piece of work!' exclaimed the super, striding across. 'I have to admit it – I thought you were going to fall down over this fellow. I suppose it's unnecessary to ask whether you've got the goods on him?'

'I got him red-handed . . . he was going to stab Peach with a TSK patent executioner's knife. I think we'll find it adds up to the weapon which was used on Stratilesceul.'

'You're an amazing fellow, Gently!' The super gazed at him with honest admiration. 'You're not an orthodox policeman, but by heaven you get the results!'

There was a cough of some penetrative power indicative of the near presence of Chief Superintendent Gish. 'I'm sure you'll forgive me for interrupting,' he observed bitterly, 'but we, at least, have still some business to transact in this affair. I take it that Chief Inspector Gently no longer has any objections to my carrying out my duty?'

Gently signified his innocence of any such desire.

'Then possibly Peach can be produced to answer a few of my irrelevant questions?'

Gently deposited Louey with Dutt and took a few steps towards the edge of the wildered garden. 'Peachey!' he called softly.

There was a rustling amongst some rhododendrons.

'Peachey . . . it's all right. We've got Louey under lock and key. You can come out now.'

There were further rustlings and then the parrot-faced one emerged. He was still trembling in every limb and his knees had a tendency to buckle, but the sight of so many policemen reassured him and he walked shakily over to the front of the house.

'That's the boy, Peachey . . . nobody's going to hurt you.'

'You got his kn-knife?' gabbled Peachey, darting a wild-eyed glance at his shackled employer.

'Yes, Peachey, we've got his knife . . . everything's as safe as houses. All we want now is a little information – just a little, to begin with! I suppose you're in a mood to do some talking, Peachey?'

Peachey was. He had never been so much in the mood before. Shocked to his plump core by his experiences in the house, Peachey had learned the hard way that honesty was his only hopeful policy and he was prepared to give effect to that policy in all-night sittings, if that should be required. Chief Superintendent Gish, however, was more moderate in his exactions. He was obstinately and snappily interested in but one set of facts – a short-wave transmitter and some records – and when he had obtained the address of same he departed in haste, leaving Peachey to waste his sweetness on the East Coast air.

'But you wanted a statement about the m-murder, didn't you?' asked Peachey aggrievedly, though with an anxious look at the silent Louey.

'We do, Peachey . . . don't you worry about that,' Gently assured him. 'We'll take you right back now and you can tell us about it over a cup of canteen tea.'

'Then there's Frenchy . . . she can b-back me up . . .'

'She hasn't been overlooked.'

'And I dare say some of the boys . . . it was only me what was sworn into the p-party.'

Gently nodded and urged him towards the gate. The super signed to his men and Dutt touched Louey's arm. From below them, through the scrub trees, came a murmur like a swarming of bees, a murmur that grew suddenly, became a frenzied roar. Louey stood his ground a moment. It was another race in progress.

And then there came a second sound, a rumbling, subterranean sound . . . like the first one and yet strangely unlike it. The roar of the crowd died down, but the second roar didn't. It seemed to be vibrating the

514

air, the trees, the very ground itself. Yet there was nothing to see. There was nothing to account for it. It was Copping who suddenly realized what was going on.

'Run for it!' he bellowed, 'it's the house – it's going over – get the hell out of here, or we'll all be over with it!'

A sort of panic followed his words. There was a general and high-powered movement on the part of one super, one inspector, four detective sergeants, ten constables and a plump civilian in a down-hill and due south direction. This left a balance of three to be accounted for and a backward glance by Copping revealed them in a snapshot of dramatic relation which rooted him to the ground. There was Dutt, sprawling on the pavement; Gently, racing up the path; and Louey, roaring defiance from the top of the steps. And the house was already beginning to move.

'Come back!' howled Copping, 'it's on its way – come back!'

Gently pulled up short some feet from the steps. A crack was opening like magic between himself and the house.

'What are you waiting for?' roared Louey. 'Come on, Mister Chief Inspector Gently – let's die together, shall we? Let's die as though we were men – let's die as though we were more than men!'

Gently measured the distance and poised himself for the leap. Louey rattled his handcuffs in ironic invitation. Then, as though his good angel had whispered in his ear, Gently flung himself backwards instead of forwards: and at the same instant 'Windy Tops', complete in every detail, lurched out frightfully into space . . .

They ran to pick him up, Dutt, Copping and two uniform men. As they pulled him to safer ground another chunk of cliff dropped thundering to the beach. Down below them a raw gap loomed, large enough to put the Town Hall in. There was a curiously unnerving smell of dank and newly-revealed gravel. On the beach was piled the debris, lapping into the sea, a cloud of dust and grit still rising from it. Gently tore himself loose from his rescuers and stared down into the settling chaos.

'Not so close!' shouted Copping, 'you don't know where it's going to stop!'

But Gently remained staring from the edge of the yawning pit. Then he turned to Dutt, a curious expression on his face. 'All right . . . fetch him up. Use that little path over there and fetch him up.'

'Fetch him up?' echoed Dutt. 'Yessir. Of course, sir. But we'll need some picks and shovels, sir, and maybe a stretcher . . .'

Gently shook his head and walked away from the edge. 'Not a single shovel, Dutt . . . not the strap off a stretcher. Poor Louey! This is his final tragedy. He thought he was big enough to play God, but when it came to the push he couldn't even commit suicide.'

'You mean he – he's *alive?*' goggled Dutt.

'Yes, Dutt, and kicking too. If we'd left the door unlocked he'd have been buried in the middle of that lot, but as it is he went down on top . . . he's sitting there now, shaking the muck out of his ears.'

CHAPTER FIFTEEN

I T WAS GREAT stuff for the press, the double arrest of Louey and Streifer. It sent the Body On The Beach rocketing right back into the headlines. There were encomiums for Gently and encomiums for the Borough Police – it was only Chief Superintendent Gish who got a cold and cautious mention. But Gish didn't mind. They were used to it in the Special, he told everyone.

All the same, it was a pity that the best angle on the story didn't come out. It drove the reporters wild to see so much delectable copy laid for ever in the freezer. There was that transmitter under a ruined pill-box down at South Shore, for instance, with its aerial cheekily installed on the Scenic Railway . . . and there were the mass arrests and deportations of agents all over the country, a major operation which the British Public had an undoubted Right To Know About. But it was no use arguing. Chief Super Gish had a heart of stone. As a result of his inhuman decree the British Public were left with the vague and erroneous impression that the Body On The Beach had to do with a gang of international counterfeiters, with an element of vice thrown in by way of a gift to the Sunday papers.

BODY ON THE BEACH — VICE KING ARRESTED declared one such. BEACH MURDER TRACED TO VICE EMPIRE said a second. And it was almost pure libel — Louey only did a bit of sub-letting. After all, even revolutionary parties have to get their funds from somewhere . . .

But it was a London Evening that produced the really telling caption. It caused Chief Super Gish to drop dark hints about people being friendly with editors. 'Body On The Beach' ran a small by-line and then, in a triumph of Cooper Black, GENTLY DOES IT AGAIN! — with one of Gently's better press photos cut in across two columns. Of course, Gently pooh-poohed it. He folded up his copy and stuck it in his pocket with scarcely a glance. But a little later, when he thought he wasn't being watched, Copping saw him perusing that paper with more than common attention.

'We didn't waste no time, when you comes to think of it, sir,' Dutt remarked with a tinge of regret, as they stood on the bridge by the station awaiting their train. 'We comes here on the Friday night to meet a stiff what nobody don't know about and by Tuesday tea-time we got the two geezers what done it, busted up a lot of bolshies and run in a sample of ponces and Teddiesall in a long weekend, you might say.'

Gently passed him a peppermint cream and took one himself. 'We certainly haven't been too heavy on the ratepayers.'

'And me, I was just getting attached to the place, sir. I reckon it beats Sahthend hollow for some things . . .

there's a bloke off Nelson Street as does a plaice-and-chips that knocks you backwards.'

Gently smiled at a distant tug with an orange funnel. 'Talking of plaice, there's some first-rate fishing goes on off the Albion Pier.'

'And them digs of ours, sir, they wasn't half bad neither. I reckon I could stand a week down here with the missus next Bank Holiday . . .'

A train-whistle sounded close at hand. Gently consulted the watch on his clumsy wrist. Beneath them an empty motor-barge came chugging past, its skipper lounging lazily by his wheel.

'But things change, Dutt . . . it doesn't take long to alter them. Do you know what struck me most while we were on this job?'

'No, sir. It ain't been like our other jobs, really.'

Gently took careful aim with his screwed-up peppermint cream bag and dropped it neatly on the barge-skipper's peaked cap.

'Well, Dutt, it was the donkeys.'

'The donkeys, sir?' queried Dutt.

Gently nodded and raised his hand in salute to the barge-skipper. 'They've done away with them, Dutt. There isn't one on the beach. If you'd known Starmouth when I knew Starmouth it would make you feel older . . . but something like that goes on all the time, doesn't it?'